Also by the Author

The Mackin Cover
As Crime Goes By
Dying Cheek to Cheek
Chief: My Life in the LAPD
(with Daryl Gates)

HIGH-HEEL BLUE

a novel

Diane K. Shah

SIMON & SCHUSTER

SIMON & SCHUSTER
ROCKEFELLER CENTER
1230 AVENUE OF THE AMERICAS
NEW YORK, NY 10020

SIMON & SCHUSTER AND COLOPHON ARE REGISTERED
TRADEMARKS OF SIMON & SCHUSTER INC.

DESIGNED BY KAROLINA HARRIS
MANUFACTURED IN THE UNITED STATES OF AMERICA

1 3 5 7 9 10 8 6 4 2

LIBRARY OF CONGRESS CATALOGING-IN-PUBLICATION DATA
SHAH, DIANE K.
HIGH-HEEL BLUE : A NOVEL / DIANE K. SHAH
P. CM.
I. TITLE.
PS3569.H314H54   1997
813'.54—DC20   96-34813
                                CIP

ISBN: 978-1-4391-9676-2

■ A C K N O W L E D G M E N T S ■

I wish especially to thank Lieutenant Kathleen Sheehan of the LAPD for her infinite patience in answering my questions and for all the times she showed me what I needed to see. I am also indebted to Officer Nina Damianakes, now retired, who helped me to get a feel for Metro Division, and to Lieutenant Tammy Tatreau, watch commander in Hollywood.

Their husbands offered plenty of help, too: Detective Mike Damianakes, currently assigned to undercover narcotics, Captain Jim Tatreau of Newton Division, and Detective Mike Sheehan. Others who endured my hounding were Officer Karla Tyson and Detective Woody Parks, both of Van Nuys Division, and retired detective Bud Arce of Robbery Homicide Division.

I am deeply grateful to Steven Downing, former LAPD deputy chief and now a TV producer and writer, for reading the manuscript and offering his wise suggestions.

If I got any of it wrong, it was me, not them.

Above all, I am beholden to former police chief Daryl Gates, who despite all of my rebel instincts made me see that police officers really can be your friends.

For Maureen, Minor, Sam, and Becca

Wednesday—April 19—8 p.m.

Curls bouncing, high heels clicking, Amelia Grant cut through the parking lot, dodging a steady stream of cars that even at this hour seemed never to let up. A tiny purse dangling from her shoulder bumped against her hip as she strode purposefully toward the Great Western Bank. Her dress—black, formfitting, and short—caught the eye of more than one motorist, and she couldn't help feeling pleased that at her age men still enjoyed taking a peek. She glanced at her narrow gold wristwatch and quickened her pace.

The bank, located at the northeast corner of the lot, was set off by itself, away from the brightly lit stores on Ventura Boulevard. As she approached it from the back, she instinctively tightened her grip on the canister of pepper spray in her right hand. The spray had been a compromise. Four months ago, when she had moved in with her boyfriend, a deputy district attorney, he had insisted she get rid of the snub-nosed .38 revolver that she had owned since her days at the Police Academy.

Now, as she passed Ralph's supermarket, Amelia dashed across the two lanes of traffic exiting and entering from Laurel Canyon, and she walked mindfully along the curb that bordered the side of the bank. Then she rounded the corner, coming out onto the wide boulevard, noticing with relief that the two Readytellers were free.

With her bank card secure in her left hand, she approached the machines. The parking spaces in front of the bank were vacant, and, for a brief moment, the traffic on Laurel Canyon came to one of those inexplicable lulls.

In the eerie silence that followed, Amelia stepped up to the Readyteller, slipped in her card, and punched in her PIN number. Trained to be alert to her surroundings, she looked to her right, then her left, before tapping WITHDRAWAL and typing in $200. By habit, she glanced up and located the bank's video camera. The machine beeped, the compartment opened, and she quickly stuffed the bills into her purse, retrieved her card and her receipt, and checking behind her, turned and walked away.

As she retraced her steps in the dark alongside the bank, she again glanced at her watch. In twenty minutes, Fred would be home and . . . then what? Playfully, all he had told her was to get dressed up. Surely he had something special planned. It was, after all, Amelia Lynn Grant's thirty-second birthday.

Unfortunately, the only party guests to show up would be the police officers and criminalists called to the scene—and the coroner's deputy on duty.

■ **O N E** ■

We were cruising along Central Avenue, looking for trouble, and had been for some time. But as darkness fell and the ocean breezes tossed a blanket of damp, chilly air over the city, the streets grew as empty as an L.A. bus. I was bored and a little bit out of sorts. The thought of a drink broke through my ennui.

I stole a glance at my watch and sighed. Eight-thirty. Three tedious hours to go.

Todd said, "You late for an appointment?" with that deadpan face he's so good at.

For a moment I listened to the drone of the squawk box and gazed hopefully out the window. But not even the trash cans were doing much business. "If it gets any slower," I said, "I may fall into a coma."

Normally we didn't do patrol; we worked special details out of Metro Division. But two nights ago, violence—a mini riot actually— had broken out at the Pueblo Del Rio Housing Project south of downtown, and we were among the extra patrols loaned out to Newton Division to help maintain calm. Our vehicle, a borrowed black-and-white, had a brake disorder.

I shifted in my seat to avoid getting stabbed in the kidney by the extra ammo case on my belt.

"You want a little action, there's a new massage parlor over on Figueroa." Todd braked for a light and raised an eyebrow.

"Yeah, right," I said.

My first two years on the department, when I was working out of Hollywood, I was sometimes used as a decoy to arrest johns anytime some City Council member felt the urge to get tough on crime. God, how I'd hated that. Hanging out in rat-infested doorways, pretending I didn't know what they were alluding to when they'd hit on me with their lame attempts at being cool.

"You dating?"

"Depends who's asking." Shifting my eyes, bored.

"Would you go out with me?"

"Probably not." A silence. Then, "Whaddaya got?" Barely flicking him a glance.

He would laugh. "I got ten inches a hot, hard loving for you, darlin'."

"So?"

"And a nice fat fifty."

I would pretend to look him over then, raising a skeptical eyebrow, saying, "Don't you want to know what *you'll* get?"

And he'd say what—half-and-half, or around-the-world, or, if it was a Latino kid with a twenty, maybe only a hand job—and I would lead him, his breath hot on my neck, up the stairs to some fleabag hotel room. Sometimes he was so eager he'd already have his money out as I softly closed the door, positioning myself *at* the door so that when the two vice cops came barreling out of the bathroom, the trick would have nowhere to go.

Once, a good-looking black man in a brand-new Mercedes slid up to the curb and, after running through the requisite dialogue, said, "What's a pretty thing like you doing this for?" And I said, "So I can have a Mercedes nice as yours." And he said, "Come home with me, I'll let you drive it," sounding as if he actually meant it.

For a split second I was tempted to tell him to beat it. But dutifully I led him into the room, a lamb to slaughter, and I could still remember the look of mortification on the poor man's face when my partners sprang out of the closet: "You're under arrest!"

At which point the man suddenly broke into tears. "My God, my God," he wailed, burying his face in his hands. "I'm a preacher! Tomorrow . . . I'm getting *married*. Oh my God. You've ruined my life!"

In a way, I *had* ruined his life, and I told him I was sorry. I still felt bad all these years later.

"Did I tell you I've been teaching Lynie to shoot?" Todd slowed automatically as we passed the projects on Long Beach, but nothing was doing here either, probably because two other black-and-whites were hogging the curb. "She seems to have a real good eye for it."

I turned and stared at the chiseled profile of my African American partner. "Lynette with a gun? You can't be serious."

Lynette Robbie, elegant, beautiful, and armed with a pair of master's degrees, had actually met Todd at one of those feel-good community meetings, when she'd stood up and harangued the officers present about the need to get guns off the street; if they couldn't do the job, she would. Then she presented her plan: through funds raised, they would pay gang members for each citizen's arrest they made that led to a conviction, with an added bonus for any guns they turned in. Before the meeting was over, the room was cheering Lynette, totally ignoring the flummoxed cops. Todd had told me the story more than once.

"Our neighbors were robbed at gunpoint," he said simply. "Lynie's tired of it."

"Honestly, Todd, there's no reason to be living in *that* neighborhood."

"It's my neighborhood. I have a responsibility to it. Besides, the people on the street feel safer knowing a police officer lives there."

"I bet Lynette and the kids sure don't."

Todd grabbed a toothpick from the box on the dash. By the end of the watch, the ashtray would be filled with chewed-up toothpicks. But it was his gleaming teeth, set against his smooth dark skin, that made his smile so alluring—on the rare occasions that he bothered to produce one.

Idly, he tapped keys on the computer terminal, inputting the plate number of the Nissan 286X in front of us. "What about Jack? He a shooter?"

I grinned. "The last time I took him to the range all he wanted to practice was how to look cool whipping his gun out." I paused. "What's that?"

Todd was already turning up volume on the police frequency. Somehow the subconscious mind instantly responds to the dispatcher's drone when the call is for you—the way a mother on a playground knows instinctively which cry is her child's. "Unknown trouble, shots fired," Todd repeated. "Three blocks from here."

I grabbed the mike and told the dispatcher we were rolling, as Todd flicked on the bar lights and the siren and hit the gas. An "unknown trouble, shots fired" was one of the most dangerous calls in the city, and the neighborhood we were in had the feel of Rollin' 60's gangsters. My adrenaline began to pump.

Todd slammed up to the curb before a decaying two-story apart-

ment house half a block off San Pedro. I jumped out. The light over
the entrance had been smashed and the brass knob felt greasy when I
twisted it. The door gave.

I stepped inside and switched on my flashlight.

Clearly, the building had once had style, judging from the elabo-
rate tile work on the arching vestibule ceiling. The rotting linoleum
floor, stained and caked with scum, told of a more recent past. A chan-
delier over the stairway to the right was dark. A door to the left
creaked slowly open. I could feel Todd tensing behind me.

A balding Caucasian in an undershirt, his gut spilling over the
waistband of his pants, peered out.

"You the cops?"

"No," I said, "we just dress like them."

Todd cleared his throat. "I'm Officer Robbie, sir, and this is my
partner, Officer Harlow. What's the problem?"

The man shuffled into the hall and jabbed the air. "Upstairs. There
was a shot. That's what it was, a gunshot. I had *Roseanne* on, so it
wasn't from the TV." He nodded knowingly. "You live around here,
you know what a gunshot sounds like."

"You didn't go upstairs," I said, "see anything?" Guessing his age
at fifty and taking in the intricate pattern of veins on his nose.

"No, ma'am. I just called nine-one-one and double-locked my
door. They don't pay me to be a hero."

"Stay put," I said. "We'll be back."

The staircase with its wrought iron railing curved gracefully up to
the second floor. The landing was dark, but from down the hall a dim
lightbulb spotlighted peeling gray paint decorated with gang graffiti
and a collection of dirt balls clumped on the floor. There were six
doors. From behind the third came the throbbing sound of heavy
metal.

I raised my hand to pound on the door, but Todd, having moved
down the hall, called, "Here!"

Unlike the others, this door was freshly painted a shiny black
enamel, and the number five had been stenciled in yellow. Even the
dented knob bore a patina of polish. The door was slightly ajar. I said,
"I'll go," and scrambled down the stairs.

The undershirt remained framed in his doorway, a three-
dimensional still life—with body odor.

"What's your name, sir?"

"Henderson, Cal Henderson. Did you find anything?"

"Who lives in apartment five, Mr. Henderson?"

"That's old Harold Biggs, why?"

"Have you seen him today?"

"No . . . I don't believe so."

"Do you know his phone number?"

"He don't have no phone." Cal Henderson pointed at a wall where a wire poked out. "Pay phone used to be there, but that was five years ago. Say, what's going on?"

"Stay glued . . . right there."

I took the stairs two at a time. As I approached Todd, he was crouching at the door, maneuvering a wire with a small mirror through the narrow crack.

"Anything?"

"I see part of a man on part of a bed and I think some blood."

"What's that noise?" I said, listening to a distinct metallic whirring sound. "A bomb?"

"More like some kind of drill, I think."

I unclipped the ROVER from my belt and called for backup. Within minutes, two patrol officers clambered up the stairs and positioned themselves in the hall. Todd and I, guns drawn, me low and to the right, Todd high and to the left, bolted into the apartment, shouting, "Police!"

"Aw, Jesus," Todd said.

Todd is one of the most unflappable men I know. I had seen him take verbal abuse from dirtbags and sergeants alike the same way he'd take in a weather report. The rare times I had witnessed an emotion leak out were when old people or children were hurt.

He holstered his gun. "Shit."

An elderly white man was sprawled on the bed, the sheets soaked with blood. The blood was still dribbling out of multiple stab wounds to his thin chest and bony throat, and some of it was dribbling from his mouth. With the back of my hand I touched the man's neck, searching for a pulse I knew I wouldn't find. Then quickly I turned away, not so much from the sight of death as from the smell of it.

The apartment consisted of one room with a kitchenette and a bath. Probably the building had been a single-family dwelling at one time, now carved into cheap rooms for rent. This room was well kept, spotless, and neat. As one officer ducked into the kitchenette and another the bath, I stepped over electric-train tracks and went to inspect a wall lined with shelves.

They were filled with model trains, old ones that had been painstakingly restored. Each gleamed and was carefully placed, as if in a museum. I reached up and ran a fingertip across a black Southern Pacific coal car.

"Look." Todd was holding the edge of a battered leather wallet. "Empty."

"Any I.D.?"

"Nothing." Todd flapped the wallet and placed it on a worn armchair. "I don't see a phone. Why don't you call for the coroner's wagon and I'll go talk to Mr. Big Ears."

" . . . who said he heard a shot, right?"

"He didn't hear nothing with that music next door."

"You think he's still got the knife?"

"I bet we find it within fifty feet of this building."

Before finding a land line to notify Newton's watch commander, I turned and looked again at the old man lying dead in his bed.

On the floor below him, a shiny blue train ground mechanically around its track.

T w o detectives from Newton Division arrived as I was finishing my chronological account. Cal Henderson, the building's rent collector and so-called janitor, stuck to his story, and despite a search of the area, no knife was found. Or any bloodstained clothing. Not that the search was a total loss: when the two men who lived next to the victim finally responded to the hammering on their door, they appeared too strung out to have committed the murder, and their music too loud for them to have heard it. Spotting Baggies of cocaine and vials of heroin strewn about the couch, the two backup officers hauled the men off to Central jail.

Our job was to go back to Newton and start on the paperwork.

"Feeling better?" Todd glanced in the rearview mirror before pulling away from the curb. "At least you got to whip out your gun and wave it at a door."

"Someone could have walked in off the street," I observed. "Maybe the guy's door was open. But I doubt it. It was the scumbag janitor. I wonder how much money he got."

"Does it matter?"

I sighed and leaned against the worn seat. The smell of the old man's blood was still in my nostrils. I'd been to emergency rooms countless times and the blood there never fazed me. This kind of blood was different. It was dead blood, some chemical change having fouled its odor. I wrinkled my nose involuntarily.

Todd said, "You're not exactly Comedy Central tonight." He glanced over at me. "What's wrong with you?"

"I think I'm getting too old for this."

"Oh brother. We're loaned out a couple of nights and you feel sorry for yourself. You ask me, you're the prima donna in the family, not Jack."

I didn't like him saying that. Others in the department sometimes did—called me a prima donna—but it wasn't true and Todd knew it. "I'm not a prima donna," I said defensively. "I'm a hot dog–ette."

Uniform duty in a black-and-white, even for two nights, always made me grumpy. Patrol was like a football game: three minutes of live action sandwiched in between interminable hours of driving around. We had been driving around since 3:30. I still wanted a drink.

Todd said, "Okay, hot dog, so how about testing me?"

"All right."

"They're on the back seat."

Maybe that was the problem. While Todd was determined to climb the departmental ladder, I was content being a street cop, a P3 actually, the highest rank in the officer category. I wanted action. Todd wanted power, and for six months he'd been diligently studying for the sergeant's exam while working toward a master's in business administration at USC. Todd Robbie might live in the ghetto but he didn't intend to work in it for long.

I grabbed the packet of Q&A flash cards off the back seat, but as I faced forward I saw, half a block up Broadway, a man coming out of a liquor store carrying a paper bag. He stepped off the curb and raised up the trunk of a gold Chevy as we rolled by.

"Slow down." I twisted around. "I know this sounds crazy, but I swear I saw a hand and an arm in that trunk."

"It's probably Monster McGrew," Todd said, referring to our captain. "He pops up in the damnedest places."

"That's what I *saw*." Though it could have been a mannequin or— a big sausage. Frankly, the guy acted too nonchalant and looked too old for it, most crimes being committed by eighteen- to thirty-five-year-olds. "An arm and a hand," I repeated. "Unless I'm losing my mind."

"You *are* bored. A guy with spare body parts in his trunk is going to display his goodies to a couple of cops?" But Todd's eyes had fastened on to the rearview mirror and he swung the car over to the curb. "Here he comes."

We let the man pass us in his gold Chevy. He was black, middle-aged, and was wearing, I had noticed before, a T-shirt over cotton shorts. He drove normally and seemed oblivious to the black-and-white now trailing at a distance.

I grabbed the mike. "This is"—instinctively, I checked the back of my left hand, where I'd penned my call number for the night—"uh . . . R-twenty-seven. Give me rolling wants and warrants and DMV on a gold Chevy, license two-Edward-Xray-Tom-five-six-three, Broadway and Main," I said, not wanting to waste time punching it into the MDT.

"Whichever sergeant responds," Todd opined, "ain't going to be thrilled."

The radio crackled. "R-twenty-seven, you're looking at a nineteen eighty-six Impala, registered to Louis Alcorn, L.O., no warrants."

Todd raised an eyebrow and glanced at me.

"So humor me. Pull him over."

"Fifty bucks it's a salami."

"Hundred if it isn't. Go."

Once again, Todd hit the bar lights, but not the siren, as he picked up speed and closed in on the Impala. The driver, seemingly confused, made a few herky-jerky movements with the car, then bumped recklessly up to the curb. We jumped out, guns drawn, using our doors as shields.

Todd shouted, "Turn off your engine! Get out and step to your right!"

The man, who had both hands on the steering wheel, something African Americans did automatically in L.A., hesitated before turning off the engine and cautiously climbing out of the car.

Todd stayed in position as I approached the man, my sixteen-cartridge Beretta pointed at the ground. He did not appear nervous. His short Afro bore a few strands of gray, but his face was unlined, pleasant, his mustache clipped; his eyes were a little bloodshot.

"Face the car, spread your legs, put your hands on the roof," I ordered. I holstered my gun and quickly patted him down, catching a faint whiff of alcohol. "May I see your driver's license, sir?"

"It's in my back pocket."

"Fine."

Cautiously, the man lowered his right hand, reached into his back pocket, and pulled out a billfold.

"Face me and take out your license, please."

Suddenly, the quiet of the empty street was shattered by a set of screeching tires. A car door slammed. Heavy footsteps. Ignoring them, I studied the driver's license: Louis Alcorn, five nine, 175 pounds, fifty-five years old.

"What's going on here?"

I said, "Do me a favor, Mr. Alcorn. Open your trunk. If what I think I saw is not there, then you'll be on your way."

"Dammit, Harlow, what is this?"

Without taking my eyes off Louis Alcorn, I murmured to Sergeant Higgins, now breathing over my shoulder, "I'll explain in a minute." Then, "Okay, Mr. Alcorn?" This was the tricky part. He didn't have to open his trunk. If he refused, we'd need a warrant. If we insisted he open the trunk without one, citing exigent circumstances, and the trunk did not contain what I thought, I would have a lot of explaining to do—mainly to the fire-breathing dragon now planted behind me.

"Harlow, the fuck are—?"

"In a minute, sir." Patiently, respectfully. But the asshole now had me by the elbow—a real breach of tactics—demanding my attention.

"Oh," said Louis Alcorn. "I can't open the trunk without the key."

"Fine," I said, pulling free of the sergeant. "Get it."

Alcorn reached into his car and plucked the key from the ignition.

Sergeant Higgins poked me in the back. "I want to know what you think you're doing, Harlow." His voice was low with rage, even though he was wrong to interfere. Todd, standing a few feet away, remained silent.

Slowly, Louis Alcorn began walking to the rear of his car. But just as he was about to slip the key in the lock, he hesitated, gave a small shrug, and laughed.

"I guess you got me, Officer!"

Then, to the surprise of everyone but me, he flipped open the lid, and there, crumpled up, lay the corpse of a young black female.

I could hear Higgins whistle through his teeth as I quickly unclasped my handcuffs. He and Todd moved in, uncrumpled the girl.

"You're under arrest," I recited, cuffing Louis Alcorn. "You have the right to remain silent . . . "

She couldn't have been more than eighteen, skinny, wearing a cheap cotton dress. Her face had probably been pretty before it had taken on the hideous contortions that came with strangulation.

I could feel Sergeant Higgins's eyes boring into my neck.

I blew on my fingers and walked away.

T h e lamp was on in the vestibule when I got home to my condo, three blocks from the beach in Santa Monica. After taking Louis Alcorn back to Newton, running his record, and booking him, I'd been too exhausted to change out of uniform, and now, as I dropped my keys on the table under the antique brass mirror, I ran my fingers through my short dark hair and inspected my face. It looked drained, my eyes red rimmed, my lipstick long gone.

As I turned toward the living room, my gaze fell upon the large framed poster that hung beside the arched doorway—the poster of Jack. He was standing, legs apart, hand on his holster, eyes squinting under the bill of his police hat. In the distance stood a black-and-white. Big red letters across the top of the poster proclaimed: NIGHT WATCH. Under Jack's feet, as if he were standing on them, were the words *Starring Jack Hayes . . . as Sgt. Matt Blaine, LAPD.*

That was the joke. He did it to entertain; I did it for real.

I switched off the lamp and moved through the dark living room and down the hall, where I flipped on another light before entering our bedroom.

Jack was lying on his back, sheet pulled halfway up his chest, the light from the hall spilling onto the empty side of the bed.

Not taking my eyes from him, I removed my thick black shoes and socks. Slowly I unbuttoned my shirt. I laid it neatly on the chair. Next came the protective vest. I unbuckled the Sam Browne with its twenty pounds of equipment and carefully draped it over the arm of the chair. I slipped off my trousers and placed them on top of the belt. Wearing only a red satin bra and bikini panties, I stole closer to the bed.

He was smiling.

I sat on the edge of the mattress and pulled the sheet up higher on his chest, pausing to curl my fingers in a clump of short sandy hair. I gazed at his wide cheekbones, the nice straight nose, the full lips, and found myself smiling back. I unhooked my bra and let it fall to the floor and lingered a moment longer. I sighed.

Then I stood.

My husband—with his eye mask on and his earplugs in—continued to snore peacefully.

I picked up his T-shirt from the floor, slipped it on, and walked out.

In the living room, without turning on a light, I uncapped the vodka and the Kahlua and poured myself a drink.

I had finished most of it before the sedative effect of the alcohol kicked in and the tension began to melt. Pulling the cashmere throw off the back of the couch, I tossed it over my bare legs and stared gloomily into the dark. The demons circled menacingly.

I'd been on the department long enough to know that every cop, no matter the rank, could name at least one superior who had been a thorn in his or her side. For the last six months, Sgt. Raymond Sebastian Higgins had been mine.

I climbed off the couch, built another drink, and remembered how hard the rain was coming down the night Todd and I had answered that radio call. Once again we were on loan—this time to Southeast—to help out with a string of liquor store armed robberies. Only, this call had come from a woman saying her son was high on PCP; would someone please come and take him away?

When we arrived at the location, 95th and Figueroa, the woman let us in. The son, a large, strapping kid of eighteen, was sitting on the sofa, glassy eyed but calm. While Todd stood in the doorway talking to the mom, I went over to the boy. "Your mama says you're not feeling so good, Jessie. We're going to take you to the doctor."

Jessie just nodded.

"Are you feeling hot?" I asked, knowing how overheated a PCP user can become. "Like you have a fever? Let's go and see what the doctor can do to make you feel better."

Obediently, Jessie stood.

Which is when our backup came barreling in. "Step aside, sister," announced Higgins with bravado. "I'll deal with this." He ripped the cuffs from his belt and told Jessie, "Hands behind your back, scumbag!"

Jessie's glassy eyes turned wild. He reached down, planted his meaty hands on the plywood coffee table, and raised it above his head. Bull-like, he rushed Higgins, screaming, "White motherfucker, I'll kill you!" He slammed the table down on Higgins, catching him on the chest and knocking him onto the living room floor.

I stepped in and used my baton on Jessie's groin. As he bent over in pain, I scrambled around behind him, jumped on his back, and began kicking his ribs. He fell on all fours. I grabbed his right wrist and forced it behind him, causing him to collapse on the floor. His left arm was thrust straight out in front of him, and as I sat on his back, I struggled to bring it around. His right arm was locked under my thigh and I tugged on his left arm with both my hands, battling against his PCP-fueled strength. Finally, as Todd sat on his head, I wrenched the long arm over Jessie's shoulder. I got the two wrists to meet halfway down his back and cuffed him, although vertically.

I got to my feet, struggling to catch my breath.

Higgins jumped up. "Where the fuck did you learn to handcuff people like that?" he shrieked.

The next day, the story spread: "The chick had to rescue the sarge!" Ignoring the secret smiles and winks of my colleagues, I kept my mouth shut and steered clear of Higgins.

But the damage was done. From that night on, Higgins, who is my squad leader, micromanaged every blink of my eye.

I decided to have one more before crawling into bed.

And made it a double.

t sounded like a siren, shrill and insistent, and it took me a moment to connect the ringing with the telephone.

Twisting in the sheets, I threw an arm over the bedside table and fumbled for the receiver. "Harlow," I groaned.

"Brenden, it's Cooper."

Cooper worked the desk. I squinted at the clock.

"Change of plans. Report directly to Metro, sixteen hundred hours. No workout."

"Uh—"

"Soft clothes, clean. Got that?"

"Yeah. Thanks, Coop."

I yawned. Already a new day, though it hardly seemed as if the old one had passed. From roll call to sign-off to roll call, one day blurred seamlessly into the next. I wondered vaguely if that's how Jack felt, day after day on the set. His days were even longer than mine, our schedules hopelessly mismatched.

I squiggled across the empty bed onto his side and buried my head in his pillow. But soon a sense of malaise began to overwhelm me. Normally a cheerful person, I had lately been moody and out of sorts. Todd had picked up on it, but my emotionally withdrawn partner never pried. And the truth was, I didn't know what was wrong. Maybe it was some kind of cop disease—the gradual disintegration of the soul.

I sighed and turned onto my back. The late morning sunlight filtered in through the plantation shutters, stinging my eyes. I squeezed them shut and tried to imagine myself long ago on the beach, lost in a novel, rotating like a chicken on a spit, savoring the musky scent of my own juices—sweat blending with coconut oil.

Instead, alone in bed, all I could see were splotches of red pulsing inside my throbbing head.

D o i n g eighty on the freeway, I shoved the Diet Coke between my legs and switched to an all-news station, searching for a tip to the sudden change of plans. A man convicted of bank robbery was now suing the bank on the grounds that *he* got robbed, citing the $342 he stole as too little to justify his sentence. I grinned. But aside from a murderous carjacking in Koreatown, there was nothing. Not that my job was ever predictable, which was one of the lures that had drawn me to Metro Division.

Considered the cream of the LAPD, Metro expected its people to be better and *look* better than the average cop. Staffed by 250 of the department's most highly trained—and notoriously vain—officers, including SWAT, Metro was known for its skill and swagger, not to mention its asphyxiating amounts of cologne.

"So, Harlow. What makes you think you're tough enough for Metro?" a jut-jawed lieutenant had snarled at me from across a table during my oral exam.

My smile wasn't nice. "Try me."

To my astonishment, Jut-Jaw pushed back his chair and rose to his full six feet three. The two other men seated beside him, a deputy chief and a captain, stared straight ahead. The lieutenant steamed around the table.

Instinctively, I rose.

"I'm bigger than you and I'm not cooperating," the lieutenant bleated. "What're you gonna do, huh, Copper?" He took a menacing step closer. "Go for your gun?"

My left hand went to my hip. "No sir. My baton. If the strap on my gun isn't unsnapped, I'll do it before I grab the baton."

Eyes flashing, Jut-Jaw took another step closer to me. "I'm still coming."

I did not blink. "No, you're not. I've just dropped you with three from the ring. In a second, I'll have you cuffed."

Right. In real life, I would have reached first for my communication skills to subdue a suspect, but I doubted that would go over well with this Marine Corps dinosaur.

The lieutenant's eyes grew hard, and for a moment I feared he would actually take a swing at me. But I knew I would not react. This wasn't a physical; it was an *oral*. He's testing my nerves, I told myself, not my skills.

High Noon lasted another ten seconds, me not taking my eyes from the lieutenant's. Then, wordlessly, he spun on his heel and returned to his seat. "Dismissed!"

Metro's mandate was big-time crime suppression. While other divisions patrolled their designated areas, Metro had a backstage pass to anywhere. Officers were dispatched on a mission-by-mission basis, often to help another division with a problem—such as a run of bank robberies—or to lend additional bodies to a troubled area, like the projects in the South End. More often, Metro tackled larger problems, like a Hillside Strangler or a Skid Row Slasher, or a case where you had to live in trees and crawl through gutters . . . waiting. We did hostage negotiations, too, or just plain talking some barricaded suspect into putting down his gun and surrendering—like O.J. that night. We were also assigned to escort visiting dignitaries around town and needed to have the wardrobe for it.

I did.

Metro's base of operations, however, hardly fit its narcissistic self-image. Rather, it occupied one floor of Central Division's station house at Sixth and Wall, an area that, although falling in the shadow of City Hall, was a grungy confluence of Skid Row, the garment district, and now—a new wrinkle—Toy Town. In recent years, Filipinos, Koreans, and Taiwanese had created block after block of toy outlets, for reasons that escaped most of the cops humming in and out of their station house, a grim, windowless, *riotproof* building that Todd called the Alamo.

Popping a couple of Motrin, I steered my black Camaro Z28 convertible into the garage, up to the second level, and—luck was with me—into a space beside a pale green Chevy Caprice.

I stepped out, opened the trunk, and collected my gear: radio, Kevlar helmet, the TAC vest that fit over the uniform, the protective vest that fit under it, the long stick—a thirty-six-inch baton for crowd control—and my 12-gauge shotgun.

I transferred my equipment to the trunk of the Caprice, shoving aside the gas masks and the ammo for the M-16. After two nights in the black-and-white, I was relieved to be back in my assigned car.

It was unseasonably hot for April, and sticky. I slipped off my beige cotton blazer and laid it across the Caprice's back seat. Then, crossing the connecting bridge to the station house, I nodded to the shoe-shine man and walked down the hall past the lieutenants' room, past the Toy Store—where Metro's sizeable arsenal of guns is kept—and into the roll call room, wondering what was up.

A cloud of noxious cologne hovered over the couple of dozen officers now taking their seats. Todd was in his usual place, in the back, studying a page of the penal code. I slid into the chair beside him. Despite the half bottle of Visine I'd poured into my eyes, they still felt grainy, and the Motrin hadn't kicked in yet. "This better not be a night of shake, rattle, and roll," I said bleakly. "My bones won't take it."

"What's wrong with your bones?" Todd turned the page. "Yesterday it was your *mood*."

I popped a stick of gum into my mouth. "You know what's going on?"

Todd flashed a sardonic smile. He was bigger than he appeared—an optical illusion due to the perfect proportions of his body. It was the body of a defensive back. Todd hadn't played since high school, but the speed and the strength still kicked in anytime he needed them.

"I hear it's a field trip to the Valley," he said. "I hope they give us a nice box lunch."

"All right, everybody. Turn on your ears!"

Sgt. Randy Rogers, a six-foot-two beanpole with a Forrest Gump haircut, grinned at us from behind the desk in the front of the room. Thirty-two officers were now in the process of getting seated.

"First item of business," Randy declared. "A Polack is making love to a woman when suddenly he stops. 'I'm sorry, honey,' he says, 'but I've got to ask you something. I was wondering, uh, have you had your AIDS test yet?'"

"A Polack?" growled a voice up front. "Aren't they on the P.C. list *yet?*"

Rogers grinned. "So the woman says, 'As a matter of fact, I was tested last week and I'm fine.'

"'Great,' says the Polack, and they finish making love."

"Tell us how!" someone hooted.

"Shut up!" Rogers snapped. "Afterwards, they're laying there and the guy says, 'I hope I wasn't being insensitive to ask you that. 'Cause you see, I got AIDS two years ago. And I don't want to get it again!'"

Groans and hisses filled the room, but nobody protested too loudly. Randy Rogers moonlighted doing stand-up at comedy clubs, and the unfortunate souls in his platoon had become his unwitting test audience, forced to endure his routines. We weren't allowed to crack a joke in his presence, a *funny* joke, unless we wanted to be banished to the desk.

"Second item of business," Randy continued. "Anyone knows a half-brained plumber, see me after. Now. This is what we got." He ran his hand through his gray Forrest Gump. "A woman was stabbed to death at an ATM in the Valley last night. Amelia Lynn Grant, age thirty-two. Turns out she's the fourth such victim in the last three months. Reason nobody's jumped on it is that two of the homicides were in North Hollywood, two in Van Nuys, and it never occurs to those rocket scientists to talk to each other. Downtown Homicide put them together and they want our help."

Rogers moved from behind the desk and began handing out packets of papers. "This is a rundown of the four. They were all committed within five or six miles of each other, all between twenty and twenty-two hundred hours. Each female had multiple stab wounds to the chest. None was found with an I.D. or cash. So far, no leads or eyewitnesses, so they've got squat."

Papers rustled as Rogers returned to the desk. "For starters, I'm sending two squads to the Valley; the others will work the phones. You Valley people will be divided among the four crime scenes. Some of you will talk to the folks in the banks; others will canvass the neighborhoods. Get all the location particulars and we'll compare notes at, say, twenty-two hundred. I want every one of you to come back with some*one* who saw some*thing*."

I glanced up from the report and realized he was looking directly at me.

"Hey, Harlow. This could be your ticket to the big time," Randy Rogers said.

D r i v i n g north on the freeway, I wondered if I would ever get to the "big time." I was only the third woman ever assigned to Metro—or Macho Division, as we called it—and I'd been there only six months. Getting in was like being asked to join the coolest fraternity on campus. You had to take written tests and skill tests, and then they had to *want* you, and anyone in Metro could actually *blackball* you.

My first day there, five officers flatly refused me as a partner ("Yeah, right. *As if* my wife's gonna go for that!"), and I wound up with a forty-four-year-old Vietnam vet who, when he wasn't talking about himself—or showing me *pictures* of himself—was putting me through the paces like a prize Chihuahua at a dog show. Our first night out, he made me climb twenty-nine roofs—in a driving rainstorm—in search of a gun that had been used in a convenience store holdup. Working gang territory the next night, he got shot in the leg. After a foot pursuit, I apprehended the suspect when he hesitated (as it dawned on him that I was a woman), and I was able to wrestle him off a fence and into a pair of cuffs.

With Rambo on disability leave, I was teamed with another misogynist, who made his feelings clear. "I don't work with women, get it? We're not doing *anything*." And for the next eight days we drove around doing exactly that: nothing. Next came Todd Robbie, a talented young officer who had grown up in Watts and who treated me with the same cool detachment that he showed everyone else. But as the months passed, he seemed to trust me, which—bottom line—was all that really counted.

T h e Valley Savings & Loan was located on Laurel Canyon, just beyond the intersection at Vanowen. I turned left into the drive-in lane and followed it straight back, past the bank's front door and around to the rear of the building. Two side-by-side automated tellers had been built into the bank's back wall. A walk, lushly landscaped with tall bushes and short palm trees, led from the machines to a parking area.

"Man, if I needed cash, I know where I'd go," said Todd, slamming the car door. "This bank was *made* for robbing."

I slipped on my jacket and caught up with Todd. The only problem was, at 5:15, the bank was closed for business. I peered through the dark glass panel windows framing the main door and spotted a blond man working at a desk in the back. Todd banged on the glass, flashing his badge—and his teeth. Cautiously, the man came forward and, after a closer look, hesitantly unlocked the door.

"Good afternoon, sir. I'm Officer Robbie, Los Angeles police, and this is Officer Harlow. Are you the branch manager?"

"Assistant manager." The man frowned. "Is there a problem? I didn't call the police."

He was one of those clean-cut types with the ever-ready smiles who lease cars, sell insurance, or hold paper-pushing jobs in banks. Only, at the moment, Mr. Assistant Manager wasn't smiling. His eyes darted from me to Todd as if he were desperately trying to recall what the bank's position would be in a situation like this.

"We're following up on the murder of Mrs. Croft," I said pleasantly. "I know you or your manager talked to the police at the time, but we're doubling back, starting all over."

The button on his blue seersucker jacket was pulling from the extra pounds that time had piled on, while his face retained the smooth, untroubled expression of a man who had never hatched an actual thought. "Um, could you come back tomorrow? I don't think I'm authorized—"

"Mr.—?" Todd cocked his head expectantly.

"Swinson. Larry Swinson."

"Well, Mr. Swinson, everybody is authorized to talk to the police when the police come a-calling." Todd winked. "It's one of your inalienable rights."

Sourly, Swinson led us back to his desk and pointed at the two customers' chairs planted across from him. He sat down with a sigh and leaned forward, trying to look authoritative. "I don't know what I can tell you," he said, aggrieved.

Quickly, we reviewed the particulars. Mrs. Alice Croft, forty-three, secretary at a computer firm, had driven into the bank lot sometime before 9:10 P.M., when her body was discovered by her seventeen-year-old son, who used the same bank and who, by terrible chance, happened to stop by on his way home from debate team practice at the high school.

"Nobody would have been here then," Swinson insisted. "I'm always the last to leave and I'm almost always gone by six."

"No security guard or janitor?" I asked.

"We have an excellent alarm system that's hooked up to the police, and the Readytellers are very well lit. We've never had any trouble."

"And the janitor?"

"Mrs. Lopez. She comes in around four and does light dusting and such. On weekends, a crew does a thorough cleaning."

"So you're saying Mrs. Lopez would not have been here that late?" I asked.

"That's right. Anyway, the police talked to her already. Look, it was a terrible thing. But it only happened once. Our customers feel very safe banking with us."

Right. Like, tough shit, Mrs. Croft, sorry you were the *exception*. Todd got up and began drifting among the desks.

"Mr. Swinson," I said, "we have a list of all the withdrawals made that night between seven and nine-fifteen. We have the account numbers and the amounts, but we don't have the customers' names."

I removed a sheet of paper from the Croft folder and laid it on the desk. "There were seven withdrawals during that period, and we'd like to know which were made by women."

Stinson glanced at the paper. "Why?"

"It will only take a few minutes. Then we'll look at the Readytellers. By the way, have you installed a camera since the murder?"

"Uh, we're checking into it. But like I said, this was just one unfortunate incident."

With that, he took my piece of paper, switched on his computer and, sullenly, began tapping on the keyboard.

S t a n d i n g in daylight, I could tell by the angle of the fixtures that the two automated tellers were well lighted, as was the path leading up from the parking lot.

"Even if someone was inside the bank," Todd pointed out, "they couldn't have seen the Readytellers. There aren't any windows in the back. So our guy hunkers down behind one of these bushes, and after the woman gets her money, he attacks her."

I turned and studied the parking lot. The drive-in from the street rounded the rear of the bank, widened into two aisles for parking spaces, and U-turned back out to the street. Behind the parking area stood a concrete block wall, about six feet high. The entire rear of the bank was secluded. Brilliant.

"I want to look at the list of withdrawals again," Todd said. "But let's go sit in the car."

I led the way back to the Caprice, unlocked it, and stood beside the open door waiting for the interior to cool off. Even this late in the afternoon the heat was oppressive, any breeze having choked on the smog and died of asphyxiation.

Eventually I slid in behind the wheel and leaned across to open the passenger door. Neither the locks nor the windows were automated. The car had 128,000 miles on it. Its only frill was the air-conditioning—when it worked.

I reached under the seat for my thermos, and for the next ten minutes sipped cold water and watched a steady stream of homebound customers drive in to use the Readytellers.

Todd tapped the paper. "Why Mrs. Croft?"

"Her size? She was what, five four?"

"Maybe. But let's look at it from the killer's point of view. Five customers made withdrawals between eight and eight-forty-seven, when Mrs. Croft made hers. Customer number three arrived at eight-thirty-one, followed by number four at eight-forty-two."

"You're assuming the killer didn't arrive at eight-forty-five and grab the first lucky soul who showed up?"

"I'm *assuming* he was here awhile. Now, look at it this way. Here's Mrs. Croft." Todd pointed to the paper. "She withdraws forty dollars. But the person before her took out a hundred—"

"It was a man."

"And the person who showed up eleven minutes before him was a woman. She withdrew two hundred."

"He couldn't have known," I pointed out. "You can't tell how much money comes through the machine."

Todd gave me his wry grin. "Brenden, it takes a lot of sweat to stab someone . . . for forty bucks?"

"What, you're worried the guy didn't make the minimum wage for the job?"

"All I'm saying is it takes a hell of a lot of work to stab someone."

"As opposed to pulling a trigger?"

"Yeah," said Todd. "That's what I mean."

T h r e e of the four customers who had used the Valley S&L Readytellers after 8 P.M. were home. All told us the same thing: they had driven to the bank alone, made their withdrawals, seen no one, and left. Nor could any recall noticing a suspicious-looking character on previous occasions.

"We still have this Marisa Ruiz," Todd said as I swung onto the freeway. "She clocked in at eight-thirty-one."

"And Mrs. Croft's son. We'll get them tomorrow."

"I'll tell you what else is wrong," he said. "Mrs. Croft's car. It was thirty feet from the Readyteller, locked. Her purse was in it with four credit cards and a checkbook. The car key was found about four feet from her body. She'd dropped it during her struggle with the killer."

"So why didn't he pick it up and go into the car? Maybe someone pulled in and scared him off."

"And this customer, seeing the body, and possibly the killer, also took off?"

"Why not?" I said.

"Because it doesn't feel right. None of it *feels* right. A guy who just happens to stumble onto one of the few banks without a camera, who cuts someone for forty bucks, and doesn't take the car?"

"So what's wrong with a gangbanger needing a little crack and using some ingenuity for a change?" I smiled.

"What's wrong is that I don't think the guy is in it for the money."

"He's in it for the kill?"

Todd reached for a toothpick. "I'd bet a fifty on it."

B a c k at Metro, notes from the four teams were collated and, using a computer-generated map of the Valley, ten additional banks with physical characteristics similar to the four murder scenes were targeted as future sites. The problem was that most banks in the Valley had similar characteristics. All were located on the few major thoroughfares where zoning permitted them, and all were well lighted. All were within a mile or two of the Ventura or Hollywood freeways. Nearly all had security cameras. Interestingly, at the three crime scenes where a camera was operative, the killer had attacked out of lens range, as the victim was returning to her car.

Surveillance tactics would be drawn up the next day. We were told to report at 1500 hours.

Walking through the garage with Todd, I suddenly started to laugh. "Exhibit A. Me. I always go to ATMs at night. After work. It's the only time I remember to." I unlocked the trunk of the Camaro.

"You're nuts," said Todd. "I wouldn't use an ATM at three in the afternoon."

"Just call me reckless." I walked over to the Caprice's trunk and picked out my radio and my spare uniform, neatly wrapped in plastic. Most partners drive to work together, saving one the trouble of constantly loading and unloading the gear, but because of the distance between our homes, we drove separately, and Todd kept the car. He parked it at the 77th Street Station, three blocks from his house, knowing it would be stripped or stolen if he left it in his driveway.

"You can forget the shotgun and the riot stick, and probably the riot helmet," he advised. "No riots scheduled for tomorrow. I checked the calendar."

I grabbed my protective vest. "Want to stop at First Base?"

"While poor Jack is pacing the floor, wondering if his *wife* is dead?"

"While poor Jack is sound asleep with his eye mask and his earplugs. That Jack."

Todd brightened. "So rip off the mask, handcuff him to the headboard, and do a slow striptease. You know how, don't you?"

I slammed the trunk of the Camaro.

"Or you might try a little pistol-whipping. Some guys like that."

"Maybe where you come from, partner. But I don't happen to *own* an AK-47."

"In that case," said Todd, "I'll be happy to lend you mine."

I squeezed the Camaro into a space on Sunset across from the First Base Saloon and cut the engine. Rummaging through my purse, I found a lipstick and applied some. I opened a small gold compact and powdered my nose. Next I produced a tiny vial of perfume, dabbed a drop behind each ear and one on each wrist. Finally, I fished out a brush and ran it through my hair. Trying to feel human again.

I smiled at myself in the rearview mirror.

Thirty-four years old, pretty face, still a great bod, that I knew.

Nevertheless . . . already coming unglued.

"**H e y ,** Johnny." I slid onto a stool as Reba McEntire sobbed from the jukebox and the shaggy-haired bartender slapped a napkin down on the bar.

"We saw *Night Watch* tonight," Johnny related. "I keep waiting for you to appear on the show."

"Yeah, they asked me to once. But I said only if I could play the homicidal maniac."

Johnny laughed. He was a transplanted Bostonian, third-generation Irish like me, and he boasted a long lineage of tavern owners and New England barkeeps. On a quiet night he would regale us with Kennedy stories and, even better, Irish-cop stories. He had merry blue eyes and a ready smile. "Same old?"

"Thanks."

While Johnny poured two shots of vodka into the Kahlua, I glanced around. The First Base Saloon undoubtedly got its name from nearby Dodger Stadium, but the bar's most devoted clientele were cops—since the Police Academy was also nearby. The bar's name spoke to us as well. *First base* was copspeak for the first stop after roll call—usually a coffee shop. This was our first stop after work. Every other Wednesday night—payday—a stately procession of black-and-whites could be seen pulling up outside as officers dashed in to settle their bills.

At the moment, a bunch of off-duty male cops stood at the bar entertaining a delegation of dewy-eyed Latina admirers. Looking through the doorway on my left, I saw a couple of guys shooting pool; several others, whom I assumed to be cops, were talking to two women, neither of whom I recognized. At the far end of the bar, to the right of the TV, was another room, the private domain of serious pool sharps.

"Here you go." Johnny set the drink in front of me. "Watch yourself."

I winked and strolled into the next room, stopping to study a framed montage of LAPD snapshots and two tired Day-Glo bumper stickers: HONK IF YOU'VE BEEN SHOT AT and DIAL 911. MAKE A COP COME.

I sat in a booth in the back, not in the mood to make small talk. But when I glanced up, Doug Romero, a veteran Metro officer, was shuffling through the doorway, hoisting a bottle of beer. I held up a hand and he slid in beside me.

"Flying solo, Mrs. Jack?"

"Don't rub it in, Dougie. How's Gloria?"

"Gorgeous as ever. She broke a tooth, did I tell you? We had to have it capped."

I sipped my Black Russian. "It's probably none of my business, but lately I've noticed a few wrinkles around her eyes. I've got the name of a plastic surgeon if you think she'd be interested. 'Course, there's always the character angle . . . "

"Wiseass. Gloria's only six years old."

"Not too early to start thinking about those nips and tucks."

"Make jokes. But tonight Gloria was magnificent. A kid carjacked a Porsche, crashed it into a Laundromat, and took off on foot. He bolted into a construction site and Gloria nabbed him cowering behind a buncha bags of concrete."

"God," I sighed, "what a woman."

"Damn right. The only canine bitch on the department." Doug Romero drained what was left of his beer. "I gotta hit the road, kiddo. Everything all right?"

I ran my tongue along the edge of my teeth. "I don't know. I've been having this toothache lately. Maybe you better give me the name of Gloria's dentist, huh?"

"*And* her plastic surgeon."

"Ouch."

For a while I watched the pool players, then I brought my gaze back to the group on my left. Three guys with big arms, cops for sure—or ex-cons—and two women, one built like a refrigerator. Possible cop. The second woman, tall, red haired, and vivacious, seemed to be keeping the others enthralled.

"Like some company?"

A round-faced man wearing a knit shirt and jeans was standing over me. He seemed slightly ill at ease, maybe some guy with the mistaken notion that First Base actually was a sports bar.

"Not really."

Politely, I glanced away, allowing the man to make a graceful exit. He didn't budge.

"I don't believe I've seen you before. Are you with the department?"

I met his eyes, brown and unreadable. "Who's asking?"

"Sorry. Adam McKay, retired, but still hanging in." He smiled nervously.

I sipped my drink. "How long were you with the department?"

"Fourteen years. Made the rank of P-three. Then I bailed to work security."

I nodded. Lots of cops went into private security, but usually they waited until they had twenty years for the pension benefits. He seemed a little on edge, probably eager to corner a live one to tell his troubles to. I decided I'd rather listen to my own. "I'm Brenden Harlow with Metro."

He stuck out his hand and I obligingly shook it. "Actually," he said, "I'm not doing much security work anymore, just enough to pay the bills."

"Uh-huh."

"Actually, I'm writing a screenplay."

Naturally. Like every other cop I knew. I said, "It's nice to meet you, but I'm just gonna finish this drink and get out of here. I've got a husband to get home to pretty quick."

"Sure. Maybe some other time." Awkwardly he turned away.

I finished my drink but felt I needed one more, so I rustled up another double from Johnny and returned to the booth. A moment later, the vivacious redhead was sliding in beside me.

"Hi, I'm Grace Randall. But the girls all call me Cookie. You're Brenden Harlow, right?"

"That's right."

"I was here when your husband was on TV. Somebody pointed you out when you came in."

"Then I guess I must be a celebrity." I smiled dolefully and lifted my glass.

"So this is what I was thinking, Brenden." She leaned forward and lowered her voice. "You've got this great-looking husband but you're not home with him. And you just blew two guys off, one after the other. I'm looking at you and thinking, Oh, man. Maybe you'd like to go out with me."

The invitation startled me, though it probably shouldn't have. Thirty, forty percent of the women on the department are reportedly gay, and stories about their more rambunctious activities shoot through the station houses quicker than a satellite transmission. The latest concerned the three caught in flagrante delicto in the Police Academy whirlpool. I'd been hit on only once, by a timid homicide detective I'd driven home one night after work.

Grace Randall was looking at me with wide gray eyes, impressing me with her directness.

"I'm really happy to meet you, Grace—"

"Cookie."

"Cookie. But the truth is, I can't imagine any woman in the whole world doing for me what my husband does. It's just one of those things. Sorry."

The redhead grinned. "I must have read the signals wrong, but you and me, I can tell, we're going to be friends. I just got transferred to Rampart, so I'm sure I'll be seeing you in here. Next time, I buy you a drink. As an apology?"

"No apology necessary." I smiled. "But I will take the drink."

Cookie stuck out her hand, shook mine, and returned to her group with a backward glance and a saucy wink.

I drained my glass and paid my bill.

It was a thirty-minute drive to the beach.

▪ T H R E E ▪

ack's fingers caressing my face woke me.

I could smell the scent of shampoo, see the smile playing on his lips.

"Hi."

"Hi."

"Don't be mad, Bren. I just wanted to talk to you." He bent down and gave me a toothpasty kiss. "You okay?"

I nodded, too paralyzed by sleep to speak.

"You were bouncing around. I thought maybe you were having a bad dream."

I closed my eyes against the spill of bright light tumbling out of the bathroom. "Are you leaving?"

"Soon." Jack sat on the edge of the bed and took both of my hands in his. "Want to have dinner tonight?"

I smiled, remembering how sometimes, on nights when the city was relatively calm, I would use my dinner hour to meet him. That was when my hours were more flexible, before I transferred into Metro, and we would take turns selecting a site: a quiet leafy road in the Hollywood Hills, a secluded spot in Griffith Park, an empty sound stage on the lot—even the back seat of the cruiser, if I could snare it for an hour or two—and we would concoct our own delectable picnics, like children escaping to Wonderland. But tonight I'd be working in the Valley. There would be no way to preplan a time or a place, nearly impossible to pry the car away from Todd.

"We just got assigned some ATM murders in the Valley." I yawned. "But I could probably come by for lunch."

We had done that, too. On days when I worked night watch, three to eleven, I would slip into Jack's trailer and we would lock the door and make love on the ugly flowered couch until he was called back to the set. It struck me now how long it had been since those impromptu trysts had been part of our routine.

Abruptly, Jack dropped my hands. "You know I can't. We're shooting at the naval yard in Long Beach." He sniffled and reached for a Kleenex from my bedside table. "Tomorrow night we're having dinner with the Rocklins. Okay?" He blew his nose noisily.

Mechanically I nodded. "I'm sorry about tonight."

Suddenly there was an insistent rap at the front door. I didn't need to look at the clock. Big Ben, Jack's driver, always arrived neurotically at six.

Jack stood. "Oh. Could you pick up my cleaning? The ticket's on the kitchen table."

I listened to his footsteps until they blended with the soft closing of the front door. After a moment I crawled out of bed and trudged into the bathroom, the air thick from his shower. In the medicine cabinet, I fished out a couple of Excedrin PMs.

To help me get back to sleep.

I n a narrow, tidy living room with white lace curtains and flowered upholstery, Marisa Ruiz leaned slightly forward and lifted a cup and saucer from the coffee table. Sparkling dark eyes, a mass of shoulder-length curls. In her mid-twenties, I guessed as I listened to her recount her uneventful withdrawal of $200 at the Valley S&L sixteen minutes before Mrs. Croft arrived. Marisa was a second-grade schoolteacher who had fallen into the habit of talking in simple declarative sentences.

"I try to go to the bank during the day," she was saying. "But that night I was shopping at the mall."

"Valley Plaza?" I inquired.

"Yes. So I drove over." She took a sip of her coffee. "I know what to do, Officer. I always look first." She laughed. "And I keep hair spray in my purse."

"Hair spray?" I said.

"Have you ever gotten it in your eyes? Mrs. Winter, the kindergarten teacher, told me to always carry hair spray." She smiled cheerfully. "It's a girl's best friend."

"The whole time you were there, you didn't see anyone at all?"

Marisa put down her cup. "Oh no, I did. Sort of. As I was walking back to my car, another car pulled in. A big car, an American kind, I think."

I masked my surprise by keeping my voice impassive. "Did anyone get out of this car?"

"No. He just kind of stopped and rolled down his window. He saw me and I guess he saw that everything was okay, so he drove away."

"What do you mean he saw that everything was okay? What makes you say that?" Quickly I began thumbing through Marisa's earlier statement.

"I mean, he was a policeman. So I figured he was checking."

I glanced up. "I don't see this in your statement, Marisa. How come?"

"They kept asking me about *suspicious*-looking people. I guess I forgot."

I studied the young woman carefully. "This policeman was in uniform?"

"Well he didn't have a hat on. But it looked like he had a uniform on."

"How could you tell?"

Marisa bit her lip, thinking. "It's been so long. He had on a dark shirt, I'm pretty sure, and somehow I just knew he was a cop."

"But he wasn't in a patrol car and he didn't speak to you?"

"No, it was a regular car and he acted like he was just passing through."

"Can you describe him?"

"Not really. I mean he was white, maybe youngish middle age." She grinned. "Whatever that means."

I sighed inwardly. Maybe the cop had jumped into his own car to run a dinner-hour errand, or maybe someone had called in something and he was actually checking. But if he were checking, why wasn't he in a cruiser? Most likely because this man was not a police officer, I decided. A police officer, after learning of the murder, surely would have reported his drive by.

I handed Marisa Ruiz my business card. "If you think of anything else, please call."

● ● ●

T o d d was parked at the curb. After dropping me off at Marisa's, he had gone to pick up dinner. As soon as I opened the passenger door, I was nearly leveled by a blast of peppers.

"I can't turn my back even for a minute," I said as I slid in.

"What? You don't like Taco Bell anymore?"

"I don't even like my husband five nights in a row."

I stared at the oily paper-wrapped lumps in the cardboard box. "Enchiladas or tamales?"

"Both. You owe me four bucks."

"You owe me a hundred. The arm in the trunk wasn't a sausage."

Todd closed his eyes and tapped a finger in the air. "That's twenty-five Taco Bell combo platters including tonight, right?"

"I'm probably going to die," I said.

T o d d ' s beeper went off just as we began questioning Mrs. Croft's teenage son. Her widower, George, a stoop-shouldered man with thinning brown hair, sat in a rocking chair in the living room with us, his empty eyes staring into space.

"'Scuse me," Todd said. "Can I use your phone?"

He was directed to the kitchen. I waited a moment, then decided to proceed. "Billy, try to think back. When you pulled in to the bank, you saw only your mom's car? No one else?"

The pale, lackluster boy blinked behind his glasses. "Uh-huh."

"And it was parked to the right of the tellers?"

"Uh-huh. But she wasn't at the tellers. And then I saw her on the ground and—"

"Brenden." Todd was already moving toward the front door. "Sorry, but we have to leave. We'll come back. Uh, sorry, really."

George Croft nodded but didn't move. Billy rose, crestfallen, and trailed us out of the house. On the front stoop I turned, and I could see the fright in the boy's large round eyes. I touched him lightly on the shoulder. "It'll be okay, I promise." I handed him my card. "This is for you to keep. Use the beeper number. Call me anytime."

Billy gulped.

"We'll be back as soon as we can." But as I trailed Todd to the car, I knew, of course, it wouldn't be "okay." Why couldn't I come up with some meaningful words—a comforting phrase or two, anything—to soothe a victim's family?

As the engine started up, a new thought occurred to me. I half turned to walk back to the house, but Todd was already flinging open my door. "Hurry up. They want us there *now*."

I wasn't tracking. "Just a minute, okay?"

"Brenden, there's been another one."

T h e usual crime-scene was being enacted at the Bank of America on Ventura, a half mile west of the San Diego freeway, when Todd nosed the Caprice through the barricades and into the blinding glare of the generator-operated spots. A traffic control officer told us to park at the Indian restaurant next door.

"Jesus," I said as I jumped out of the Caprice.

The TV vultures, their satellite trucks camped along Ventura, were shoving their mikes into the face of Cmdr. Stan Willsey, LAPD's official spokesman, as he stood rigidly in front of the bank. There were always reporters with scanners who raced to crime scenes, but they didn't come equipped with satellite trucks. And Willsey rarely ventured out from Parker Center.

I noted two ATMs in front of the bank as we ducked under the yellow tape and trotted down a long drive-in lane that ran alongside the bank. It led to a large enclosed parking area and three more ATMs on the bank's back wall. A dozen specialists were combing the lot, pigeons bobbing for crumbs, in addition to the usual gaggle of cops who show up out of instinctive curiosity. Ten feet from the money machines, a woman lay curled on her side, asleep forever in a pool of her own cooling blood.

"Why would she have driven back here at night," Todd asked, "when she could have used the tellers on the street?"

"Parking," I said. "In L.A., it all comes down to the automobile."

We retraced our steps past the corpse, which had drawn a crowd, and back out to the boulevard. Through the bank's glass front doors, I spotted Higgins conferring with the captain of Van Nuys Division. Captains rarely showed up at crime scenes. We flashed our badges and hurried inside.

Across the room from the brass, a shell-shocked gray-haired man was trying to comfort a hysterical woman. Nearby, an agitated long-haired young man paced back and forth, an unlit cigarette stuck in his mouth. In a third tableau, toward the back of the bank, two men in suits spoke in hushed tones.

We hiked up to the brass.

"What happened?" I said.

Sergeant Higgins measured me with cool eyes. He was medium height with thick dark hair, a mustache exactingly sculpted to LAPD's hair code, and a body preserved from 1974, when he had won the state high school wrestling championship.

"Captain Logan, Todd Robbie and Brenden Harlow. They're in my squad."

We nodded dutifully at the slender, blue-eyed Logan and got a curt nod in return.

"About fifty minutes ago," Higgins recited, "the guy with the cigarette discovered the body. Same story. Stab wounds. A receipt for $300 but no cash. Car keys in her pocket. We got one criminalist on scene, and the medical examiner's supposedly rolling."

"How did the media get here so fast?" I asked. "You said fifty minutes ago?"

"Some clown heard it over the police frequency. But it would have come out anyway." Higgins paused. "Victim's Sheila Dann."

"Who?"

"Brenden only watches one TV show," Todd jumped in, "and it ain't during the day."

"An actress?" I said.

Todd held up three fingers. "Emmy Award–winning actress. A hat trick."

It still didn't ring a bell. I shook my head.

"*All My Husbands.* You'd like it," Todd said.

I stared at the lifeless body of Sheila Dann as the criminalist finished making his notes. What had been, only a short while ago, a vibrant, breathing twenty-eight-year-old beauty was now a rigid, blank-eyed broken doll, carelessly cast away. The gruesome transformation always unnerved me.

A man in tan cords and a brown jacket, whom I took for a detective, sat on his haunches studying the corpse. "Why is it I always get to put the good-looking ones to bed *after* they're dead?" he asked, tapping his notebook.

"I'm not gonna touch that," I said. "How many wounds?"

The detective just looked at me.

"Sorry. Brenden Harlow, Metro. I won't get in your way, Detective." I paused. "Are those handcuffs?"

The detective followed my gaze to the woman's right foot. "Cute, huh? He leaves them as calling cards. Always under the victim's right foot. She was stabbed three times. Two chest, one stomach. Haven't turned her over yet, but if it's the same perp, he doesn't cut 'em in the back. This one, even if she'd been attacked in the emergency room, they couldn't have saved. Guy practically ripped her heart out." Wearily, he stood. "I'm T. J. McCall, and I'm still working on the guy's third victim, Andrea Wright."

Interesting. At Metro we hadn't been told about the handcuffs. But then, detectives often don't share information, even with one another.

"What I don't get," I said, "is why he doesn't stab the victim from behind. She falls to the ground, he grabs the money and runs. Even if she lives, chances are she wouldn't have seen his face. But this way, confronting her head-on, there's bound to be a struggle."

McCall snapped his notebook shut. "Serial killers don't think in terms of convenience, Harlow."

So Todd was right. The killer was hooked on murder, not the cash reward. And he wanted it to be a game, which accounted for the hand-cuffs—his party favors. Worse, he had chosen as his killing grounds a most public place, frequented by nearly everyone at least once a week.

"Okay," I said, "so he's after a thrill. In this case, I suppose it's either the terror on the victim's face or the challenge of making a kill head-on. In a very public place."

McCall cocked his head and gave me a long appraising look. "You like danger, Harlow?"

"Controlled danger." I grinned. "I'm picky."

He pulled out a card. "My number. In case you need it."

As I looked again at Sheila Dann, I tried to guess, as I always did, if she had felt any foreboding as she marched up to the Readyteller.

I pocketed McCall's card—and wondered why I'd need it.

Jeffrey Posner had finally broken down and lit the cigarette dangling from his lips. He was seated on a couch at the front of the bank, sandwiched between Todd and T. J. McCall. Both were taking notes. I slipped into a chair across from them and listened.

Even though it was unlikely that Todd and McCall had ever met, they had automatically fallen into the good cop–bad cop routine. Mc-Call played the heavy. He was a large man with curly brown hair, a hawklike nose and, at the moment, a decidedly threatening manner.

He held up a wallet. "You only got eighteen bucks in here, Posner. That corpse out there, *before* she was a corpse, got three hundred outta the machine."

He was a good-looking kid. Nice build, cute nose, all jaw, and shoulder-length black hair, which he kept raking with his fingers. "I didn't take her money. I didn't do anything! I just saw her lying there—"

"That's what happens when you kill someone, shit head. They just lie there," T. J. McCall said.

"Maybe," Todd offered, "he saw it go down, you know? Saw the guy plunging the knife into Sheila's chest. I bet if you ask him, he'd give us a real good description. I think he wants to help."

"Fuck it," McCall said.

"Look, I didn't see anything," Posner wailed. "I was just trying to be a good citizen. I called nine-one-one from my car. Then I waited. I thought I should wait."

Todd nodded. "He's got a point. The killer wouldn't wait."

McCall stood up in disgust. "Let's go, Jeffrey. You're a real entertaining guy. Let's see how your act plays at the station."

As the anguished young man let McCall escort him out, Todd closed his notebook and frowned. "His act won't play at all. He didn't do it. You agree?"

I got up. I could still taste the peppers. "Do you have any Tums?" I said.

W e regrouped at Metro and reviewed our latest game plan, which wasn't much of an improvement over the old one. Five stabbings and we still had nothing. As Todd and I were walking out, Bill Turley, the lieutenant in charge of Metro's B Platoon, our platoon, intercepted us in front of the administrative offices. "Brenden, got a minute?"

"Sure, Lieutenant."

"Captain and I want to talk to you."

Uh-oh, I thought as I rolled my eyes at Todd and followed Turley through the administrative offices and into the private domain of Capt. Martin McGrew. Although my dealings with Monster had been few and always pleasant, I privately believed he was most comfortable in the ranks of men and had accepted me into Metro purely to appease the equal-opportunity screamers.

McGrew, broad shouldered and barrel chested, was seated behind a large desk at the narrow end of his brick-walled, pie-shaped office. On the wall, where a window should have been, he had drawn one and framed it with real curtains. He rose as I entered. Despite thick glasses and pockmarked skin, he wasn't a bad-looking man, if you factored in the boyish smile and mellifluous voice. What accounted for his nickname was that, because of the thick glasses, no one could be certain if he was looking at them, or something across the room.

"Captain."

"Have a seat, Brenden. Bill, you too." McGrew sat down and, to my dismay, proceeded to remove his glasses. He placed them on the desk. Now I felt even more discomfited. Like, could he even see me?

"Brenden, as you know, there are situations when we believe the best way to nail a suspect is by using a decoy," Monster began. "When there's a series of bank robberies, we'll put people inside as tellers because bandits like to make return engagements. But with serial killers, decoys are rarely used, since it's impossible to predict when or where the killer will strike next."

He paused, and I, thinking I ought to say something, said, "Right."

"I just got off the phone with Captain Ragsdale of Robbery/Homicide. He told me, despite the odds, he was thinking of using a decoy anyway. And since our killer only attacks females, the decoy would have to be a female."

This time when McGrew paused, I said nothing.

"Frankly, I don't like it. As you know, this department has always been slow to use female decoys in dangerous situations. Call it sexism, but even with men we always try to weigh the benefits of the strategy against the danger to an officer's life."

I spoke quietly. "I know that, sir."

"Ragsdale specifically asked for you. I won't order you, Brenden. I'm only asking you to think about it. Would you be willing to serve as decoy in this case?"

Unaccountably, McGrew popped his glasses on. His right eye now appeared to stare directly at me while his left eye wandered out the make-believe window. He said, "You can be frank with me. If you say no, I'll understand. You'll be given deep, deep protection."

"I understand, sir."

Lieutenant Turley cleared his throat. "If I might say something here . . . Brenden might want to talk to her husband first."

"Oh definitely," Monster agreed. "Fact is, Brenden, I would never let my wife do anything this dangerous, and I'm not ashamed of it either."

At once I understood their concern. Police officers were instinctively more protective of the weak and the defenseless, and that meant women and children. Some officers I had worked with literally had to jam their hands in their pockets to keep from opening doors for me or pushing me to the ground when confronting an armed suspect.

"Captain." As Monster's eyes zeroed in on me, I made an effort to meet them—both of them. "You wouldn't be asking me to do this if you didn't think I could. And I wouldn't be in Metro if I didn't think I could. So why don't you just tell Captain Ragsdale you've got a live one here? I'll do it if he says okay."

McGrew glanced at Turley and, for a second, I caught the apprehension in both men's eyes. Monster hesitated. "You sure?"

I grinned. "Absolutely."

But as I headed for the garage I couldn't help wondering: Why had Ragsdale, whom I didn't know, specifically asked for me?

Jack was still awake when I arrived home. On Friday nights, with his weekends free, he often waited up for me. He was in bed reading *Sports Illustrated* and drinking a cup of tea. Crumpled pieces of Kleenex littered the floor. He smiled as I walked in, and blew his nose. "Hey, darlin', you're alive."

"Just barely," I said. "When they had me pinned to the wall, I told those gun-happy bastards I had to get home to Sergeant Matt Blaine, Mr. *Night Watch* himself."

Jack put down the magazine. "They fell for it?"

"They do every time." I gave him a kiss. "How are you?"

"Someday, after you lock up all the carjackers and drug dealers, you guys'll go after the real criminals in life. Writers!"

"Uh-oh," I said automatically. Jack was always battling his writers, seemingly with good reason. I opened the door to the walk-in closet and started to undress. "As long as they don't try to kill *you* off."

"Listen to this, Bren." Jack put down his tea and sat up straighter. "So I'm pulling alongside this guy, yelling at him. Like through a speaker or something? Creep doesn't slow down, so now I'm sup- posed to shoot his tires out. I mean, I went freaking nuts, right? I said no cop's gonna shoot out someone's tires doing ninety on the freeway! And they said, 'This is TV!' I said, 'Yeah, well, it's also supposed to be L.A., not fucking Moscow.'"

I laughed as I slipped on a black silk pajama top. In the beginning I would actually try to help Jack by suggesting alternative scenarios. But my input, I would soon learn from Jack's irate voice on his cell phone, only resulted in more battles on the set. My husband is not exactly a diplomat when it comes to informing his producers that the writers are idiots.

"Be right back," I said and popped into the bathroom.

When I came out, I halted in the doorway. Jack was fingering a pair of handcuffs. Slowly, I walked over to him. The drawer to his bedside table was open. I lifted out a second pair of cuffs.

"You mean it?"

"It's why I married you," Jack said.

I snapped one of the cuffs onto his left wrist. "Is it?" I pried the other pair of cuffs from his hand.

"Okay, that and your Irish soda bread."

I slipped this cuff onto his right wrist. "And they say love is a complicated thing."

His breath was coming quicker now. "Whatcha gonna do?"

Raising his arms, I secured each cuff to the brass rail running across the headboard. "I don't know. Todd says some guys like to be pistol-whipped."

"Yeah?"

I reached over and switched off the lamp. We had done this once, fooling around, just for the sheer silliness of it. And Jack, unable to use his hands to touch me, helpless to do anything but writhe beneath me, to trust and to wait, never knowing what I would do next, swore that he had actually died in a blaze of white light. When the tables were turned and I was cuffed, or tied to the bed with long silky scarves, I too felt a heightened degree of passion. It was as if the partner who was free of constraints instinctively became more attentive and caring to the one who was helpless.

We abandoned the dual blindfolds, though, the night the bedside lamp came crashing down on Jack's head.

Now, sitting astride him, I began sucking his nipples, and then I bent down, fitting mine onto his, then sliding up him and running the tip of my tongue across his face. "You know what they say at the academy," I murmured. "A happy prisoner won't make trouble."

"I won't," Jack promised. "Oh, Brenden."

S o it was hardly the time to tell him that I was about to become a sitting duck for a deranged slasher. I would have all of Saturday to do that. Only, Saturday morning, as I opened my eyes, Jack bounded into the bedroom with a breakfast tray. It contained a cup of coffee, which Jack always brewed just right, orange juice, and—plunked for-lornly in the middle of a paper plate—a stale bagel.

"Change of plans tonight," he sang as he climbed onto the bed. Sitting cross-legged in his nylon warm-up suit, he broke the bagel in two and took a bite. The president of the network that airs *Night Watch* was in from New York and had insisted on hosting a dinner. "At Spago," Jack said. "The East Coast guys still have to go to Spago."

"Do *we* have to go?"

The president of entertainment, the head of programming, et cetera, et cetera, would also be there. "It's really an honor to be in-cluded," Jack said, "don't you think?"

"I thought we were supposed to see the Rocklins." Jay Rocklin was Jack's agent, and his wife, Suzy, was probably my only real friend outside the department.

"I already called and explained. Oh, and listen. Ronnie Harris's wife will be there. You can talk to her about getting on the committee for the ball."

Ronnie Harris was president of the entertainment division, and each fall his wife, Cee Cee, organized this $1,000-a-plate extravaganza known as the Florence Nightingale Ball to raise money for whatever illness was the rage that year. Those on the West Coast who worked for the network, or were under contract to the network, felt obliged to cough up the money and attend; who knew the ramifications if they did not? I hadn't minded the blackmail—variations were played out in the police department, though on a pitifully smaller scale—but Jack's insistence that I cozy up to a bunch of social-climbing sharkettes for the sake of his career always made me nuts.

I put down my cup and reached for his hand. "Jack? You're going to hate me."

He narrowed his aquamarine eyes. "You're coming tonight, Bren. I don't care what—"

"No, of course I am. But starting tomorrow . . . "

Jack began sniffling noisily.

"Do you have a cold?" I asked.

"I think it's an allergy. A spring allergy," Jack stressed. Usually when he wasn't feeling well he treated his condition as an emergency room event. But at the moment he seemed merely annoyed.

"Anyway," I continued, "I'm going to be tied up with this ATM thing, which involves—"

Jack pulled his hand from mine and climbed off the bed.

"There's Kleenex right here."

But he was already heading for the bathroom. "We have to be there at eight."

I felt my frustration rising. "I need to talk to you. It's important."

The bathroom door swung shut, a fitting symbol, I decided, of our deteriorating marriage and divergent interests. When we met, eight years ago, I'd been on the department two and a half years and I was working patrol out of Rampart Division, a tiny, twelve-square-mile area west of downtown that was home to ninety languages and the highest crime rate in the city. My partner, a hip Latino, was thrilled when we were asked to baby-sit an actor doing "research."

I was not. Gang violence was breaking out almost every night, and the last thing I needed was some hotshot talent flossing his teeth in the back seat.

Only, Jack Hayes hadn't been like that. Quiet and respectful, he had asked the right questions and hadn't tried to impress us with a bunch of Hollywood bullshit. After his last night with us, he invited me to dinner.

He was four years older than I and his career was stalled in the guest-appearance stage in weekly dramatic series. The two-week ride-along had been in preparation for a TV movie in which he played a lawyer defending a cop. The role won him an Emmy nomination and, according to Jack, I had brought him the luck of the Irish. We were married the following December.

Two years later he landed the lead on *Night Watch,* a ratings hit now finishing its fourth season. Which is when the problems began. It was becoming a little difficult to come home after dealing with the sad or murderous souls who populated my day, only to be hauled off to one of Jack's glamorous parties, where his friends expected me to perform clever tricks. "Are you really a cop? Show me! Wrestle me to the floor!"

Or, seizing on a possible use for me, they would follow with the predictable security questions: Would I drop by and check out their alarm systems? Should they get a gun? What kind? What *else* should they do? And Jack, floating in some nether reaches of the host's estate, would resent my pleading glances to go home. Upon reflection it seemed like a petty gripe, these parties; only, in my darker moods they seemed to portend a deeper, richer vein of problems festering under the surface.

The bathroom door flew open and he barely flicked me a glance as he strode past the bed.

"Jack?"

At the door he turned and, for a moment, our eyes locked. I knew that his refusal to talk about my assignments was due to fear, fear that I was abandoning him, just as his mother had abandoned him—at least in Jack's eyes—when she had been forced to get a job to support them. That I, like his mother, could wake up in the morning and go through the day content in my work, leading a life without him, unfailingly served to terrify him.

"And do something with yourself, okay?" he said. "I want you to look *right* for a change."

His words hit me so hard that it took me a moment to catch my breath. Even then I didn't speak immediately as I stared at him uncomprehendingly from across the room. "Meaning what?" I said quietly.

"Meaning," Jack emphasized, "don't look like a cop."

F o r once, I was grateful the restaurant was noisy.

I was seated between Alex Grodin, the network president from New York, and Jack. Jack was preoccupied with Cee Cee Harris, to his right, so for most of the dinner I talked to Alex and his wife, a quiet, gracious woman named Katharine. Given the noise level, it was nearly impossible to carry on a conversation with anybody else at the table. Which was fine with me.

Despite Jack's affront, I had only to flick a glance at the other women to know, childishly, that I had won. I was younger than they were, and none could compete with my well-toned body or the black Spandex dress that encased it. My proud carriage kept me from looking like the skimpily clad bimbos who occupied other tables, but I had never much cared what I wore anyway. As a cop I had learned how to fit in anywhere; it was my body and how I moved it that announced who I was.

Alex Grodin picked up on that immediately.

From the moment I sat down he made a genuine effort to draw me out, and I found myself relaxing, soothed by his charm and his lightning-quick wit. He asked insightful questions about police work and listened intently to my answers. From time to time he would nudge the conversation back to the network, and in the spirit of sharing a private joke, he made light of his job and of the television industry itself.

"Most people would agree that you do something constructive for society," he said as the main-course plates were whisked away; "whereas most people would agree that I do something *destructive*."

He had laughed. But once the dessert orders were taken and it occurred to me that I was actually enjoying myself, Mr. Network TV threw me a sucker punch.

"Brenden," he said gravely, "I want you to give this some thought."

My attention was diverted as Cee Cee Harris laughingly stood and excused herself. I started to say something to Jack, only he jumped up and followed her. I turned back to Alex. "Sorry."

"With your knowledge of police work, you could be a major asset for us," he said without preamble. "We could hire you as a consultant for our crime shows. Down the road, maybe you'll come up with a concept for a show and you could produce it. You're smart, savvy, and I think you could have a lot of fun."

Whether it was all the wine I had consumed or the noise, I was slow to catch on. "But I couldn't," I replied sincerely. "My days are long enough as it is."

Alex showed me his bonded white teeth. "I'm not asking you to moonlight, dear. I'm talking full-time job." He drummed his fingers on the back of my hand. "The money would knock you out."

Only then did it sink in. My God, I thought, had Jack put the network president up to this? Here, at Spago, on a Saturday night, surrounded by the cream of network TV—had Jack actually colluded to ambush me?

I looked into the warm, questioning eyes of Alex Grodin and said, "Thanks for the offer, but I'm not ready to leave the department yet. Especially to do something so *destructive*." I gave him a nice smile.

Abruptly, he pulled his head back and spoke to his wife, as if this conversation had never taken place. I turned just as Jack reappeared and sat down. A moment later, Cee Cee Harris swept back to the table. As she was about to pass behind me, she suddenly leaned down and put her head between mine and Jack's. "Brenden," she said gaily, "your husband's a real hoot." With a giggle, she moved away.

A hand bearing a plate swept under my nose and deposited a warm chocolate puddle decorated with a white squiggle. I reached for my wineglass.

I sat there, listening to the bright, noisy chatter—feeling thoroughly alone.

▪ F I V E ▪

T he six banks we're targeting tonight are within a three-mile radius," Sergeant Higgins was saying. "At each location, we'll have two people stationed at observation posts. We'll also have a layoff man within a hundred feet. Got that?"

It was standard procedure. I began to doodle. I made a stick figure of a wino sitting on a curb holding a bunch of droopy flowers. Which is what a layoff man was, more or less. That is, the worst-looking, most unlikely person on the street. A wino, a bag lady, a grungy kid on skates with a headset, someone like that. Once, I sat on a curb for eight straight days holding a sign—NEED WORK TO FEED MY BABY—while a well-dressed male cop strolled the area, flashing his Rolex and diamond pinky ring (borrowed for the occasion from a jewelry store), hoping to arouse the interest of a thief known as Gold Digger Dan. He never did. Meanwhile, the only offer I got, as I kept my eyes peeled, was from an elderly man with a cane who asked me to help him clean out his garage. "Maybe next week," I told him and, as he glared at me, I felt really bad.

"Naturally we'll have a chase car at each location," Higgins continued. "We're gonna try to have shit details combing the areas for possible suspects, but it'll depend upon manpower availability. Another thing, people. From now on, we'll be working out of Van Nuys Division. Roll call will be at sixteen hundred hours."

This was Monday. Over the weekend, the newly minted ATM Task Force had been assembled. Heading it would be senior Detective Marty Walters from Robbery/Homicide. His number two in the joint effort, unfortunately, was Higgins. Walters would be the brains; Higgins, his legs. Over them would be a lieutenant named Thomas Inman. Under them would be a lead complement of detectives from Robbery/Homicide, a couple more from either Van Nuys or North Hollywood, where the five murders had occurred—and my platoon from Metro. Basically, we would provide the bodies to hunt down the assailant. While the unit may have looked impressive on paper, a task force frequently brought out the worst in the LAPD. Often they were run by wannabe generals and staffed by cops with their own inimitable quirks, one being their creative interpretation of "the rules." Rather than operating like a well-oiled brigade, we often acted like escaped characters from *M*A*S*H*.

I raised my hand.

"Yeah, Harlow."

"Sarge, I'm gonna have to wear a sweatshirt, maybe a denim blouse or something. A jacket or a bulky sweater will look funny in this heat. So I'm wondering—"

"Right. No protective vest." Higgins grinned. "We're still scouring the city for a steel-plated bra, though. I hear they have 'em at Trashy Lingerie."

"And you would know, sir," I said sweetly. I could feel Todd stiffen beside me.

Higgins ignored my remark. "We did get you a fanny pack with Velcro 'stead of a zipper. That'll be the best we can do. Go to the Toy Store and pick up a .380 Sigma. Anything else?"

"No sir."

"Then see Mack after. He'll wire you up."

The night before, in preparation for our Valley exercise, Todd and I had visited the six locations we'd be working. We drove the routes from bank to bank and figured where, in each bank's lot or on the street, I might park. We studied the lighting near the ATMs and tried to guess from which direction the attacker would come. Then we drove to Rent-A-Wreck, where Todd "tried out" the backseat floors of at least a dozen sedans, with the fussiness of a man purchasing an eighty-foot yacht. Finally he chose a beat-up Taurus. Then, as the clerk was drawing up the papers, Todd changed his mind and went for an even more decrepit Intrepid.

Sgt. Mack Maloney was waiting for me in the Toy Store. Stocky, and with a nose that looked as if it had once taken a healthy right cross, he'd been brought in from the field years ago and now found or designed whatever exotic equipment Metro or SWAT might need.

He is good at it. He is also an indiscriminate bigot, who despises any officer who isn't white, male, and, like himself, slouching toward retirement.

"Sarge?" He was sitting on a stool at the workbench that ran along one side of the long narrow room, flipping through *Playboy*. The top of his head was slicked with the few strands of black and gray hair that remained.

"Yeah, Harlow." He tore his eyes from the magazine, held it up, and shook out the centerfold. "You ever wish you looked like *that?*"

I studied the buxom goddess. "Gee, I don't know. I'm not really into plastics." I checked the workbench. "Is my transmitter ready?"

With a thud, the magazine landed in a drawer. I was wearing khaki shorts, running shoes and socks, and a navy sweatshirt. As Maloney got to his feet, his eyes covered every square inch of me. Then he snatched the transmitter from the workbench and slipped it into the pocket of a narrow black cloth harness.

"Take off your shirt. Unless you want it in your panties." He gave me a hard-edged stare.

"I'll tape it to my left side, sir. I know how to do it." Asshole.

"It's got to be done *right*. You think I haven't seen tits before?"

Real ones? I nearly shot back. But I held my tongue and extended my hand. "I'll take care of it, Sarge."

"Look, Harlow, you wanna be a cop, act like one. A guy needs to be wired up, he takes off his shirt. Positioning the transmitter and securing it is tricky. It's my ass if it's not done right."

Some guys I wouldn't have minded. But Mack Maloney was a self-anointed standard bearer for the old boys who still ran Metro and staunchly battled to keep women and gays out. While I resented being harassed in front of other cops, I found one-on-one confrontations like chasing down a suspect; you simply had to outsmart 'em.

I said, "Okay. So draw me a diagram. I'll tape the transmitter, you can run the wire up. I'm kind of in a hurry."

Maloney didn't move. But the muscles in his neck did. And the silence between us grew heavy.

A footstep sounded behind me. "Brenden, you ready?"

A baseball cap that said *Red Car* on it poked through the doorway in the hands of Lieutenant Turley. He gave it a twirl on one finger. "Lucky cap," he declared. "It's from the old trolley car days and it has a history. All the officers who've worn it over the years have come back unharmed." He handed it to me.

I slipped it on. "Thanks."

"It'll keep your hair in place. You wired yet?"

Calmly, I walked over to Maloney and took the transmitter and the harness from his hand. "I was just on my way to the locker room, sir." A roll of flesh-colored tape lay on the counter; I grabbed that, too. "You got some scissors?" Without a word, Maloney opened a drawer and handed me a pair.

"Be right back," I said.

"Hat looks cute," Lieutenant Turley said.

B e c a u s e he would be cooped up on the backseat floor all night, Todd won the right to drive to the Valley, which meant thirty-five minutes of doing the five o'clock freeway two-step.

As we sat in traffic on the 101, he reached for his fifth toothpick, a sure sign that Todd was nervous.

I wasn't. So much of police work was tedious that I sometimes wondered why I bothered. Then something like this would come along—or a middle-of-the-night phone call—and I'd be like a kid going to the circus. I was ready to rock 'n' roll.

The freeway wasn't. I popped a piece of gum into my mouth and stared at the red Fiero in front of us. It was still stopped, even though our lane had begun to creep forward. Impatiently, Todd honked.

The driver, fixated on his rearview mirror, didn't move. Todd honked again.

I handed him a stick of gum. "Can't you see he's flossing?" I said.

W e needed to wait until dark, so we played gin rummy in the parking lot of a fast-food place on Lankershim. Then we headed out.

I was at the wheel, Todd on the floor in back. I had already checked my equipment. A tiny mike was attached to the shoulder harness I wore under my sweatshirt, and a second mike was clipped to the sun visor. Our car radio was set to a special frequency. Todd had a ROVER with an earplug. At least a dozen people would be able to hear me through the mike or speak to me or Todd over the designated tactical frequency. Higgins, who would be calling the shots, would be riding in a van with a Metro officer and a technician from our Scientific Investigation Division. A second sergeant and an officer were in a dual-purpose Metro car—the chase car—and would precede us to each location. They would do a quick drive-by surveillance, then park nearby.

The traffic was heavy as I swung onto Laurel Canyon heading north. I stopped for a light at Magnolia and could see the Bank of America across the intersection. It was our first stop. Although it stood alone, it was surrounded on two sides by an L-shaped strip mall. As I waited for the light to change, Higgins's voice crackled over the radio. "Circle the block. Someone's at the machine."

Driving past the location I could see the single Versateller on the west wall of the bank. A man in a suit was standing at the machine, folding bills into his wallet.

Behind him were parking spaces, and beyond them, a row of shops. All appeared to be closed except for a liquor store. I continued driving to the next cross street and turned right. When I circled back to Laurel Canyon, I reported to Higgins.

"Okay," he said, "pull in. Park in front of the pay phone past the machine and remember to leave your window down."

I turned into the narrow strip of asphalt that separated the bank from shops behind it. An Asian in a white apron was, at the moment, sitting on the curb in the alley beside a Chinese restaurant, cutting vegetables, even though the restaurant was closed. He would be our lay-off man. The van and the chase car would be nearby. As I rounded the corner of the bank and pulled into the slot in front of the phone, I glanced across the street at the Lucky supermarket. Somewhere in the parking lot that fronted it would be a car—the observation post— where two officers with binoculars would be watching. In the alley behind the Chinese restaurant, or perhaps even in the tree near the Versateller, two more cops with ROVERs would be ready to move if the OPs told them to go. Despite my eagerness, I found myself tensing.

Three tall light stands illuminated the parking area, and a light on the overhanging roof above the bank shone down on the single Versateller. I turned off the engine.

From the street came the drone of traffic and the occasional high-pitched squeal of a fast-accelerating car. I flipped through the plastic cards on the passenger seat and found the one for Bank of America. Instinctively, I checked the rearview mirror; two abnormally large green eyes stared back. I licked my lips and got out, slamming the door behind me.

Eyes straight ahead, I walked up to the ATM—and nearly jumped; but it was only the explosive backfire of a motorcycle. "Calm down," I told myself as I fed the card into the slot. I pressed the computer screen for English, then punched in the code *1234*. For once, someone in the department had used common sense, keying all the cards to the same easy-to-remember number.

I pushed the spot marked WITHDRAWAL. As a new screen appeared listing various amounts, it struck me how exposed my back was and, to my surprise, I found my hands trembling. The tiny mike inside my sweatshirt rested between my shoulder and my clavicle. I wondered if Higgins and all the others tuned in could hear my belabored breathing—or the pounding of my heart.

I punched *$20*. The words flashed, ONE MINUTE, PLEASE.

I gripped my fingers to keep them still. They were ice cold.

Suddenly . . . the sound of a car pulling in. I squeezed my fingers harder and . . . a door slammed. Footsteps sounded. The machine began to hum, then it burped. A door slid open and a twenty appeared. There was no way they could talk to me, only I to them. The prearranged signal for danger was two honks of a horn. Despite the protection and the precautions, I couldn't remember ever feeling so vulnerable. The footsteps were now close behind me.

Carefully, I removed the money. I stuffed it into my shorts pocket and, with a deep breath, I turned.

A blond woman about my age stood there rummaging through a large purse. I walked to the Intrepid, switched on the ignition, and rolled up the window. The woman was stepping up to the machine. Turning on the radio, I said, "R-seventeen. All clear."

"Take your time proceeding to the second location," Higgins responded. "I want to make sure this woman is all right."

"Check."

"And R-seventeen?"

"Yes?"

"Relax."

So he had heard my ragged breathing. Well, screw it. It was my back that was unprotected, not his. I jammed the car into reverse and backed up.

The woman was still at the machine. I drove past her but idled at the end of the drive, pretending to wait for the traffic to clear. I kept my eyes on the rearview mirror. When the woman began walking to her car, I turned onto Magnolia.

"Okay," I said, "you've got some stretch time."

Todd's head bobbed into the rearview mirror. "I knew it," he declared. "I should have been an astronaut. Least then I could have had *fun* being scrunched up like a sardine."

"Sardines aren't scrunched up. They're packed in."

"Exactly. Astronauts get to float around."

"But you'd have to forgo tamales and sex, maybe for weeks. You'd never survive."

"How do you know they don't have sex? Maybe they just don't tell us that stuff."

"Right," I said. "Sex in a space shuttle. With the guys. What a turn-on. A bunch a dicks flapping in the ionosphere . . . Oh shit."

I had totally forgotten the open mikes. I bit my lip. "Um, Sarge? Strike that, okay? I'm only trying to humor my partner here."

A profusion of static crackled over the radio.

"You're humoring half the department," Sergeant Higgins said.

B a n k number two was a Citibank, deeper into the Valley, solidly in the territory commandeered by the Central Americans. Around here, I was more likely to get riddled by a gang's bullets than slashed by a psychotic killer. I kept my eyes moving and warned Todd we were approaching the location.

This bank was situated on the corner of Van Nuys and Vanowen, in an area that still showed signs of earthquake damage; or maybe the boarded-up stores were casualties of the dogged recession. I was instructed to drive past Vanowen and park a few feet along on Van Nuys. Down Vanowen—twenty yards past the two Readytellers—a van with blackened windows stood at the curb. It would be ours.

Palming the Citibank card, I crossed the street. A tall woman in jeans and a gold motorcycle helmet nearly barreled into me. "There's a man in the lot," she breathed and kept walking. With surprise, I realized the woman was Cookie Randall from the First Base Saloon.

Now, standing in front of the machine, I hesitated. I knew, from our surveillance, the bank's lot was behind the building. If the guy wanted to come for me, he would come from the lot. I angled my body slightly to the left so that I could see him out of the corner of my eye. Then I slid the card into the slot.

The card popped out.

I tried again. This time the machine swallowed it and the computer screen lit up. As I punched the appropriate squares, again hitting *$20,* I was aware of how desolate the streets were, how quiet it was. Despite its aerobicized glossy image, Los Angeles remained an unhip town that worshiped the sun and slavishly kept the sun's hours.

I heard a sound and glanced quickly to my left. No one. My eyes returned to the machine, which was still WORKING ON IT. A car with a radio blaring roared up Van Nuys just as the bill pitched through the chute. With relief, I lifted the compartment door.

"I'll take the money, lady."

I flinched. It was the voice of a male Latino and it came from my *right*. Leaving the money in the chute, I turned slowly. A guy, five-six and wearing a soiled T-shirt and jeans, stood five feet away, pointing a semiautomatic at me. He must have come off Van Nuys; why hadn't anyone seen him? Shit. No protective vest, and I wouldn't be able to uncork the little .380 semi in my fanny pack fast enough. I said, "No problem, mister. You can have the money."

As I spoke, my eyes traveled over the guy's shoulder to the Intrepid thirty feet away. The rear door was opening.

"Gimme it now."

"It's in the machine. I walk away, you take it."

He was smug. He'd probably been taking other people's money since his hands were big enough to wrap around a gun. Todd was out of the car now, gun drawn. I'd give him twenty feet.

I said, "Okay? You take it, it's yours."

The scumbag grinned and came toward me. "Maybe I take more, huh, *chica?*"

"There's two hundred in the machine. Take it."

Like a cat, he sprang and wound fingers of steel around my left wrist. I started to bring up my right knee when—inexplicably—his eyes widened and he let go of me. He stepped backward, hesitated, then he took off.

There was a loud pounding, then a *whoosh* as Cookie flew by and threw herself at the fleeing thief. As he hit the sidewalk with a jaw-cracking *thwack*, she knocked the gun from his hand and was on top of him in a flash, snapping on the handcuffs. Within seconds the guy was surrounded by cops.

I looked at Todd. "Where'd he come from?"

"Around the corner. I didn't see from where."

Cookie scrambled to her feet. "He was in a Toyota, a few doors down Van Nuys. I saw him get out. I ran back through that drive-in on the other side of the bank and cut through the lot. You okay?"

"I'm fine."

I watched the guy as he was being led toward the squad car. All the starch had gone out of him and he looked as if he were about to cry. He was probably an illegal with an unregistered handgun. He'd be booked, maybe serve a couple of months, then he'd be back on the street. With a different name.

Higgins spoke to one of the officers, then started toward me. As he approached, I prepared for a bunch of lip. But all he said was, "You want to take a breather?"

"I'm fine." I wasn't. On only the second bank of the first night I had learned just how "deep" my protection was. I remembered Monster's admonition that even a split second could mean disaster, but I had naively expected better than this. And the danger hadn't even come from the slasher.

I felt my anger rising as I watched the handcuffed man being ushered into the squad car, and it was all I could do to restrain myself from going over and leaving a few marks on the creep. He was on my turf, probably illegally, and he had threatened my life for a lousy twenty bucks.

With blood roaring in my ears, I walked to the machine, grabbed the twenty, and crossed the street to the Rent-A-Wreck.

A s I drove to the third bank, my pent-up anger reconfigured into a burst of euphoria. The tension that had been building in me had been released during the attempted robbery, along with whatever those endorphins are that make you feel giddy. The chances of meeting up with the killer on the first night, I reminded myself, were slim to none. According to the information we'd been given, he had struck two times on Tuesday nights, once on Wednesday, and twice on Fridays. And always when there was a half-moon. Tonight there was a quarter moon. I often wondered if killers actually planned their attacks according to such criteria. From what I gathered, they responded to unstoppable urges rather than devious plotting techniques. At the moment, our man was probably sitting in some dark, depressing room staring at the tube.

I was wrong.

The third bank, located on Riverside not far from Fashion Square mall, attracted a steady stream of customers. Higgins told me to move on to bank number four.

This one, a Glendale Federal Savings, was on a dark stretch of Ventura in Sherman Oaks. Although its one ATM was located on the boulevard, the bank sat on the southwest corner of a residential street. A car wash, closed, was located on the west side of the bank. A restaurant across Ventura had its main entrance and parking in the rear. There were no other businesses open nearby.

Instead of stopping in front of the ATM, I made a right and parked just short of the turn-in to the bank's lot. A wall separated the lot from an alley that ran behind it. On the other side of the alley was a house.

"I like this," I said softly. "Ready?"

"Ready," said Todd.

Taking my time, I got out of the car, rounded the corner, and walked along Ventura to the machine. I slipped the card in. Immediately it came back. I inserted it again. Only, there it was again. I studied the card and realized it was the Citibank card. Jesus. As I turned to go fetch the Glendale Fed card from the car, my toe struck an object.

I looked down and my heart began to beat faster. On the sidewalk, not five feet from the machine, was a pair of handcuffs.

I kept walking. Inside the car, I locked the door and switched on the radio. "Sergeant, I think he's been here. There's a pair of handcuffs next to the ATM."

A crackling silence followed. "It's his calling card," I added.

Still nothing. "Come in, Mobile Two." Had our communications broken down already?

"Stand by, R-seventeen." Then, "Leave the premises immediately. Drive half a mile east on Ventura and park."

"Roger."

I slid the key into the ignition and made a U-turn. Again I could feel the surge of electricity. Would they find another body? If so, why weren't the handcuffs under the victim's right foot, like that detective T. J. McCall had said? Or was it possible the killer was changing his game? No, I thought, he couldn't know we'd be out tonight, know our plan, guess our route. He couldn't. Then again, I was not one to step up to the counter and buy coincidences.

I parked in front of an espresso place with the cute name Cuppa Chino. "You or me?" I asked Todd.

"Me. Cappuccino?"

"A double," I said.

A few minutes later, as Todd returned, Higgins again crackled over the radio. "R-seventeen, return to Metro right away."

Todd and I glanced at each other as he got in the passenger seat. I said to Higgins, "Did you find anything?"

"A wallet. Empty. A couple of detectives are on the way."

My adrenaline, which had been causing mood shifts all night, now tapped into a new emotion: despondency. As I caught a glimpse of the quarter moon glimmering through the murky Los Angeles sky, I thought about all the women, now getting ready for bed, whose destinies would place them in the killer's catastrophic path.

He would strike again.

I could feel it in my bones.

T h e First Base Saloon was unusually busy for a Monday. Perhaps the Dodgers had played an important game or, more likely, had sponsored a giveaway night. I elbowed through a clot of people congealed at the entrance and was within a single human of reaching the bar when I spotted Cookie Randall coming out of the ladies' room. I managed to get Johnny's attention just as she pulled up.

"Hey," said Cookie.

"Hey, yourself."

"Whatever you ordered's on me, remember?"

I smiled. "I owe you one for tonight. You handled it just right."

"Follow me."

I picked up my drink and trailed the tall redhead through the poolroom to a booth she had previously snagged. She picked up her gold helmet and black leather jacket from the table, tossed them onto the seat, and slid in. "They pulled us out early," she said. "What happened?"

It occurred to me that I didn't know how much I could tell. When I left Metro the orders were firm. The evidence, if that's what it was, found at Glendale Federal had to be kept under wraps. The lab had gone to work immediately on the handcuffs and the wallet. No fingerprints on the cuffs. Some on the wallet. Even better, the wallet, though empty of cash, did contain identification. Detectives were tracking down the owner now.

I sipped the Black Russian and tongued an ice cube into my mouth, crunching it to pieces. "When we got to Glendale Fed, there was evidence of a robbery. Sarge decided to call a halt till they could check it out. There's probably no connection." I took another sip and began to feel the relaxing effects of the vodka. "How'd you get roped into this, anyway?"

Cookie chugged the Corona right from the bottle. "Probably because when I was working Harbor, I did a bunch of stakeouts." She grinned. "Or maybe I just got lucky."

"I'm the one who's lucky. You were the only one on the ball tonight." I mashed another ice cube. "The guys in the van were a little slow on the draw. I suppose they were busy playing poker."

"Speaking of lucky"—Cookie raised her eyebrows and smiled mischievously—"I hear you may be getting a new captain."

"I am?"

"How well do you know Lucy Robinson?"

I shook my head. "I don't. She joined Metro a couple of months ago. Fourth woman in the division. I guess they thought that was too many, so they assigned her to Mounted."

Cookie lowered her voice. "They assigned her to Mounted to keep her away from McGrew. But he keeps showing up smelling like horses. The word is he's going to Harbor when Captain Traynor retires in July."

I hiccuped. "Monster McGrew! Go on."

"I'm serious. If they'd reported their affair to Personnel, it would have been okay, right? But he couldn't, 'cause of his wife. The last time she caught him having an affair she sewed up all the flies in his undershorts."

I nearly spit out the liquid in my mouth.

"I hear they tried to warn him to keep his paws off Lucy, but"— Cookie laughed—"the man is in *love*."

"He must be," I deadpanned. "Lucy's got those unfortunate teeth." In fact, the joke around Metro was that Lucy was destined for Mounted, given her horsy face. Normally I steered clear of office gossip, since much of it was straight out of the eighth grade. And I particularly steered clear of remarks made about women. But this was a morsel too delicious to pass up. "Since you know so much," I teased, "tell me this. Does he make love with his glasses on, or *off?*"

"Off," declared Cookie. "So he can only see half of her at a time."

I tossed back the last of my drink. "Come on. How do you know this stuff?"

"Girlfriend, Cookie knows everything she's not supposed to."

"I'll remember that." I looked at my empty glass. "I should run."

"Oh have another." Cookie glanced away. "And there's Adam." She stood up and whistled.

The ex-cop began making his way toward us. As Cookie greeted him, I excused myself and headed out front to get a refill. But the crowd at the bar was still three deep.

As Willie Nelson wailed "You Were Always on My Mind," I pushed open the door and stepped out into the thick gloom of night.

That gloom soon descended on Operation ATM.

As one week rolled into the next, the few leads we dredged up proved as dry as the Los Angeles River bed, and our collective mood darkened. While a detective attuned to the finer points of astrology plotted the course of the moon, those of us more grounded battled the effects of prolonged stakeouts: bad jokes, cramped bones, mounting frustration, crankiness, indigestion, and—worse jokes.

By now we had moved the operation to Van Nuys Station, which became our new headquarters. Metro officers were nomadic, moving from division to division depending upon the nexus of our mission, and we thought of ourselves as Old West gunslingers following elusive trails of dust. Or at least we did when we were in a *good* mood.

But increasingly we were not. Adding to our woes were the dozens of tips phoned in daily by well-meaning citizens—or nutcases—and none amounted to anything except a wisp of smoke. Moreover, because of the murder of Sheila Dann, media infestation of the Valley reached epidemic proportions. More than once we drove up to a targeted bank only to encounter, under glaring spotlights, some razor-cut hair doing his nightly stand-up. Not to mention Todd, who, thanks to his contortions on the Intrepid's back floor, had developed a pinched nerve in his neck—and a disposition to match.

"I'll tell you what you're doing wrong," Det. T. J. McCall informed me as he hunched over the bar and unlawfully lit a cigarette. I watched his silver blue exhaust balloon overhead. "And only because I like you," he said.

"I suppose catching the sucker isn't a priority?" I was weary and not particularly eager to have my work critiqued at 12:45 A.M.

McCall shrugged. "We'll catch him." He eyed the Black Russian on the bar in front of me. "How can you drink that shit?"

I swept a strand of hair off my face. "Right now, Columbo, I can't tell you why I do anything I do, except that I do, okay?"

After the thirteenth fruitless night of running the Intrepid uselessly around the Valley, I had stumbled into the First Base Saloon looking for a little comic relief. I had found the crusty detective sitting at an otherwise deserted bar. He had struck me as the type of veteran who could spin a yarn and produce a laugh. I was wrong.

"For starters, you shouldn't be wearing those sneakers," he said grievously.

I stole a glance at my scuffed Nikes. "What's wrong with them?"

"If you'd read the reports, you'd have seen all the victims were wearing some kind of high-heeled shoe. I say 'some kind' because Andrea Wright wore white boots. But they had a stacked heel. Two wore standard black pumps. The other two had on sandals with two-inch heels."

"That wasn't *in* the reports," I said defensively. At least not those I had been given. The oversight didn't surprise me. Although LAPD was, at this late date, scrambling to install computers, few detectives could be coerced into sitting down and actually inputting useful information. Word of mouth was still our most sophisticated technology. "What else am I missing? Perfume, lipstick, strands of hair in lockets?"

"No." T.J. tapped the ash onto the floor. "And their looks and their ages don't show a pattern, either. But here's the thing that did. They all wore skirts. I think our killer chooses women in high heels and skirts because it's harder for them to fight back."

"Christ." I lifted my glass. "You could have told somebody."

T.J. grinned. "Yeah, right. You people in Metro have your gorgeous little heads up your perfect round asses."

I suppressed a laugh and released a small smile instead. "Since you like me so much, what else should I know?"

Two quick puffs, then T.J. squished the cigarette with his heel. "Let me ask you a question, Harlow." He turned his deep brown eyes on me. "You ever go to an ATM at night?"

"Of course."

"And you got your eyes peeled, I assume."

"Sure."

"Okay. Now forgetting you're a cop, you pull up, you see a guy hanging around. What do you do?"

"I probably stay in the car till he's gone."

"Right. Now suppose you're making a transaction and you hear footsteps behind you. Or maybe you've finished and you're starting back to your car. A guy approaches. A guy under forty."

"All systems on alert."

"Do you have a can of pepper spray in your hand?"

"No. But if I didn't have a gun on me I sure might."

T.J. nodded, keeping his eyes on me. "Amelia Grant, the fourth victim? She had pepper spray in her hand." T.J. lifted his glass and inspected its contents as if concerned about quality control. "Never used it."

"What?"

"So all systems weren't on alert. Same as they wouldn't be on alert for you"—T.J. took a gulp of scotch—"if the person approaching was a woman."

I blinked. "No way."

"No? Three of the victims were under five five. Small women are especially wary. Sheila Dann, who was five eight, was terrified of men, which is probably why she was so good at playing the vixen. Acting out. Furthermore, it would occur to a woman, more than a man, that women in high heels are even more at a disadvantage, which this killer, if it *is* a woman, would probably welcome. Unless she has unusual strength."

"We're talking about a *knife,* Columbo."

T.J. reached into his pocket and counted out some bills. "You cook, Harlow? Women are no strangers to wielding knives." He stood, hiked up his pants, and gave me a salute. "You need me, you beep me." He headed for the door.

I swiveled around on my stool. "Hey, how come I haven't seen you in here before?"

McCall kept walking. "'Cause I never needed to *talk* to you before." The door slammed shut behind him.

T h e next afternoon, shod in a pair of high-heeled shoes, I arrived early at Van Nuys Station and went looking for Lieutenant Turley. I had spent the morning at a shopping mall trying on dozens of shoes until I found just the right pair. Taupe, and made of a heavy faille and spandex-type weave, they fit my feet like gloves. The heels were a chunky two-and-a-half-inches tall. I also purchased two short cotton pleated skirts. I found Turley on the third floor, in the homicide detectives' office that Operation ATM had commandeered, and dropped the bills on his desk.

"Why wasn't I told the victims wore high heels and skirts?" I pulled up a chair and sat down. "It wasn't in the reports and somebody should have told me."

Turley put down the Mexican take-out menu he'd been studying and reached for a bottle of Snapple. Tall, but with a growing roll of fat around his waist, he had recently gone on a Jenny Craig diet and shed twenty pounds. In celebration, he now came to work in perfectly cut suits. I had a sneaky suspicion that his gray hair had turned just a little bit browner.

He sighed and tapped the menu. "Lulu's Taco Stand. Man, do I miss Lulu."

I wasn't in the mood to humor him. "Why wasn't I told?"

"It wasn't in the reports, Brenden, because we're trying to cut down on leaks. That new guy at the *News* has been breaking stories faster than we can find them." The Snapple came up to his lips. "But, yes, somebody should have briefed you."

Typical. Ever since Rodney King, LAPD had become so obsessed with its image that it went to ludicrous lengths to craft it, often at the expense of its officers. Clearly, nobody wanted to blow this case. I moved on. "I was given the information by T. J. McCall, who also said—"

Turley put down the bottle. "Who?"

"T. J. McCall. Detective Two, Van Nuys? He's working three of the murders."

Turley simply nodded.

"He said one of the victims died clutching a can of pepper spray, which she didn't use, and it was his theory that the killer might be a woman."

Turley grinned. "Detectives always fall in love with their theories. You talk to another detective, he'll swear the killer is an escaped dwarf from the circus." He raised an eyebrow. "Anything else?"

"No sir."

Turley leaned back in his chair and studied me with his long-lashed limpid eyes. "How are you holding up?"

"I'm fine."

"You need a day off, you holler."

"Lieutenant—why haven't we been told anything about the wallet and the handcuffs at Glendale Federal?"

His eyebrows bunched. "Oh. You didn't see the report?" He began shuffling through a stack of papers. Media leaks aside, it was beginning to look like another example of too many chiefs and not enough grunts. With Robbery/Homicide, two divisions, and Metro all working on the case, the information pipeline needed a good shot of Drano.

"Here." He glanced at a single sheet of paper. "The wallet belonged to a James Tashjian. He lost it, or was robbed, while Christmas shopping at the Beverly Center." Turley looked up. "Doesn't know how it got to the bank. It was found under some leaves at the edge of the parking lot, and its deteriorated state suggests it had been there a long time. It was a coincidence."

"Are the handcuffs a coincidence, too?"

Turley leaned forward. "Let me give you a tip, Brenden. Don't think. We got too many damn people thinking. Your job is to react." He smiled thinly. "That'll keep you busy enough."

As if women couldn't react *and* think at the same time.

"Sure. Thanks for the advice, Loo." And I walked out.

T h e brain trust plotting our nightly rounds shuffled the banks like cards in a casino deck. New banks were added, old ones revisited, and Glendale Fed—"coincidences" notwithstanding—became a daily stop. At least someone in authority thought the killer might have been signaling his intentions. Or hers.

"And tonight, boys and girls," Sergeant Higgins announced with glee, "we have a half-moon!"

The roll call room erupted in a chorus of baying as we groaned to our feet and headed for the door. In the hallway I caught up with Todd. "I'm going to get wired up. Meet you downstairs in ten?"

"Want me to go with you?"

I knew he was concerned about Mack Maloney, but I was determined to deal with the toad myself. Like the rest of us, Maloney was now operating out of Van Nuys, and for the past week he'd resorted to giving me the cold shoulder. This was preferable to being harassed, but wasn't the result I wanted either. "What I really need is a Coke," I told Todd. "Diet or cherry. Okay?"

"Sure. Meet you downstairs."

The Scientific Investigations office that Maloney worked out of was located on the second floor. Small and cluttered, like all our undersize offices, the room was filled with electronic equipment. Maloney was standing in front of metal shelves filled with VCRs. My transmitter was on the desk. Every night I returned it to Maloney so he could change the batteries and check its condition.

"Hi, Sarge."

He turned away from watching the tapes we had removed from Glendale Fed's video camera and gave me his usual, impassive stare.

I perched on the edge of the desk. "Mack, I was wondering if you could do something for me."

Maloney finished printing out a frame from the video and switched the machine off. "You look like a tart, Harlow. They got you going after johns now? More your line of work, I'd imagine."

I picked up the transmitter and studied it. "There's been a new development."

"Yeah? What's that?"

"All the victims wore skirts and high heels." I met his eyes. "Do you think you could make a thigh holster for me?"

I raised my skirt a few inches. "See, right around here, midthigh. And I'd want the gun on the outside of my thigh. That way, I'd just run my hand up my right leg and whip the gun out. I'd save a couple seconds on the fanny pack. I just don't know if you can make something like that."

Well of course, he could. Maloney could make anything. But I needed to arouse his ego.

He put down the photo and stared at my thighs.

"I'll wear the fanny pack tonight, but—"

"You're not wearing stockings."

"I don't like them."

"Wear them." He pulled open a drawer and searched it. "Not a holster. I'll make some kind of garter, I'm not sure out of what. It'll fit snugly around your thigh. Panty hose—the stretch kind—will help keep the garter in place and give you a little protection against rubbing." He turned to me. "Stand up."

From the drawer he removed a tape measure. "Come on, Harlow, let's go."

I stood and raised my skirt. Maloney crouched. With thick, dirty fingers, he ran the tape around my right thigh.

"There," I said. "That feels about right."

"Higher," he said. He moved the tape up another inch and studied it. "Christ, your legs are thin. I got eighteen inches here. Who ever heard of a cop with eighteen-inch legs?"

He straightened. "But they're nice legs. Too bad they're wasted on you."

I smiled. "That's what your wife says about you."

For one brief second, I caught a flicker of amusement in Mack Maloney's eyes.

It was a start.

I headed for the ladies' room to harness myself up.

"It isn't a woman," said Todd with certainty. "Marlene says that unless a woman did hand-to-hand combat in the military, she can't think of a possible scenario." He lowered his visor against the glare of the setting sun. "And Americans didn't do hand-to-hand combat in the Gulf War."

I checked to make sure my gun was properly loaded. It was, just as it had been ten minutes before, when I last checked it. I shoved it back into my fanny pack. "Well from what I read, women in the navy are forced into hand-to-hand combat just to get to the mess hall."

"You know what I mean," Todd was meandering along Riverside at a snail's pace. Todd always drove like the end of the world was at the next stoplight. "Marlene isn't ruling out a gangbanger though. A fourteen-year-old kid."

In a high-speed chase, God forbid we should ever get into one, the suspect would come up *behind* Todd. "Well Marlene doesn't know shit," I said.

Marlene was a professor at USC with a doctorate in criminal psychology with whom Todd had struck up a "professional friendship." I didn't question the woman's knowledge, but academics routinely missed the off ramp to the real world.

"For one thing," I said, "these knifings appear too perfectly executed to have been done by a kid. And from everything we know, the killer stayed calm and methodical throughout."

"Like . . . a surgeon," Todd put in. "Jeez, Bren, why not? A goddam surgeon."

"A plastic surgeon," I said with conviction. "They seem like the type."

"I'm serious. The guy could be wearing one of those white coats, stethoscope around his neck? Even if he were black, would such a person scare you?"

"Speaking of scary black persons," I said, "if you don't get this buggy up to thirty miles an hour, I'm going to jump out."

"Hang on," said Todd, "I'll open the door for you."

But he had an interesting point. A wacko surgeon. Sam Sheppard had been an M.D. An actual surgeon might be a first.

" T h e r e ' s a male black at the machine," Higgins announced over the radio. "You may proceed."

I hesitated. "Proceed, sir?"

"Confirm."

I wanted to ask why but did not. In the past I was always told to drive around the block if someone was using a machine. To be a tempting target, I had to be alone. Perhaps Higgins knew something I didn't. Which made me feel even more vulnerable, not to mention cross. It was the last stop of the night.

"Turning in," I said quietly to Todd. "Lone male at the machine. His car will be four spaces from ours, passenger side."

I didn't like it. Pulling in so that my car faced away from the machine, limiting my visual inspection of the teller to the rearview mirror. But had I backed in, it might have tipped the killer off, if the killer were indeed watching. I switched off the ignition and glanced in the mirror. The man at the ATM was wearing a plaid flannel shirt and a cap with the bill turned backward. He was still hunched over the machine. I picked up the First Interstate card and opened the door.

When I stepped out and slammed the door, the man did not react. He was thirty feet away and still at the machine. I began walking toward him, the *click-click*ing of my heels echoing menacingly through the silence. A cool customer, not to even turn around.

Five feet behind him, I stopped, my hand resting lightly on the fanny pack. A good six feet tall, broad shoulders, feet planted apart, shoelaces on the left sneaker not tied—a promising sign. An occasional car drove past, offering a degree of comfort in the thickening silence. The seconds ticked by. If this was the killer, he would wait until I had made my transaction, I reminded myself. I squared my shoulders and inhaled deeply. The machine beeped twice.

And then he turned around.

The flannel shirt was hanging open over a white T-shirt and jeans. It was a long shirt. Long enough to cover a sheath hooked onto the side of his belt or something jammed in a back pocket.

Our eyes met. His hands were at his sides. My hand was on my fanny pack.

"Machine's a little slow," he said pleasantly.

I nodded in response. Maybe thirty, hard to tell. Six two, for sure; 215, 220. How fast could I get the gun out—one second, two? I was remembering what they taught us at the academy. A bullet through the heart, and still the person has six seconds to react before the body quits. Six seconds to deploy a knife. I knew from my training it could be done.

He took a step toward me. I forced my nerves to remain steady. A truck rumbled by; a breeze ruffled my skirt. Another step closer to me; my hand slipping into the fanny pack. Weight on the balls of his feet now.

Then, rapidly and without warning, he moved to his right and swept past me.

I let my breath out evenly and approached the machine. As I jammed the card into the slot, I heard the car door creak open. I was no longer wearing Turley's lucky cap because it would have looked odd with my skirt and heels, but now, foolishly, I wished that I had it.

I began working the machine. But I was listening hard for the sound of a door slamming, an engine starting up. Normally, in decoy situations, I would have in my sights someone undercover who would use a hand signal to warn me of danger. But facing into an ATM alcove, I would have no such help. I could only hope for the honk of a horn.

Still no sound of a door slamming. I pushed the spot on the computer screen for *$20*, then smoothly slid my gun out of the fanny pack.

A sound now—a footstep? Yes, footsteps. He was coming back. I could feel the goose bumps raised on my arms, a breeze tickling the hair on my neck. He won't stab me in the back, I told myself. Unless this was a different killer, or a killer with a gun.

A horn sounded in the distance—once, twice. Was it ours? I stared at the Readyteller. Hurry up, hurry up, hurry up.

Now I could hear him breathing as the machine beeped and a single bill appeared in the chute. I removed it with my left hand, stuffed it in my pocket, and almost forgot my card. I took a breath and tore it from the machine. Then, bringing my right hand down and burying the five-inch barrel in the pleats of my skirt, I turned.

He was eight feet away and coming. With a shiny metal object in his left hand.

"Did I leave an envelope there?" A friendly smile.

Is that how he did it? Momentarily catching his victims off guard as they would instinctively turn their eyes back to the machine, helpfully, as he launched his murderous assault.

The shiny object in his left hand was flat and narrow.

I shook my head.

Which is when his right hand disappeared under the flannel shirt. Slipping off the safety, I brought my gun up.

The eyes grew wide; his hands shot out in front of him; the shiny metal—with keys attached—flew to the ground. "Jeez, lady. Whatcha doin'?" His voice cracked, his face froze with fear.

I held the gun steady, two-handed style. "I'm a police officer. Pull back your shirt. Slowly." Todd was out of the car now, and two shadowy figures had emerged from behind shrubs.

The man's fingers shook as he lifted the blue plaid shirt and showed me his belt. Only there was no belt, only the empty loops of his jeans. No bulges in the front pockets. "Turn around, mister. Keep your shirt up."

"You want money? Hey, take it."

Nothing in the back jeans pockets but the square shape of a billfold. I could see him flinch as he noticed Todd twenty feet in front of him and the two other officers hanging back, one to his left, the other to his right. He probably thought he was about to get the shit kicked out of him.

"All right, you can turn around." I checked the safety and slid my gun into the fanny pack as the man stared uncomprehendingly at me, the whites of his eyes large and luminous. "I'm sorry to have frightened you, sir. There's been some trouble at this bank. You can go now." I smiled apologetically. "I hope I haven't ruined your evening." But, of course, I had.

He continued staring at me, and I could see the sudden flash of anger in those frightened brown eyes. He said, "LAPD?"

"Yes. Officer Harlow."

He snorted. "Well, Officer Harlow, pardon my fucking black ass." He stooped to pick up his keys and marched stiffly away.

I glanced over at the Intrepid, where Todd was silently watching. As I approached, I had trouble meeting his eyes.

"Why don't you drive?" was all I could think to say.

The gym at the Police Academy was crammed with sleek sculpted muscles laboring under clanking metal equipment remanded from an earlier time. Harsh light and the sour odor of old sweat suffused the room. The department apparently chose to funnel its resources into its crime-fighting equipment, figuring our bodies were *our* problem. I hauled mine over to the weights.

Without a lot of effort, I could run ten miles in seventy-five minutes on sand, and tried to three times a week; but as with most women, it was my upper-body strength that proved a struggle. I stepped over a couple of undercover narcs and found an empty bench. I eased onto my back and began working with the lighter hand weights first. It never got any easier.

"Slide your feet in closer to your butt. Better for your back."

I looked up into the crinkly eyes and flushed face of Chris Leiter, one of SWAT's leading attractions. He had a body designed by Michelangelo, and a face that made women weep and men look twice. Even his sweat glistened exquisitely. He blotted some of it off his neck with a towel and said, "Spinach. Eat your spinach. They say it's a girl's best friend."

"I'm old-fashioned. I prefer guns." I dropped the hand weights. "Help me with the barbell?"

Chris lifted one barbell off its pegs and lowered it into my hands. Then he added a twenty-pound plate to either end. At forty he was still blond and boyish, with the kind of facial-bone structure usually reserved for movie stars. In fact, he often got hired to train actors for action roles, and once he landed a bit part for himself and got to say three lines. Now he uttered one. "I hear you had a little excitement last night."

I began pumping the barbell. The tendons strained in my neck. "Tell me something." I huffed and puffed and raised some more. "With suitcases on wheels, remote controls, and those sweet-shooting semi-automatics, why does anyone even need arm muscles anymore?"

"Grocery bags?"

"Delivery boys."

"Injured partners?"

"Backup."

After three more lifts, my wobbly arms raised the barbell and slid it into the grooves over my head. Groaning, I sat up.

"This guy pulled into a bank just before I did, and Higgins decided to run his plates. Turns out he was wanted on suspicion of robbery. So Higgins sends me in hoping the guy would mug *me,* and then they would pick him up." I made a face. "Higgins."

"Did they? Pick him up?"

"Higgins misread the plate. The guy was Judge Terry's son."

"Ouch." Chris grabbed a set of hand weights and began working his triceps. "By the way, that Amazon dyke Cookie was looking for you a while ago. She's bad news, Brenden."

I stood and began stretching my back muscles. "She seems okay to me."

"If ever there was a female Lothario, Cookie's it. She loves 'em and leaves 'em." Chris looked at me meaningfully. "Word is, she's got her sights set on you."

"Really. And you don't warn me off men who have their sights set on me? What's the matter, Christopher? You jealous I might be collecting from both sides?"

Chris's muscles rippled under the strain of the hand weights. "A citizen filed a complaint against her."

"For what?"

"Sexual misconduct." He gave me a smile tailored for a close-up. "A *female* citizen. Claimed Cookie took a long time patting her down."

I said nothing.

"And you've heard about the girlfriend, haven't you? A vice cop who, in a little lover's quarrel, tried to *shoot* Cookie outside the Phoenix airport last year?"

I just looked at him.

The hand weights clanged to the floor.

Mr. SWAT strutted his stuff away.

T h e roll call room at Van Nuys Station was deserted when I walked in, forty-five minutes early. I poured a cup of rancid coffee and slid into a seat in the front row.

Earlier, I had cornered Lieutenant Turley in the detectives' office and managed to pry all of the ATM murder reports from his clutches— "To help me react better" is what I said. In truth, since I was familiar only with the details of Mrs. Croft's killing and Sheila Dann's, I *thought* (oops, there I went again) I might learn something useful by boning up on the other three victims.

Mary Shaunessy was the first.

At 3 P.M. on a Tuesday in February, she had arrived at West Valley Community Hospital in Encino to begin a five-hour turn of volunteer duty. According to her husband, Frank, she worked at the hospital three days a week, talking to terminally ill patients. Two years before, her five-year-old son had been treated at West Valley for spinal meningitis. The boy died, but Mary felt profoundly grateful for the efforts the staff had made. As a result, and perhaps to keep the memory of her son alive, she had taken up volunteer work.

On that Tuesday she had left the hospital at 8:15. Frank, who played poker on Tuesday nights, arrived home shortly after ten to an empty house. Concerned, he had phoned the hospital, plus two of Mary's friends, and then he called the police. Told that it was too soon to worry—and to call back the next day if she were still missing— Frank set off to look for his wife himself. He stopped at a grocery store and drove past the Bank of America branch where the Shaunessys kept their accounts. Distraught, he returned home at one.

Four hours later, Patrol Officer Leon Martinez of Van Nuys division noticed a 1993 green Acura in the lot of a Home Federal Savings on Colbath, just off Ventura, near Woodman. Twenty feet from the ATM, he also found Mary's body. The guess was that she had passed the bank on her way home and decided to stop there rather than drive to her branch, which was a mile past her home in Toluca Lake.

Apparently it had been a slow night at the ATM. The receipt found in her pocket showed she had withdrawn $100 at 8:26 P.M. It was the bank's final transaction of the night. Mary was forty-one.

She was wearing a black skirt, a black cardigan over a hospital candy striper's top, and black high-heeled pumps. Her purse had been locked inside the Acura, the key in her pocket. The $100 was missing. Mary Shaunessy had been stabbed four times in the chest and once in the abdomen. The coroner also noted a punctured Adam's apple. He concluded that a single-edged hunting knife with a six- or eight-inch blade had been used as the murder weapon.

As I sipped my coffee, Todd's half-joking remark about a surgeon leapt to mind. I considered it. Why not? I thought. Why not someone Mary knew from the hospital, someone who had followed her from the hospital to the bank?

Which led to the next question: How would this person know she would stop at a bank? Had she told him? Or had he been following her for some time . . . waiting for his big chance?

Except . . . that would have made it personal. Serial killers, I had been told, almost never knew or targeted their victims.

I put that thought on hold as cologne wafted into the room and members of my platoon began to trundle in.

I t proved another fruitless night for Operation ATM. As I pulled out of the Van Nuys lot, I decided to go straight home to finish reading the murder reports. I put Mary Chapin Carpenter on the tape deck, and eighty on the speedometer, and cruised down the 405 freeway, beginning to unwind.

Mary had just broken into "Going Out Tonight" when a yellow light on my dashboard began to blink urgently. My car, it indicated, was running on fumes. A gambler's instinct carried me past two freeway exits before I veered off the Wilshire ramp in grudging concession.

The station I drove into was deserted. I paid for the gas and was jamming the hose into the tank when a McDonald's up the street caught my eye. A black Ford Ranger pulled in. It drove to the far end of the gas station, turned around, and sat there idling, its headlights beaming straight at me. So much for civility.

Minutes later I was bouncing into McDonald's. The only customers, a man and a woman, were eating burgers at a table. I paid for a double cheeseburger and a Diet Coke, and as I climbed back into my car, I noticed the same Ford Ranger now parked, and seemingly vacant, four spaces over. I bit into the burger and pulled onto the street.

The possibility that our killer stalked his victims continued to haunt me and, once or twice, sent my eyes unreasonably darting to the rearview mirror. Police are notoriously indifferent to the advice we give to the public—like fastening seat belts (almost never) or staying alert for follow-home robbers (yeah, right).

The next time I checked the mirror, my eyes lingered. What appeared to be the same black truck was now several car lengths behind me. I picked up speed and veered onto the freeway. The truck veered right along with me.

Its lights made it impossible to see the license plate or the driver. But surely it wasn't following me? I turned up Mary Chapin and accelerated to eighty. Two miles later, when I cloverleafed onto the Santa Monica, it was still on my tail.

It stayed glued there until I exited the freeway at 4th Street and the trailing headlights disappeared. I stuffed the last of the burger into my mouth, crumpled the paper, and drove slowly through the quiet residential streets of Santa Monica.

When I turned onto my street, lights again flared in my mirror. I slowed, but the vehicle, now at some distance, did not seem eager to pass. Unable to tell if it was the truck, I drove past my building's garage and turned at the next corner. Then I parked at a curb and waited. No lights appeared.

Alone on the still streets, I returned to my building and used the remote control to raise the iron-grill garage door. After the door came down, I killed the engine and again waited. Five minutes later, satisfied that no one was lurking outside, I parked in my designated slot and climbed tiredly up the stairs.

T h e condo we occupied was one of six in a three-story building on 3rd near Idaho. The apartments, newly renovated when we moved in, were airy and spacious. The halls were thickly carpeted and there was an elevator that I rarely used. At the time we bought the condo, Jack and I used what money we had as down payment. I had always loved the beach, and Jack had already been living in Santa Monica for some time. The view of the ocean from our living room on the third floor was the deal maker. Although we now could afford something larger, Jack—always cautious with money—preferred to wait and someday buy a ranch near Santa Barbara.

He was sprawled on the living room couch when I walked in. The TV was on, sound turned low, and he was talking into the cordless phone. A slight frown crossed his face, and as I closed the door he abruptly hung up.

Smiling, I walked over to him. "Howdy, stranger. This is a surprise."

He was wearing a sweatshirt and jeans and he stretched his arms behind his head and yawned. "You're home early. Did you catch the killer or something?"

"Not even close." I dropped the reports folder on the coffee table and sat down beside him. "What about you? Isn't it past your bedtime?"

He reached for my hand. "We wrapped tonight for the season."

"God, already?" I had, in truth, totally lost track of days, even weeks. Late April or early May was when most TV series went on hiatus for two months.

I pulled off my shoes and slipped the gun from the elasticized garter Maloney had made for me. It was his little joke, I supposed, that he had made it flaming purple. I placed the gun on the table and leaned back with a sigh. "You look amused. Do you like my newest prop?"

Jack stood up. "I'm going to get a beer. Want anything?"

"A glass with ice, thanks."

I watched him disappear into the kitchen. Ever since the dinner at Spago we hadn't so much not gotten along as gone our separate ways. This wasn't hard, given our schedules and my preoccupation with Operation ATM. These little marital interruptions, as I called them, had occurred before, but this time I sensed something different—a sort of aloof detachment. Maybe we were both a little bit tired.

I could hear Jack moving about the kitchen as the minutes ticked by. "Can't you find the ice?" I called out.

A moment later I heard the freezer door close and he walked back into the living room, saying, "Want me to fix you a drink?"

"Thanks. Vodka and Kahlua."

He smiled faintly. "I haven't forgotten."

I watched him measure out the vodka. "So what are you going to do all summer, lucky boy. Maybe I can get away for a long weekend. My lieutenant said anytime I want days off, just ask."

Jack added the Kahlua and handed me the glass. "Cheers." His eyes lingered on my face. "You look tired."

"I am."

He sat down beside me and rubbed my cheek. I sank into his body. "The more I think about it, the more I like the idea of going away," I said. I turned my head up and looked at him. "It would be good to go away, don't you think?"

Jack took a sip of beer. "Unfortunately, I am going away. To Hawaii. Tomorrow."

"Tomorrow?"

"That's why I wanted to wait up for you. Paramount's shooting its big Christmas movie, and Billy Orso dislocated his shoulder. They want me to audition. It's a great part." He paused as his eyes searched mine. "What do you think?"

I felt my stomach knot as I put down my glass carefully on the table. "How long?"

"If I get the role, three weeks, maybe four, total. I think the Hawaii shoot'll be two weeks, but I'm not sure."

"Could I come with you? For a few days?"

Jack reached over and stroked my hair. "Maybe later. Right now I'm nervous and I'll be very preoccupied. I hear the director eats actors for breakfast."

"You sound pretty sure of yourself."

"I know what I want, Bren. I'm going to get the part."

I reached for his hand and wove my fingers through his. "What about your wife? Do you still want her?"

"Don't be silly, of course I do." He paused. "At least till something better comes along." He kissed my cheek.

My eyes wandered to the TV, where Errol Flynn was swashbuckling through a black-and-white movie. "I really think we need some time together, Jack. I don't feel very connected to you right now."

His aquamarine eyes sparkled. "That's because I don't go around slashing women to death."

"I'm serious."

"I know you are, but what do you expect? That I'm supposed to sit around for two months waiting till you come home so I can hear your tales of derring-do?"

With my free hand I reached for my drink. "Is that what this is about, my job?"

"Come on. It's about nothing. I mean, all I want is to be in this movie. Is that so terrible?"

"But what did you think you were going to do all summer?" More and more, I was beginning to sense that I was getting only half the story. "This just came up today?"

"A few days ago." A look of uncertainty crossed his face.

"A few days ago?"

"Well, last week maybe. But it wasn't final until last night. I mean that I'd get the audition." For a moment he fell silent. "Let's not part fighting, okay?"

I helped him pack, and we made love, but there was something mechanical about it, as if neither of us was paying strict attention. His demeanor fluctuated from endearing warmth to cool indifference, and at times I wasn't sure he was even in the room with me. As I tossed sleeplessly beside him I tried to convince myself that maybe his solution was better than mine: go away from each other for a while, then see who showed up at the family reunion.

He had promised to wake me before he left. But when I awoke the next morning, it was due to the shrill beep of the alarm clock. He had set it and left it on our dresser, across the room, beside a bright arrangement of flowers that, I suspected, his driver had fetched. The scribbled card read:

> Bren,
> I need you more than you know. Don't give up on me. And stay away from those lecherous cops.
> All my love, Jack

As a final touch, he had taken the two pairs of handcuffs from the drawer, placed them on the dresser, and intertwined them.

I stayed in the shower a long time—as the steamy water washed the tears from my face.

T . J . McCall had interviewed Frank Shaunessy three times.

He asked routine questions—among them, What did Frank know about his wife's relationships at the hospital? Frank had cited two young interns whom his wife had invited to the house for dinner several times. Frank described the young men as pleasant, burbling with hospital stories, and typically exhausted from lack of sleep. McCall interviewed them, too; both were on duty when Mary was murdered—and could prove it. T.J. also contacted the service people who regularly visited the Shaunessy house: the maid, the gardener, and the pool man. Nothing.

I got up from the kitchen table and refilled my coffee cup.

Alice Croft was victim number two. Since her investigation was handled by another division, North Hollywood, the two detectives assigned to the case did not think to inquire if she had any dealings with West Valley Community Hospital. I made a note to call Mr. Croft.

Andrea Wright was number three. Age thirty-four, African American, recently divorced, mother of an eleven-year-old son and an eight-year-old daughter. Apparently she had lost her husband and her stenographer's job the same month and had moved in with her mother, Florence Gibbons. Two weeks before her death, Andrea had been hired as a receptionist at a health clinic in Reseda. "High number of abortions performed," T. J. McCall had noted.

My reading tempo picked up. Andrea had left the clinic shortly after 7 P.M. on a Thursday night in March and, her mother insisted, would have taken the Ventura freeway east to the Hollywood north, exiting at Victory and driving west to the corner of Coldwater Canyon, where Southern California Savings Bank was located. According to the director of the clinic, staff was paid on Thursdays, and Andrea had stopped at the bank to deposit her check. Her mother said Andrea would have gone next to the grocery store. She expected her home no later than 8:15.

An actual witness came forward to declare that he had seen Andrea pull into the bank lot. Stanley Green, who worked as a night watchman at Tower Records five miles away, had used the automated teller and was climbing into his pickup when a woman who fit Andrea's description drove in. He said another woman was using the teller—a gray-haired woman. He saw Andrea park and open the door of her car. Then he drove off.

Interestingly, the bank's computer noted Stanley Green's withdrawal of $40 at 7:26 P.M. It did not show another transaction until 7:50 P.M., when a Donald Gruber withdrew $200.

At 7:58, a call was made to 911 by an unidentified male from a pay phone half a mile from the bank. The caller reported that a black woman was on the ground and looked bloody. Det. T. J. McCall interviewed Donald Gruber, who claimed he saw no dead woman when he used the Readyteller. Yet when the police arrived, they found Andrea Wright in the lot, twenty-five feet from the ATM. According to McCall's notes, "It was possible to miss her, I guess, if Mr. Gruber was in a fog and staring straight ahead." Gruber also insisted he had not made the call to 911.

Andrea Wright had approached the Readyteller with purse in hand. It was found beside her body. It contained her paycheck, $9.41 in cash, two credit cards, and her car keys. McCall wrote: "According to Jamal Kulil (the branch manager), the deposit function on the Readyteller may have been stalled. All subsequent transactions that night were for withdrawals."

My eyes skipped past the coroner's report to additional notes from T.J. But if he connected Andrea Wright's job at the clinic to Mary Shaunessy's volunteer work at the hospital, he did not record it. I made a second note to check with him.

The name of the fourth victim did not immediately ring a bell. Amelia Lynn Grant, physical ed teacher at Kennedy High School in Granada Hills. Single. The viciousness of her stab wounds indicated she had put up a fight. The coroner counted eight thrusts to her chest, three to her abdomen, and two to her neck. As a final flourish, the killer had sliced off her left nipple.

I stared at my half-eaten bowl of cereal, picked it up, and carried it to the sink. I took a long drink of water to calm my stomach. Then I returned to the table.

On a Wednesday night in April, Amelia was dressed to go out— short black dress, high-heeled shoes, Chanel No.5. According to her boyfriend, Fred Lumley, they had dinner reservations that night to celebrate Amelia's thirty-second birthday. He had called her around 7:30 to say he'd be leaving his office shortly. A prosecutor, he worked in the Criminal Courts Building downtown. He and Amelia, he said, were engaged, and she had moved into his house in Sherman Oaks at the beginning of the year.

During that phone call, Amelia had complained of a splitting headache and said she was going out to get a refill for the Empirin with Codeine she took for her migraines. She drove to a Sav-on drugstore near the northwest corner of Ventura Boulevard and Laurel Canyon and entered the parking area behind the stores. The pharmacist on duty reported that she dropped off her prescription and was told it would take about ten minutes to fill. Amelia said she would be back. He believed she had left the drugstore through the rear door into the parking lot.

The parking area was a block long and surrounded on three sides by shops and banks. Amelia had cut through the lot, moving northeast until she came to a Great Western Bank that fronted on Laurel Canyon.

Although it was set off from the other stores and offered two not-well-lighted tellers, it was within ten feet of a steady stream of traffic.

Amelia withdrew $200, put her bank card and the money into her purse, and began to retrace her steps. The killer must have been waiting near the rear of the bank, which was not lit at all. Although cars traveled in and out of the lot along the south side of the bank, no one came to her aid or reported the attack.

Fred Lumley told detectives he arrived home at 8:25. When Amelia had not returned by 9:15, he called the drugstore and spoke to the pharmacist. The prescription was still waiting to be picked up. Fred then called an LAPD detective he knew from court. The detective agreed to meet Lumley at the drugstore right away. As soon as he pulled into the lot, Fred spotted Amelia's red Honda Civic. Ten minutes later, he and the detective found her body behind the bank, obscured by bushes.

I finished my now-cold coffee and wondered if Amelia, in her capacity as a gym teacher, had dealings with West Valley Community Hospital. It wouldn't be convenient to the high school, but it was only a few miles from her home. Then my eye caught the detective's final note. "Victim was accepted into L.A. Police Academy but dropped out after five months."

Oh Christ. It hit me then. She had been Amelia Rodriguez at the time. I thumbed through the rest of the papers and found a snapshot of her taken at Kennedy High School. Of course, I remembered her now. Sparkling black eyes, thick, curly hair worn in a ponytail. Talkative and eager. She had done well, I recalled, but was under the strain of rushing home to care for her sick mother. Her teenage brother—it now came back to me—had been killed in a gang shoot-out and that was why she had decided to become a cop. The first day at the academy, she had stood up in front of our class of sixty-five and had said that. Seven months later, when we graduated, fifteen women and nine men had dropped out.

I couldn't remember why Amelia had.

▪ E I G H T ▪

t's been twenty-one days since the last one," announced Todd from the floor of the Intrepid. "He's out there. I know it."
I slipped my gun into my thigh holster and drove out of the station parking lot—for another night of bank hopping. I was feeling somewhat ill. "Nobody knows," I said.

"He'll strike tonight," said Todd with conviction. "I've got a hunch."

"But an ill-timed one. It was a month between number three and number four, two days between four and five."

I had thought I was okay about Jack's running off to Hawaii until I discovered, among a stack of magazines in the bathroom, last week's issue of *Entertainment Weekly*. TV COP TURNS HIS MIRRORED GLASSES WEST, the blazing headline read.

"I doubt the stabber's tuned into your calendar," I said sullenly.

"Shit, Brenden, this is *show time*. You're always fussing about being bored. Now you've got the lead role in the movie. Lighten up."

Just the word *movie* made my stomach clench.

"Maybe he's out of handcuffs," I said.

In between cash withdrawals, I told Todd what I'd learned from the murder reports. It seemed a harmless enough diversion—something to help relieve the monotony that grows out of a prolonged stakeout. At the academy, they devote an hour to it—the psychological effects of stakeouts—but I'd forgotten what they had said.

Todd's hunch proved bogus: no bodies, no handcuffs. Not even a

drop of congealed blood. Had the stabber discovered our operation
and retreated? Been arrested for another crime? Left town to continue
his spree in a distant locale? I began to envision thick yellowish folders
gathering dust in the department's archives as Operation ATM took its
place among LAPD's unsolved homicides.

My cheerless reverie was interrupted by Higgins's staticky voice as
I returned to the Van Nuys parking structure. "Harlow, meet me in
Lieutenant Turley's office right away."

"Sure. Do you want to see Todd, too?"

"No," said Higgins ominously. "Just you."

Apprehensively, I rode the elevator to the third floor. Turley was
seated behind a borrowed desk in the homicide detectives' office, his
jacket off, but his white shirt still, somehow, fresh. Higgins was
perched on the next desk, swinging his legs. "Close the door," Turley
greeted me.

Their grim faces were unnerving. I stood midway between their
desks trying to look dignified, despite the way I was dressed. My feet
hurt from the shoes and I wanted to sit down, but I wasn't sure it was
okay. I clasped my hands behind my back and waited.

Turley cleared his throat. "Brenden, are you sure you understand
what your duties are?"

The question confused me; what was he talking about? I said,
"Oh, absolutely."

"You requested copies of the reports on the victims yesterday and
I handed them over, not thinking."

"Yes sir."

"I'd like them back. Do you have them with you?"

"They're at home, sir."

"Then bring them in tomorrow."

Only the next day was Saturday, a day off. "Is something wrong?"
I said.

"I told you before, we have a dozen detectives working this case.
You drive, you withdraw money, you react. That's it."

Shit. Higgins had overheard me discussing the reports with Todd
in the car. During the long hours we rode around, I often forgot they
eavesdropped.

"Sir," I said, "it's only natural. You live something day and night,
you get obsessed with the details."

Higgins snorted. "Like I've been telling you, Loo, Harlow thinks

she's Jane Wayne. Hell, I don't even know why we have eight thou-
sand cops. She can protect the city all by herself."

I stiffened. It seemed to me I had been playing the dutiful soldier
to perfection, but even that apparently didn't mollify Higgins. "I'm
sorry, Sergeant, if I stepped out of line." I hesitated. "Did I step out of
line?"

"See what I mean, Loo? Wiseass."

"All right," Turley said, suddenly yawning. "The point is, Brenden,
you've got enough to deal with. Return the reports and let the detectives do their job. Chances are they'll be the ones who catch this guy.
You're really just window dressing."

It took all of my restraint not to fly across the desk and punch
him. *Window dressing?* Why, my life was on the line every single
night. And they were telling me—these two who held jobs that never
put them in physical danger, and were making two or three times what
I did—that I was *window dressing?*

"Anything else, sir?"

"Yeah," said Turley. "You want to take the detective's exam, go
see Captain McGrew."

T h a t morning I had beeped T. J. McCall from home, but I had
never heard back. Shamelessly, I used T.J.'s possible presence to in-
duce Todd to run into the First Base Saloon with me. Even so, I practically had to arrest him to coax him through the door. "I came here
once when I was at the academy," he said darkly. "It nearly made me
decide *not* to be a cop."

"Which is why," I added, "you became a *sport.*"

Once past the jukebox, I angled him into the poolroom, where,
through a thicket of boisterous people, Cookie hailed us from a booth.
There were no empty ones, or a way to avoid her; my ulterior motive
for dragging Todd in here—the need to talk about Jack—would have
to be put on hold.

"Hi," said Cookie, "you know Adam McKay, right?"

Todd was introduced and we all squeezed in. Before leaving Van
Nuys I had changed into jeans, a red V-neck sweater, and a pair of flip-
flops. Cookie still had her work clothes on. Tonight she was a bag
lady, wearing a shapeless flowered dress fashionably torn in several
places, a bandana over her head, and artful smudges under her eyes.

"I see the life appeals to you," I said.

Adam, who was sitting to my right nursing a beer, said, "Are you all in this together?"

Todd smiled beneficently. "It's a minority kind of thing."

Adam looked at us, not knowing if Todd was serious. He said, "You think your killer is of, uh, privileged descent?"

I grinned. *Descent* was the newly minted term for race; *privileged* was law-enforcement speak for minority. "The thing is," I said, "who in this city isn't privileged? Blacks are a minority, whites are, Asians are, gays are, and then there are the Hispanics, who may or may not include the Mexicans, who certainly don't want to be confused with the Central Americans. The non-Hispanic whites and the non–African American Hispanics . . . or is it non-Hispanic African Americans . . . ?"

"Oh, man," said Todd, "that's good for a three-day suspension right there."

I shrugged. "I'm an Irish hyphenate, what do I know?"

"Anyway, this killer is an equal-opportunity slasher. Or should I say, he's behaving politically correct," Cookie put in.

"So if he's caught and convicted," Todd inserted, "does he get time off for politically correct behavior?"

"And he hasn't attacked a man, right?" Adam said suddenly. "Men are *not* politically correct."

I finished my double Black Russian and began mashing the ice cubes. Adam struck me as kind of a dork. What I never understood about dorks was why, knowing they are dorks, they didn't just shut up?

"Still," Adam said, "this guy must have an M.O. I'm sure they've been looking into links between the women. I remember a case I once worked. The West L.A. rapist? He attacked something like twenty-three women. The only thing they had in common—listen to this—they were *Democrats.*"

"Was Reagan governor then?" Cookie asked. "Or Jerry Brown?"

"The guy worked at a polling place?" Todd sounded intrigued.

"Nope," said Adam, with a faint smile. "He let his fingers do the walking. He probably called hundreds of people. When a woman answered, he'd say he was conducting a poll for the state Democratic Party. If the woman said yes, she was a registered Democrat, he'd proceed. Find out what he wanted to know, like did she live alone, and decide if he liked the sound of her voice. Then what he'd do, he'd say he'd like to send a questionnaire to learn more about her concerns, what was the address?"

"I knew it!" declared Todd. "They never should have given women the vote."

I held up my empty glass. "I need another. To drink to Todd and affirmative action."

Adam jumped up. "Boy, am I glad I'm not in *your* car. Anyone else want anything?"

Todd smiled across the table at me. Cookie ripped off her bandana. "I'm beat. Have they got anything at all to go on yet?"

"Todd thinks it's a black surgeon with a reassuring stethoscope," I noted. "T. J. McCall thinks it's a woman. Me? I think it's your garden variety wacko. Straight white male."

Cookie rolled her eyes. "Well, starting tomorrow night, they're adding a second decoy."

"They're sending you in?" I said, surprised.

"No. But I heard them talking. Some gal from Hollywood Division, I think." Cookie looked angry.

"What's the matter, you wanted the job?"

"Me? I'm five ten, one fifty five. Who'd attack me?"

"I don't know," I teased. "But I've heard stories."

"Don't humor me, Brenden. I'm in a bad mood. Sweet Pea moved out two days ago." Cookie looked down at her beer miserably.

Todd just looked at me. I shrugged. I had never heard of Sweet Pea. Adam returned with my Black Russian, then excused himself. I turned to Cookie. "What else did you overhear?"

"They're expanding the surveillance area. They'll probably put one of you in the van, then alternate you."

Turley could have told me. If he hadn't been so enthralled with yanking my leash, maybe he could have thought of something meaningful to relate. I took a long drink and sank deeper into my gloom.

While Todd tried to get the inside scoop on Sweet Pea, I kept checking my watch and looking out at the bar for T.J. After a while, I excused myself. I needed the bathroom and a refill.

As I turned left and started toward the restrooms, I suddenly caught sight of a familiar back standing with Adam McKay at the bar. *Higgins.* What the hell was *he* doing here? Although there were no regulations reserving First Base for rank and file, superiors rarely wandered in.

Both stalls in the ladies' room were in use, so I stood over the sink and stared into the mirror. My eyes looked slightly bloodshot, but I was pretty sure the lighting was designed to make everyone look debauched. When I finally went out, I found Todd standing there, looking glum.

"Tired?" I said sympathetically.

"Tired, stiff, and old. Man, this job makes you old. How about you? Ready to roll?"

"Not yet. I'm going to have one more and see if T.J. shows up." I burped. I pointed a finger down the bar where Higgins and McKay were huddled. "You ever seen Higgins in here?"

"I told you," said Todd, "I don't come in here."

"I don't like him being here. He could go somewhere else."

"Then leave with me now. Go home, get a good night's sleep. In fact, I'll be happy to drive you home."

I was feeling slightly dizzy. I leaned against the wall and peered at my partner. "What? You think I can't drive?"

"Not if you have another one. Not on the freeway. It's Friday night."

I smiled and squeezed Todd's arm. "You're sweet. I'll be fine. Talk to you tomorrow. In fact, let's do something tomorrow. Let's go rent a brand new wreck."

"Dammit, Brenden, I'm serious. Leave with me."

"I'm just gonna have one more. Give my love to Lynette, okay?"

Todd sighed, his eyes clearly unhappy. I probably had made a mistake bringing him here. He was a little tightly wound. He said, "Call me when you get home?"

"And wake up your whole household? Stop being an old fuddy-dud."

I moved past him and stepped up to the bar. "Johnny, I'm *dying.*"

I guess Todd left, although I didn't see him walk out. I spoke to Johnny for a minute; then, carrying a double vodka, no Kahlua, I began working my way through the crowd to the poolroom. An arm circled my shoulders. For a frantic moment I feared it might be Higgins.

"Let's get out of here," T.J. said.

I was hung over, my hair was in disarray, my flip-flops flown. Despair had set in. Creakily, I sat up on the couch and—unlike in the movies and the books—I knew exactly where I was. T. J. McCall's apartment.

I put my elbows on my knees and my head in my hands and stared bleakly at the overflowing ashtray on the coffee table, then at the vodka bottle, the scotch bottle, and finally the two glasses, each partially filled with dead ice cubes. I sat very still.

It was an overcast day, judging from the weak light seeping through the parted curtains over the two front windows. It looked like the kind of living room a man might inhabit after splitting up with his wife. The couch appeared new, of dark gray quilted material, and it stood on lighter gray carpeting. The wooden coffee table looked beat. A worn upholstered armchair flanked it on one side. Across the room a big-screen TV sat forlornly on the floor. Stacked along the walls were cartons, mostly unopened. There was track lighting on the ceiling and a floor lamp at one end of the couch. I gathered from the branches outside the windows that the apartment was on a second or third floor.

I not only knew where I was, I remembered what had transpired. There had been the usual cop talk: whining litanies of all that was wrong with the department—broken-down equipment, weak leadership, the lowering of standards to pander to any old ladies or midgets who wanted to become cops. "They should just give me a truck and a sanitation route," T.J. complained at one point. "We're the city's janitors, always cleaning up everyone else's messes."

"Well, that's poetic," I had responded.

It was during the Operation ATM part of the dialogue that T.J. captured my full attention. "It's coming together fast now," he had said.

T.J.'s theory sounded somewhat leaky, though I didn't know whether this was due to the wishful thinking of the speaker or, by then, the inebriated state of the listener. But as best I could now recall, it went something like this:

All of the victims had ties to children. Alice Croft, the secretary at a computer firm, had a son; Andrea Wright, the health clinic receptionist, had a son and a daughter; Mary Shaunessy visited sick children at the hospital; and Amelia Grant taught phys ed to high school girls. Sheila Dann, the actress, was on the board of the Make-A-Wish Foundation, a charity that raised money to offer terminally ill children a wish come true. Whether she had simply lent her name or was active, T.J. still wasn't sure. Nevertheless . . .

"Don't you see, Harlow?" he had said as I returned from a trip to the bathroom. "The handcuffs. That's the connection."

I had some trouble following.

"I'm betting they all bought handcuffs for children at the same outlet."

"As if you can't buy handcuffs every five feet," I had inserted.

"Gun stores, sex shops. You can probably even join a handcuff-of-the-month club and get them delivered by UPS."

"That's not—"

"Personally, I buy mine at the Police Academy store, which is open to the public. Where do you get yours?"

"Shut up, Harlow. I think it has something to do with kids. Which fits my lady killer theory. We've traced all the cuffs to the same manufacturer. They're going to fax me a list of outlets, preferably toy stores, that sell them in L.A. County. Then we narrow it down to the Valley."

I said, "Uh-huh," thinking his plots were as bad as Jack's.

It was then, I believe, that I raised the possibility of linking the victims to the West Valley Community Hospital, or finding some other medically related connection. Or maybe I just thought I said this because now I couldn't remember T.J. addressing that possibility at all.

Actually, what I think I said was, "Have you checked to see if they're registered Democrats?"

The apartment was as silent as a black hole. The digital clock on the VCR read 12:07 P.M. I was going to have to face myself sooner or later. I stood up and smoothed my wrinkled sweater. There was no sign of T.J.

After a while, I found my flip-flops next to the front door.

W h e n I walked into my apartment, the red light was blinking on the answering machine. I plugged in the coffeemaker and waited for the reassuring gurgle before I pressed the play button.

There were five messages, four of them from Todd. The fifth was from Jack. "It's raining. I miss you. I'll call again." He left his number at the hotel.

I dialed Todd's number and got *his* machine. Our machines were some kind of subpartners. "I'm not in intensive care," I said. "I just need some."

After I showered, I began searching the kitchen for something to eat. The freezer looked promising. But my stomach didn't respond to the sun-dried-tomato-and-mushroom pizza or Jack's supply of chicken pot pies. Buried in the back, under a plastic container of tomato sauce, sat a square foil packet. I was prying it loose, wondering what it might contain, when my beeper went off.

I picked it up off the counter and glanced at the number. I didn't recognize it. I went back to the freezer, but once again the beeper sounded. Same number. I succumbed and dialed it.

A hesitant voice breathed, "Hello?"

"You beeped me," I said. "Who is this, please?"

There was no reply, only the sound of breathing.

"This is Brenden Harlow."

"Oh." The voice stopped. "Um, yes. Hi, Sergeant Harlow. This is Billy, Billy Croft? My mom . . . " His voice trailed off.

From the freezer, I removed the foil packet. It was secured with freezer tape. "Hi, Billy. What's up?" Cookie dough maybe?

"You said I could call you."

"Sure. It's Officer Harlow, by the way. Is anything wrong?" I tossed the packet back into the freezer and moved to the counter, where I could write.

"Um." There was a long pause, then: "I'm afraid, okay? The man who killed my mom? I think he's gonna kill me, too."

The pen was rigid in my hand. "What makes you say that?" I asked softly.

"The phone keeps ringing and nobody's there and my dad went to his store and won't be home til tonight and—"

"What store?"

"Huh?"

"Where your dad works."

"Um, an office supply store. He and Uncle Larry own it."

I glanced out the kitchen window. The sun had finally broken through the low cloud cover and was shining splendidly. Damn.

"Billy," I said, "do you have a phone machine?"

"Uh-huh."

"Turn it on. If your dad calls, you can pick up. I'll be there in about an hour. Will you be okay til then?"

I could hear the relief in his answer. "Yes. Yes, I will. Thank you, Sergeant Harlow. Thanks *a lot.*"

I sighed as I hung up. My sun-starved bones and my stomach would have to be put on hold.

illy Croft's oval face appeared in the living room window like an apparition, the shadows hollowing out his cheeks, his skin a deathly pallor. The face didn't move until I rang the doorbell.

"Hi," I said as the door cautiously opened. I had forgotten how frail looking he was, tall and thin with a chest curved in like a comma. His striped T-shirt was tucked into a pair of jeans, the belt pegged at the last hole. He blinked at me from behind the thick glasses.

"Maybe I shouldn't have called," he said. "You don't have to stay if you don't want to."

There was no entry hall, only the living room with its overstuffed furniture and brightly colored throw pillows. I closed the door behind me and said, "I could use a Coke, if you have one. We'll chat for a bit anyway."

"Sure."

The living room seemed strangely empty, as if the death of Mrs. Croft had robbed it of its personality. I wondered what she had been like and found myself drawn to the fireplace, where, on the fake stone mantel, a grouping of photographs had been arranged. A woman with a round face and short brown hair proved a happier resemblance than the death scene photos I had studied. Even so, it was not a flattering pose, Mrs. Croft squinting into the sun.

"Here's your Coke." Billy handed me a glass. "I didn't know cops drank Coke."

I smiled. "Cops do just about anything you could think of. We're really pretty ordinary."

Ordinary, maybe, but not normal. A normal person would have gone to the beach, not plowed relentlessly through heavy Saturday afternoon traffic on a fruitless mission, as I assumed this to be.

"So let's sit," I said, "and you can tell me why you think someone wants to kill you."

I chose one end of a red-flowered couch and motioned to Billy to sit at the other end. I noticed his feet, large feet, tucked into black high-topped sneakers. A dorky kid on the debate team whose one concession to coolness was his footwear.

"I thought 'cause he killed my mom, he'd try to kill me."

Was that all, I wondered. A lonely kid's scary imagination? "Chances are," I said, "he doesn't know you exist. Your mom is one of five women he's killed since January, did you know that?"

Solemnly, Billy nodded.

"If he had been planning to kill your mom, he could have followed her—possibly for months—and never caught her at a bank at night alone. So we believe he's opportunistic. See what I mean?"

"Uh-huh."

There you are, I thought. No one had followed Mary Shaunessy from the hospital either, not with the intention of killing her at an ATM. I had just disproved my own theory. The killer chose randomly.

"He may not even know who he's killed," I continued. "He only takes their cash, not their credit cards or any I.D."

"My mom's name was in the *Daily News*."

I sipped my Coke. "Billy, have you talked to Detective McCall?"

"Um, I don't think so."

"Did your mom ever buy you things at a toy store?"

A toothy grin. "I'm too old for toys. I'm seventeen."

"What about games or sporting equipment?"

"I have computer games, but my dad buys them, or I do. There's a computer store at the mall."

Still, T. J. McCall was an experienced detective. If the killings were so blatantly opportunistic, why was he convinced there was a link? Which reminded me. "Did she ever go to West Valley Community Hospital, or see a doctor there, do you know?"

Billy crinkled his nose as he stared at me with confusion. "Um, she didn't go to the hospital," he said at last. "Her doctor's name is on the emergency number list in the kitchen. I went to see him once. For a sore throat."

"Where's his office?"

"In Glendale, I think."

A car drove by and Billy's eyes flew nervously to the windows. He jumped up. "I forgot to lock the door."

"So is it only the phone calls that scared you? Have they happened before today?"

Billy came back, shaking his head.

"Do you feel like someone's been following you?"

"I'm not sure." His eyes were even more evasive than his words, flitting to the window and all around me, but he rarely looked directly at me. Something was frightening him, something he didn't want to tell.

"All right. Let's go back to the night of the murder. Maybe it will help, okay?"

"I've already said everything," he protested mildly. "She was dead when I got there."

He sounded almost resentful and I wondered if relations with his mother had been strained in the way that relations between parents and teenagers often are. I said, "Tell me, Billy. After you drove into the bank and around to the back, you saw your mom on the ground, right? What did you do?"

"I went over to her and, uh, she was all bloody and not moving or anything and then I think I screamed."

"Did you touch her?"

Billy shook his head, tears welling in his eyes. "I stood there and I screamed."

I thought about that as I sipped my Coke. A panicked scream was usually an involuntary reaction to a terrifying circumstance, a sound people were often unaware they were emitting. But Billy twice stated that he had screamed, which was even more unusual coming from a boy. Typically, males did not scream. They shouted; they swore; they muttered. Or they fell mute. I said, "What did you do next?"

"I ran out to the street and waved my arms and a car stopped. It was a man. I said there was, um, an accident and I needed to call 911. He said he'd drive me to the mall. I got in and he had a phone right there. But he said it would be better if I called from the mall."

"I see."

"He drove me into the mall right up to a pay phone in front of the drugstore. He even gave me a quarter. I called 911 and I walked back to the bank. The police were there by then."

The report had merely noted that Billy had hailed a passing motorist, but now it struck me as odd. A rare motorist who would stop to pick up a stranger but wouldn't allow him to use the car phone? Most people, had they even stopped, would have made the call themselves and driven on.

I said, "Do you remember what the man or the car looked like?"

"No."

"Come on, Billy, you can remember something. Was it a four-door car, light or dark in color, a convertible? Was the man white, black, Hispanic?"

"It was a four-door car, I think dark. No, I'm not sure. It was real messy inside. Like there were clothes and things on the back seat. He was white."

"Young, old, glasses?" I wasn't sure why I was having trouble buying the story.

"Old, I guess. No glasses. He had on a sweatshirt, I think, and running shoes. They were kind of muddy."

"White-haired old, or teacher old?"

Billy smiled thinly. "Yeah, he could have been like a teacher. He had a baseball cap on."

"Did he tell you his name?"

"Uh-uh."

"Do you know how long you stood on Laurel Canyon waiting for someone to stop?"

"Hardly any time at all. He was coming around the corner and he stopped."

The corner. I closed my eyes and tried to remember. "You mean, he was on a side street north of the bank, or right there at the corner of the bank?"

"North, I guess."

The report hadn't gone into any of this. Either the detective hadn't included the details or he hadn't thought to ask for them. But the motorist's behavior intrigued me. "Did he happen to say his car phone wasn't working?"

"No. He just said he'd take me to the mall."

Billy had discovered his mother's body half an hour after she withdrew her money. How long would it take to stab a person to death? Five minutes, five seconds? Was it reasonable to assume the killer would have waited until the body was found, waited in his messy car with muddy—bloody?—shoes? No, I told myself. This was a stranger who simply didn't want to get involved. Or maybe he was in a hurry.

I looked at my watch. Forty minutes had passed and the phone hadn't rung once. I wondered if Billy was telling the truth about the hang-ups. Either way, it was clear the boy was scared. And that he wasn't going to tell me why. I stood.

"I'm glad you called. Call me anytime."

Reluctantly, Billy got to his feet. "You're going now?"

"When will your dad be home?"

"He always comes at six-thirty."

It was just past four-thirty. "You'll be okay? Maybe you can turn the TV on."

"Sure," Billy said. "But what if he calls again?"

I looked at the boy carefully. "Who, Billy?"

"The guy that's been hanging up."

I smiled. "It could be a girl, you know, a girl from school who secretly likes you. I used to do things like that."

Billy turned bright red. I left him pondering this new—and probably far scarier—thought.

S i n c e I was in the neighborhood I decided to drop by the Shaunessy house. I knew perfectly well it was only an excuse to put off going home to an empty apartment. But it was good enough to convince me.

A stocky man with a reddish brown beard responded to the ringing of the bell. He was wearing a green plaid shirt and jeans, and he held a book in one hand. He eyed me warily. "Yes?"

"Frank Shaunessy?"

"That's right."

I held up my badge. "I'm Officer Harlow with the Los Angeles police. I'm working with the task force assigned to your wife's murder and I happened to be in the neighborhood."

He had one of those indelibly friendly faces, the kind that would have crinkly eyes and an easy smile. I could see that, even though the dark eyes held a profound sadness that would never entirely disappear. "Do you have some news?" he asked hopefully.

"I'm sorry, only more questions. Do you have a few minutes?"

His broad shoulders visibly sagged. "Please come in."

The living room that he led me into was filled with cartons that he seemed in the process of packing. In one corner, a TV spoke in low tones. He moved some books off the couch and invited me to sit down. "I'm in the middle of packing," he said unnecessarily.

"Are you moving?"

He pulled up a chair. "On Monday. I thought it would be good for me to start over somewhere else."

"I'm so sorry."

He shrugged, as if he were tired of hearing how sorry people were. "So now what? Every time I turn around the police are back, always someone different. How many of you are on this thing anyway?"

"Probably forty or fifty," I said. "Sometimes we step on each other's toes, but believe me, we're throwing all we've got into finding the killer. And we will."

Frank Shaunessy said nothing. He looked to be in his mid-thirties and already he had lost his son to meningitis and his wife to a madman. I doubted LAPD's problems would mean a thing to him. I said, "One of the other victims worked at a health clinic. One theory we're pursuing is that the killer may have been connected with the medical profession."

And still he said nothing.

"I know you mentioned the two interns who visited your home, but I was wondering if your wife knew a surgeon or—"

"It's the mayor, isn't it?" he said accusingly.

"Excuse me?"

"That's why you people keep coming around, acting like you're doing something. The mayor's putting pressure on your chief and the public is screaming. So you keep coming around bothering the victims' families instead of arresting the bastard who did this."

"Mr. Shaunessy—"

"He'll strike again, too, dammit. Tell me, Officer, how many women have to die before the LAPD does *something?*"

I felt my own anger rising. Having no rational explanation for his wife's murder, he was lashing out at us. It was LAPD's fault that his Mary had stumbled across the killer's path; why weren't we there to protect her?

I looked at him calmly. "What I was hoping you could tell me, Mr. Shaunessy, was if Mary had been friendly with any of the staff doctors."

His eyes narrowed. "Are you insinuating that my wife was having an affair—"

Interesting leap there. "Now sir, why would I think that?"

"Because if you are, you're wasting your time."

He was right. I stood. "I realize I shouldn't have come unannounced. I just had some free time and—"

"Goddam police," he grumbled as he trailed me to the door. "I hear it costs the taxpayers more than a billion dollars a year to support your department, is that right?"

I turned. "I'm not exactly sure."

"And the only thing you people seem to do well is beat people up, innocent people. The criminals you just let go."

I studied his angry face. "You've had bad experiences with the police?"

"You mean outside of the rude assholes who give you tickets?" He snorted contemptuously. "No, but Mary did. Some of you should be locked up yourselves."

"What happened?"

"There was an abortion rights demonstration at Rancho Park, and this cop started hitting a guy with his club. Mary tried to intervene but the cop shoved her away. She got his name and badge number and reported him. But, of course, nothing was ever done."

"If it was a use-of-force violation, he would have gone before a Board of Rights," I offered.

"Yeah, that's what they said. But they ruled it inconclusive. I love that. A guy gets beat up but it's inconclusive." Angrily he opened the door.

"By the way," I said, "have you given us your new address?"

"Yeah. Santa Monica." Frank Shaunessy paused. "I hear the cops there are almost as bad."

I picked up a broiled chicken and a salad from a place on Broadway and even opened a decent bottle of chardonnay. But I didn't consume much of either.

My first reaction to the *Entertainment Weekly* article had been surprise. Jack always showed me everything written about him, anxiously asking my opinion—was the story okay, what did I *really* think? So I was puzzled that he hadn't mentioned it. When I read it, I understood why. In a fairly lengthy and flattering profile there was a single, dismissive mention of me. "Yeah," said Jack, "she's a cop. But she doesn't help me with my work any more than I help her with hers. We meet up at the house once in a while. What more can I say?"

I knew what more Jack would say. He would say, "Brenden, you're being ridiculous. I told that reporter a lot about you, only she didn't print it. God, you know how reporters are, they want to turn everything into a scandal."

But more than his cavalier dismissal of me, what really stung was the paragraph announcing that Jack would be replacing Billy Orso in *Paradise Found*. If the magazine had known about it two weeks before, when the story would have been reported, why hadn't I? I picked up the phone and called Suzy Rocklin.

"Brenden!" she sang. "How are you?" Suzy laughed. "I was hoping this would be Jay."

I fingered my glass of wine. "Where is he?"

"Maui, dummy, with your husband, doing the mother of all deals. But then, aren't they all?"

I hesitated, mulling this over.

"Jay's been over there for four days," said Suzy. "Where've you been?"

"Jack didn't tell me anything until Thursday night," I admitted. "I don't know what's with him lately."

I could hear a sharp intake of breath, Suzy lighting a cigarette. Then the exhaling. "Why don't you fly over? You know how actors are. They love to be pampered when they're working. Surprise him."

I studied the glass of wine. "Suzy, what's going on?"

"What do you mean?"

"I don't know what I mean. I just know something is wrong."

I measured her silence and didn't like it. I didn't like it that too often, Suzy, through Jay, knew more about my husband than I did. But I had held her hand once or twice in the past; now she could hold mine.

"The only thing I can think of," Suzy said, "is Cee Cee Harris. I think she's real bad news."

Cee Cee Harris? As in—when they both disappeared from the table at Spago? But Cee Cee was one of those nightmarish women who sat on the board of a dozen charities, redecorated—or added on to—her house every other minute, ran her kids all over town, gave eighteen dinner parties a week, and always managed to look stunning. I doubted she'd have time for Jack.

I said, "What are you getting at, Suzy?"

Over the line came an insistent beep; another call. "Listen," said Suzy quickly. "They're not having an affair, no way. So stop worrying like a wife and start acting like a cop. Talk to you later."

What the hell was that supposed to mean?

But the line went dead.

Maybe she meant to say stop being a cop and act like a wife. In other words, go to Hawaii. I tried reaching Jack, but he wasn't in. I left a message on his hotel voice mail.

By nine o'clock I was soaking in the tub, sipping my third glass of wine, and letting the roiling waters of the Jacuzzi swirl around me. Eventually I crawled into bed and dreamed I was having my tonsils out.

The weight room at Van Nuys Station was even more depressing than the one at the academy. It was deserted when I walked in and scribbled my name on the clipboard. Since Metro people are the only ones who actually get paid to work out as part of their watch, we have to make it official. I tossed a mat onto the concrete floor and began with a series of stretches.

A black woman wandered in and turned on a radio. I hopped onto an Exercycle and did fifteen minutes, trying to ignore the loud, throbbing music. The woman began lifting weights. Every once in a while I would catch her looking at me; not a casual glance, but intently, as if she were studying me. I moved over to a bench on the other side of the room and lifted weights. I could feel rivulets of sweat snaking down my body under my tank top. A second black woman entered, nodded at the first, and climbed onto the Exercycle. She, too, stole glances in my direction. I was beginning to feel slightly uncomfortable when two men walked in. One, a muscular Latino in a turquoise tank top, went over to the radio and turned it down. "Mind?"

The woman on the bench shook her head.

I returned to the mat to finish with my usual fifty sit-ups. I was almost done when the beeper on my elastic belt went off. The number on the screen had an 808 area code; Hawaii. I went over to the clipboard to sign out.

"Say, are you Brenden Harlow?"

I put down the pen and turned. The second woman who had come in was standing behind me, eyebrows raised questioningly. She had pretty, almond-shaped eyes and her hair was pinned to the top of her head with a red plastic clip. She rubbed her neck with a towel.

"Yes, I'm Brenden."

She smiled. "I'm Dorrie Green. From Hollywood Division? I've just been loaned to the task force."

"Nice to meet you, Dorrie. Did they say what you'd be doing?"

"I think decoy."

"You've worked undercover before?"

"Not since I became a detective thirteen months ago. Before that I did drug buys. But I'm a single mom with two kids. I figured enough was enough."

"Then you've come to the right place," I said. "About the only excitement we get is reading the tabloid headlines in the 7-Eleven. But let's talk later. Right now I need to make a call."

I crossed the hall to the locker room and took a quick shower. While I was dressing, the first woman from the weight room came in, stared at me boldly, and headed into the shower. I pulled on my garter, slipped in the gun, and ran a comb through my wet hair; I'd have to come back later and dry it.

I rode the elevator up to three and started down a long hall, searching for a phone. Near the end of the hall, a tiny gray-haired woman was coming out of an office. I said, "I'm with the task force. Is there a phone I can use?"

"Try the lieutenants' room. I don't think anyone's in there right now." She pointed across the hall.

I ducked inside and found a set of back-to-back desks on either side of the large, square office. I stood over the desk closest to the door and made a credit card call to Hawaii.

"Paradise," a man sang.

"This is a call from hell."

"Excuse me?"

"Is Jack Hayes around? I'm Brenden, his wife."

A moment later Jack came on the line. "Bren," he exclaimed, "I've been trying to reach you for two days. There's been a storm and the phone lines have been down. You okay?"

"Sure. How are you?" I sat down. "Are you hired?"

Jack laughed. "Yes. And right now I'm in the middle of wardrobe. We start shooting tomorrow. I've got so much to tell you, but I can't now."

"I understand. Are you pleased?"

"Yes and no. If I don't reach you tonight, I'll try tomorrow. But the shoot here is only ten days. Then we come back to L.A."

"That's good," I said.

"Look, I'm really sorry I took off in such a hurry. You sure you're okay? How's the stakeout going?"

"Like a bad day on the set. Same scene. Lots of takes."

"I can't say I'm unhappy about that," Jack declared. "I worry about you all the time."

"Thanks. I miss you."

"I miss you, too, Bren. Talk to you later."

As I was hanging up, the woman who had directed me into the office appeared in the doorway holding a sheet of paper. "You're with the ATM Task Force?"

I nodded.

"A call came in an hour ago. A woman claiming she knows something." She handed me the paper. "That's her name and number."

The name was Rosa and the area code signified a Valley location. Tons of tips were being called in, but because I was working in the field I was spared having to deal with them. The thing was, occasionally one paid off.

This one didn't. Rosa, who was twenty-one, wasn't sure but kind of *thought* maybe her boyfriend was the ATM Stabber. Right. If husbands and boyfriends the city over only knew how often their angry partners called them in. Rosa wanted money for her information. I said sure, stop by anytime.

Damn. Even though it was a bogus tip, now I'd have to make out a report. Add it to the fat file of other false and goofy leads. I stood up.

"Officer?"

The woman, who I assumed was a secretary, again stood in the doorway. "I have another call. I'd take it myself but I have a report to type up for the captain."

I looked at my watch. Twenty minutes until roll call. "All right. Can you transfer it?"

This one identified herself as Ms. Smith.

"Officer Harlow. How can I help you?" I began.

"I think I may have seen the man who stabs women at ATMs," Ms. Smith stated matter-of-factly. "I saw him at the Bank of America on Ventura, where Sheila Dann was murdered."

I sat down and picked up a stray pen. This one sounded older, her voice more sure of itself. "When was that?"

"Five nights before the murder."

"What did you see, Ms. Smith?"

"Well, I parked my car in front of the bank on Ventura. No one was there at the time. I used one of the tellers right there on the street to make a deposit. When I was walking back to my car I noticed a security guard standing just around the corner, where the drive-in lane is that goes to the back. He said, 'How are you this evening, ma'am?' I said I was fine."

"What time was this, do you remember?"

"About eight-thirty. I thought it was odd that I hadn't seen him when I arrived, but then I thought maybe he'd been patrolling the tellers in the back."

"Go on," I said.

"Well a few days later, actually the day Sheila was killed, I went into the bank to use my safe deposit box and I told the manager I appreciated the security guard." Ms. Smith paused. "He said they don't have a security guard."

"This man," I said, "what was he wearing?"

"A light blue shirt and dark pants and a hat. Not a baseball cap, but a hat like a policeman wears."

"Did he have a gun?"

There was a pause. "I don't think so, at least I don't remember seeing one."

"What made you think he was a security guard?"

"He had a yellow patch on his shirt with blue lettering. But I didn't see what it said. And the way he was standing, feet sort of apart?"

"Can you describe his face?"

"He was in the shadows at the corner of the bank and the bill of the hat made it difficult. He didn't have a mustache. But I can't tell you what color his hair is."

"Could you tell what descent he is?"

"You mean race? He's white."

"What about his age?"

She laughed softly. "I'm forty-four. Everybody looks young to me."

"And when you were walking back to your car, did you see anybody else?"

"Not that I remember."

"All right. I or someone else will call you back. Tell me your full name, please."

"Terry Smith." She gave me her address and both her home and her work numbers.

I ran my fingers through my damp hair and hurried downstairs to the roll call room.

S i x people were introduced as new members of the surveillance team, including Dorrie Green. As decoys, Dorrie and I would each visit eight banks a night, Sergeant Higgins explained, working in tandem. While I was driving the Rent-A-Wreck and withdrawing money, Dorrie would wait her turn in the van. Then we would trade places, although she would use her own rental. Todd would provide backseat security for us both. We went over the hand signals we used to coordinate between myself—and now Dorrie—and those in the field.

"Next," said Higgins, "Art Bannister from Robbery/Homicide is going to bring us up to date. Detective."

A dark-haired, beefy man in a beige sport coat walked to the front of the room. He tacked an eight-by-ten photo onto the bulletin board. It showed a man with thinning dark hair, a long, narrow face, and a scraggly beard.

"Afternoon," Bannister began. "You're looking at Donald Abernathy. Male Caucasian, five ten, goes about one-sixty. Thirty-seven years old. We like him as a suspect for two reasons. One, he was a janitor at Home Federal Savings, where our first victim, Mary Shaunessy, was killed. He'd worked there sixteen months. Three weeks before her death, he was laid off. Two, he then gets hired at Great Western, where Amelia Grant, our fourth victim, is killed. Donald's got a real nice profile for it. High school dropout, juvenile arrest record. Two robberies. One a liquor store, one a woman's purse. Served two years in the army; had problems getting along with his superiors, made no real friends. Since then he's held a series of manual labor jobs, the longest being eighteen months. Lives alone in a garage-type apartment in Sunland. Eight years ago a girlfriend reported him for threatening her with a knife. But she dropped the charges. Five years ago he was convicted of auto theft. Served eighteen months. Reason why I'm alerting you is, a week ago, he stopped showing up for work at Great Western, and it appears he hasn't been home. We've got his apartment under surveillance. But I want you all to be on the lookout. Any questions?"

I raised my hand. "How recent is that photo?"

"Recent," Bannister said. "Great Western took it for his identity badge when they hired him."

Other questions followed, but Bannister had given out all the information he cared to. I assumed he had additional reasons for suspecting Donald Abernathy, beyond what he had divulged. When the meeting broke, I went up to Higgins. He was standing over a table, organizing a sheaf of papers.

"Sarge, do you have a minute?"

"Yeah, Harlow. What's up?"

I had refrained from mentioning Terry Smith in the meeting for fear that Higgins would again accuse me of hotdogging. But I thought the tip important enough to alert him. "Just before roll call I spoke to a woman who may have a possible lead."

Higgins glanced up. "We just got our lead."

Speaking in a monotone, I went ahead and told him about Terry Smith's sighting of the security guard anyway. "Although she specifically said he didn't have a mustache; maybe she should see the picture of Abernathy," I concluded.

Higgins fixed me with those hard unyielding eyes. "Did you return the reports to the lieutenant?"

I shifted to my other foot. "I was about to, sir, when I was asked to take this woman's call." I hesitated. "Do you think it's worth following up?"

Higgins scooped up the papers. "What I think, Harlow, is that you should fill in a clue slip and turn it in like everybody else." He looked pointedly at his watch. "Isn't it time for you to do your *assigned* job, Officer?"

"Right," I said, even though taking phone tips was part of a Metro officer's *assigned* job.

But Higgins had already spun on his heel and walked out.

W a n t i n g to avoid Higgins's big ears, I told Todd about Terry Smith before I wired up. I was taking the first shift; Dorrie was in the van. Typically, Sundays produced little ATM business. People picked up weekend spending money on Fridays and Saturdays, then returned on Mondays to fill up for the week. On Sundays, apparently, they rested.

Now, as I drove out of the second bank's lot, I said to Todd guardedly, "Four of the five banks had security cameras. Not one captured anything, right?"

Todd was on his back, knees up, feet on the floor behind me. I knew my transmitter couldn't pick up his words as he said, "Sure, a security guard would know how to duck a camera. But don't forget, serial killers are furtive animals. The reason they're serial killers is they don't leave many traces, so they're able to go right on killing."

"It fits nicely though, don't you think?"

"She said no one else was around. Why didn't he strike?"

It occurred to me then that I had forgotten to ask Terry Smith what she'd been wearing. If she had worn pants, would that have disqualified her in the killer's eyes?

The radio hiccupped. "R-thirteen? Can you hear me?"

I realized then that Higgins must have been trying to raise me, but Metro people get a new unit designation each day, and sometimes I get stuck in yesterday's mode. I turned up the volume. "Twenty. This is R-thirteen. Go ahead."

"Okay, at the next intersection the street is blocked. Construction. Take your first left and go over to Lankershim, then take Chandler to Coldwater. Do you read me?"

"Roger."

"Maybe it was a neighborhood watch guy," Todd theorized. "You know, the kind that go to community policing meetings, have milk and cookies with a cop, then run around their neighborhoods like Clint Eastwood hoping someone will make their day?"

"I don't know," I said. "Those wackos are usually harmless."

"What?" said Higgins over the radio.

"I just turned onto Lankershim," I replied quickly, "and I'm gonna stop right here at a Citibank. It's my bank and I need some cash."

I made a quick U-turn and parked in front of the bank. It sat on the corner of a small side street but its two ATMs were on Lankershim, artistically hidden by trees and bushes. Most of L.A.'s architecture lacked anything resembling esthetics—except for banks. I said, "Twenty, do you read me? I'm at Lankershim and Otsego and I'm stopping at Citibank. I'll only be a sec, okay?"

"As long as you don't hold the damn place up," Higgins grumbled. "All our manpower's being used."

I blinked. Was that a joke? Higgins never attempted humor with me. I never even suspected he had any. I shook my head and opened the door.

"I'll jump out, too," said Todd. "I'm gonna go behind the bank and take a whiz."

It was a picture-perfect spring night, the air fragrant with the scent of magnolia bushes and night-blooming jasmine. It was a night to barbecue and drink margaritas, not drive around in a heap looking for scum, I thought as I retrieved $200 from the machine and stood on the corner idly watching the traffic on the busy boulevard. Out of habit, I began rotating my shoulders and neck. I hadn't had that much wine the night before, maybe half a bottle, but I was feeling lethargic.

"Brenden."

Todd was rounding the corner with that look of controlled anger I knew so well. My first thought: a black man lurking behind a building—had someone given him a hard time?

I grinned. "Your fly stuck, partner?"

"Goddam fucker."

"What?" I said anxiously.

He grabbed the front of my blouse and shouted into the mike. "This is R-fourteen. Twenty, do you read?"

I could see the beads of sweat on his forehead.

"Yeah, I just found number six."

The communications traffic on our frequency, the volume now turned loud, attracted the attention of a man in shirtsleeves locking up a fast-photo operation three doors past the bank. He turned and studied us with interest.

Todd called out, "We're the police. Have you heard or seen anything unusual in the last hour or so?"

The man was dark complected, possibly Middle Eastern, and he walked toward us, nodding. "There was a commotion in the back. I heard a sound but I couldn't tell if it was someone crying out or a dog wailing. I went to my back door and looked out and I saw a man running."

"What did he look like?"

"It was dark. He had on a light blue shirt, that's all I could tell."

"When was this?"

"Maybe fifteen, twenty minutes ago."

While Todd talked to the man and waited for Higgins and others to arrive, I grabbed a flashlight from the car and, gun drawn, went into the alley that ran behind the stores. I could see now what had happened. Todd had gone around the back of the bank. A maroon station wagon was parked in the alley, the driver's door flung open. She must have been getting in when the murderer came up from behind and yanked her out. Five feet into the alley, her brutally slashed body lay on the blood-soaked ground.

I stood there a moment trying to make sense of what I was seeing. I couldn't even be sure this mess of spongy red tissue had been a human. She was half sitting against the base of a tree, her head tilting to the left as if she had fallen asleep. Under a twisted piece of cloth that had been the skirt of her dress, a patch of flesh on her right thigh had been skinned off. Her stomach had been slit open, the intestines exploding out.

I gulped air through my mouth and quickly turned away.

Along the right side of the alley, the blacktop merged with a gravel strip. Maybe five feet wide, the strip backed up into a high chain-link fence. Garbage bins stood on the gravel. Apparently shopkeepers came out through back doors and left their garbage for pickup.

The distant sound of sirens rang through the night as I probed further into the alley. Four stores past the bank, I thought I heard a noise up ahead and to the right. I shined my flashlight on a Dumpster near the fence. Then, from the far end of the alley, a pair of headlights began moving slowly toward me. I lowered my gun and waited.

The car crawled forward. As it drew closer I saw that it was a beat-up bronze two-door. A man was behind the wheel, a woman beside him. I signaled with my flashlight for the car to stop.

The man, a Latino, rolled down his window.

"You'll have to turn back," I said. "The alley's blocked up ahead."

The man frowned and turned to his wife. She spoke softly to him. I aimed my flashlight at the back seat. It was filled with grocery bags.

"Comprende?" I said.

The man nodded and began to back into a parking area behind one of the stores. Out of the corner of my eye I saw a flash of color accompanied by the sound of gravel crunching.

The son of a bitch had been hiding behind the Dumpster, and now he was taking off. I took off after him. "Freeze," I shouted. "Police!"

I was too far away to call for Todd, and I didn't know if Higgins was still in position to hear me through the transmitter. I tried anyway, breathing hard. "This is R-thirteen. Code two. Possible suspect in the alley behind Citibank, Lankershim and Otsego. Possibly armed. Repeat, need backup immediately."

Damn. I didn't have my cuffs. Despite my high-heeled shoes I was gaining slightly. "Stop now or die!"

The man ducked behind another Dumpster. I pulled up short and trained the flashlight on the grungy metal container. "I want to see your hands first, then the rest of you. Like now."

Behind him stood the chain-link fence, and I didn't want to have to go over it. I shined the light high on the fence, hoping to squelch any ideas he might have of trying it.

"Come on, asshole, I don't have all night."

A rustling sound. Slowly, hands raised, a man emerged from the side of the Dumpster.

"Keep your hands up," I said, planting myself fifteen feet from him and keeping my gun trained on him. The flashlight beam showed he was wearing jeans and a sleeveless black T-shirt.

I now realized the bronze car had turned around and had stopped behind me. I waved my flashlight. "Go on, keep moving."

Reluctantly it rolled off. I turned my attention back to the man. "What are you doing here?"

"Nothing."

He was a Caucasian, about five ten, muscular, with dark greasy hair and stubble on his face. He was clutching something in his raised left hand.

"What's that?"

"I don't know. A glove."

"Drop it."

"Okay, okay, don't shoot."

The item fell to the gravel.

"Turn around slowly." No gun or knife sticking out of his waist-band. "On your knees, hands up." The man obeyed. "Now drop to your stomach. I want you spread-eagled, face on the ground."

I kept my gun pointed at him. "What's your name?"

"Fuck you."

Two patrol officers were jogging toward me. I walked over to what the guy had dropped and shined my light on it. It was a partial black glove, the kind that serious bodybuilders use to lift weights.

I looked up. "Cuff Hulk Hogan here. I want this glove for evidence."

As they dragged the man to his feet and led him away, I walked back to the first Dumpster and opened it. The stench nearly gagged me. As I shined my light over the rotting garbage and debris, it took about a second to spot the purse. Red leather bag on a strap.

I left the Dumpster lid open and waited. When two more officers arrived, I told them to collect the purse and to search for a knife and a blue shirt.

Then I walked back to the street, jumped behind the wheel of the wreck, collected Todd—and led the caravan back.

nder normal circumstances, Mr. X would have been our collar. We would question him, decide whether to book him
and, if so, write up our crime-and-arrest report. But these
were not normal circumstances. While Todd baby-sat the
suspect on a wooden bench inside the back entrance to the
station, I got on the phone to Robbery/Homicide downtown.

It was 9:30 on a Sunday night, and ordinarily no one would have
been in. Detectives more than other cops keep regular office hours.
But because of the murder, I tried anyway. When I got no answer, I dialed Detective Headquarters, which operates a twenty-four-hour command post out of Parker Center and would know where to reach a
task force detective. The sergeant I spoke with told me to reach Marty
Walters, the lead detective on the case. I found him at home and explained our situation.

"Yeah, I heard," Walters said. "I'm getting ready to roll out to the
scene now. Go ahead and question the guy. If he smells good, hold
him. I'll stop by when I'm finished at the scene."

I returned to the rear lobby grinning and told Todd, "He's ours."

Todd unshackled the scowling man from the metal rings on the
bench and we led him up to a second-floor interrogation room. It was
as cramped and miserable as one would expect in a decaying, out-
dated station. Van Nuys didn't have the rat problem some of the older
inner-city stations had, but the too-small offices—with sporadically ac-
quired computers wedged into any available space—the drab paint
job, and the harsh lighting spoke of a station dying for major cosmetic
surgery.

The interrogation room was no more than six feet by eight, domi-
nated by a table and four straight-back chairs. There were two ther-
mostats: one that worked the air-conditioning, which didn't work; one
that shielded a hidden mike.

"I want a Coke," the man announced as soon as he sat down.

"Sure," said Todd. "Just as soon as the waiters arrive." He flipped
open his notebook. "A hundred forty-three bucks. Nice walking-
around money, pal."

We still didn't know how much the victim had withdrawn from
the ATM, and needed to wait for the bank to contact us. But we had
found $143 in the suspect's jeans.

"Otherwise," said Todd, "our friend has no I.D., no driver's license, no credit cards. The keys in his pocket are for a Ford."

"And a comb," I added. I had been present when Todd went
through the guy's pockets before putting him into the wreck. "A greasy
comb."

"Man likes to keep up his appearance," Todd said.

I removed the handcuffs from the suspect and slid into a seat
across the table from him. "We'll start with your name," I said.

"Get me a cigarette."

"Sure," I said. "After you answer the first ten questions. Correctly.
Starting with your name."

The man slouched in his chair and glared at us defiantly. He
looked dirty and he smelled even dirtier.

I said, "No name? Resisting arrest. That's the first charge against
you. And so far, the only one."

The guy sniffled. "George James."

I scribbled that down on a field interview card. "Address?"

"Who gives a shit where I live?"

"The victim's family and friends, I suspect."

"I didn't have nothin' to do with that woman."

"Then how do you know the deceased is a woman?" I asked.

"A bird told me."

"Address, George."

The guy shifted his eyes to Todd, who was standing by the door.
Todd smiled sweetly. "Just put down the Van Nuys jail."

"Fuck. I'm staying with friends, but I don't remember the address."

"But you do know their phone number, right?"

"Naw. I just got in today."

"Fine," I said. "We'll go ahead and book you on suspicion of mur-

der. You'll get a court-appointed lawyer and he or she can help you remember these bothersome little details."

"One-oh-four Hiawatha Street."

"Where's that?"

"Chatsworth."

"North of the one-eighteen?" Todd asked.

"No. South. Near Devonshire."

Todd nodded. "He knows what he's talking about."

"Now can I have a cigarette?"

"How long have you lived there?" I continued.

"Three months."

"Are you employed?"

George inspected his fingernails then looked up with a grin. "I
took early retirement."

"You mean you were laid off. From where?"

"I work in landscaping."

"What's the name of the company?"

"It has no name. It's my brother-in-law's."

"What's his name?"

"Bob."

I yawned. "I can stay here all night, Todd. How about you?"

"Sure," said my partner. "I like all that time and a half. And this
guy's only looking at time."

George shook his head in disgust. "Bob Gomez."

"You ever been arrested?"

"'Course not."

"How many times? Once, twice?"

"No."

I stood up. "Be right back."

I scrambled down the stairs to the first floor to run a computer
check on George James. Whether it was the hour or the computer, the
machine took its time coughing up the information I was looking for.
Surprise, surprise. There was no George James in our records, nor one
residing at the address he had given. Nor one listed at the DMV. I
stopped in the lobby and asked the desk duty officer where I could
rustle up some decent coffee. He looked about eighteen, a clean-cut
California beach boy, and he gave me a nice smile. "If you play your
cards right," he said, "I'll direct you to the cappuccino machine."

The hell with the bad paint job; this station had its priorities right.
"Where?" I said eagerly.

He pointed. "The food room, such as it is. It's in the coffee machine. Thirty-five cents."

When I got back up to the interview room, I gave one paper cup to Todd and sat down with mine. "Bad news, mister. We're going to have to rehearse it from the top."

"Shit," said Todd.

"Yeah," I said. "The asshole wants to play games. The thing is, I wonder if he knows we can arrest him for giving false information to a police officer. You knew that, right?"

The man's eyes darted from one of us to the other. "I don't know nothin' without a cigarette."

"I'll go," said Todd. "I think I saw a machine downstairs."

As soon as the door closed, I leaned forward. He had a big tattoo on his right bicep and another curling around his left wrist. But they weren't gang tattoos. I doubted his muscles came from a gym; probably from construction. Or prison.

I said, "Now, either you're innocent and you can get out of here lickety-split, or you're guilty and you'll want a lawyer. You want a lawyer?"

He rubbed his tongue across his teeth and said nothing.

"How did you get to the alley?"

"I took the subway." He grinned at his little joke.

Actually, the subway *was* a joke. L.A.'s belated, pathetic attempt to build one had become a civic scandal. At last report, it had begun to tunnel its way into the Valley, collapsing entire streets in its wake.

"Are you working in construction on the subway?"

He hadn't expected that, and the faint flicker in his light brown eyes made me think I'd got it right.

"There's no George James listed at the address you gave us."

"I'm renting from a guy. I forget his name."

"What's the name on your driver's license? Man, I hope you've got a driver's license. Big trouble if you don't."

"James George."

"Cute."

"James Allen George."

"Your family doesn't believe in last names?"

"Junior," he added with a sly grin. "James Allen George Junior."

I pulled out a fresh card. "Birth date?"

"November twelfth, nineteen sixty-two."

"Where's the Ford you were driving?"

"Who says I was—"

The door opened. Todd tossed down three cigarettes and a plastic ashtray, but he kept the matches. "How's it going?" He struck one. The guy accepted the light and exhaled lustily.

I said, "Let's go get some dinner. I could use a steak." I looked at my watch. "I'm sure we'll be back by midnight, don't you think?"

For the first time, a look of concern crossed our suspect's face as he flicked his eyes around the claustrophobic room.

"Naw, spaghetti and meatballs," Todd said. He lifted his gray sweatshirt and patted his flat stomach. "I'm starved."

With a crash, Junior jumped up and tried to flip the table over on me. I caught it as the ashtray came crashing into my lap. Todd, standing by the door, lunged, grabbed the guy by the neck, and slapped the side of his head.

"Ouch!" James George said, rubbing his red right ear.

"Or," said Todd, "we can all sit down and finish up now."

Once again, we arranged ourselves at the table. For round three, the guy produced the same name, a different address, an age of thirty-one, and exactly the same job story: brother-in-law Bob. This time, Todd offered to run his record, and alone again with the creep, I proceeded with the matter at hand.

"What were you doing in the alley?" I couldn't directly ask him if he had killed her. For if he had, and said so, he could later claim the confession had been coerced. We hadn't read him his rights yet, so we had to tread carefully. "Did you follow that woman in?"

"Of course not."

"Someone says you did."

"Yeah? Who?"

"Eyewitness. Gave a pretty good description. By the way, what did you do with your shirt?"

"What shirt?" He plucked at his black T-shirt. "This is my shirt."

"What were you doing in the alley, James?"

He stubbed out the cigarette and stared sullenly at the ashtray. There was a knock at the door. I went to open it. A dark-haired uniform with a bristly mustache said, "Harlow?"

I nodded.

"Can I see you for a moment?"

I stepped into the hall and closed the door. The name plate on his uniform read *Whiteside*.

"Thought you'd like to know there's more than one set of prints on the purse. Lab's running it now."

"What was in the purse?"

"Makeup, what looks like house keys, no wallet, no money, no credit cards or I.D."

"But you ran the plates?"

"Yeah. Michael Lloyd. Age thirty-six. Canoga Park. Probably the husband. Someone's on the way to see him now."

I paused, thinking about the guy. Watching TV, or maybe putting the kid to bed, waiting for his wife to come home. The sudden knock at the door.

"Did you find anything else? Like a light blue shirt?"

Whiteside grinned. "Yes, ma'am. In a dumpster behind the photo shop. Also a mate to that glove on the gravel. Lab's got everything. By the way, what's your guy's name?"

"It was George James. Now it's James George. My partner's downstairs checking it out."

Whiteside nodded. "Next time try Mike. The shirt had a yellow patch over the pocket. Says *Mike's Security* in dark blue script."

"Blood?"

"Oh yeah."

"Thanks."

I went back into the interrogation room and said, "Things don't look good, James. We found your shirt. Bloody mess. When my partner gets back, we're gonna have to fingerprint you and leak a little blood out of you."

"What for? I didn't have no shirt. And I didn't kill that woman."

And I didn't like the fact that from the waist up, he bore no scratches, bruises, or bloodstains. Over his left eye he had a fresh pink scar, but not fresh enough. His fingernails were caked with dirt, but his hands looked clean. The money in his pocket did not appear to have blood on it, but the lab would check on that. I scribbled a note on one of the cards to have a detective go back to the alley and check for water spigots. Maybe one of the shops had one out back.

I studied James. Longish dank hair. Fuzz on his face. Small, close-set brown eyes. Bulbous nose. Thin lips. Even cleaned up he would have been no Mr. America. But he could have put on a uniform and passed for a security guard. Well-developed arms and pecs. His long thin fingers were roughened.

I said, "You look uncomfortable, James. Why don't you relax, put your feet up on the table? When my partner gets back, we'll see about that Coke."

Smirking, James maneuvered his legs out from under the table and thumped his sneakers on top of it. I couldn't tell if the dried, cakey material on the bottom of the jeans was mud or blood. But I had no trouble identifying the dark reddish brown spots on the white soles of his shoes.

He reached for a cigarette. "Where's the damn matches?"

"So what were you doing back there? It's Sunday night, it's dark. Doesn't sound right to me. Hey, James, what am I *supposed* to think?"

He threw down the cigarette. "What was I doing back there? I was being a good citizen. I heard a scream. I thought maybe I could help. The fuck? Is that a crime now?"

"Where were you when you heard her scream?"

"I was coming out of the liquor store and walking toward that corner."

"Walking north or south?"

"Uh, south?"

"What did you buy in the liquor store?"

"Bottle o' beer."

"And that's all you bought, one beer?"

"Maybe a pack of cigarettes, I forget."

"I remember. You didn't buy cigarettes. If you had, you wouldn't be sitting here begging for one."

He said nothing.

"What did you do when you heard the scream?"

"I went into the alley."

"Was anybody else there?"

"The lady, the lady was already dead."

"How do you know that?"

"Christ, did you see her?"

"How close did you get?"

"Pretty close."

"Why, if you knew she was dead? She looked horrible. She *smelled* horrible."

James studied his hands.

"What did you do with the knife, James? Did you throw it over the fence? We'll find it, you know. They're out there looking right now. Help us a little bit, we can help you."

"Fuck you."

"Where'd you get the money?"

"It's my money."

"'Cause as soon as we dust it we'll know if the woman's prints are on it, too."

"I didn't take no damn money."

"What about her credit cards?"

He cleared his throat and looked at me uneasily. "That's what I was looking for when I saw the man."

"Oh, now we've got a mystery man?"

"He was behind that Dumpster. I heard a noise and I ducked behind the woman's car. Then he left. He went back to the street. I waited, then I went over to the Dumpster thinking maybe he'd thrown away a purse or credit cards or something."

"I suppose you didn't get a good look at this man?"

"Uh . . . He was in black. Yeah. Like a black sweatshirt? He had the hood pulled up. That's why I knew he was the killer. Who would have a hood on in this weather?"

I stood up. "That's a real nice story, James. But before I get back, you might want to dream up another one. A better one."

His eyes widened. "Where are you going?"

"To get the paperwork so we can book you. We'll read you your rights, fingerprint you, and toss you in the roach motel." I paused in the doorway. "I just hope we can find a pillow for once that doesn't have dried vomit on it."

The next hour produced a flood of information. The name James Allen George Jr. could not be traced to any known source or verified. The occupants of the second address he gave were a sixty-year-old widow and her three cats. The owner of the liquor store on Lankershim did not recall ever seeing our man.

I gave up the cappuccino and switched to straight caffeine. We fingerprinted our suspect, and within thirty minutes we had him nailed. Using VIPAC, we ran his prints and hit the jackpot. Justin James Allen, thirty-three. Parolee, six months out of Chino state prison. His record was rich with crime. Two armed robberies (liquor stores), three assaults with a deadly weapon (all against women, but oddly, no charges of sexual assault), and, his crowning achievement, manslaughter for the stabbing of a coworker at a construction site outside Bakersfield six years before. And yes, he was currently working construction on the subway.

Along the way, we matched his prints, naturally, to the glove he'd had in his hand and to the purse in the Dumpster. No prints were found on the second glove, which was retrieved from the second Dumpster, and prints cannot be lifted from a cotton shirt. We were still waiting for results from the money.

Higgins didn't think we had enough to book him for murder; in fact, we had little evidence to connect him to the murder, except possibly the money and the blood on his shoes. The dead woman had withdrawn $200, so where was the rest? But the money, even if it had her prints on it, would not prove he killed her.

In the end, we booked Justin James Allen for not identifying himself as a parolee to a police officer—a violation of his parole good enough to send him back to prison—and threw him into a cell in the first-floor jail wing of the station.

N o sooner had I fallen asleep—or so it seemed—than the phone rang.

"It's Marty Walters. Sorry if I woke you."

I cleared my throat. "No problem, Detective. I'm tracking."

I wasn't. Police officers are supposed to come equipped with this special wake-up device that makes them instantly operational no matter how sound asleep they are. Through some factory oversight, my batteries had not been included. I always had to fake it.

I glanced at the clock—7 A.M.—and silently groaned.

"I'm going over your report," Walters said. "This Terry Smith. When did you talk to her?"

"Yesterday." I inched my legs over the side of the bed. "She sounded okay."

"Good. We'll want her to come in for a lineup. Problem is, I'm a little shorthanded right now. Think you could do it?"

"Sure." I reached for the pen and the pad of paper I kept on my bedside table. "Give me her number."

An hour later, showered, dressed, and primed with industrial-strength coffee, I was plowing through northbound traffic on the San Diego freeway.

T e r r y Smith lived in a sizeable two-story white frame house in the Valley's fashionable Encino neighborhood. Fashionable in that it was once home to Michael Jackson and his backyard zoo. Plenty of other celebrities lived in the area, but I didn't know who or, at 8:20 on a Monday morning, care.

A tall, statuesque woman with stylishly cut gray hair and a subdued red suit greeted me at the door. She was holding an attaché case.

"Officer Harlow?"

In a celebratory mood, I was wearing a short navy dress, belted, and a pair of high-heeled navy shoes. I held up my badge.

"You don't look like a police officer," Terry Smith said with a smile. "But then, I've been told I don't look like a building contractor."

"Least not like any of the screwups I've ever dealt with," I said. "I bet *your* word means something."

She laughed and closed the door behind her. "I'll follow you in my car, if that's okay."

"Actually, it would be better if you rode with me. I know it's inconvenient but I want to talk to you. I'll drive you back, okay?"

Terry Smith consulted the man-size gold watch on her left wrist. "I've got a ten-thirty downtown."

"Delay it." I gave her a meaningful smile. "Your police department will be grateful," I said.

I n the car, Smith removed a cell phone from her attaché case and placed a call, presumably to her secretary. When she broke off, she said, "What did you want to talk to me about?"

I had been debating, the 101 freeway versus Ventura Boulevard. It was rush hour. I opted for the surface street and said, "Just out of curiosity, do you remember what you were wearing the night you saw the security guard?"

She glanced at me with a frown. "Heavens no. Why?"

"It would help if you could remember."

"I would understand if you wanted to question my eyesight. But my clothes? Gosh, it was weeks ago."

"Maybe you could remember if you went straight to the bank from work," I prompted, "or you stopped home and changed first."

"Hmm." Once again the attaché case flew open, and Terry Smith removed a leather day planner. "Let's see. I told you it was several days before Sheila Dann was murdered."

"Try five. I think you said five."

"Okay. Wait. Was she killed on the twenty-first or the twenty-eighth?"

"The twenty-first," I said.

"So five days before would be Monday. Here we go. I had a five o'clock meeting with the Arco people at the California Club. Then I drove out to a construction job in . . . " She paused. "I'm thinking I probably went straight to the bank." She looked at me again. "But what did I wear?"

I glanced at her tailored suit. "Do you generally wear a suit or a dress to work?"

"I'm afraid I don't understand."

"Ms. Smith, all I can tell you is the victims wore similar types of clothing. You said you were alone at the bank, and I'm wondering, if you'll forgive me, why this man didn't attack you. Maybe he isn't the killer. Or maybe you simply weren't dressed for it."

"Oh heavens. Oh, I see." She bit her red-stained lip. "I usually wear a suit to work. Unless I'm going to a job site. Then I'll wear pants or even overalls. But because I'm a large woman, I find it less off-putting to men if I'm dressed feminine."

"So if you met with the Arco people, then went to the job site, you might have been wearing a skirt?"

"You're right. That late in the day, I probably wouldn't have changed."

Or maybe she had and forgot. On the other hand, she was a large woman, and the victims had been smaller, so maybe Mr. Stabber had thought better of it.

I glanced at her as I turned left onto Van Nuys Boulevard.

She had a gold compact open and was checking her lipstick.

It was only 8:45 when I pulled into the station, but already the streets surrounding it were clogged with TV vans. The news vultures would, by now, know of murder number six. But I didn't think they would have been told that we had a live one in the tank.

"Officer Harlow!"

Three women and a man, all microphone equipped and attached to trailing cameramen, pounced on me and a startled Terry Smith.

"You arrested the ATM Stabber last night! How does it feel? Tell us about it!"

So much for LAPD's ability to keep its mouth shut. "We're holding a possible suspect," I said, "but not a confirmed one."

I tried to move away but someone vise-gripped my elbow. I turned quickly and was confronted by the woman from Channel 2. Her cameraman practically screwed his lens into my face. "You ought to let go of my arm," I said darkly. "It costs the taxpayers plenty to maintain it."

The woman didn't even have the grace to look embarrassed. "Brenden. It is Brenden, isn't it?"

I took Terry by the arm and tried to edge forward.

"You can't run away from being a hero!" the newswoman screamed.

I turned back and gave her a broad *News at 11* smile. And then, below camera range, I gave her the finger.

I led Ms. Smith up to the third floor and, unsure where exactly to park her, I ushered her into the outer office of Captain Logan, whom I'd met at the bank the night Sheila Dann was murdered. Logan spotted me standing at his secretary's desk and came out. "Brenden, congratulations. Good job."

The icy blue eyes appeared a bit melted this time. "Let's hope we've got the right guy," I responded. "Captain, this is Terry Smith. She's here for the lineup."

"Ms. Smith?" Logan shook her hand. "Won't you sit down? I'll let Detective Walters know you're here. Brenden, why don't you come with me?"

I followed him down the hall. "I'll try to update you," he said as we walked toward the elevator. "We located Allen's car, or at least the car he had the keys to. Stolen vehicle. His prints are all over it, so we can nail him for that. Uh, morning, Bill. His prints are also on the victim's purse. There was a bloodstain on the money and a bunch of partials. They're still working on those." He poked the elevator button.

"Has he said anything yet?"

"That's the bad news. He's sticking to his story. Heard the scream, saw the body, saw a guy in a black hood, who ran. A couple of detectives are searching his apartment now."

The elevator door slid open.

"Were there handcuffs?" I inquired.

"Damn," said Logan. "I forgot something."

I trailed him back to his office wondering about the handcuffs. I hadn't seen any beside the victim, but it had been dark, and the bloody mess of her body was all that had captured my attention.

Terry Smith was perched on a chair, talking into her cell phone.

The investigating detectives had worked quickly. They had found five light blue shirts and five police hats and put them on four prisoners, pried out of their cells, and on a freshly shaven Justin James Allen.

Terry Smith, staring through the one-way glass, said, "The light is so bright in there. It would help if I could study the men in shadows."

Right. As if we had a lighting director. This produced a minor crisis until Captain Logan suggested we draft one of the TV cameramen parked outside to help light the lineup. By now, Higgins had turned up and was standing at a distance sipping coffee. He seemed intent on ignoring me.

I walked over to him. "Morning, Sarge."

"Harlow."

"I'm wondering what's the game plan for today. Will roll call be here or at Metro?"

Higgins blew on his coffee and still managed to give me a small, sardonic smile. "I suspect here. I don't imagine it'll be long before they kick Allen and we can get back to work."

"Kick him?" I said. "Completely?"

"Oh, they've got things to book him on, so they'll keep him. But I don't think they'll keep him for murder."

I raised an eyebrow. "I see," I said, and turned away.

The prick. I doubted Higgins would know more than Captain Logan, and from what Logan had said, Allen was still a live one. I decided to be insubordinate. I rode the elevator back up to three and found Logan sitting behind his desk. When he saw me outside, he called, "Are they ready to go yet?"

"Not quite, sir. I can't find my address book." I frowned and pirouetted, pretending to search for one. "It's probably in my car."

"Have someone call me when they're ready," Logan said.

"Sure." I inched toward his doorway. "You know, something just occurred to me. We may have two other witnesses who could I.D. Allen."

Logan tilted his head. "Who? Come in, Brenden."

"Alice Croft, the second victim? Her son."

"Sit down."

"Thank you, sir." Man, now I was really walking into smelly stuff—leapfrogging over my sergeant. "Billy Croft," I said. "And a school-teacher named Marisa Ruiz." I told him about the "just checking" guy Marisa encountered at the Valley S&L and the man who picked up Billy and drove him to the mall. "I know it's a long shot," I added, "but maybe we should check with them. I should have thought of this before."

"Did Billy give a description of the driver?"

"White guy, baseball cap, sweats, clothes piled on the back seat."

Captain Logan nodded. "Thank you, Brenden."

W h e n the artistically lit lineup again got under way, Terry Smith studied the men carefully. Then she told Detective Walters to ask each one to say, "How are you this evening, ma'am?" She contemplated them some more. "It could be number four," she said, "but I couldn't say positively."

Number four was Justin James Allen.

"Thank you, Ms. Smith," Marty Walters said. "You can go now."

As I escorted her out, I noticed Logan, Higgins, and a detective I didn't recognize conferring in a corner. Higgins glanced at me expressionlessly as I passed by.

D e s p i t e Higgins's prediction, we did not go out on Operation ATM that Monday night. There were a number of developments. For instance, a pair of handcuffs had, in fact, been found at the scene, under the corpse's bunched skirt. Since the killer's fondness for handcuffs had not been released to the public, we could assume the dead woman, identified as Michelle Lloyd, age twenty-eight, was his sixth victim.

The search of Allen's apartment did not, unfortunately, turn up a stash of cuffs or anything else to link him to the mayhem.

The blue shirt with the Mike's Security patch contained the blood of the victim and no one else's. No firm called Mike's Security could be found.

Billy Croft and Marisa Ruiz were invited to stop in the next day for another lineup.

With time to kill before roll call, I drove over to the Police Academy to use the firing range. Most officers were required to be tested every other month; in Metro it was every month. I was about due and I wanted to get in some practice.

I walked up the hill behind the academy to the firing ranges and pulled out protective gear from the shed. A training instructor was just finishing with a group of recruits. "Can you spare some time?" I asked. "I want to run through the combat range." I walked toward him. "Brenden Harlow, Metro."

"Hi, Brenden. I'm Len Wilkinson. You want the bonus-shoot course?"

He was a tall, muscle-sculpted sergeant with a thick black mustache and a look of patience on his face. "That would be great," I said.

The bonus course probably meant something once, say before inflation was invented. Depending on how you qualified—marksman, sharpshooter, expert, or distinguished expert—you'd get a few more bucks in your paycheck. I was a sharpshooter, and to keep that designation, I had to score 340 out of a possible 400 points.

The course consisted of six phases—forty shots total—and required you to shoot from varying distances in so many seconds. The hardest was the first—firing four rounds in three seconds from seven yards at two paper targets that bladed away.

I got three head shots out of the four. Next I had 3.5 seconds to fire six shots. Four head shots, two chest. I was on a roll. The next phases were at ten yards, seventeen, and finally twenty-five.

"You always this good?" Sergeant Wilkinson asked when I had finished. "Three hundred fifty points, girl. I think I smell an expert looming."

"I'm always better in practice," I admitted, removing my ear protectors. "But thanks."

It was now two o'clock and I was starved. I walked over to the academy cafeteria, where the food is edible and the prices are cheap. At this hour, I pretty much had the place to myself. I was working on a chef's salad and thumbing through a stray copy of *Los Angeles* magazine when a tall, thin man with a dark beard slipped into my booth.

He was wearing a long-sleeved blue shirt, a tie, and khaki slacks. He said, "Brenden? I'm Steve Offerman with the *L.A. Times.* Sorry to drop in on you like this." He smiled mischievously. "I've been chasing you all day."

I took a swallow of Coke. "Then you've been wasting your time. I'm not at liberty to talk."

"I just need to plug a couple of holes in my story. Detective Walters said to talk to you."

I highly doubted that. But then I figured, What the hell? "Get yourself something to drink if you want to."

"Thanks."

He held up his hand and the waitress came over and said she'd be right back with his coffee. He pulled a notebook from his hip pocket and bit off the cap to his pen. "It's about Justin James Allen, okay?"

I put down my fork. "Then you probably know all there is to know already. You probably know more than me."

He grinned. "Probably. But I don't know how you found this character. Can you fill me in on that?"

I went back to my salad and thought it over. The department had clamped down on its flow of information to the media, decreeing that all interviews had to be cleared, and anything else had to come from Cmdr. Stan Willsey and his flack commandoes. But explaining how we had found the suspect didn't seem like a state secret. "I can tell you how we found him, yes," I said at last.

My account was short and sanitized. Offerman's coffee arrived, and as he poured milk into it, I told him how Todd and I had stopped to get some cash, how Todd had discovered the body, and how I'd discovered the suspect. I said nothing about money, gloves, a purse, or a bloody shirt.

"Were you scared?" Steve Offerman asked.

I grinned. "Come on. What citizen would want to read that a cop was scared? Of course I wasn't scared. When you're in it, you're never scared. It's only before or after."

"What does your husband think of this?"

"My husband? What husband?"

"You're married to Jack Hayes, right?"

So that was why I was getting all this attention. And Jack—Jack wouldn't even know what was going on. "He's in Hawaii," I said, "on location. I haven't had a chance to talk to him yet."

"What made you join the LAPD anyway?"

"A long-ago boyfriend. And maybe a broken heart."

"Really? That doesn't sound like a liberated woman talking."

I smiled sweetly. "Liberated from what? Me, I like to think of myself as a perpetual prisoner of love. A lifer, so to speak."

"Tell me more," Steve Offerman said.

I hadn't thought about it in a long time. I bit into a roll and remembered Bill Modine. "When I was in school," I said, "I'd hang out at the beach. I'd bring a book, a radio, some food, and spend my afternoons reading. This guy just started talking to me one day." I saw that he was taking notes. "Just kidding," I said.

"Aw come on. This is good stuff. A human police officer."

"Nope. I won't talk for publication."

Steve Offerman put down his pen. "All right. But don't leave me dangling, okay?"

It was between my sophomore and junior years at Cal State Northridge. Bill was a homicide detective working out of Pacific Division. We started dating, and he would regale me with his colorful cop stories. At the time, he was working on the mysterious death of the fourth husband of a Pacific Palisades socialite with a penchant for inventing new varieties of roses. The socialite's first three husbands had also died.

"Arsenic," I said. "Bill found traces of it in her potting soil. She put it in the muffins she baked. It would usually take eighteen months for enough arsenic to accumulate in the husbands' systems to kill them."

Bill took me to the bars where cops hung out, and I really enjoyed the life. Eventually he quit the department to go to law school— and unfortunately quit me as well. I changed my major to social work. After I received my degree I realized I would need a master's.

My father, Sean Harlow, owned a bakery on Fairfax, the only Irish-owned bakery in the then solidly Jewish neighborhood. My mom had helped out, and the bakery had served as my nursery, day-care center, after-school hangout, and much later, place of haphazard employment. Now they were gone and the bakery was an Ethiopian restaurant.

"My dad said I'd have to earn my own tuition," I went on. "I began working for a government-funded program that ran a child-care center in Echo Park. One day, without quite being aware of what I was doing, I found myself driving up to the academy. LAPD was operating under a court mandate to hire more women. I was athletic, had never used drugs, and—presto—I was a cop."

Steve Offerman played with his pen. "Now you're one of the few women in Metro division. Think you showed the guys a thing or two last night?"

Oh Christ. What was this guy doing? The last thing I needed was for him to foment sex-related trouble for me. "Don't get carried away," I said quickly. "We do this kind of stuff all the time. And it was my partner who found the body."

The reporter, chin in hand, nodded encouragingly.

I glanced uneasily at my watch. "I'm gonna have to run now, Steve. You take care, huh?" I slid out of the booth.

"Hey, Brenden."

I stopped and saw him raise his hand. Suddenly, a photographer leaped out of thin air and began *click-click*ing.

"See you, fellas," I said, and hip-hopped away.

J u s t i n James Allen was scheduled to be arraigned in Superior Court at ten o'clock Wednesday morning. That gave detectives forty-two more hours to come up with enough evidence to convince a judge we had sufficient reason to charge him with first degree murder in the death of Michelle Lloyd. Or any of the five previous victims, if we could find some proof of it.

"So hit the goddam Valley like the beaches of Normandy," Sgt. Ray Higgins exhorted us, "and come back with a nice big goodie bag. This is our D-Day, people. Dismissed!"

We collected our glossy eight-by-tens of Justin, and the whole ATM clan—make that a battalion—rolled out.

Although the "beaches of Normandy" had been combed before, police work dictated repeating the same tasks until the story turned out the way we wanted it to. Todd and I had been given a list of people to visit—among them the fiancé of Amelia Lynn Grant and residents of the building where Sheila Dann had lived—and we had to make stops at two banks where murders had occurred. The branch managers had been notified to call in all personnel who had worked in the banks in the weeks prior to the killings.

As Todd crept along Van Nuys Boulevard, he adjusted his sun visor and said, "So what do you think? Did Allen do it?"

"Why not? He was in the alley and he doesn't exactly strike me as the kind of good heart who would rush to a woman's aid. I don't know why Higgins is even making us do this."

"I keep thinking maybe there really was a guy in black. Like he said."

"Sure. Like maybe someday you'll get stopped for speeding." I opened my bag and fished out a pack of gum. "Do me a favor, okay?

Don't play devil's advocate with me." I handed Todd a stick of spearmint Care Free.

"You *are* worried we've got the wrong guy."

I leaned against the headrest and closed my eyes. The five hours of sleep I'd managed, sandwiched between a lot of stress, was catching up with me. "He was in the alley, Todd."

"So was I," Todd emphasized. "If I'd stopped to use the Readyteller, then decided to take a leak, someone could have found me lurking in the alley, too."

I said nothing.

"Tell you what else bothers me," he said. "This Justin doesn't seem clever enough for it. He manages never to get caught on the bank's video, and their ranges and angles are all different. And no eyewitnesses?"

"Whenever I go to an ATM," I said, "I'm almost always alone. Whatever the time of the day." But in fact, Todd's point about the cameras had been worrying me, too. That, plus where was the knife? He could only have gotten rid of it in the vicinity of the murder, and someone should have found it by now. Also, while I wasn't an expert on serial killers, Justin James Allen seemed somehow lacking. Right now I could give him no better than a fifty-fifty probability.

I opened my eyes and discovered we were caught in a major traffic snarl due to road repair work. "Don't you think it's odd how they're always tearing up the streets?" I said. "What I think is, they're planting earthquake seeds. It's a plot to destroy Los Angeles."

Todd shot me a look. "Maybe you should call the president."

"He's probably behind it. Anyway, you're just annoyed that our suspect isn't a black guy with a stethoscope. Admit it."

"Wrong. I'm disappointed he isn't a *she*. I bet Lynie dinner at the Pacific Dining Car."

I switched on the radio to a golden oldies station. I needed an outside stimulus. What I got was Ken and Kevin taking calls on the best way to dump a girlfriend.

I turned to Todd. "One of these days we're going to have to do something about your gambling problem," I said.

D e p u t y District Attorney Fred Lumley lived in a dark-stained ranch house on a pleasant street in Sherman Oaks, south of Ventura Boulevard. A Border collie sniffed us suspiciously as Fred led us into the living room. He was wearing a white shirt, a loosened tie, and khaki slacks, his light brown hair slicked back behind his ears. The living room, like the Crofts', seemed sad.

"Please sit down, guys," Fred said. "You ready for some coffee?"

I declined on the theory that I had a long night of sleep ahead of me, but Todd said yes. Fred returned with coffee, a beer for himself, and a bag of potato chips. "It's called dinner. Brenden, can I get you anything?"

I smiled. "If I'd known you were serving, I would have waited."

Todd placed our photo on the coffee table. Fred glanced at it and shook his head wearily. "What's the thinking?" he asked. "All random?"

"Random fits a serial killer profile," I said. "And the way these attacks occurred, I don't see how they could have been planned. Why?"

"I keep wondering if the guy was someone I prosecuted. He could have stalked Amelia. Waited for an opportunity."

"If she suspected she was being stalked, wouldn't she have said something?" Todd asked.

"It would have been more like Amelia to deal with it herself. She came from a broken home. She was always on her own."

"I knew her a little from the academy," I put in. "Even though she was there only a few months, she made an impression on everybody."

"Shit." Tears welled in his eyes. "Life's a bitch, isn't it? Amelia starts out to become a cop because her brother was murdered. Then she ends up a statistic. If you believe in fate, you have to believe her whole life was preordained." He blew his nose.

"Did she ever say why she left the academy?" I asked.

"She said she was disappointed in the people she met there. Not so much her classmates, but the instructors and the command staff. She thought maybe she'd become a social worker. But she liked physical activity, and the job at Kennedy High was perfect for her."

"Disappointed how?" I asked. "Sexual discrimination, harassment, what?"

Fred shrugged. "She never really said. But Amelia was idealistic. For some reason, the LAPD didn't live up to her expectations. She wanted better than that."

"One other thing," I said. "When was she married?"

Fred showed genuine surprise. "Amelia was never married. Why?"

"Because I knew her as Rodriguez, not Grant."

"Oh right. Her father, Rodriguez, ran out on the family when

Amelia was a child. When she turned twenty-one, she decided to take her mother's maiden name."

There seemed nothing more to say. I stood and Fred walked us to the door. "Thanks, guys. Um, listen, something's been on my mind."

We turned expectantly.

"I made Amelia give up her gun. I simply don't believe we should all be running around carrying. But it haunts me at night. If she'd had her gun . . . "

"Forget it," Todd said. "All the victims seemed totally unaware they were in danger until the moment of attack. Amelia would have needed the gun in her hand, cocked."

"She did have pepper spray," I pointed out. "And she obviously made a habit of being alert. So you can stop beating yourself up."

I paused. "It's almost as if this killer is invisible."

The phone was ringing when I got home, and I managed to grab it before the machine picked up.

"Trying to get a cop to respond to a citizen's call is damn near impossible," Jack said sunnily.

"How many cops have you called?" I kicked off my shoes and sat on the floor. The cord didn't stretch to the kitchen table.

"Just beautiful green-eyed ones. How are you?"

"Beat. We've got a suspect in custody. There was another murder last night. We found this guy about thirty feet from the body."

"We?"

"He wasn't armed. I was. I'm fine, just tired."

There was a silence. His voice had been so clear, he could have been in the next room. But now, during his interlude, I could hear a soft static. "Remember," said Jack, "how we used to say what worked so great for us was that I was the dreamer and you were the realist, and together we got it just right?"

"Mm-hmm. So what are you dreaming these days?"

"That we need to reinvent our lives."

"And?"

"Haven't gotten that far yet."

"But somehow it involves one of us giving up his or her gun and badge?"

Jack laughed. "Maybe. But not the handcuffs. And at the moment, I think it ought to be me. This is turning into a bitch."

"I want to hear," I said. "But can you hold a minute?"

I scrambled to my feet and trotted into the living room, grabbed the vodka and Kahlua, and brought them back to the kitchen counter. I picked up the receiver. "Go ahead."

The cord did stretch to the freezer and the glasses cabinet, and I mixed a double as Jack listed his litany of woes: an action-filled script directed by a man who could supervise explosions but not people, and dialogue that was dumb. The director, whose name was Harry something, didn't mind Jack's script changes, which, I had come to believe, were generally good. "But he doesn't understand what difference it makes," Jack complained. "He doesn't know a clever line from a trite one. He just wants to get on with the next piece of business."

"Ask him if he knows Sergeant Higgins," I suggested. "They might be related."

"Anyway, we're already four days behind on this shoot, and I'm not sure when I'll be back. It's supposed to rain again tomorrow. But I'll keep in touch, okay?"

No, I thought, it was not okay.

"Talking to you," Jack continued, "always makes me feel better."

But not seeing me? I could feel my disappointment rising. I decided to send him off with a shot of his own medicine. "I may take a few days off, Jack. I'm really tired. If I go somewhere, I'll let you know."

There was a pause. "What do you mean go somewhere? Where?"

"I don't know yet. But I need to get away. I may drive up the coast or something. I'll let you know, okay?"

He sighed. "We really need to change our lives."

"I'm going to bed now," I said. "Love you, and sweet dreams."

But my anger followed me into the bedroom. It was long into the night before I fell asleep.

I awoke to bright sunlight pouring into the bedroom. I stretched and breathed deeply and bounded out of bed, happy for the light. I started the coffee machine, drank a glass of juice, and on the way to the shower, I stopped to open the front door.

The lead story in the *Times* was the arrest of the man believed to be involved in the ATM stabbings. I flipped the paper over and there— in the lower right-hand corner of the front page—was the headline AN OFFICER AND A LADY COLLARS STABBING SUSPECT.

Oh shit, I thought. It never even occurred to me that I was being interviewed for my own story. Like an idiot, I had bought Steve Offerman's line that he just needed to complete a piece on the arrest. Worse, right beside the story, a picture of me leaped out. I was turning away from the camera, looking like I was on the move (undoubtedly off to make another collar) wearing a small, self-satisfied grin. Shit. Shit.

I went back to the kitchen, poured a cup of coffee, and sank into a chair.

The guy had done his homework. Aside from printing the details of the arrest—and my goofy recitation of how I had become a police officer—he had noted that I was an only child, had starred on my high school soccer and basketball teams, and was a decent student with, according to my homeroom teacher, "an attitude"—always up to mischief.

A couple of officers I'd been partnered with early on said complimentary things about me. Todd was quoted as saying, "She covers my back like a three-eyed octopus. She's a pro." And Monster had even weighed in with, "I can't think of another woman in the department who would have taken the risks she did." Which was sure to inflame only about twelve hundred other women.

Gloomily, I headed for the shower, anticipating the field day Metro would surely have with me.

"**O t h e r** than my glowing testimonial in the paper, I don't think you came off so hot, frankly. But then, that's what I'm *paid* to do. Save your sweet ass."

I had been on the Exercycle in the academy gym when Todd waltzed in. He stood in front of me, his fingers wrapped around the handlebars, grinning. I ignored him.

"Okay. Why don't we go for a walk?" he said.

I followed him out behind the building, up some stairs, and into the rock garden, where retirement parties are often held. We each sat on a rock beside a gurgling fountain.

I blotted my face with a towel. "Like an octopus? A three-eyed *octopus?*"

Todd looked repentant. "Yeah, Lynie said I probably *thought* it sounded poetic, but she thought it sounded pathetic. It was supposed to be a compliment. Don't I get credit for that?"

"Sure. Now I'm gonna have to wrack my brain figuring out what to tell those vultures about *you.*"

"Handsome, articulate, brave, sensitive . . . "

"Phew. And I thought I was going to be caught tongue-tied." I snapped my towel playfully at his chest. "So what's up?"

"The lineup was a bust."

I blinked. "I thought the lineup was at three."

"They changed it to noon. The kid swore Allen was not the driver who picked him up. And Marisa Ruiz couldn't be sure."

"Which doesn't prove—"

"Which doesn't prove Allen's not the killer. It only means he didn't pick up the kid or pose as the security guard. There's other news, too."

"Okay."

"Michelle Lloyd once worked at the USC County Medical Center. She's an RN. She worked there two years, going back eight, nine years ago. Then she got a job in the emergency room at St. Joseph Medical Center in Burbank, where her husband is a thoracic surgeon."

"Oh, I get it. He's black, wears a stethoscope, and murdered his own wife."

"Brenden, will you shut up?"

"Sorry."

"So they're taking Allen's photo to all the clinics and hospitals."

"But what would be Allen's connection? We've found nothing that indicates he ever held those kinds of jobs. Unless he hung around, scouting victims."

"Anyway, I've got to go work out." Todd stood. "Coming?"

"As soon as I untangle my tentacles," I said.

T h a n k s to Todd's poetic turn of phrase, I was now known in Metro as Ms. Octopus, although I suspected, behind my back, it was more like Ms. Octopussy. Higgins wondered aloud at roll call how many tentacles it took to get a man off in bed and invited me to the front of the room to lecture on the subject.

When the guffaws subsided, I respectfully declined. "Let's just say it saves wear and tear on the gums," I said.

And that was that. For the time being.

Once again we would spend our watch as clue dogs. Todd and I were dispatched to St. Joseph's to show the evening shift Allen's photo and to ask if anybody had seen anyone or anything unusual. A cherubic looking woman in a wheelchair, recuperating from a knee operation, motioned frantically to me and swore she had.

"Last Friday night, I went out to the garden for some air," she reported. "And I saw him. He was smirking. An evil smirk."

"Who was, Mrs. Rodebaugh?"

"Him. The ATM Stabber."

I glanced at Todd. "Where exactly did you see him?"

She pointed to the ceiling.

"Upstairs?"

"No, silly." She wheeled closer to us and raised a finger to her lips. "On the moon. I saw his face on the moon."

" **B e l i e v e** me, you don't want to hear my problems," Cookie Randall said as she stared morosely at her Corona. "Besides, you'd never understand."

Tuesday night the First Base Saloon could have been a church: just a handful of dead-eyed strangers slumped at the bar waiting for salvation. We were alone in the poolroom, and dispirited as Cookie was, I was grateful for her company. "What makes you think I wouldn't understand?"

She looked at me with rheumy eyes. Cookie had obviously been here for a while. She said, "Tell me something, Brenden. You ever had a problem?"

I screwed up my face, pretending to think. "Not really. Which, of course, is a problem. Skipping merrily through life with a ray of sunshine always bouncing off my head."

"Sorry." Cookie began to pick at her fingernails. "I mean love problems. This girl I was living with—" She glanced at me. "You sure you want to hear this?"

"You mean Sweet Pea? Sure. And I will understand."

Cookie leaned back in the booth and sighed. "I picked her up at the academy about four months ago during a softball game. She was watching. You couldn't miss her. Long blond hair, big blue eyes. And you know, she was *there.*"

By "there," I knew, Cookie was referring to the Softball League, a women's league that played up at the academy on Saturdays. Players were assumed to be gay. Most of the people watching were also assumed to be gay.

"She's twenty-two," Cookie said. "A rookie working out of Devonshire."

"Go on." I was trying not to feel uncomfortable. If a man were telling me this story, I knew I wouldn't mind. But although I could accept Cookie's painful predicament, I couldn't help feeling squirmy.

"I pursued her for about a month, sending her flowers and little notes, things like that," Cookie said. "Finally, one night, I made love to her. She told me she was Catholic and felt a lot of guilt. I told her we all do."

Cookie lifted the bottle to her lips and drained most of it. "She moved in with me, and then last week she moved out. I'm not kidding, Brenden. I seriously thought of blowing my brains out."

I squeezed her arm. "Why did she move out? Are you sure it's so hopeless?"

Cookie nodded. "She said she wasn't gay. She'd been going with a guy, they had a fight, broke up. I suppose I was her revenge. Anyway, he came back and she was gone in a flash. Left me a little thank-you note saying never to call her again."

A tear broke off and streamed down Cookie's face. I was at a momentary loss. I sipped my drink, and after a while I said, "It's probably none of my business, and you can tell me so. But have you ever made love to a man?"

"Yeah. My uncle. Who raised me. For five years. Until I escaped to the LAPD."

I worked on my drink and watched two guys come in and take up pool cues. One looked over at me and winked. "Two on two?"

"We're not players," I said, "sorry."

Cookie finished her beer. "I'm glad you told me," I said quietly. "And if it's any consolation, I think you're terrific. You're a great cop and a really good person. Good things happen to good people, Cookie. I know it sounds corny, but that's my safety net. Not my badge or my gun. Just that belief."

She looked at me with brimming eyes. Through the tears I could see the gratitude in them.

"And on that note," I said jumping up, "I'm going to get us another round."

Later, only when I felt fairly certain that Cookie would not go home and swallow her gun, I suggested we leave.

I paid for our drinks, gave Cookie a hug good-bye, and was stuffing my wallet into my shoulder bag when a man I had not previously noticed called my name. He was sitting at the far end of the bar and he stood as I turned toward him.

"Bob McNally," he said, coming over and extending his hand. "Long time no see."

McNally was a retired sergeant who worked security on the set of *Night Watch*. He also served as technical adviser. Whenever I visited Jack at work, I would have a few words with Bob.

"Hi," I said with surprise. "Gee, on your salary, surely you can afford better than this?"

He was a husky six-footer, gray haired and with a fleshy face. He was wearing a lightweight jacket over a shirt and cotton pants. Despite his new line of work, he still looked like he could take up a baton at any moment.

"Sure I can. But on your salary, *you* can't." He laughed. "Or does that weasel of a husband share some of his loot with you?"

"I steal it when he's asleep. What's going on?"

"Come on, Brenden. I'll walk you to your car."

I was parked about a block from the bar and as we started east on Sunset, he took my arm and said, "This is awkward. I suppose I could lose my job over it, but I decided to risk it anyway."

"You're in trouble?"

McNally shook his head. "I know Jack's in Hawaii. I thought it would be best to talk to you when he was away. Maybe give you some time to think about it."

I grinned. "A marriage proposal?"

"Unfortunately, it's not. It's serious, shitty business."

He said nothing more until we reached my car, and then Bob stood on the sidewalk, feet apart, facing me. "He's doing coke, Brenden. Did you know that?"

"Jack is?"

"Yes. Jack is doing coke. I won't put you on the spot by asking what you know or how much you know, but it's my opinion your husband needs help."

I looked into Bob McNally's eyes as I would a suspect's, trying to determine if he was feeding me a line. Only this time, everything seemed to freeze—my brain, my breathing, this moment in time. "I don't understand."

Bob placed his hands on my shoulders. "You and I don't know each other very well, but I'm very fond of Jack. He's a good man. He works hard and he treats people nicely. But he started doing coke the beginning of this past season. At least that's when I became aware of his habit. Yes, Brenden, he has a habit."

"You've seen him?"

"Everybody's seen him. So far, I can't say it's affected his work. I don't know why the hell he's doing this to himself."

"Like once or twice or what?" I swallowed, but I couldn't seem to get this information to go down.

"A day. That's how often I see him doing it."

"Oh man."

I walked away from Bob and sat on the hood of my car. "Where does he get it, do you know?"

"Sure, I know. There's a guy who supplies several people on the show."

I nodded, unable to speak, too busy trying to juggle my shock, anger, and fear.

"I tried talking to him about a month ago, when he learned he might have a shot for a role in *Paradise Found*. He was worried about the drug test."

"What drug test?"

"Every year when his insurance policy gets renewed . . . you know he takes a physical, don't you?"

"Sure."

"Well apparently he cleans up for that. But studios require actors and directors to have physicals before they'll hire them for a movie. Jack asked me how long it would take to get the crap out of his system. That's when I did a one-on-one, telling him to straighten up. I said it wasn't just his career that was at stake, but his wife's."

I closed my eyes and felt a cool, moist breeze blow across my neck. Department policy had loosened over the years on the matter of marijuana. At one time, no person would be accepted into the academy if he or she had smoked so much as a joint. But increasingly that policy had become impractical; too many candidates who had done dope in school were being eliminated. So they made exceptions for former casual users. But once you were in, being caught in possession of any kind of drug was grounds for immediate dismissal.

I looked again at Bob. "Thanks."

He began to walk away. "Oh, and Brenden? When you sort this all out, feel free to call me. Here, let me give you my number."

He pulled out his billfold and extracted a small white business card. "I'm not going anywhere else with this information." He handed me the card. "You didn't know, huh?"

I glanced briefly at the card then hopped off the car. "Maybe I did, Bob. I just don't know."

I n the anger and confusion that consumed me on the drive home, fragments of telltale signs whistled through my memory. The sniffling and nose blowing, the mood swings, his mysterious disappearances at parties for long periods of time, a certain evasiveness he had never shown before. And finally Suzy Rocklin's odd words on the phone: "They're not having an affair" and "Stop worrying like a wife and start acting like a cop."

My first thought as I stormed into the apartment and headed for the freezer was that I would jump on the next plane to Maui and confront Jack right away, even if that meant making a horrible scene.

My fingers trembled as I tore open the mysterious foil packet I had discovered the other day. The Baggie, carefully taped, contained what looked like ten grams. Son of a bitch. I ripped open the plastic and I tossed the contents down the disposal and let the scalding water wash hundreds of dollars into the Santa Monica sewer system.

Later, as the night turned to dawn and exhaustion wore me down, I decided to sit tight. I saw no sense jeopardizing Jack's career. I needed his cooperation, not his resentment. And he would need my love.

The courthouse in which Justin James Allen was due to be arraigned was next door to Van Nuys Station. Without a whole lot of sleep, I had managed, nevertheless, to arrive by 9:45, fifteen minutes early. What I hadn't thought about was the throng of reporters lined up in the hallway waiting to be let in. Judging from their numbers, not all would. Steve Offerman from the *Times* was third in line, and he touched my arm as I passed by.

"Big day, huh?" he asked, giving me a wink.

"Excuse me." I showed my badge to the marshal guarding the double doors. He pushed one open and I entered the courtroom.

A dozen or so people were already flitting about—lawyers and prosecutors attached to other cases. Behind the prosecution table on the right side of the room, a black woman in a beige suit was conferring with Det. Marty Walters, T. J. McCall, and Art Bannister. I guessed she was our district attorney on the case.

I slipped into a seat three rows behind the table and wondered if anyone else from our task force would show up. An arraignment is merely a rubber-stamp affair. Late yesterday afternoon, the detectives brought their case to the D.A., describing the crime and citing evidence that fingered Justin James Allen as the killer of Michelle Lloyd. Apparently they had come up with something new to implicate him, but as of yet, I hadn't heard what. If the D.A. agrees there is a case—make that a winnable case—he or she files a complaint. In today's proceeding, the judge would decide if the complaint was valid, then ask the defendant for a plea. There would be no drama and no need for us to show up. But this was my first big case and I felt proprietary towards it. I crossed my legs under my skirt and let my shoulder bag slide to the floor. After a few minutes, T.J. slipped into the seat beside me.

"We got him, Harlow, and we got Judge Freedman. You tell Judge Freedman a guy looks squinty eyed, he'll bind him over." He thumped my knee. "Your decoy days are history."

I hadn't seen T.J. since the night I had passed out on his couch, and I wondered if he would mention it. I decided somebody should. "You were a good listener the other night, T.J." I gave him an uncertain smile. "I think."

"So buy me dinner tonight. I'm off. Can you cut loose for a couple of hours?"

"Maybe."

"I could use one of Harry Henderson's steaks. I'll be there at six-thirty. Beep me if you're not coming."

With that, T.J. stood up and went to sit in the front row. A moment later, Higgins and Lieutenant Turley walked in and took seats in the row in front of me. Higgins turned his head sideways. "Roll call's not until *fifteen-thirty,* Harlow. Nice to see you're early."

The jerk.

I smiled a pretty smile that he did not see and said I would certainly be there.

M y Metro platoon, momentarily at loose ends, was assigned to a night of shake, rattle, and roll in Hollywood, which meant book everything that moves except traffic. At times, when the sight of hypes, prostitutes, transvestites, gangbangers, drunks, and self-styled freaks got to me, I wondered why the city didn't just bulldoze the place. Despite Hollywood's seediness, movie-struck tourists from around the world continued to bus in to gape at Hollywood and Vine and Mann's Chinese Theater. Sometimes I would catch the look of confusion or disappointment on some of their faces, and it made me feel sad. The Hollywood of the movie studios wasn't here, it was located elsewhere—in Burbank, Culver City, Universal City, and Century City. Even Paramount, which was only a few miles from the geographical Hollywood, was technically located in Los Angeles. And although some moviemaking did occur on studio soundstages and backlots, much more was done in far-flung locales. Like Hawaii, where tourists could actually eyeball an action thriller in the making, and one of its stars doing coke.

I asked Todd to drop me at Harry Henderson's Steak House on Melrose and to come back in an hour and a half to fetch me. It was seven-thirty when I called in a Code 7 and jumped out of the Caprice.

T.J. was sitting alone at the tiny bar in the front of the restaurant. I slid onto the stool beside him. "Hi there."

"You always so punctual?" he greeted me.

He looked nice. He was wearing a navy sport coat over a white open-necked shirt and jeans, and some kind of pleasant but not over-bearing scent. "Always," I said. "I hate making people wait."

T.J. stood up. "Let's get a table. I'm starved."

He left his half-filled glass on the bar and walked over to the maître d'. Harry Henderson's has been around since the forties, and its dark wood paneling, red leather booths, bare wooden floor, and faded photographs evoke that long-ago era. The maître d', a man who looked like an authentic World War II relic, doddered ahead of us to the first booth.

"Okay," I said as I sat down, "I'm sorry. I would have been on time, okay, except that two blocks from here we came across a trans-vestite who complained of stomach cramps and demanded to be taken to a gynecologist. This intrigued my partner, who fancies himself an armchair sociologist, and he wanted to know more. The transvestite, who was wearing a dress I would kill for, went into a long account of morning sickness and then keeled over in a dead faint. We revived her and she mentioned she was bleeding, I quote, 'down there.' Todd tried to check but she slapped his face and said only I could look—'girl to girl.'" I sighed. "Could I have a drink, please?"

T.J. just sat there frozen faced.

"Pretty please?"

"Shit, Harlow, you're a *cop*. Cops don't have to explain. Why did you explain? All I wanted was to celebrate. Jesus H. Christ."

I grinned. "A bottle of wine then?"

"You're going back to work?"

"Such as it is." I caught T.J.'s dubious look. "I'll only have a glass or two. Am I buying?"

"Yes, ma'am."

"Then get someone over here and order me a sirloin, medium rare. I need to go wash my hands."

The steak was perfect, the wine—a California cabernet—went down real smooth, and I listened as T.J. filled me in on some late de-velopments.

"Michelle Lloyd worked in the ER of St. Joseph Medical Center, as you know," he told me. "In February, Justin James Allen was driven to the same ER after a branch fell off a tree and hit him on the head."

I looked up from my napkin, which I'd been tearing into little pieces. *"Excuse me?"*

"Pipe down, Harlow. Allen was working for a tree-trimming service, and one of the trimmers trimmed as Allen was passing under this tree."

"I thought he worked for the subway."

"He does. He also works for his brother-in-law's gardening service."

I poured a second glass of wine.

"He had a deep cut over his left eye and needed some stitches. We got hold of his chart, and Michelle Lloyd was the attending nurse."

At least it backed up the scar I had seen. "Anything else?"

"We found someone at the hospital who overheard Michelle offering to drop Allen off somewhere."

I relaxed. "You do good work, you know that?"

"Mm-hmm. And the night is still young."

"Uh-oh. What's that supposed to mean?"

"It means why the hell are you married?"

I studied him for a moment and for the first time I noticed a fleck or two of gold in his deep brown eyes. It was as if the eyes had seen too much but the little glimmers of light still held out hope. "You have designs on me?"

"Of course I have designs on you." He grinned broadly. "Any on me?"

"No." I laughed. *"No.* Finish your steak. Think about dessert." I looked at my watch. "I wonder what happened to Todd?"

It was nine-twenty. I had given him the number of the restaurant, so he would have called if something had come up. Maybe nothing had come up and he was generously allowing me extra time.

T.J. said, "You like being married, Brenden?"

I raised an eyebrow. "Brenden? So now we're on a first-name basis? Gosh, you must be *serious.*"

"Fuck you." T.J. looked up. "Anyway, here's your ride."

"Evening, folks," said Todd curtly. He frowned. "Brenden, move over."

"I was beginning to think maybe you liked life without me," I said. "Want a glass of wine?"

Todd shook his head as he slid in next to me. "We've got a problem."

I said, "Higgins thinks I went AWOL?"

"No. I mean we *all* got a problem."

I felt my hand tighten around the stem of the wine glass. "Oh no," I whispered.

"Oh, yes. They just found number seven," Todd said.

N u m b e r seven seemed to me far worse than the others. Suki Kahn was twenty-four years old, and even in death you could see her delicate beauty. Straight black hair; Asian, almond-shaped eyes; an oval face; thick eyelashes; and a heart-shaped mouth; her ruby red lipstick not even smudged. Her slender legs were caked with blood. Her purple dress was twisted around her waist above the small pouching of what had been her stomach.

The stomach had been ripped open and looked, forgive the description, like a watermelon at the end of a picnic. The only other wound apparent as Suki Kahn lay in a pool of darkening blood was a gaping cut straight through the heart.

It seemed far worse than the others, partly because finding this victim when our supposed killer was locked up tight was like having scaled a mountain, using every last drop of energy for the final ascent—only to discover yet another peak looming up ahead.

But more than that, Suki Kahn had been six months pregnant. Baby Kahn was number eight.

As if to taunt us, the psycho had widened the kill zone. Downey Savings was located in Encino. It occupied a corner lot on Ventura, next door to a Coco's. The single ATM was on the east side of the bank, facing the rear wall of the restaurant. A tree obscured the ATM from the street. Suki had parked her Toyota Camry within fifteen feet of the teller. Once again the murderer had struck as she returned to her car, out of range of the security camera.

The murders brought out hundreds of grim-faced officers and even the chief. For once nobody was engaging in corpse humor, and a strange hush fell over the scene. Higgins, coordinating with the watch commander from West Valley Division, in whose territory this killing had occurred, dispatched teams of us to scour the area for witnesses. Numbly, I climbed into the car with Todd.

We stayed out until 2 A.M., fueled more by anger than the prospect of turning up any eyeballs. By the time I got home I was so drained and dispirited that I downed a shot of vodka straight. Without bothering to turn on a lamp, I sat on the couch in the living room and stared into the vast darkness of the ocean.

Even though I had spent twenty minutes in the shower, I could still smell the blood . . . and the image of the young woman still stared me in the face. This was the time when a police officer needed a friend. Not to talk to, but merely to sit beside in the despairing urgency to hear the sound of someone breathing. This was police work at its worst, posing far more danger than an armed criminal: the blackness, the emptiness, the haunting, silent aloneness.

The kind that made you reach out to a bottle.

T h e vultures had alighted on the Suki Kahn murder in time to make the morning papers.

From what I knew about newspapers, they must have scrambled to rip up the front page, yank the big headline off the arraignment story, and hastily substitute an even bigger headline for the late-breaking showstopper. PREGNANT WOMAN IS STABBER'S SEVENTH VICTIM: JAILED SUSPECT PULLS A HOUDINI is what the *Times* not very nicely splashed across the top of its front page.

The story was written by someone named Marcy Goldstein, and I followed the jump to an inside page. There I found a second story, by Steve Offerman, titled "How the LAPD Captured the Wrong Man." Even before I got through the first paragraph, my stomach began to churn.

According to Lt. Thomas Inman of Robbery/Homicide, who was in charge of the ATM Task Force, there had been serious questions about the guilt of Justin James Allen. "We could place him at the scene of the crime," Inman said, "and that blurred some of our people's judgment."

I blinked. Well, what about yours, Lieutenant Hotshot?

"For instance," Inman was quoted as saying, "the money we found on him, $143, had his prints on some of the bills, but none of the victim's, which should have raised a flag. True, there was a small blood smear on one of the bills, but that could have been transferred from the victim's purse, which Allen admitted rifling. We finally traced this money to a Coast Federal Bank down the street. Allen had withdrawn $120 from his own account prior to the murder."

Stunned, my eyes kept darting along.

"Secondly, Officer [Brenden] Harlow encountered Allen in the alley near the body less than twenty minutes after Citibank's computer indicates Michelle Lloyd withdrew $200. It seems unlikely this man would have left the scene to spend $57, then come back. So we had a problem. Even if he went off to dispose of the murder weapon, why would he risk coming back?"

Well, I had wondered that, too.

The story then made a sharp turn and took direct aim at me. An unnamed source "close to the investigation" revealed that "Officer Harlow was alone with the suspect for at least ten minutes in the alley. During that time, she told us, he started to confess. She stopped him. He hadn't been read his rights yet. After he was read his rights—and that was well into the interrogation—Allen denied having anything to do with the stabbing of Michelle Lloyd. It was only several hours after the arraignment that detectives learned the money found on Allen had come from his own bank."

Confession? *What confession?* Allen hadn't confessed to being on the planet Earth. Why would this unnamed source have said *that?*

The next sentence, from a *second* unnamed source, added, "Brenden's always been a hot dog. I don't know whether it's because she wants to prove she's as capable as the men or if it's her nature, but too often she doesn't understand that LAPD regulations apply to her, too."

Well there certainly was no mystery about that quote. Higgins's name was all over it. But the statement about the confession didn't sound like something even Higgins, in his dislike of me, would plant.

Plant.

Yes, that's what it was, a plant. I got it now, of course. Someone high up the command had decided to save the department from having egg on its face by putting the egg on me.

I had brought my first cup of coffee and the paper back to bed, and now I lay there stupefied, unsure what to do. My thoughts drifted to T. J. McCall. Wouldn't he have known the money didn't have Michelle Lloyd's prints on it? Or heard about the "confession" and mentioned it to me? But even as suspicion and paranoia filled my brain, I could not believe T.J. had been party to a setup of me.

The phone rang. I put down the paper and haltingly reached for the receiver on the bedside table.

"Brenden? This is Kathy. Captain would like to see you at noon. Can you make it?"

With a sinking feeling, I told Monster's secretary I could.

• • •

M o n s t e r McGrew greeted me with a warm handshake and his glasses on, for which I was grateful. I sat in the chair opposite his desk. Several morning papers were stacked on it and looked as if they had been read.

"Sir," I began, "I'm at a loss to explain the references to me in the *Times*. The insinuation—no, the assertion—that I claimed Justin James Allen had confessed is ridiculous. My report noted quite clearly that he said very little in the alley. I am also frankly insulted that anybody would suggest I do not follow regulations precisely. It's hardly my fault that Robbery/Homicide did not learn until after the arraignment that the money came from his own bank. I would like to know what's going on here."

Monster calmly removed his glasses and began polishing them. "Brenden, you're very upset." He gave me a patronizing smile. "All I can say is, welcome to the world of the media. We've all been attacked unfairly. Sorry it happened to you." He put on his glasses and stared at me crookedly.

"Captain, with all due respect, I was attacked by someone inside LAPD. The reporter did not make up those quotes. I want to know why I'm being made the scapegoat."

Monster sighed. "You're a good cop, Brenden, everybody knows that. I think you're overreacting. Maybe someone was misquoted or the reporter misunderstood. You've been under a lot of strain. We all have."

He leaned back in his chair and fixed his right eye on me. "You weren't here then, but this is a lot like the Hillside Strangler case. For thirteen months those guys had the city in a panic and the department in turmoil. The only thing you can do is roll with the punches and keep working the case."

"You're not addressing the issue, sir. One of my superiors deliberately libeled me in the press. I really want to know who and why."

Now Monster came forward and folded his hands on the desk. "Tell you what, Brenden. I'll look into this. In the meantime, I'm going to suggest you take a break from Operation ATM. The minister of trade from Taiwan is coming in tomorrow to meet with the mayor and some of our local business people. I'm going to assign you escort duty." He smiled beneficently, as if he had just rewarded me with a three-day cruise on the Carnival Line.

I scowled. "But I don't want to be taken off the case. What I want is a retraction in tomorrow's paper. And I don't want to go waltzing around town with the minister of trade from Taiwan." I paused and straightened my shoulders. "Besides, if I don't show up my whole squad will believe I screwed up."

Monster stood. "No one's going to think you screwed up. Take today off and report tomorrow at nine A.M. We should have the minister's itinerary fixed by then. It'll be good experience. You haven't done escort duty yet, have you?"

"I was passed over for Yeltsin and Gore." I had been, too—by Higgins. Assignments were made by seniority, and both times I had been overlooked in favor of Metro guys with less time in Metro than I had. "I'm psyched over this stabber, sir. I want to stay with it."

Monster came around his desk and patted me on the shoulder. "You'll be back with the task force by Monday," he said reassuringly. "Meantime you'll get a little experience under your belt. I'm sure the minister will be very impressed with you." He paused. "As we all are. Kathy!"

He started for the door. "Call Robbery/Homicide and tell Lieutenant Inman to ring me after lunch." He turned. "See, Brenden? We'll get everything straightened out." Then he was gone.

I stared at the empty doorway and wondered if he was en route to his love nest with Lucy Robinson.

Or maybe it was a haystack.

had no idea what to do with myself. Even though I tried to convince myself to think of this as a day off—with regular day off things to do—once I got home I sat in the kitchen and sulked.

Eventually I put on a pair of shorts and a T-shirt, strapped on my Rollerblades, and skated recklessly toward Palisades Park—wondering diabolically how many citizens I could flatten in an hour.

When I returned, somewhat calmer, I found Jack's voice on the answering machine and a number on my beeper. Jack said, "Call me at the hotel after ten tonight, my time. Miss you," followed by a noise that I supposed was a kiss. The number on my beeper meant nothing to me. I filled a glass with ice water, drank it, refilled the glass, and dialed.

The phone rang six times. As I was about to hang up an indistinct gruff voice barked, "Yeah."

"You beeped me within the last hour," I began pleasantly.

"So? I beep a lot of people."

Great. A crank call. "Perhaps I misdialed."

"Not if you're with the department."

The voice sounded strange, as if it had been somehow altered. "Go on," I said. "I might get interested sooner or later."

"You fucked up, Miss America. Leave the case alone and you won't fuck up again."

The line went dead.

I dropped the receiver onto the cradle and stared out the kitchen window. Then I called the Metro desk.

"Metro. Officer Whelan speaking."

"Hi, Tim, it's Brenden. Can you look up a number in the backwards book?"

"Sure. Give it to me."

I read him the number I had just dialed and waited patiently.

"Gee, Bren, nothing here. But let me give you a number at the phone company. Ready?"

I took down the number and dialed again.

"Security, Mimi speaking."

"This is Officer Brenden Harlow, Metro Division. I need to run a number."

"I.D.?"

"Two-two-seven-oh-seven."

"Hold on." I knew she was confirming my identity on her computer screen. We weren't supposed to call the phone company without authorization, but I knew there were certain extensions we could call that produced results. Mimi came back on the line. "Number?"

"It's a two-one-three," I said and read off the next seven digits.

"That sounds like a pay phone. Want a location?"

"Please."

"One moment."

A crank call coming from a pay phone didn't surprise me. But that a guy would sit there for up to an hour did.

"Looks like a box at the entrance to the zoo. Does that help, Officer?"

"No. But thanks."

It was now close to five. I had been out between, say, 3:45 and 4:45. That would eliminate any of my colleagues from Metro or Operation ATM who would have been in roll call at Van Nuys, then moving out through North Hollywood, Van Nuys, and now, with the murder of Suki Kahn, the West Valley. Unless—Mack Maloney?

I jumped as the phone rang. Cautiously, I lifted the receiver. "Yes?"

"Brenden? Tim Whelan again. A message just came in for you."

I held my breath . . . the crank caller?

"Fred Lumley from the D.A.'s office. Need the number?"

"Please." I thanked Tim and called Amelia Lynn Grant's fiancé. A secretary answered and put me through.

"My condolences about the crap in the paper," Fred began. "That was unfair."

"Thanks. And my condolences that we screwed up. We'll get it right next time, I promise."

"I hear things," Fred said, lowering his voice.

"Such as?"

"Such as suspicions about security guards. You wouldn't believe how many cases we prosecute against security guards. The demand for private security is so great that companies have become pretty damn lax in their background checks." He laughed self-consciously. "I guess you know that."

"I do," I said, "but I think you're trying to tell me something."

"Right. There was a guy at Kennedy High School, worked during school hours. He hit on Amelia several times and was generally rude and obnoxious. They let him go, gosh, maybe February or March. You could probably get his name if you called the administration office."

"Will do. Which reminds me. Do you know if Amelia went to a hospital or a clinic, either for herself or maybe with a kid?"

"Why?"

"Some of the victims had ties to hospitals or clinics."

"If she went with a kid, I wouldn't know. Maybe the school would. As for herself, there's been nothing serious, except for migraines. A doctor would have prescribed her pills. In fact, hell, the night she was killed she was having a prescription filled, remember?"

"You'll check the bottle?"

"Tonight. Thanks, Brenden."

A t 10 P.M., with the Dodgers idle, the First Base Saloon was deader than my chances of promoting to chief. I pulled up a bar stool, ordered my usual, and shot the breeze with Johnny.

"Don't be upset, Brenden. Think of yourself as finally famous. In your own right," he said, referring to the story in the *Times*.

I lifted my glass—"Bully for me"—and glanced at my watch.

"When's Big Jack coming back?" Johnny religiously read *Variety,* for reasons I did not understand, and therefore knew of my husband's whereabouts.

"Soon," I said. "Maybe next week. If the rain over there lets up. Another?"

Johnny gave me a reproving look as he swept up my glass. "Slow down, kiddo. The night's young, okay?"

"Okay."

Ten-thirty now. T.J. had said ten o'clock sharp when he reached me earlier this evening. I got up and studied the selections in the juke-box. I slipped in a dollar and punched an old country western favorite, "Take This Job and Shove It." I grinned and went back and sat down.

"Hey, hi."

Adam McKay slipped onto the stool next to me.

I yawned inwardly and gave him a tin-plated smile. "How you doing?"

"Pretty good. Hey, Johnny. A Corona?"

Johnny slapped a new cocktail napkin on the bar and set down my drink. As he did so, he raised an eyebrow. Johnny was good like that, silently asking me if I wanted company. If I indicated I did not, he would somehow remove McKay. I gave a small shrug.

"I was beginning to feel kind of lonesome." McKay inched closer to me.

"So, how's the screenplay coming along?" I leaned away from him.

He was wearing a long-sleeved red-and-white checked shirt, black slacks, and shiny black loafers. A silver link bracelet hung loosely around his right wrist.

"Good, I think. I finally figured out the second act, which, as you know, is the ballbreaker. Now I'm into the third. Thanks," he said to Johnny. He poured the Corona into a glass. "Maybe at some point you could read it?"

He looked at me disingenuously.

"Gee," I said, "I still haven't learned how to read a script. Like, when Jack wants my opinion on something? He sort of has to perform it for me."

"No problem," Adam said swiftly. "I'd just like your thoughts on the basic plot and the characters. Especially the female detective. They say it's hard for a man to write from a woman's point of view." His right elbow, on the bar, planted itself against my left forearm.

I sipped the Black Russian. "A shoot-'em-up, huh?" I lifted my arm to smooth my hair.

"Yeah," said Adam. "Something like that."

And then he'd want Jack to read it. After that he'd want Jack's advice on selling it to a studio. It wasn't like any of this was new to me. Half the cops on the force were feverishly writing TV scripts or screenplays. They all figured they could improve on the stuff that was being made.

"It's actually about a mail bomber."

I grinned. "That's original."

"I know. It's hard to compete with real life," Adam said dejectedly.

"Sure."

"On the Writers Guild Bulletin Board—that's something I plug into through my computer—they discuss the problem of creating innovative plots. A writer comes up with one, and by the time he finishes writing it, it's getting round-the-clock coverage on CNN."

"What is?" T. J. McCall came up and shook a cigarette out of his pack. "You mean the Valley thing?"

"No," I said, hopping off the stool. "We haven't reached disaster status yet. Only eight dead. To get on CNN, you need a minimum of . . . I don't know. After Oklahoma City, it might be in the hundreds."

"Adam McKay," Adam said, speaking to T.J. "Retired."

"Though not from screenwriting," I put in. "Well, Adam, you take care. T.J. and I are going to run along."

I opened my purse to get some money, but Adam held up his hand. "Hey, it's on me. With pleasure."

Sullenly, I left the saloon, annoyed at being indebted to the scheming Adam McKay.

T . J . knew a poisonous Mexican food joint down the block, but it was nearly deserted and we weren't going to eat anyway. We both ordered Coronas.

"So what's up?" T.J. took a gulp from the bottle. "You said it was important."

"It is important. Getting smeared in the paper is always important."

T.J. nodded but said nothing.

"Do you know how it happened?"

"How what happened?"

"What I mean is, did you know something I didn't?"

"About the case? Of course. I know plenty of things that you don't."

"Things like . . . we had the wrong guy? Did you know that?"

T.J. shook his head. "Robbery/Homicide has the lead on this case. I'm just doing some of the vacuuming. I didn't know that Allen *didn't* do it. I just knew that some of our pieces didn't quite fit the puzzle. But that happens all the time. You find a cache of acorns, you conclude a squirrel did it. Only it turns out to be a pack rat. That kind of thing."

I gave him a level look. "Bullshit."

"Hey." T.J. put down his bottle. "Don't get mad at me. Nobody from the *Times* talked to *me*. I wouldn't have told them shit. First thing I learned as a cop: never talk to a reporter."

"First thing I learned as a cop: never talk to a detective."

"Jesus. Calm down, will you?"

"Well, *someone* is out to get me." I had raised my voice, and a guy near the kitchen mopping the floor paused and looked over at me. I sighed. "I'm sorry, T.J. I'm not sure what to do."

"Why do anything? It's not like you're suddenly public enemy number one. I bet the number of people who actually read that far into the paper is about four. Just mind your business and keep plugging along. That's all you *can* do."

"Well that's thrilling."

"Look, Brenden, this isn't *Night Watch,* where you roll out after the commercial break and wreak vengeance." T.J. lifted his bottle. "Welcome to the real LAPD."

A waiter came over and asked if we wanted to order. We both shook our heads. "Okay," I said, "so here's the thing." I reminded T.J. that it seemed a number of victims had connections to hospitals or clinics, and I said that Fred Lumley was going to check Amelia's prescription bottle. "He said we could call Kennedy High to find out if she took a kid to a hospital. Oh. He also said something about a lecherous school security guard."

"Hank Harper. Raped a thirteen-year-old neighbor girl. He's awaiting trial in Men's Central Jail." T.J. gave me a lazy smile. "You knew that, right?"

I dropped a ten on the table and walked out.

M y car was parked a few doors past the saloon, and I debated sticking my head in to see if anybody new had turned up. But the idea of going home, crawling into bed with a nightcap, and seeing what was on TV appealed more.

This time no doubting question marks loomed in my mind. I picked up the headlights as soon as I made a U-turn across Sunset, and it made one, too. The same truck that followed me home a week ago was on my tail again.

I dawdled, driving east toward Figueroa, but the Ford Ranger lagged just far enough behind me so I couldn't read the plates. I arrived at Figueroa in the center lane as the light was turning yellow, but rather than make a sudden right, I moved slowly into the right lane, stopped, then signaled my turn. I was curious.

I followed Figueroa to the 110 south and took it to the Santa Monica. As before, the truck stayed five or six car lengths behind me. I exited at 4th Street, drove to Ocean Boulevard, and turned right. The driver, confident he knew where I was going, dropped back and let three cars slip in between us. I began to pick up speed. As I approached San Vicente I made a sudden U-turn and slammed into a parking spot on the west side of Ocean. Then I jumped out and waited for him to pass.

He was too clever for me. He rode the coattails of the car in front, preventing me from seeing the plates. As he passed, he turned his head away from me, offering me only the view of a cap pulled low and a shirt collar turned up. I darted into the street only to discover the truck had no rear plates. His taillights vanished into the fog.

After I entered my apartment, I chain-locked the front door, switched on the alarm, and called Jack. Once again, I communed with his voice mail. I crawled into bed with a soothing Black Russian, set my alarm, and mindlessly watched Letterman interview a skinny blond actress who giggled.

▪ S I X T E E N ▪

There was a profusion of chatter I could not follow as I watched the rumpled man at the intersection begin to lurch my way. He was holding a cardboard sign that read: A DOLLAR WILL BE OK.

He flattened the sign against my window, but the light changed and we escaped.

"The minister wants to know who that man was," said the translator in the back seat.

I glanced at Edward Chang at the wheel beside me. He shrugged. I turned my head. "He's a bum," I said. "Possibly a homeless one, but you never know."

More singsong chatter, then, "The minister asks, A beach bum? Where is the beach?"

Edward rolled his eyes. He was the young Metro officer partnered with me for this escort duty. In the hour we had been together he had told me that although his grandparents had fled China in 1938, he knew no more Chinese than I did. Edward said, "No, not a beach bum. A beach bum is somebody who spends a lot of time at the beach. This man is poor and wants money."

"The minister wonders, Why does this man not have a job?"

"Oh, look," Edward exclaimed. "There's the Convention Center. That's where the trade show will be. And that's where your next appointment is, Minister."

We had commandeered one of Metro's Crown Victorias for the occasion. Our package also included a squad car in front and another Crown Victoria behind filled with members of the minister's party. We caravanned in to the Convention Center with military precision. It was only eleven o'clock, and already I was bored stiff. I swallowed a yawn and hopped out of the car.

The six of us from Metro escorted the minister's entourage to the proper office, then Edward and I sat down on two folding chairs in the hall to wait.

"What do you think?" I said, dumping my shoulder bag on the floor. "Chinatown?"

A devilish glint sparked in Edward's eyes. "I was thinking Little Tokyo. In the spirit of multiculturalism."

"We're supposed to *prevent* incidents, not cause them, Edward."

"Well, there's a place in Beverly Hills. The Mandarin?"

Even though Edward had done the advance work for the minister's three-day visit, the minister's translator had told us that today we should pick a place for lunch, a place that was special to Los Angeles. Outside of Disneyland, which was on the itinerary for tomorrow and which wasn't in Los Angeles anyway, I couldn't think of a place that was special to L.A.

"You've got something against Chinatown?" I asked.

"I hate Chinatown," Edward said adamantly. "I go to a restaurant, they see my face, and they think I'm stupid when I can't speak Cantonese. Or Mandarin. Or whatever."

"Oh, I see." I sighed. "Well, I've lived here my whole life and I can't think of anyplace that's typically L.A.ish. It's not like we have an Empire State Building or something."

Edward grinned. "The Watts Towers?"

I grabbed my purse and stood up. "I'm calling the Cultural Affairs Department. We do have one, don't we? I think so. They'll know what to do."

"Just make sure the restaurant has forks and knives, okay?"

I fished out some coins for the phone. "I think you are the sorriest excuse for a Chinese person I've ever met," I said.

"But I do have nice slanty eyes," Edward said.

T h e Cultural Affairs Department solved the problem by sending us clear across town to Gladstone's 4 Fish, which was on the beach in Santa Monica. It had nothing to do with Chinese food and I'm not sure how it reflected L.A., but the minister seemed content with a paper bib tied around his neck, eating a lobster. I meanly wondered if he were plotting how the Taiwanese could copy the lobsters and sell them more cheaply.

Next was the garment district downtown, where the minister "observed" how Americans mass-produced clothes. I wasn't sure how many actual Americans staffed these factories, but a Spanish-speaking translator materialized and spoke to the Chinese one. Everyone seemed pleased.

During the week prior, LAPD had converged on the district hoping to shoo the criminals away. There had been a recent string of murders in the area, and the possibility that the minister might stumble upon a corpse had produced a burst of departmental activity along the streets surrounding the warehouses.

"The thing is," I whispered to Edward as we drove the minister away, "a corpse would be reflective of L.A. I think we missed an opportunity here, don't you?"

At City Hall, we deposited the Taiwanese into the glad-handing clutches of the mayor, who had arranged a late-afternoon "tea" for the minister and local business leaders. A bouncy young woman in a canary yellow suit—"Hi, I'm Maria Santana, Special Events"—led the rest of us into a conference room set up with soft drinks, coffee, and an assortment of cookies and cakes. "I'll be back to check up on you," Maria sang, "and try to give you some warning when things are winding down, okay?"

I trailed her out the door. "Could you tell me where the ladies' room is, please?"

"Sure. I'll take you to the one for guests. I don't suppose there'll be many women at this thing. Are you with Metro?"

"Yes. Brenden Harlow."

"Okay, Brenden, right through there," Maria said. "Is there anything else I can do for you guys?"

I shook my head sadly. "Unfortunately, not a thing."

The ladies' room was decorated more like a powder room, except the two toilets were enclosed. Placed on the counter around the sink were soaps, hand creams, small bottles of perfume, and a can of hair spray. I began brushing my hair. It felt nice to have a moment to myself.

After I washed my hands and rubbed on some hand cream, I looked again at the day's itinerary. The minister would have an hour to rest at his hotel before attending a diplomatic dinner hosted by Taiwan's consul general. The day seemed endless and my muscles felt stiff. I stepped back from the sink, planted my right foot on the counter, and leaned into a nice, deep stretch.

I was working on my left leg when the door flew open. A woman entered and gasped.

"Oops," I said with a foolish grin.

"Officer . . . Harlow?"

I hadn't really looked at her in my embarrassment.

"For goodness sake," she exclaimed.

"Oh," I said, "Terry Smith." I lowered my left foot to the floor. "I guess I could say this is a surprise."

She was wearing a tweed jacket, probably a silk-and-cotton blend, over a beige skirt and matching calf pumps. I guessed her height with heels at six feet, but her broad shoulders—and the enclosed space—made her seem even larger. She dropped her handbag on the counter and ran her fingers through her short gray hair. She smiled. "Okay, I'll go first. What are you doing here?"

"Special detail. The trade minister from Taiwan."

"We have a lot in common then. That's why I'm here, too."

I lifted a brow.

"I'm building a toy factory for a Taiwanese firm. But why you?"

"Fate. It dogs me everywhere I go."

She opened her bag and pulled out a compact. "I saw the papers. They pulled you off the case, didn't they?"

I couldn't exactly interpret her tone. The harsh note might have been disapproval, or maybe the result of her own bad mood. I said, "Not at all. From time to time everyone gets taken off a case for a day or so to stay fresh."

Her eyes met mine in the mirror. "A girl like you has a lot to prove, I'm sure."

I reached for my own bag. "I'd better run." I smiled. "Good luck with the minister."

She uncapped her lipstick and said almost casually, "You know, I saw him again."

"Saw . . . the guard?"

"That's right." She began applying her lipstick.

"When?"

"Last night, as a matter of fact."

"Did you report this?"

"Not yet." She laughed. "I haven't had time."

"Same circumstances?"

She dropped the lipstick into her purse and turned to face me. "I can't keep the minister waiting."

"Terry," I said. "Tell me. What time last night? Were you alone again?"

"Yes. It was late. Somewhere around ten o'clock, I think. I was making a deposit when I heard footsteps. I turned and he was walking by. Said good evening and kept walking."

"Where did he go?"

She shrugged. "I was nervous, so I didn't withdraw any money. I just grabbed the deposit slip and hurried to my car. But he was nowhere in sight. Then I think . . . yes. A car pulled up with two people. I remember feeling relieved."

"Did you get a better look at him?"

"Not really. Maybe." She pulled open the door.

"We may ask you to come in and talk to our sketch artist."

She gave me a brief smile. "Anytime." The door closed behind her.

I took a moment to freshen my own lipstick. What was with her, anyway? Was she playing mind games with me, or . . . I put down my lipstick and entertained a thought. A sudden untethered thought. I stared at my reflection and listened to drops of water *plink-plink* into the sink.

What if a woman *had* committed the murders? A large woman . . . a woman who worked in construction. A woman who, perhaps hoping to raise the danger stakes, had called in a bogus tip—simply for the sheer thrill of it—and now, quite unplanned, had found an opportunity to do it again.

It was a daft thought sparked by nothing I could put a finger on. A glance, a tone, who knew? But these were the hunches you listened to—the hunches that could break a case.

If you could ever figure out how to prove them.

I straggled through my front door shortly after eleven, brain dead and beat. I turned on some mind-numbing pseudoclassical jazz that Jack kept in the CD cabinet, poured a vodka, and drifted into the bedroom. I kicked off my shoes and called Hawaii. Again I left a message. I realized that Jack had been gone only a week, and already he had started to seem like a stranger. Or maybe he'd been a stranger longer than I cared to admit. I had put off searching the apartment for more packets of coke. I stretched out on the bed and thought, Tomorrow I will look; or maybe some other day.

On impulse I dialed T. J. McCall's home number. My purpose was to tell him about Terry Smith, but I wondered if that were the real reason. Maybe I needed to hear a voice.

"Hello?"

"Hi. It's Brenden."

A pause. "It's late."

I glanced at my watch. "Is it? Can you talk for a few minutes?"

"I could've talked last night but you had to have a snit. What's up?"

"I had a detective's hunch today. But I'm not a detective and I can't do much about checking it out."

"There are many detectives who could check it out," T.J. said, aggrieved.

I hesitated. "Are you mad at me, or are you busy?"

"Both."

"Okay. Sorry I bothered you. I'll talk to you another time."

"Fine," said T.J. and hung up.

I stuck a second pillow under my head and stared at the ceiling. No one ever said detectives were normal. The ones I'd dealt with tended to be moody and unpredictable, if not flaky. Eventually I worked up the energy to take off my clothes. I hung my suit in the closet and put on a navy kimono. Then I wandered into the den in search of a yellow legal pad. It was a cozy room with a big leather chair and ottoman, a desk with a computer on it, a TV, and bookshelves filled with scripts and videos. Jack had insisted on putting speakers in the walls in each room, and all speakers were individually controlled. I lowered the sound of the crescendoing music, climbed onto the leather chair, and began doodling on the notepad. How, I wondered, could we ascertain Terry Smith's whereabouts on the nights of the murders?

I sipped the vodka and thought about it. If she were the killer it seemed unlikely she would have stalked her victims. Running a construction company, she would have a busy schedule. Which meant she was an opportunistic killer, preying on smaller women caught by chance alone.

Unless—yes, of course—she did her stalking at night. Sitting in her car or, really macabre, posing as a bank guard, she could preselect her victims. Perhaps—and we would have to try to establish this—her victims visited ATMs around the same time each week. Then all she would have to do was to wait to catch her target alone. I smiled. I liked it.

When the phone rang a few moments later, I jumped up and grabbed the desk phone, expecting to hear T.J.'s voice. Instead, I heard Jack's.

"Well, well," I said. "You live and breathe after all."

"Just barely," said Jack. "How's the cream of the LAPD?"

"Curdling." As always, I found myself brightening. Even through my anger at him, he still had that effect on me. I sat down and swung my feet onto the desk.

"We could elope," Jack said. "But this time it's your turn. I'm on the sixth floor, you'll need a rope."

"Don't they have stunt people for that type of work? Even for you, I don't think I could manage it."

"Don't be coy," Jack said. "I haven't been gone so long I can't recall the steel in those sinewy arms."

"You really need to be rescued?"

"Puleeze."

"Then I'll notify SWAT. What are the circumstances?"

"I'm being held hostage by a brutal, sadistic director who feels a take isn't a take unless it's the seventeenth one. There's a lot of physical action and my muscles are sore, my throat's sore and—"

"Poor thing. I think you are very brave and heroic."

And how much coke are you doing, baby? is what I really wanted to say.

"If I kill Patty Lang," Jack said, "will you promise not to turn me in?" Patty Lang was the movie's female lead.

"Oh dear. Don't you have any friends?"

"The stunt guy's okay. Good for a beer or two. And they've got the screenwriter here. We commiserate. God, I miss you."

"Well, I'm sorry to inform you, but you've got competition. I'm spending the weekend with the trade minister from Taiwan. He's already offered to send me a new wardrobe. At least that's what his translator said."

"Stop," Jack moaned. "I don't want to hear about the chopsticks. I'll move my room to the ground floor. Can you manage that?"

"Maybe."

"It looks like it'll be another ten days." He hesitated. "Are you still thinking of taking some time off?"

"The time-off gods have not been friendly. We arrested the wrong guy and the killer struck again. Someone in the department bad-mouthed me in the *L.A. Times*. The minister has halitosis. I'm not having a good time."

"Wait'll I get home. The money I'm making for this film? We'll do something great. And Jay's negotiating a better deal for me on the series. We'll be able to do whatever we want forever."

I began playing with the sash on my kimono. I knew what was coming. I could quit my job, he'd say, although with the series, my salary had been meaningless for some time. He'd mention moving to Santa Barbara, having children, da-da, da-da, da-da. I said, "Talking to you isn't helping. I need to see you, Jack."

"Soon . . . I love you, Bren."

"I love you, too."

I hung up and tried to tell myself the coke in the freezer had to be someone else's. Bob McNally was wrong. My husband wasn't doing drugs; he wouldn't. It was all a crazy misunderstanding, I was sure of it.

I picked up my dead vodka glass and went to revive it.

he phrase *clue slip* conjured up a sliver of paper upon which a police officer could scribble, well, a clue. Like—the candlestick-in-the-library sort of thing. But as with so much else in the department, the phrase was misleading. What I was rigorously working on at the moment was an eight-by-eleven sheet of paper containing a zillion boxes, all needing to be filled in. My eyes began to cross before I had completed a third of the page.

I had, however, over the weekend, obtained from Maria Santana the name of Terry Smith's construction company. A phone book gave me an address; I already had the number. The DMV gave me her vehicle plates and the make of her car, a Mercedes 300E. I guessed her height and weight. I didn't want to leave even one box blank. All this so I could alert Operation ATM that Terry Smith had again spotted the bogus security guard.

The Metro desk officer who had phoned at 7:15 A.M. told me there would be no stakeout tonight. Instead, I was to come in at noon with my squad and pursue leads by phone, or maybe trek out to the Valley to hunt one down. This was normal procedure; a stakeout could not be conducted night after endless night. It would produce massive burnout no matter how many of our bodies they used. The lead detectives on the case liked to be present as we made our ATM rounds, and this was not always the best use of their time, or ours. So they said.

The problem was—and you'd think someone might have solved it decades ago—Metro officers had no desks. So, as usual, we had to scramble to borrow some. I was put in the lieutenant's room with two other guys; Todd found a desk in the administrative offices.

After I completed the "clue slip" I picked up the phone and called Robbery/Homicide. Technically, I should have gone through Higgins, but I had an excuse.

"Detective Walters, please," I said.

One thing that always struck me about LAPD is that no caller was ever questioned. Either you were put through, if your party was present, or the desk person took your name and number and passed it along. No one asked who you were or why you were calling, which I found interesting. To get past a secretary at any company in America, you had to state your business, if not your entire life story.

"Walters."

"Hi, Detective. It's Brenden Harlow in Metro."

"Say, Brenden, what's up?"

"Terry Smith. I ran into her Friday. She says she saw the same alleged guard patrolling the bank grounds Thursday night. I filled out a clue slip, but I'm wondering if there isn't more here than meets the eye."

"I'm listening."

"Okay. If you take her word for it, then other customers must have seen him, too. She said as she was leaving, in fact, another car was pulling in. So that's an obvious avenue, which I'm happy to follow up."

"And if you don't take her word for it?" Walters was quick.

"She's a very large woman who owns a construction company."

"Anything else?"

"It would take some digging to pin down her whereabouts the nights of all the murders."

"I hear you. Fax me your clue sheet. You got someone you can go to the bank with?"

"I can ask my partner, Todd Robbie."

"You got anything better to do?" Walters chuckled. "Don't answer."

"No, I'd like to. And another thing. I told Terry Smith that we might want her to come in and see the sketch artist."

"What's her number?"

I gave it to him.

"You got a pager?"

"Yes." I gave him that number also.

"Okay, Brenden, we'll see how fast we can rope Terry Smith in to do a sketch. When we get one, we'll run it out to you."

"Okay. Um, by the way . . . " I hesitated. "Would you tell Sergeant Higgins you're asking us to do this?"

"Will do. Talk to you later."

• • •

A t the Bank of America, we asked the branch manager for permission to question customers and, for the next few hours, Todd and I took turns moving from the street ATMs to those in the rear. Had anyone seen a security guard?

Late in the afternoon, quicker than I had expected, a patrol officer brought us an artist's sketch of Terry Smith's guard.

At 7:45, Ron Josephson and Bill Munoz, both members of our Metro squad, arrived to relieve us, and Todd and I, after getting pasta in Chinese-food cartons from a Mexican drive-through, headed downtown to Metro.

At 9 P.M. we walked into Lieutenant Turley's office bearing a list of three customers who said they had seen a guard, too.

T h i s line of inquiry continued the next day. Officers with sketches took up posts at all seven banks where murders had occurred, and you could palpably feel the department's adrenaline pumping. In an effort to stem the charges of LAPD incompetence that the media had been spewing forth, and to quell the queasy stomachs of the female population, the chief held a news conference to trumpet our progress and to display the suspect's sketch on local TV. The immediate result was to unleash a torrent of phone calls from L.A.'s lunatic fringe—and swarms of news vultures to the banks we were surveilling. A civil war nearly broke out between police and reporters, who found themselves elbowing each other to interview the same bewildered bank customers.

Todd and I were assigned to the Great Western Bank on Laurel Canyon, where Amelia Lynn Grant had been killed. By four o'clock, however, we had not found a single taker. No one working for the bank, or doing business inside the bank, or using the ATMs could recall seeing a guard or anyone who resembled the man in the sketch.

It was the Tuesday before Memorial Day weekend, and the strange weather patterns that had afflicted the Southland all spring had wackily reversed themselves. The too-early heat spell had broken into a series of cool, overcast days, and now big swollen clouds threatened to burst into a downpour.

I was talking to a teenage girl in a T-shirt and jeans who glanced at my sketch and giggled. "Hey, I know that guy."

I moved a step closer. "You've seen him here at the bank?"

"Naw. But I saw him yesterday."

"Where?"

"At school."

"What school?"

"Grant."

"He's a security guard there?"

The girl snapped her gum. "Naw. Mr. Lansing's my science teacher. Gave me a fucking F." And she giggled and bounced away.

Which is when my beeper went off.

Happy for a break in the tedium, I walked into the bank and used someone's phone to call Robbery/Homicide. I was put through to Marty Walters. "Anything?" he said.

"Zero."

"Then come on in. Have Robbie drop you off and he can go back to Metro."

"Be there in half an hour."

I usurped the wheel from Todd's clutches and blasted downtown to Parker Center. I jumped out on Los Angeles Street and dashed through the now steady rain into the stark, cavernous lobby of police headquarters. If you weren't a criminal when you came in, the dim lighting made you look like one. I flashed my badge at the desk officer and rode the elevator to three.

A dozen or so detectives sat at various tables in the Robbery/Homicide office, many of them working the phones. A secretary planted near the door pointed me toward a small room at the back. As I entered, Marty Walters turned from a bulletin board and saluted. "Welcome to the War Room."

In the forty years since Parker Center had been built, crime had grown but LAPD's space had not. Several desks were pushed together in this cramped back office, and all the wall space—a blackboard, bulletin board, and faded paint—was covered with maps, charts, lists, and—sadly, on one wall—pictures of the stabbing victims in life and in death.

Art Bannister, the beefy detective who had briefed us on the since-forgotten Donald Abernathy, rose and said, "Hi."

I nodded. The other man in the office was T. J. McCall. He was wearing a polo shirt and was speaking softly into a phone.

Walters pointed to a black-crusted pot. "Coffee?"

"Thanks," I said. "I'll get it. What's up?"

Walters walked over to me and lowered his voice so he wouldn't disturb T.J. "So far," he began, "the only people who have seen Terry Smith's guard are customers at Sheila Dann's bank. We had two more today. Now, this is just a crazy hunch." Walters walked over to the desks, picked up a glossy eight-by-ten photo, and brought it to me.

"Terry Smith," he said.

"Where did you get this?"

"When she came in yesterday, we told her it was standard procedure. Photograph or videotape anything that breathes as a result of Rodney King. Anyway, now look at this."

He went back to the desk and returned with a series of charcoal sketches. The first resembled the photograph of Terry. The second added a police hat. The third gave her short sideburns. I glanced up sharply at Walters.

"Like I said, a hunch. What do you think?"

So he had leaped to the same conclusion I had; maybe it wasn't so zany after all. I merely smiled.

"We've been checking her out since yesterday," Walters continued. "When T.J. gets off the phone, you two will start surveilling her."

I said, "Besides this hunch, is there anything specific to go on?"

Walters laughed. I liked him. He was probably around fifty, with prematurely white hair and merry blue eyes set in a face that had remained unlined and youthful. By reputation I knew he was one of our best homicide detectives. He had worked on many high-profile cases and almost always solved them.

"This bank where she saw the guard is two miles from her home," Walters said. "She lives alone. Her housekeeper leaves at six. Even when her husband was alive, she was never known to socialize. Apparently, she was the business brains behind the company, while her husband was the dreamy-eyed architect."

"How did he die?"

"Lung cancer."

I perked up. "When?"

"Two years ago."

I perked up some more. "Michelle Lloyd's husband is a thoracic surgeon at St. Joseph's."

Marty grinned. "Thatta girl."

"What else? She's forty-four. Isn't that a little old for it?"

"Only if you look at the male criminal population. Female killers tend to be older. And three nights a week she works out with weights at a gym. She runs ten-K races and finishes high in her age category. Her mother doted on her younger sister, and Terry, I'm told, has never had any use for women."

I blinked. "How did you find all that out?"

Walters smiled broadly. "Look at this face. Wouldn't *you* tell it your deep, dark secrets?"

"Frankly, I wouldn't tell it the time of the day."

"Then do me a favor. Don't commit a homicide."

"Are you going to bring her back for questioning?" I asked.

"Nope. I'd say we've got her right where we want her."

"Where's that?"

"Grinning from ear to ear," Marty said.

I f she were grinning, I was not. Stuffed inside T.J.'s aging Caprice, the rain pouring down, I was hungry, fidgety, and damp. We were on a little side street off Ventura Boulevard, fifty feet from the entrance to the parking lot at Jim's Jungle Gym. Somehow T.J. had ascertained the time Terry would be leaving her office downtown and, friendly cops that we were, we shadowed her here.

"How long does she work out?" I asked. "Did you find that out, too?"

"An hour to an hour and a half. But tonight she has her massage after."

"Probably she stretches out on hot coals and has some Asian guy walk on her back." I cracked the window. "She strikes me as the type."

"In addition," T.J. said, ignoring me, "we're trying to locate two guys. One worked as an architect for her firm for ten years. He left a year ago. Harry Altman. The other was a foreman type. They had some kind of blowup and he's gone, too."

"Is it a big company?"

"Midsize. She does commercial jobs, office buildings, warehouses, but not shopping malls or industrial parks. She usually has about five projects going at once."

"How big is her staff?"

"Two secretaries and three project engineers. There's a business manager, a lawyer on retainer, and an accountant. Aside from Altman, she's always hired architects freelance, but that's another direction to go in. See if any of them have anything unusual to say." T.J. jabbed the car cigarette lighter.

"But you have nothing to tie her to the murders?"

"Nope. But I have a couple of things to connect her to the victims. If you behave yourself, I might tell you."

I rolled down my window another inch as he lit up. "Is that how you talk to your male colleagues? If they behave themselves, whatever *that* means, you'll tell them things?"

"Of course not. But they don't put on lipstick every ten minutes either."

"No, their *cologne* lasts all day."

"For chrissake, Harlow."

"Anyway, I'm sorry if my lipstick unnerves you. I forget you're a guy."

After I got T.J. calmed down, he sulkily told me that Terry's firm had built the clinic where Andrea Wright was working at the time of her murder, although he could not say if the two women had ever met. He also noted that Terry was a member, like Sheila Dann, of the Make-A-Wish Foundation. "And," he said triumphantly, "Dr. Michael Lloyd did operate on her husband."

It had been only a hunch. That the pieces were starting to fit together sort of amazed me. "So what do we do now? We still have at least an hour to go."

"We hope like hell some woman isn't getting mutilated at an ATM," T.J. answered. "And you shut up and let me think."

"Um, one more question." It had been bothering me ever since Monster assigned me to decoy duty. "Did you suggest me to Ragsdale?"

"Once in a while," T.J. said sourly, "even I make a mistake."

F r o m Jim's Jungle Gym we trailed Terry Smith to a large two-story house on Louise Avenue set well back from the street. The second story had a balcony opening from one of the rooms, and the whole house was artfully framed by towering California maples. We waited forty-five minutes to see if she would stay put; judging from the light patterns inside the house and the red light that flashed on her outdoor alarm panel, we assumed she would. T.J. dropped me at Metro. I retrieved my car and headed for the First Base Saloon.

It was a lousy night. The rain was pouring down in sheets, and I knew I should have just bagged it. Instead, I stepped up to the bar and ordered a double. When I stuck my head in the poolroom, I found Cookie Randall and Dorrie Green.

"Welcome to girls' night out," Cookie sang. "Dorrie's kids have gone up north to be with her mom, so I thought she should see how the other half lives."

I studied the delicate-looking detective and wondered if Cookie had designs on her. She was quite striking, with her almond-shaped eyes and broad, winsome smile. "How old are your kids?" I asked, sliding into the booth.

"My son is ten and my daughter is seven," Dorrie said. "Marcus is the little man of the family trying to take care of his mama. Kathleen is a handful. If there's a way to get into mischief, she finds it." Dorrie sighed. "Just like me."

"Oh, are you trouble?" I said.

"Let's just say I'm a ghetto kid who learned to stand up for herself and doesn't always know when to quit."

"What made you join the department?"

Dorrie fingered her glass. "About the fifth time I called the police to get my husband to stop beating on me, I met a nice sergeant who told me the department could use people like me. I assumed he meant female and black. Once I got into the academy, I realized I had other qualities that make me good at what I do. But as soon as I get my twenty years in, I'm going to work the system from the other end."

"Instead of locking kids up," Cookie asked, "try to make sure they don't get arrested?"

Dorrie nodded. I noticed she was drinking Perrier. She took a small sip, then put down her glass. "Higgins is over there eyeballing us. He got a problem?"

I turned and looked through the doorway, and sure enough, there he was at the bar, standing with Adam McKay. "He's got it in for me," I said. "I'm wondering if that's why he comes here. Cookie, has he always come in? I could swear I never saw him here before a week or two ago."

Cookie broke out one of her devilish smiles. "I hear marital problems. Maybe he's a little down on women right now."

I leaned closer. "Marital problems? But how would you know?"

"What I don't know, cutie pie, you could put on the head of a pin."

"What *do* you know?" asked Dorrie unmoved.

"They haven't built the computer memory for it," Cookie Randall said.

•   •   •

T o my surprise I was assigned to work with T.J. again the next day. The rain was still sledgehammering the city, swelling the Los Angeles River—such as it is—and causing hillside residents to throw down sheets of plastic in an attempt to keep their yards from running away. Sandbag crews were out, LAPD was prepared to go on an all-alert, and the city was holding its breath.

Once again, we were imprisoned in T.J.'s car, this time in a cavernous parking structure under the Broadway Plaza on South Flower. Smith & Company Builders was located on the twenty-seventh floor. We were located within sight of Terry's gunmetal gray Mercedes. I still didn't understand why T.J. wanted me with him. A woman on surveillance was a good idea, but not one Terry Smith would know if it became necessary to walk in on her.

T.J. had put on a pair of glasses and was reading a report. "This is interesting," he said, tapping it. "That clinic that she built? Apparently she didn't finish the job. The building was financed by a private group of doctors on the West Side. It would be a nonprofit clinic for people without insurance. Each doc volunteers one day a week. Here's the screwy part. When Terry found out they intended to do abortion counseling and perform abortions, she said her conscience wouldn't let her have any part of it." T.J. looked over his glasses at me. "The doctors threatened to sue, but eventually they settled with her and hired someone else to finish the job."

"I doubt Mrs. Shaunessy had an abortion, if that's what you're getting at," I said.

"People are *shooting* abortion doctors," T.J. pointed out.

The concept seemed rather far-fetched, but even the thought that someone would stalk and kill women who had undergone abortions gave me a chill.

"Maybe," I said softly, "she was never able to conceive."

T.J. punched the numbers on his cell phone and told someone at Robbery/Homicide to check with the victims' gynecologists. When he hung up, he smiled playfully. "Guess what your job is?"

"This is too weird." I got out of the car and slammed the door.

I glided up two escalators to the building's massive lobby, which also contained a mall of shops, and found a phone booth. I pushed in a quarter and dialed Terry Smith's office. A pleasing female voice answered. "Smith and Company. May I help you?"

"Good morning," I said. "This is Jeanie in Dr. Harmon's office? I'm afraid doctor's going to have to cancel Ms. Smith's appointment tomorrow at ten A.M. He has to do a cesarean." I paused. "He could see her Friday, if that's convenient."

"Dr. Harmon?" echoed the woman. "What kind of appointment are you referring to?"

"I believe it's for her yearly exam."

"Pelvic exam? I don't understand. Ms. Smith goes to Dr. Bernstein."

"Harriet Smith?" I said.

"No," said the woman with relief. "Terry Smith."

"Gosh. I'm sorry. I wonder how that happened. Well, thank you." I hung up.

Naturally, the phone did not have a phone book, so I called Metro and asked the desk officer to check our special directory of doctors. I glanced at my watch. I'd been gone eight minutes. I wondered how many Bernsteins there were.

"I'm putting you on hold," the desk officer said.

I turned and watched the people in the lobby, people who were dressed for offices and carried briefcases. Ten minutes. And then she caught my eye. Wearing a black pants suit and polished black tie shoes, Terry Smith hurried into a Humphrey Yogart shop.

I hung up and trotted to the escalators. She hadn't been wearing a raincoat or carrying an umbrella. So either she was on her way to the garage or she was just grabbing some yogurt. I scrambled down one escalator, then another, and jumped off at level P2.

I jogged along the row of cars until I came to ours.

Or where ours had been.

The space was empty.

I turned and looked down the aisle for the gray Mercedes.

But it was gone, too.

A s if launched by Mission Control, I was hurtled up through the wind tunnel and ejected onto the twenty-seventh floor. At the end of the carpeted corridor, I pushed through a pair of wooden doors. A young man in a narrow suit was sitting behind a glass desk.

His dark hair was slicked back behind his ears and, as he looked up, I noticed the long dark lashes. A single red rose poked bravely out of a slender crystal bud vase.

"May I help you?" He folded his hands on the desk and I noticed his French cuffs, a rare affectation for L.A.

"Is Ms. Smith in, please?"

"I'm afraid not. She's stepped out. Is there something I can help you with?"

Stepped out. That could mean she would be returning momentarily and could catch me in a lie. On the other hand, if I lied, it might prove useful. I wanted to know where she was.

"Gee," I said, "she told me to stop by. Do you suppose I could wait?"

Middle ground. Not an irreparable lie.

Narrowed eyes now. "May I ask your business?"

"It's about a job." Definite lie. Though I could have defended it: it was about *my* job.

The man held up his finger and reached for the phone. "Smith and Company Builders, may I help you?"

I turned and studied the anteroom. I was standing on plush maroon carpet. Two couches in a maroon print sat at ninety-degree angles to each other in one corner. There was a square table piled with building and design magazines, and on the dark wood-paneled walls some interesting black-and-white photographs of L.A. in prehistoric times. It was the kind of decorating that would make men feel comfortable, and I assumed it was men whom Terry Smith mainly saw. Behind the young man another set of double doors stood firmly closed.

He scribbled a message, thanked the caller, and hung up.

"I'm afraid both Ms. Smith and her secretary, who could perhaps help you, are not here," he said at last. "If you'll leave your name and number, one of them will get back to you." He pushed a notepad across the desk.

"Sure," I said, as he handed me a pen. "By the way, is Harry Altman around?"

I lowered my head and carefully printed the name Candace Lake.

"Harry Altman?"

"Yes. Doesn't he work here?"

The man pursed his lips. "I'm afraid not. He hasn't been here for over a year."

I made up a phone number and handed the man the pad. "Oh, I didn't realize. Perhaps you can tell me where to reach him? We used to be neighbors."

"I believe he's at Merckenstein and Company, Ms. . . . uh, Lake. I'll be sure to give Ms. Smith this message."

"Thanks."

I tossed him a friendly grin. At least I had found out that much.

B u t — where was Terry Smith?

Had she only been getting yogurt, she would have been back. If she had gone down to the garage, I would have seen, at the very least, her car pulling away.

I descended to the lobby, found an empty pay phone, and dialed T. J. McCall's cell phone. Busy signal. I dialed Metro and began scribbling down the Bernsteins the desk officer recited to me. Not as bad as I thought. Seven gynecologists named Bernstein in L.A. County. One in Long Beach, whom I dismissed as geographically unsuitable. One in Woodland Hills, a possible. Two in Beverly Hills, one in Santa Monica, one with offices at Cedar Sinai, and one at UCLA.

Finding out if Terry Smith had been unable to conceive and had thus channeled her rage at women who had undergone abortions was nothing but a straw in the haystack. But even Rumpelstiltskin, they had reminded us at the academy, had woven straw into gold. I ducked into Humphrey Yogart's, bought a cup of frozen Malty Falcon, and returned to the phone with a handful of quarters. I tried T.J. again and this time a recorded voice told me he was either out of the area or out of the car. I called Robbery/Homicide and gave the desk officer the number of my pay phone and the one next to me. Then I started on Bernsteins.

Four of my six inquiries were answered by receptionists who said I had the wrong Bernstein. A fifth, the UCLA Bernstein, was answered by a service; the message taker told me the office would reopen at two. One Beverly Hills Bernstein had a phone machine that informed me he would be away for the next two weeks and his associate, Dr. Bender, should be contacted in case of an emergency.

She had now been gone for an hour. I walked across the lobby to a waste bin and tossed my empty yogurt cup. I debated whether I should try to reach Harry Altman. I wasn't a detective, and in a case this sensitive I didn't want to proceed without permission. I decided it would be okay to try to locate him, and then, if T.J. was still missing, I would check with Marty Walters.

Information gave me the number for Merckenstein. I dropped another quarter, and when a receptionist answered, I asked if Harry Altman was employed there.

"One moment, please."

I hadn't intended to be put through. I had intended only to get the firm's address. Instead, a voice said, "Altman speaking."

"Harry Altman?"

"That's right."

"Sir, I'm Officer Harlow with the Los Angeles police. Are you the same Harry Altman who was formerly employed by Smith and Company Builders?"

There was a moment of stunned silence. "Why yes," he finally replied. "Did you say the police?"

"Don't be alarmed, Mr. Altman. We may want to talk to you. Will you be in your office all afternoon?"

"Uh, no. I have several appointments. Can you tell me what this is about?"

"Not over the phone, sir. But this has nothing to do with you. We were just hoping you could provide us with some information. Would it be all right if we called back to set up an appointment?"

I could have asked him to drop by Parker Center, third floor, Robbery/Homicide, but then he would definitely demand to know what was going on.

"Uh, sure, I guess so."

"Thanks, Mr. Altman. We appreciate your cooperation."

As I replaced the receiver I became aware that someone was standing behind me. Jamming the paper with the phone numbers into my pocket, I turned, half expecting to find Terry Smith.

A man with no teeth showed me his gums. "Can you spare some change, lady?"

"**S o** I located Altman in West L.A., and I narrowed the list of gynecologists to two Bernsteins," I said.

T.J. picked up a moldy white towel from the back seat and was rubbing it over his damp hair. A steaming cup of coffee rested on the console between us. The strong aroma tempted me.

"Gosh. And I forgot to bring my box of little gold stars," T.J. said peevishly.

I looked at the coffee. "May I?"

T.J. grunted.

"Tell me what happened. I don't understand how she beat me down here."

"She didn't. A man got into her car and drove off. I figured he was going around to pick her up in front of the building. Which he did."

The coffee was too hot to swallow so I just held the cup in my hand. "In the rain? She walked out the front door and down all those steps in the rain?"

"Maybe she doesn't do garages."

"So where did Terry Smith and her driver go?"

"It was quite thrilling, Harlow. He dropped her off in front of a building. He put the car in a lot about twenty yards from the front door and waited. I waited. Forty-five minutes later she came out."

"You didn't go in? You didn't find out who she went to see?"

"I'll figure that out when we get back to Parker Center."

"How do you know?"

"Because," T.J. said. "Parker Center is where she went."

T . J . phoned Robbery/Homicide and asked that someone interview Harry Altman. The only thing he let me do was make a food sprint up to the lobby. I got a turkey sandwich for him and a cold pasta salad for me, plus a double cappuccino to boost my spirits. After that, all I got to do was sit in T.J.'s car, breathe Marlboro fumes—and wait.

A little before six, his cell phone rang. He listened, made a face, and hung up. "Fucking reception. Run up to the lobby and call Arlie McFadden. He'll tell you about his interview with Harry Altman."

I started to get out.

"Wait. You better take my cell phone. If I'm not here when you get back, I'll use the ROVER to get a message to Robbery/Homicide. Then they'll call you." He tilted his head. "Think you can handle it, Harlow?"

"I doubt I'd even know where to begin."

This time the lobby was awash with people escaping for the night. It reminded me of a laboratory in which a deranged scientist unlatches all the cages and hundreds of mice come scurrying out. Too many of them scurried to a phone. I flashed my badge and comandeered one.

Arlie McFadden was brusque.

"Altman was her chief architect for ten years," he began. "Said they got along okay once he figured out how to deal with her. She's got a steel-trap mind and doesn't suffer fools—or mistakes. She demands respect, competence, and total dedication. Occasionally she'll lose it, throw a fit. But he learned that if you leave her alone, she'll snap out of it, no harm done. He said he knew nothing of her private life or her marriage. The woman is all business."

"How come he left?" I asked.

"He felt his salary wasn't commensurate with his importance to her company. He asked her for ten percent of the company in class A stock. She refused. He said the negotiations were pretty straightforward, nothing nasty. He decided to see if he could do better elsewhere."

"That's it?"

"Pretty much."

"How did you explain why you were asking questions?"

"I told him she had provided important information for an investigation we were conducting and it was standard procedure to do a bit of a background check on a key witness. He seemed okay with that."

"Anything you want me to tell T.J.?"

"Nope."

After I hung up, I looked at my watch. Six-fifteen. Time for all good workers to go home. I pushed in another quarter and dialed Terry Smith's office. I would say I was with building operations and we were planning to turn off all electricity for half an hour starting at 6:30. Hopefully, I would get some idea of when Terry planned to leave.

Only the phone was answered by a machine. The machine, in the voice of the male receptionist, announced office hours were from 9:30 to 6; please leave a message or call back.

Damn.

As I started toward the escalator, it occurred to me that despite the machine Terry could still be up there. I did an about-face and headed for the elevators. Waves of people poured out of them, but none were her. I stepped into one and pushed *27*. Once again I was launched into the stratosphere of the skyscraper, and once again I lurched off. I turned down the hall to Terry's office but could determine nothing. With the heavy wooden doors and the thick carpeting, there was no slit for light to seep through.

I pressed my ear to the door. No sounds. Carefully I tried the knob. The doors were locked.

Double damn.

I returned to the lobby and headed for the escalator. I was sick of this cold, glass-and-steel building. Now I might have to hang around even longer if T.J. had taken off. On level P2, I walked along the emptying rows of cars until I came to the Caprice. I looked down the row. The Mercedes was there, too.

I opened the passenger door and slid in. "I think we have a problem," I said.

A n o t h e r hour and fifteen minutes passed. T.J. didn't see how we had a problem; Terry Smith was obviously still in her office. "Of course, she'd lock the doors," he said. "Alone in a place like this, wouldn't you?"

"No," I said stubbornly. "I would forget to."

"That's 'cause you're a cop. It's planted in your twisted little mind-set. Come on, mister, make my day."

I turned in my seat and stared at him. "You're kidding, right?"

Which is when his cell phone rang.

T.J. had kept the police frequency turned off to prevent drawing attention to ourselves, or possibly to prevent brain damage.

"Yeah."

In the shadows of the garage I could not read his face.

"Uh-huh. I've got it. I'll get back to you pronto." He clicked off and reached for his doorknob.

"Maybe just a teeny weeny hint?" I said.

"A woman's been shredded. I'm going to see if our squirrel slipped away." Clutching his cell phone, he took off on the run.

I sat perfectly still. I had no idea who had been killed, but it didn't matter. In a case like this one, you begin to take each murder personally. The shock I was feeling provided the same electric jolt to the system that would come with the news of a loved one's death.

Eventually, I switched on the police frequency and tried to piece together what was going on. I learned that the location of the stabbing was the Valley Savings & Loan on Laurel Canyon, the same bank where Mrs. Croft had been killed. The killer had doubled back.

I had no idea what to make of that. I folded my hands in my lap and waited.

T . J . was talking into his cell phone as he got in and closed the door. "Yeah, okay. You want me to wait? No, listen. I'll head out in that direction. Call me after you've checked. Right."

He tossed the phone into my lap and started the engine. As he backed out of the space, he said, "Unless she's dead at her desk, she's not there. Arlie's en route to her house now."

I reached for the ROVER. "R-twenty-one. Need to notify R-twenty am en route to the location. Over and out."

Neither of us spoke as T.J. steered up the ramp. Two trucks were parked near the booth where we were supposed to pay. T.J. flashed his badge instead of cash and we turned onto Hope Street.

"Jesus," I said.

"What?"

"A truck. A construction person has to have a truck. It didn't come up on the DMV, but maybe it's registered to her company. I don't know why I didn't think of this before."

"And I should have had her house put under twenty-four-hour surveillance."

Angrily, he switched on the windshield wipers.

"Not necessarily," I said. "If she drove her truck out of here and went straight to that bank—"

Again, the cell phone rang. I handed it to T.J. His face showed no

expression as he listened. After a minute, he clicked off. "Congratulations, Harlow. A truck is parked in her driveway. When Arlie called her
house, she answered. Now we've got to hope someone saw the truck
pull in and can pin down the time."

Even that would be useless as arrest bait. We had no warrant to
search it. And unless she'd left her business card with the body, we
still had next to nothing.

"Buckle up, Brenden. I won't be observing the rules of the road,"
T.J. said.

y the time we arrived at the scene, winds were whipping the rain almost horizontally. The criminalists had erected a small tent over the woman, but any evidence and most of her blood had undoubtedly washed away. Inside the tent a lantern was burning, illuminating the killer's gruesome handiwork.

Higgins came out of the tent and straightened. He looked grim and very tired. "Hello, Harlow. Wanna take a look?"

"Better let me go first," T.J. broke in. "Mind?"

I shook my head gratefully. Already the smell of blood, or what was left of it inside the corpse, was making me uncomfortable. I said to Higgins, "I heard it was the most vicious attack yet."

"Yeah. Let's get out of the rain."

He led me around the side of the building and in through the front doors. The bank was crawling with police officers, many of them lookie-loos. But one, a plainclothes detective, was sitting behind a desk interviewing two men. I recognized the younger of the two, Larry Swinson, the assistant branch manager who had insisted Alice Croft's murder was "an aberration." Higgins headed straight for a coffeepot on a small table. He filled a cup for himself then looked questioningly at me.

"Thanks."

He handed me the coffee along with an uncharacteristic smile. "It's a bitch, huh? You do any good today?"

"Apparently not." I sipped the coffee. Someone at the bank must have made it recently, because it was actually drinkable. "I located her former architect, nothing there, and narrowed the list of her possible gynecologists to two."

"Gynecologists?" Higgins looked skeptical.

I explained T.J.'s antiabortion theory and added wryly, "The bottom line is she got away. She drives to work in a Mercedes and leaves in a truck."

My eyes drifted to the front door, where a pale man and a sobbing woman were being ushered in by a uniformed officer. He took the woman's arm and led the couple to the rear of the bank.

"Who's the victim?" I said.

"A woman named Sally Sloane," Higgins replied. "Or can I say girl? She was eighteen. Lived in Encino, daughter of a doctor. Her high school graduation is in three weeks."

"Not Kennedy High?" Amelia Grant immediately came to mind.

"No. Marlborough, the private girls' school in Hancock Park."

Sally Sloane would make the fifth medical tie-in of the eight victims, excluding Suki Kahn's unborn child. Mary Shaunessy volunteered at a hospital, Andrea Wright worked in a clinic, Sheila Dann was on the board of Make-A-Wish Foundation, and Michelle Lloyd was a nurse. It occurred to me then that I still hadn't heard from Fred Lumley about Amelia's prescription for painkillers.

I said, "Hancock Park and Encino. This bank isn't convenient to either one."

"Go look at her, Harlow. It's quite a sight. She's damn near decapitated."

I blinked. "Her throat was slashed?"

"Butchered would be more descriptive. Go look. You won't see this kind of wound very often."

"But the other victims were stabbed in the chest and stomach," I said. "Sometimes thigh. Could it be a different killer?"

"Not unless there's someone else with a handcuff fetish. There were handcuffs. You really ought to take a look."

He was obviously baiting me. But there would be enough legitimate lookers poking their noses into the tent, and I was not trained to analyze crime scenes or wounds. I sipped my coffee and said nothing.

"Well," said Higgins, "I'm going back out." He started to turn away. "Oh, by the way. Tomorrow, roll call's at fifteen-thirty. We're going to hit the streets again. Unless, of course, we get something out of the witness."

I felt the cardboard cup bend in my right hand.

"Oh, didn't I tell you? They're interviewing the witness at Van Nuys right now."

They were in one of the interrogation rooms on the second floor. As I approached it, I passed the listening room. Five or six officers were crammed inside, and another half dozen were crowded in the narrow hallway listening to the voices that were being piped in. I wedged my way past them, rapped on the door of Room 2, and stuck my head in.

A bedraggled soul sat huddled in a chair across the desk from Marty Walters and Art Bannister. Walters glanced up and motioned me in. "Is T.J. with you?"

"No. He's still at the bank."

"Have a seat, Brenden. I may want your input."

I closed the door. The boy was wearing an oversized brown sweater and jeans. A soaking tan windbreaker hung on the back of his chair. His blond hair was slicked against his skull. His lips were blue.

"Jason, this is Brenden Harlow. She's one of the officers working this case."

The boy merely blinked. His nose was running, but nobody, including him, was doing anything about it. There was a box of Kleenex on the windowsill. As I squeezed into the one empty chair, I reached for the box and put it on the desk. But the boy was staring down at the sketch of the elusive security guard that was placed in front of him.

Marty Walters said, "Brenden, this is Jason Cosgrove. About a half a mile north of the bank he ran out of gas. He picked a good spot for it because there was a gas station across the intersection. Only he didn't have any money. He was on his way to the bowling alley on Riverside where he works the eight-to-midnight shift. So he starts walking to the bank thinking he could use his ATM card to get some cash."

I glanced at Jason, then returned my gaze to Walters. I needed to know if Walters believed this story.

"He walks up the drive-in lane, walks alongside the bank, then rounds the corner to where the machines are."

I nodded.

"Okay. The victim parked her car parallel to the curb in front of the machines. The lights are on, the motor running. As Jason rounds the corner, he sees the girl scampering down the walk back to her car. The driver's side door is closest to the bank. She's reaching for the handle when she seems to hesitate. Jason's thinking, Oh my God, she locked herself out. Then, from out of nowhere, a man appears. He grabs the victim—"

"I'm sorry," I said. "From which direction?"

"South. The direction the car was facing, the opposite direction from where Jason was standing. Jason sees this man raise his right arm. There is a flash of metal. He sees the attacker strike the girl. She crumples to the ground. Jason realizes if the man looks straight ahead, he'll see him. So Jason starts to backtrack. When he gets around to the front of the bank he hides in the bushes. A minute or so later, a car speeds out from behind the bank using the exit lane to the street."

Jason was staring at his lap. "I shoulda yelled or something," he said softly. "Then he would have stopped hitting her."

The poor kid had probably seen too many *Terminator* movies. I said, "Jason, you did the right thing."

"Our killer is blessed with near-perfect timing," Walters continued. "As Jason was running down the drive-in lane to get help, a car pulled in. Say, a minute after the killer had gone. The driver used his cell phone to call 911."

"So the killer parked his car on the other side of the bank in the exit lane?" I said. "That sounds right. He could stand at the corner of the bank, or sit in his car with the lights off. People driving out of the bank in this rain probably wouldn't even notice him."

"Normally, I doubt he'd take that chance," Walters said. "But you're right. In the rain, he'd know tire marks or bits of rubber or even fibers from his floor carpeting would be washed away."

Art Bannister glanced at his watch.

I said, "What about license plates or make of car?"

"Jason says the headlights were off," Walters answered. "But he believes it's a gray four-door vehicle. Big. Probably American made."

Marisa Ruiz, the second-grade school teacher who had withdrawn money from the same bank shortly before Mrs. Croft did, had said a man she thought was a cop had driven by in a dark four-door American-made vehicle. And Billy Croft had described the vehicle that picked him up similarly. Some shades of gray were dark and appeared black at night.

I nodded and said, "And the car that drove in after?"

"A red Beamer," Bannister replied.

There was a sharp rap at the door. Walters got up and opened it. A large man in a rain slicker stood in the hallway. Walters stepped out, leaving the door open. The two men spoke for a moment, then Walters returned and closed the door.

"That was Arlie McFadden. He found the tow-truck driver who hauled away a Saab three doors down from the suspect's place. The driver said he noticed the truck in her driveway on his way to pick up the car. He can't pin down the exact time he saw it, but according to his log, he got the call to pick up the car at six-thirty-nine and he arrived at Studio City Saab on Ventura at seven-thirty-five. He says he guesses it took him about twenty, twenty-five minutes to drive to the address on Louise. So let's say he got there at seven-ten."

The girl had been killed at seven-fifteen, according to the ATM receipt found in her pocket, the eyewitness, and the call to 911. But given that the killer had been driving a sedan and not a truck, the time frame meant nothing. And although Terry's sedan was gray, no one in these parts ever mistook a Mercedes for an American car, and besides, the Mercedes was still downtown.

"I'll check the DMV again," I said. "Find out how many company vehicles she owns, except—"

"What?" Walters said.

"I'm trying to remember what time Arlie called her house. I believe it was after eight."

The boy, who had appeared to be drifting off into his own world, suddenly perked up. "Hey, that killer was no woman. It was a man."

"Describe him again, Jason, will you?" Walters said as he sat down across from the boy.

"He was big and he was wearing a funny kind of rain hat. A black floppy one, like a woman would wear. But it wasn't a woman. He had big shoulders like a man. And he grunted like a man."

"The killer grunted?" I repeated.

"Yeah. When he struck her. He grunted, then he bent over her. And he had on, like, this sweatsuit with a zipper jacket. It was black or navy."

"And gloves?" I asked.

Jason frowned. "Yeah. I think so. Yeah, that's it. Gloves."

Marty Walters said, "Why are you hesitating? Picture again this man raising his arm. You saw a flash of metal, remember? Now, try to see the handle of the knife."

"But that's how I know he was wearing gloves," Jason said with certainty. "See, at first I thought the man was black. Then I saw part of his face, under the hat, and it was white. His face was white. So he must have been wearing black gloves."

Or she, I thought. The killer most definitely could have been a she. And Terry Smith would have had all the time in the world to drive to the bank and drive home. If we could connect her to another gray car.

I said, "If our suspect left her office after six and went out through the lobby, it's possible she may have had to sign out at the security desk."

"She would have had to sign out by six-thirty-five at the latest," Art Bannister said, "for her to get to the bank. Probably even earlier, considering the rain and rush hour. And we can't assume that she got to the bank and just happened to find her target right off. We're looking at a pretty narrow window here."

Again the door opened, and Mack Maloney walked in. "I picked off the best shots and enlarged them as much as I could, boss." He put several sheets of paper in front of Marty. "You want to look at the tape, let me know."

We all craned our necks. For the first time the killer had been captured on video. Apparently, Valley S&L had finally installed a camera. Unfortunately what we saw was pretty much what Jason described. A figure in black hacking away at Sally Sloane. Marty looked up. "Keep working on the face, Mack. It's worth a try."

Maloney nodded and left.

"All right," Walters said. "Let's get Jason home. Brenden, where's your car?"

I gave it some thought. The day had been so very long and, in my mind, indistinguishable from yesterday. "Parker Center," I said finally.

"Good. I'm going back to the office. I'll drop you. Have you had dinner?"

I looked at the detective helplessly.

I honestly couldn't remember.

I had planned to run up to Robbery/Homicide to see if T.J. was back. But once we pulled into Parker Center, I didn't have the energy. I said good night to Marty and walked slowly to my car. Did I have dinner? Um, yes. The pasta salad. I began to yearn for a real dinner served at a nicely set table. As it turned out, I wasn't even allowed to fantasize about one, because just as I was unlocking the Camaro, my beeper went off. The number was Suzy Rocklin's.

I drove down Los Angeles Street to the freeway, and after I had hooked onto the Santa Monica, I gave her a call.

"That was fast," Suzy said when she heard my voice. "You sound like you're in your car."

"Heading home, what's going on?"

"Jay and I feel terrible we haven't had you over since Jack's been gone. What does tomorrow night look like?"

I smiled to myself. "Mind reader. I was just thinking how long it's been since I had a real dinner."

"Our house then. What time's good?"

"I can't, Suzy. When you turn on the news you'll find out there's been another one."

"Shit. Where?"

"Laurel Canyon. Eighteen-year-old girl. We're going nuts." Even over the car phone I could hear Suzy inhaling a cigarette.

"You've got to come tomorrow," she said urgently. "We'll wait if we have to. Or we'll meet you somewhere. It's really important that we see you, Brenden. Say you'll try."

"I'd like to, but roll call's at three-thirty, and the way things are moving, I might not even have dinner."

"Three-thirty? Then how about lunch? One o'clock. We'll pick a place near you."

"That would work. Sure. Call me at noon. You guys okay?"

"We're fine," Suzy said. "But we miss you. Talk to you then."

It wasn't until I clicked off that I remembered to check my rearview mirror. The rain had turned to a fine drizzle, but as I got closer to the beach, I ran into a heavy fog that made driving treacherous. No one was on the freeway.

It was the kind of event the Chamber of Commerce could have sold tickets to.

I missed the eleven o'clock news, and both Letterman and Leno, in nasty conspiracy, broadcast reruns. I hated Ted Koppel. I paged through *Newsweek* and sipped a Black Russian. But horrifying images of the figure in black hacking, hacking, hacking cut through whatever I was reading. Despite my exhaustion, I was stuck in the usual place; I needed another human. So when the phone rang, shortly before midnight, I picked up the receiver with relief.

"Hi," I said.

There was silence, followed by static. Good. T.J. on his car phone. I waited for his voice.

"Like I said, hotshot, this case is too big for you."

I tensed. It was the same gruff voice that had phoned me from the zoo. Only now, somehow, the bastard had gotten my unlisted number.

I held my breath.

"I got you handcuffed, cutie cop. And your pals ain't gonna solve it, no one is. Remember the Zodiac Killer in San Francisco? Sweet dreams."

Carefully, I replaced the receiver and jumped out of bed. Either this was the work of one sick cop or . . .

My money was on the slasher.

In the den, I dug out my address book from the one desk drawer Jack allotted me. Higgins answered on the first ring, his voice uncommonly mellow.

"Sarge, it's Brenden. Sorry to bother you."

"Harlow." He grunted. "Where are you?"

Where was I? Where the hell did he think I was? I sat down and tried to collect my thoughts. "I'm home. I just got a crank call, my second. Maybe I'm paranoid, but . . . " The words stuck.

"So what's new?"

I waited a beat. "The calls could have come from the slasher."

The silence that followed made me wonder if he had been asleep or otherwise distracted. I said, "Please indulge me for a minute. This person mentioned something I believe only the killer would know." I hesitated. "Sarge?"

"Hang on, Harlow. Let me switch to another phone."

I could feel the adrenaline go to work; not cop adrenaline, but the common, ordinary, frightened kind. The bastard had my phone number.

"Sorry," Higgins said. "Tell me again."

"Maybe I'd better backtrack. Last Thursday, I got a beeper call. I was out at the time and had left the beeper at home. When I called back, someone with a gruff voice answered. I can't be sure if it was male or female. The voice said, 'You fucked up, Miss America. Leave the case alone and you won't fuck up again.' The number I called was to a pay phone at the zoo."

I waited for him to reprimand me for not going through channels to use the phone company. It didn't come. Instead, Higgins said, "He called you Miss America?" He sounded amused.

"And this same person just called me again. Not on my beeper, but to my unlisted number. Actually, we have two unlisted numbers, and Jack and I are very careful about giving these numbers out."

"What did the man say?"

"The man, or woman, said, 'This case is too big for you, hotshot.' Then—"

"He called you hotshot?" Higgins was clearly enjoying this. I fell silent. "Sorry, Harlow, go on."

"Thank you," I said formally. "He said, and I quote, 'I got you handcuffed, cutie cop. And your pals ain't gonna solve it, no one is.' He said, 'Remember the Zodiac Killer in San Francisco?' Then he said, 'Sweet dreams,' and hung up." I paused. "Sir, the mention of handcuffs . . . no one *knows* about the handcuffs."

"The task force does," Higgins said blandly. "And the task force would have your number. I wouldn't worry too much about it."

"Except, consider this. After the first phone call I realized this person had to have been waiting at a pay phone for up to an hour. It would have been between three-forty-five and four-forty-five. There was a three-thirty roll call at Van Nuys that day. Van Nuys is nowhere near the zoo."

"Of course," said Higgins agreeably, "not all of your colleagues are on the task force, but look, let's not take a chance. You want company? Is your husband there?"

"I don't need protection, but . . . okay, there is one other thing."

"What?"

I told him how a truck had twice followed me home after work. "I'm not worried this person would try to break in," I said. "But I was thinking we might put a trap on my line."

"Sure," Higgins said smoothly. "I'll take care of it. If you're worried, unplug your phone. Thanks for letting me know. Good night, Harlow."

He hung up.

Unplug my phone? That's what a cop tells a citizen, not another cop. If you believe you are communicating with a suspect, you don't cut off the line of communication.

I sat staring at nothing in the empty silence of my apartment. I could feel my heart pounding.

I chewed on a fingernail—and wondered when the caller would ring me again.

reinvented version of the old Beachcomber had sprung up on Ocean Boulevard, and when I waltzed in, only ten minutes late, Jay and Suzy were already seated at a primary patio table. Jay was agent perfect in pleated beige linen pants and a long-sleeved white linen shirt. Suzy provided the right auxiliary touch with her black-and-white polka dot backless minidress and black patent sandals. Both jumped up as I drew close and smothered me with hugs and almost-kisses.

"You look tired," Jay said.

"She does not," Suzy objected. "She looks beautiful."

"Beautiful, but tired." Jay always had to have the final word. I smiled at them. I was happy to be in a place with people who were not cops or corpses, but were ordinary real people—or at least as real as Hollywood people get.

"We ordered you a lemonade," Suzy said. "The lemonade here is divine."

"No sugar," Jay added quickly, as if fearing the health gods were lurking in the potted palms. "We checked."

"Well," I said, sitting down and lifting my glass, "here's to lemonade and old friends."

Jay proceeded to slip on a pair of microscopic black-rimmed reading glasses. He had just turned forty, but already he was having trouble with the small print. Like everything else he did, Jay made a production of the glasses as he opened the menu.

"The tuna carpaccio is a must," he announced. "If you like raw fish."

"I think Brenden, of all people, is capable of ordering for herself," Suzy chided. She smiled at him then looked at me. "So what's with this killer? Why can't the police catch him?"

"If Jack were here, he wouldn't permit me to talk about my work," I said slyly. "Let's pretend Jack's here."

Jay peered at me over his glasses.

"Have you talked to him?" I continued. "He sounds like he's not having fun."

Suzy and Jay exchanged quick glances. "Um," said Jay, "really? What's wrong?"

"Oh, the usual. He's working with Director Too Many Takes, and he doesn't like what's-her-name, the actress, and it rains all the time, and his muscles hurt." I smiled. "You know. Jack stuff."

A slim blonde in a hula skirt floated over and asked if we were ready to order.

"I haven't looked at the menu," I said, not making a move to open it. "Can you come back?"

"Have the Tiki salad," Suzy urged. "I'll have the Tiki salad."

"Tuna carpaccio for me," Jay announced and promptly removed his glasses.

I shrugged. "Okay, the Tiki," and wondered why the hurry.

After several minutes of catching-up talk, I began to sense something was going on with the Rocklins. They were going through the motions of lunchtime conversation without hearing a word that was being said. This was not like them. I wondered if they were in the middle of one of their legendary quarrels or if their edginess had something to do with me.

"So," I said to Jay, "have you talked to Jack lately?"

"In fact, I just got back from Hawaii. Last night."

"Last night?" I echoed.

Suzy cleared her throat. I looked from one to the other suspiciously. "All right, people, what's up?"

Again they exchanged glances. Suzy coughed. Jay played with his glasses on the table.

"Okay," Suzy said. "I'll start. Brenden, there's a problem. I mean, Jack is having a problem. Jay flew over because he's concerned. He got nowhere with him. We need to band together to figure out what to do."

I am not one for hedging. "Are you talking about a cocaine problem?"

Jay brightened. "You know about it?"

"I'm learning about it. How bad is it?"

"Bad," said Jay. "This isn't going to be fun. But I told Suzy I'm not going to keep you in the dark any longer."

"He did," Suzy testified. "He said that just before you arrived. Tell her about the physical, honey."

Jay nodded unhappily. I had never seen him look so . . . human, if that was the right word. I am very gifted at reading people, especially people's faces, and Jay's was always compulsively arranged in a smiling mask. At the moment, the mask had slipped to reveal genuine discomfort.

"I love Jack," said Jay, sounding apologetic.

"We all love Jack," Suzy added with passion.

I was growing increasingly anxious, not only over my errant husband but at being played as the trusting, empty-headed wife, the last on the block to know. On the other hand, perhaps I had only myself to blame for that.

"Go on," I said. "Tell me."

"Or you'll give me a lie detector test?" Jay smiled weakly.

"You know I trust you. Tell me."

Jay took a deep breath. "Okay. He's high practically all the time. I think he used to do coke now and then. But they say you just keep needing more. As you know, actors have to take physicals before they sign contracts. Jack kept putting his off. He figured he needed three days to clean out his system and he just couldn't stop the drugs."

"This surprises me," I said in a calm voice. "Considering how well he sleeps at night. Coke keeps you up forever."

"Seconal. He takes Seconal."

I fell silent. Hell, was he hiding prescription drugs, too?

"Anyway," Jay continued, "this goes on right up until he's supposed to go to Hawaii. Then he remembers there's a nurse in the doctor's office who seems really friendly to him. He convinces her to submit her own urine to the lab. She agrees. He gets a clean bill of health."

So that was why he sprung the Hawaii trip on me at the last minute. He wasn't sure he could pass the physical.

I felt my anger rising. "So what did this nurse get out of it?" I said sarcastically. "An autographed picture?"

This time Jay cleared his throat. Suzy studied her lap.

"She won a free trip to Hawaii," Jay said miserably. "I'm sorry, Brenden."

Everything seemed to stop then. It was as if the restaurant ground to a halt and all the people in it became statues. My eyelids did not blink, my blood came to a roaring standstill. "Are you saying . . . ," I whispered.

"I'm telling you this because we have to help him," Jay pleaded. "He's been screwing up on the set and—"

"Screwing her brains out in bed?"

Jay and Suzy both looked at me forlornly.

"Brenden, think of Jack as being sick," Suzy tried bravely. "We'll help. We're going to make him better, I promise. We'll be right there with you both every step of the way."

I realized then I was twisting the cloth napkin viciously in my lap.

"I've got three reservations for tomorrow morning," Jay said quickly. "Flight leaves LAX at eight-thirty. We arrive in Maui at eleven. We'll confront Jack, have an intervention. Convince him he must go to Betty Ford when he finishes this movie. We'll get rid of the nurse. Then we'll catch the three o'clock flight home. Or the red-eye. You'll only have to miss one day of work. Please, Brenden, you have to come."

Before I could say anything, the waitress arrived bearing our plates. She placed them before us, asked if we wanted anything else, and floated away.

I stared at the mound of lettuce, chicken, coconut scrapings, Chinese noodles, and mango sections.

"Well, Brenden, what do you think?" Jay asked with a heroic smile.

"Will you excuse me?" I said. "I'll be right back."

I walked calmly into the ladies' room. And then I threw up.

S e r g e a n t Higgins, his chest puffed out inside his formfitting uniform, paraded back and forth in the front of the roll call room waiting for us to settle down. Although I had arrived early, he had made no attempt to speak to me. I turned to Todd. "Do you remember the Zodiac Killer in San Francisco?"

Todd was looking as disreputable as he is capable of, which meant a sparkling clean sweatshirt and pressed jeans. This had become his Rent-A-Wreck stakeout attire.

"Sure," said Todd. "I took a course in criminal behavior in college. We spent half the semester on him."

"Never caught, right?"

"Never caught. He was a killer with a conscience, though. He always phoned in his crimes to the police."

"How many?" I said.

"No one is sure. He says thirty-seven. Every few years a new murder spree is linked to him, but his last known killing was maybe twenty-five years ago. Why?"

"I think our killer views him as a role model."

"He's been calling them in?"

Higgins was impatiently drumming his fingers on the low table in front of him. The room fell silent.

"Tell you later," I whispered.

"Afternoon," Higgins began. "Last night's homicide makes three murders in the past nine days, nine altogether. Even though our killer seems to be on a tear right now, he's never struck two nights in a row. So we're canceling tonight's stakeout. Instead, we'll hit the phones and the streets. But first we're going to hear from Detective Walters."

Marty got up from the front row and went to stand beside Higgins. He was wearing navy slacks and a short-sleeved white shirt. For the first time, I noticed circles under his eyes. He smiled briefly and began.

"We've been targeting a woman named Terry Smith. Last night's murder has dimmed our enthusiasm for her somewhat, but not totally. Sometime after two-thirty yesterday afternoon, she slipped our surveillance. We didn't reconnect with her until eight P.M. Now this is what's interesting. Prior to our losing her, she went to Parker Center to meet with Assistant Chief Ron McManus. She made the appointment a week ago. On the phone she was vague, saying only there had been increasing criminal activity near some of her construction sites. Chief McManus has known her for years and told her to drop by. But a few minutes before she arrived, the mayor phoned and asked McManus to go to City Hall for a budget conference. He told his secretary to apologize to Ms. Smith and to reschedule her appointment."

Marty paused and lifted a cup and drank from it.

"Now here's the interesting part," he continued. "Ms. Smith got to Parker Center and signed in at the front desk at one-thirty P.M. She went up to the sixth floor and spoke to the secretary. But she did not exit the building for another forty-five minutes. So, where the hell was she and what was she doing?"

"How do we know when she left?" came a voice from the back. "I mean, people just drop their visitor's badges in a box and walk out. Half the time, people don't even do that."

"Right," said Marty. "Only we had a guy on her. T. J. McCall. He saw her leave Parker Center and get into her car. We've put out the word to see if anyone else in the building saw or met with her."

"She's the only suspect?" someone else inquired.

"We got a little lucky last night. Our first eyewitness. A kid. He believes the assailant was a man, but we're not discounting Smith, who looks man-size, at least from a distance. As I said, we know where she was at eight P.M., but not at seven-fifteen, when Sally Sloane was murdered. All right, let's get to work."

I did not see T.J. in the room. Marty Walters made no attempt to speak with me.

The son of a bitch Higgins had not taken my crank call seriously.

I watched him darkly as he moved about the room dispensing assignments. When he got to us, he handed Todd a sheet of paper. "The detectives are drowning in tips. Would you mind talking to Sally's family? Find out the usual: Has she been threatened, followed, harassed? Did she have any knowledge or connections with the other victims? Talk to her friends, teachers, whatever." Higgins clapped Todd on the shoulder. "Got it?"

Todd glanced at the paper, then back at Higgins. "Are you asking me to do this, or me and my partner?"

Sometimes I really love the guy.

"Sure," Higgins said. "Take Harlow with you. See you back here at ten-thirty. Unless you find a pot of gold."

"And if we do?" I inserted.

"Then pick up the phone," said Higgins mockingly, "and call it in." He walked away.

"Jesus," said Todd. "What was that all about?" He narrowed his eyes. "What'd you do now, Brenden?"

"It's what I *want* to do," I whispered. "What's that term when a soldier shoots his commanding officer in the back?"

"It's called insanity."

"Right. Give me a minute."

I went up to the front of the room where Marty was chatting with two detectives and asked if I could have a word.

"Sure," said Marty, taking me aside. "What's up?"

"I've received two phone calls that—"

"Yes, I know. Higgins told me."

"He did?"

"Called me this morning."

"What about a trap on my phone?"

"It's on our list, Brenden." Marty smiled pleasantly. "Let us know if he calls again."

Mystified, I walked away.

I was silent in the car driving to Encino. My thoughts kept hop-scotching from the slasher to my husband. It has always been my theory, which I believe has Irish roots, that two concurrent crises are better than one. Then you can devote only half as much misery to each. At the moment, Jack was taking a back seat to the slasher. I didn't know if this was because the Jack situation was too painful even to think about, or if it was my habit to put work first. I didn't want to think about the implications of that, either. ·

"So what's happening, woman?" Todd reached for a toothpick. "You have that wrist-slashing look about you again."

I stared out the window and noticed how the rain had washed the city clean. The trees and shrubbery sparkled, and the air was so clear I could actually see the sharp outlines of the San Gabriel Mountains in the distance. I said, "You don't want to hear about it. Besides, I wouldn't know where to begin."

"Then may I remind you of our rules? Rule number one. If something's wrong that doesn't concern your partner, and you don't want to talk about it, then don't *take it out* on your partner. Remember?"

"Yes. But I forget what the penalty is."

"Misbehaving partner buys cheerful, sensitive, understanding partner five dinners of good partner's choice."

I looked at Todd. "Are you sure?"

"Yep."

"Then I have no alternative. If you liked palatable food, I might pay the fine."

"I think there's a penalty for insults, too," Todd said.

"No, there isn't. I've received two threatening phone calls that might be from the killer. You interested? Because I don't think anybody else is."

"Not really." Todd slowed to glance at a street sign. "Where do we turn?"

"Two blocks."

The toothpick somehow crossed from one side of his mouth to the other. I had no idea how he did that.

"What makes you think it's the killer?" Todd said.

T h e Sloane house was a one-story whitewashed mini mansion—or maybe it was a whole mansion, I wasn't sure of the distinction. But it occupied only a fragment of the rippling lawn. Cars filled the driveway and lined the curbs on both sides of the street. Now that I was familiar with the area, I realized the Sloanes lived less than half a mile from Terry Smith.

We parked up the street and walked slowly back to the house. It was always difficult to interview someone who had lost a loved one, but it was worst of all when the loved one was a child.

"Maybe you should deal with Dr. Sloane," I said, as we started up the front walk. "You have the nicer manner. I'll talk to anyone else who looks like a winner."

"I agree with your assessment," Todd said. "But I want you to sit in with me when I talk to Sloane. They're usually more composed when there's two of us." He nudged me. "Just don't talk."

"Jesus," I said.

"Brenden, I was *joking.*"

"No, no. See that gray Mercedes? It's Terry Smith's."

Fifteen feet across the lawn, sandwiched into the driveway, stood the Mercedes with the plates I knew by heart. I stopped.

"Do you see what I see? Driver's window open. Car unlocked."

"Like maybe she left handcuffs or a knife on the front seat?"

"I'll occupy her inside," I said. "But keep an eye out. Someone entering or leaving the house may recognize Terry's car and wonder why—"

"A dangerous black man is in it?" Todd concluded.

"Then I'd have to arrest you. How many times have I arrested you?"

I had, in fact, actually gone through the pretense of arresting Todd several times when it suited our purposes. I was good at it.

"I'll sue the department *and* your ass for false arrest and violating my civil rights," he calmly replied.

But then, Todd was good at it, too.

● ● ●

D r . Sidney Sloane and Terry Smith were among the crowd of mournful people assembled in the living room. They were standing near each other at the far end beside a table piled with food.

To my amusement, Terry slid up and introduced me to Sloane before I could do so myself. I was dressed poorly for the occasion. While everyone else had on dark, serious clothing, I was wearing my stake-out best: short pleated red skirt, black T-shirt, and those ridiculous taupe shoes.

"One thing you can say about our LAPD," Terry crooned. "When they're on a case, they're on it. Poor little Brenden. It's a wonder you get any sleep."

"I would have last night," I responded agreeably. "But a crank call woke me up."

Dr. Sloane just looked at me, but I doubt Terry's words, or mine, had registered. Terry shook her head and went, "Tsk, tsk, tsk."

"Dr. Sloane," I said, "I'm so sorry about your daughter. And I apologize for my intrusion. But we need to talk as soon as possible. Would you have a moment now?"

His wife, a small, grief-stricken woman, materialized at Sloane's side. She had short taffy-colored hair, reddened blue eyes, and appeared to be wearing no makeup. Her tailored black linen dress was wrinkled. She looked directly at me.

"Are you Mrs. Sloane?" I inquired.

"Yes. Do I know you?"

"I'm Brenden Harlow with the Los Angeles police. Forgive my timing, but I was hoping to have a word with you and Dr. Sloane."

Mrs. Sloane put her arm through her husband's. "Is that how they dress policewomen now? You could show a little respect for the family."

Her anger was predictable. Most people we deal with are angry. We don't exactly make a habit of turning up at joyous occasions. "I was called away from something," I answered nicely. "Is there somewhere we can talk?"

I glanced through the living room archway into the front hall, hoping for a sighting of Todd. Dr. Sloane broke out of his private misery. "We don't mean to be rude. Would you like something to drink?"

"A glass of water, thank you."

Terry Smith said, "I'll get it," and walked away.

I said, "Small world. Even in a city like Los Angeles. Did you know Terry Smith has come forward with some information about a possible suspect?"

Dr. Sloane blinked. Mrs. Sloane continued eyeballing me with malice. I did not go on, for I noticed, then, Todd walking into the living room. I gave him a brief wave and he came over. The Sloanes looked at him but did not speak.

"This is my partner, Officer Robbie," I said. "Dr. and Mrs. Sloane. I was just suggesting we find a place to talk."

"Yes, well, I suppose my library," Dr. Sloane volunteered. He turned and led the way. I raised my eyebrows and shrugged at Todd as we followed the couple along a white marble hallway and into the library. The walls were lined with bookshelves glamorized by a rolling set of circular steps that seemed more pretentious than practical. But it was a nice touch, I supposed. There was also a tufted leather couch, a low table, and two matching leather armchairs. Without a word, the Sloanes sat down on the couch.

"Here's your water," sang Terry from the doorway. "Shall I sit in?"

Strictly a judgment call here. But I doubted she would add much —or give anything away. I accepted the glass with a polite smile and answered, "Give us a few moments alone."

I sat in one of the leather chairs and sized up Dr. Sloane. A tall, athletic-looking man with blond hair and a ruddy complexion. His daughter had probably been in perfect health with an expected life span of eighty years. Sixty-two of them had been stolen from her less than twenty-four hours before. I had no idea how one could learn to deal with that.

Mrs. Sloane, apparently deciding it would be safer to talk to a black man than a bimbo, turned her body to face Todd. "Sally was our only child," she said. "She was a good girl."

Todd nodded with understanding. "Was it her habit to use the ATM on Laurel Canyon?" he asked. "Usually people choose the branch closest to home."

"There's a branch on Ventura," Dr. Sloane said. "Isn't that the one she normally uses?" He glanced at his wife.

"Yes." Mrs. Sloane began to cry.

"So, help me reconstruct this," Todd said. "Do you know where she had been, where she was coming from?"

"She said she was going to stay after school to work on her speech." Dr. Sloane paused. "She was her class valedictorian."

Oh shit, I thought, and involuntarily gulped. Mrs. Sloane broke down completely. But Todd, cool as always, went on. "Did she plan to come home after?"

Mrs. Sloane nodded. "For dinner. Sally was a good girl."

Yes, I thought, they always are. It's the assholes who live to be ninety.

"Gee," said Todd. "I'm mystified. She's all the way across town in Hancock Park. On a rainy night, she gets off the freeway several exits early and goes to a bank that's out of her way. Can you think of why she would have done that?"

"Oh, what difference does it make?" Mrs. Sloane fumed. "Sid, I can't deal with these people." And she got up and walked out.

Dr. Sloane cleared his throat. "Nora's distraught," he said without apology. "But I was wondering that myself. Then Nora mentioned there's a shopping mall on Laurel. Sally might have planned to stop there for something."

Right. Like a dress for a graduation she would be too dead to attend. I said, "Had Sally said anything about being harassed, followed? Were there any crank calls or callers who hung up?"

"No."

"Anyone at school giving her a problem?"

"Marlborough's an all-girls school, you know. They socialize with the boys from Harvard-Westlake, Loyola, and the Brentwood School, but Sally never complained about anyone."

"Did she have a boyfriend?" I asked.

"You know how kids are today. They seem to date in groups. I can give you the names of four or five friends she hung out with."

"That would be helpful," Todd broke in. He pulled a sheet of paper from his notebook. "Now, sir, I'm going to read you the names of the other victims and see if any of them ring a bell."

"You think there's a connection?"

"Not necessarily. But we're looking at this situation every way we can. Some of the victims had connections to hospitals or clinics. Here we go. Mary Shaunessy?"

Todd ran through the list and extracted only baffled looks from Dr. Sloane. But when he mentioned the Make-A-Wish Foundation in association with Sheila Dann, the doctor held up his hand. "Yes, I'm on one of the committees. But I only saw Sheila once or twice at fundraising events. Quite a few celebrities lend their names but don't actually participate."

"By the way," I said, "do you know the name of your daughter's gynecologist?"

"I'm sorry?"

"Was she seeing one, Dr. Sloane?"

"Why yes. Dr. Roger Bender. He's in Beverly Hills. He and Paul Bernstein have a practice together on Crescent."

Bingo. Paul Bernstein. He was one of the two Bernsteins whose offices had been closed when I was trying to track down Terry Smith's gynecologist. If he were Terry's doctor, then maybe we had something after all. Todd was looking at me quizzically. I stood and went to close the library door. "And Terry Smith," I said. "How do you know her? Is she a patient?"

"Terry? No. I'm a cardiologist. Why?"

I used Arlie McFadden's line. "As I said before, she's given us some information and it's our practice to check out people who supply us with leads. Have you known her long?"

"Quite a while. Her late husband was our architect."

"For this house?" I showed my surprise. "I thought she only deals in commercial real estate."

"Yes, Terry does. But her husband stayed away from that. He was strictly an architect, and he designed homes. He built this for us, gosh, ten years ago."

"And you've kept up your acquaintance with Terry?"

"I wouldn't call her a close friend. We tried to look in on her after Mac died. MacDonald was actually his first name. But she didn't seem receptive to our invitations. We see her around. She often jogs by our house in the evenings. I understand her firm does very well."

I looked at Todd. "Except for the names of Sally's friends, I can't think of anything else."

We waited in the library while Dr. Sloane went to consult his wife. He returned with a slip of paper containing six names and phone numbers.

Todd stood. "If you think of anything that could help us, Dr. Sloane, here's my card. But I'm sure we'll be in touch."

As we walked through the house, my mind was whirring with all the directions the case could go and the dozens of leads that could be followed.

After Dr. Sloane saw us out, I noticed the Mercedes was gone.

y car, seemingly equipped with a mind of its own, over-rode my intentions to go home and sped off in the direction of the First Base Saloon.

I decided three times I would not go to Maui with the Rocklins in the morning. I would deal with Jack when he returned, I told Suzy when I phoned her from Van Nuys Station at 8:30 P.M. Todd and I had been holed up there questioning Sally Sloane's friends by phone; none had anything promising to say. In fact, nothing promising transpired at all. Todd's search of Terry Smith's car had also produced nothing. My attempt to reach Dr. Roger Bender had ended with me leaving an emergency message with his service. Finally, at 9:15 he rang me back.

I explained we were investigating the murder of Sally Sloane and while I could not, unfortunately, share details with him, we were checking all victims for abortions.

There was a stunned intake of breath. "You want to know if Sally Sloane had an abortion?" he said in disbelief. "My God, she was barely eighteen. I doubt she ever had sex."

"Okay, here's another question." I paused. "A sensitive one."

"Concerning Sally? Look, I know her father professionally, but I know—I guess I should say I *knew*—little about the girl. I'd only seen her a few times."

"Actually," I said, taking a flyer, "this is about one of Dr. Bernstein's patients. A Terry Smith. I don't have his home phone number and I must speak with him."

"Paul's on vacation," Dr. Bender said. "He's in Italy. In an emergency, I could reach him. But he wouldn't have his records with him."

I said nothing.

"What is it you're looking for? I mean, I know Terry. But I really can't discuss another doctor's patient. Why don't you speak to Terry yourself?"

"That would be awkward."

As I had hoped, this aroused Dr. Bender's curiosity. Long ago I had learned that in star-bloated L.A., even doctors could be persuaded to reveal their famous patients' secrets. Terry was not famous. But loosened tongues were a professional habit.

"Is this about an abortion, too?" the doctor asked. "I don't understand. Terry wasn't a victim, thank God, if that's where you're going."

"I can only tell you she may have been very lucky in that regard."

"My God," the doctor exclaimed.

"I know that she is childless," I went on.

"Are we off the record?" Dr. Bender said.

I wasn't sure what that was supposed to mean. "Absolutely," I swore.

"She had a miscarriage about seven, eight years ago. She was afraid to try again after that. Dr. Bernstein talked to her many times about not giving up and how there are many, many new techniques, including implanting of eggs, et cetera. Terry said she'd think about it. Then her husband died, and I guess that was that."

"Dr. Bender, you've been very helpful. And let me assure you, Terry will never need to know that we spoke."

"I'd appreciate that," he said.

After we hung up, I mulled over what he had told me. The miscarriage could, possibly, bolster the theory that Terry might be taking out her anger on women who had undergone abortions or, in the case of Suki Kahn, had succeeded where she had failed. This did not, however, explain the murder of Sally Sloane.

At 9:40 I phoned Suzy Rocklin for the third time and told her, for the second time, that I would go to Maui. "But if I'm not at the airport, go without me if you want."

"Brenden, be at the fucking airport," Suzy snapped. "This man needs your help. He's your husband. If you were in trouble, wouldn't you expect Jack to be there for you?"

She slammed down the phone.

Two hours later I walked into the First Base Saloon looking for Cookie Randall. Cookie, I was convinced, would know what to do.

• • •

T h e assumption that last night's downpour had kept everyone housebound would explain the multitudes tonight. The bar was jammed. Even before I attempted to order a drink, I stuck my head in the poolroom. It, too, was packed, but I didn't see Cookie. I did, however, notice Dorrie Green, bent over the pool table sighting down a cue. Johnny, meanwhile, had spotted me, and several pairs of hands passed along a tall Black Russian. I took a swallow gratefully and made my way over to Dorrie.

"You take to slumming magnificently," I said.

"Hey, there." Dorrie straightened. "Give me a sec, okay? I've got these boys almost beat, and I want to collect."

Pool was a game I'd never taken up, but I could see the smoothness with which Dorrie banked her shots. Like a lot of guys I'd known, she'd probably spent her teen years hustling pool for spending money.

Grinning widely, Dorrie moved around the table to a man with a coplike build and held out her hand. A twenty was transferred into hers.

"All right, I just got my drinks paid for," she said to me. "Let's try the end of the bar."

We found some space under the TV bolted to the back wall, and we each dug out a bit of elbow space. "Have you seen Cookie?" I asked.

"Back at Van Nuys I did. She was all fluttery over a hot date. I doubt we'll see her tonight."

"You knew Cookie before?"

"For several years. We worked at Harbor together." Dorrie smiled. "I've been called plenty for late-night counseling."

"Girl troubles?"

Dorrie rolled her eyes. "More than you'd care to know. As a matter of fact, one of her exes has been stalking her. Gwen Dixon? You know her?"

I shook my head.

"She's here tonight. Probably looking for Cookie. After Cookie broke up with her, Gwen tried to shoot her."

I put down my glass. "Outside a restaurant? I heard about it."

"No, outside the Phoenix airport. They'd gone down there for gun school. I guess Cookie gave her the cold shoulder and Gwen didn't like that. So she fired off a shot from her service pistol as Cookie was walking into the airport."

"What happened?" I asked, fascinated.

"Cookie reported her and she was fired." Dorrie grinned. "Cookie has a knack for finding off-balance women."

"I'm beginning to think everyone's off-balance," I said. "Point her out to me if you see her. I'm curious what a Cookie girlfriend looks like."

"Beautiful," Dorrie said. "Over there. Girl with the waist-length blond hair?"

I spotted Gwen near the jukebox. Small, slender, with a heart-shaped face and all that golden hair. "Oh sure," I said. "She always wins awards at the sports banquets. Or used to."

"Mm-hmm. And here come Dumb and Dumber."

Squeezing in through the front door at that moment were Higgins and Adam McKay. It was a dismal development. "I take it you're not impressed with Higgins either."

"No, no," said Dorrie. "*He's* Dumb. Adam's Dumber."

"What'd Higgins do to *you?*"

"Asked me out."

"Figures."

"He said I wasn't really in his command so there'd be no problem. I said I thought there'd be a *big* problem." Dorrie made a face. "I'm so sick of these guys. They fuck you on the job then think you'd be thrilled to fuck *them* afterward. You're married, so I don't know if you have the same problem."

I finished my drink. "Want another, Dorrie?" I caught Johnny's eye.

"No. I've got to get going. Now that I've delivered my big speech I have to confess I'm seeing a detective." She smiled and put down a ten.

After Dorrie left, I enjoyed a fresh drink by myself before Adam McKay inevitably closed in on me. "Hi, there."

I gave him an imperceptible nod.

"Bad day?"

"Maybe my days are none of your business, okay?"

The affable grin vanished and for a moment he managed to look hurt. But instead of *getting it* and walking away, he planted an elbow on the bar and lowered his voice conspiratorially. "Thought you should know. Higgins was asking Johnny how much you drink."

"You don't say."

"It's not a big deal or anything," Adam said pleasantly. "Higgins isn't a bad guy, really. Years ago we worked the same division. Then I ran into him here one night. I think he's kind of lonely."

Instinctively, my eyes drifted down the bar. I watched Higgins put down some money and leave.

Adam said, "Maybe this will cheer you up."

A manila envelope thumped onto the bar. I looked at it with dismay.

"My screenplay. No hurry. But when you have a chance, I'd love to know what you think."

"Sure."

McKay smiled gratefully. "Can I pay for your drink?"

"No. Good night, Adam."

He got that toadying, hangdog look he was so good at, but he finally walked away.

Later, when the bar began to clear out, Johnny came over with a final drink. "Take your time, kiddo. This is it for tonight."

I smiled ruefully. "Sergeant's orders?"

"Mine. You got problems, take them elsewhere. I've seen too many cops wreck themselves, and they're way older than you." Johnny's eyes fell on the envelope. "What's that?"

"A script. By Higgins's best bud, Adam McKay."

"Yeah, that's a puzzler, isn't it? But then, tonight I felt like I was emcee at the Olympic Auditorium. On the undercard we had Cookie's trigger-happy ex. The main event was the almost-fight; two neighborhood guys, a Mexican and a Chinese, got into it over the Dodgers. Shows you how this country has slipped. The word *bums* wasn't used even once."

I grinned. "They probably haven't mastered the finer points of English yet."

I picked up a tabloid that somebody had left and scanned the front page. A thirteen-year-old girl, playing softball, had hit an inside-the-park home run and, as she was sliding into the plate, punctuated the event by suddenly giving birth. The dateline was China.

I wondered if this was another example of how America had slipped.

I had parked about a block west of the bar. As I walked slowly toward it, I don't know what made me turn as I passed the twenty-four-hour minimart, but something did. And when I glanced in through the plate glass windows, there was Adam McKay standing at the counter, his back to me, chatting with the Chinese owner.

I glanced at my watch. Surely Adam had left the bar quite some time ago. And then I had a thought.

Once, when I was a second-year cop, I had attracted a stalker. For three months Mr. Whoever sent me revoltingly detailed (and often misspelled) love notes at work, left flowers at the apartment building where I was then living, and phoned me repeatedly. When he began sending snapshots of myself—proving he was frequently close enough to shoot them—I asked the department for help. The stalker proved to be a nineteen-year-old kid I had helped rescue from four club-swinging Latino gang members.

But as I glanced quickly up and down Sunset searching for a black Ford Ranger, I found none.

I drove home, taking care to pay attention to the night.

T W O screwdrivers helped me to sleep most of the way to Maui. I didn't know if Jay used upgrades to get the first-class tickets, or figured what the hell, his client would pay for them, but I was grateful for the comfort and the quiet of the first-class cabin. Before we began our descent, I ate the fruit the flight attendant placed in front of me and drank two cups of coffee. I was ready.

Although not, it turned out, ready enough.

As we stepped into the lounge, I spotted Jack immediately, standing at a distance. He was leaning against a railing, one hairy leg crossed in front of the other. A colorful Hawaiian shirt hung over his tan shorts. He wore sunglasses and a smile.

"He knew we were coming?" I whispered to Jay. "I thought this was supposed to be an *ambush*."

"I spoke to him last night. I thought it would be good if he had the night to think about it." Jay bolted ahead and raised his voice. "Hey, man!"

I hung back and watched them clumsily hug. I never understood why men even bother, since they do it so badly. Suzy, in her stylish platform sandals, nudged me along. "Look like you're happy to see him," she coaxed, pasting on a too-big smile as if to demonstrate.

"He's the actor, I'm not," I said rigidly.

Jack came forward and did a better job of hugging Suzy. I dropped my gear bag on the floor and caught Jack's eye over Suzy's tousled head. He squeezed her shoulders and stepped aside.

"Hi," I said.

He pushed his sunglasses up on his head and gave me one of his dazzling smiles as he walked toward me, arms outstretched. I didn't want to be hugged, but I wasn't going to make a public fuss. His arms came around me and he pulled me to him and buried his face in my neck. "I'm so glad you're here and I'm so sorry . . . Bren?"

He straightened and looked searchingly at me. I could see now the sadness in his eyes and the strain lines on his face. "Are you okay?" he said.

"Sure." I managed a tight smile. "I'm fine."

He picked up my bag and took my hand. "Thank you so much for coming," he said.

Jack being Jack, he had managed to leave his car right at the curb. The four of us piled into the BMW and Jack started the engine. "Is anybody hungry?" he inquired.

"No," I said.

"Yes," Jay said. Suzy giggled self-consciously.

"Okay, this is what I thought we'd do." Jack checked the rearview mirror. "There's a beach club about twenty minutes from here. I've rented one of the cabanas. Sound good?"

"You're not shooting today?" Jay inquired from the back.

"No. I worked it out," was all Jack said as he pulled away from the curb.

I spoke little during the ride but Jack managed to keep my hand in his. My body was tense; I felt neither anger nor relief at seeing him, just a strange discomfort. I stared straight ahead and studied the scenery and tried to keep my mind blank. As an actor, Jack was a master at reading body language. We used to play a game. He would deliver various monologues, then he would break off and make me notice, limb by limb, how I was arranged and, thus, what emotions I was feeling or thoughts I was thinking. A blank mind and good posture would confuse him.

Jay and Jack talked idly about the movie, how it was going, when they would finish filming on the island. It struck me then—and this shows my state of mind—that the last time I had been to Hawaii was on my honeymoon. Beginnings and endings. Life's inviolate rhythms. Is this how it worked?

Jack turned to me. "Remember how we got lost that night looking for Haleakala Crater?"

Jack. The body-language mind reader. I sighed and relaxed against the seat and nodded.

Yes. I remember . . . yes.

T h e cabana Jack had rented consisted of a large, airy room with a king-size bed, walk-in closets, a small kitchen, and a great big marble bathroom. The main room was filled with rattan furniture covered with thick white cushions, and the tables were covered with vases of flowers. A silver bucket contained ice and bottles of expensive water. The refrigerator was filled with fruit and a platter of sandwiches and bowls of salad. Jack had created the perfect set.

Jay kicked off his sneakers and stretched his arms. "Do you two want to talk first? 'Cause I thought maybe we would talk as a group, get everything out in the open."

I spoke up. "Yes. I'm sure we all want to hear what Jack has to say." I sat down on a chaise longue and lay back.

Suzy provided everyone with tall glasses of ice water decorated with lime slices. Then she sat down beside a round table. Jay sat on the other side, and Jack stretched out on the bed, his arms folded comfortably behind his head.

"Okay," he said. "I've got a problem. A major problem. I do a lot of coke. Some methamphetamines. No heroin, not ever. Nothing with needles, nothing weird. Just coke. Wine, naturally." He paused. "I'm in trouble, guys."

An awkward silence followed.

Then—"That's good," Jay said eagerly. "I mean, that's a good start." He squiggled uncomfortably in his chair.

"And you want our help, don't you?" prompted Suzy.

"I do," replied Jack sincerely. "I love you all and I don't want to hurt any of you again." He let his eyes linger on me.

"So we looked into Betty Ford," Jay said.

"Jay can pull strings," Suzy said. "Get you at the top of the list. I have friends who have gone. They say it's the best."

Suzy. She could have been talking about a ski resort or where to dine in Italy. But then, the whole scenario was surreal. It was like a badly scripted movie that caused you to wonder how the hell it ever got made. And then I realized the truth of the situation. The three of them had no idea how to deal with Jack's problem or even how to stage an intervention. They were mouthing the words of the bad movies because that's all they knew to say. Of all of us, it dawned on me, I was the one with the expertise. I had learned about drugs at the academy, and afterward through refresher courses the department periodically offered. In my day-to-day duties I had dealt with pushers, overdose victims, victims of drug-related crimes, and people who had turned into animals in search of their next fix. I had been to seminars on intervention, studied reports rating which programs had the best success rate, and seen too often the disastrous results of methadone.

And it was me, the police officer *and* the wife, who was going to have to take charge.

Still, I did not. I listened attentively, uttered an occasional sentence, and kept my eyes on Jack.

After an hour, when he began sounding like a sinner who had just found the Lord, I got to my feet.

"Rocklins, go for a walk."

I went into the kitchen and put a sandwich on a plate, grabbed a bowl of salad and some silverware, and walked back into the other room. I put the food on a glass dining table and returned to the kitchen. I came back with sourdough bread, another bowl of another kind of salad, and a plate for me.

The door closed behind the Rocklins. Jack stood in the middle of the room looking helpless.

"Come and sit down," I said.

He glanced at me questioningly.

"It's okay." I smiled. "I'm gonna beat your brains out *after* I eat."

I pulled out a chair and sat down.

Slowly, Jack came over, sat down, and fastidiously arranged a napkin on his lap. He picked up half of the sandwich. "So how's work going?"

"Not as bad as my marriage, but almost."

Jack put down the sandwich. "Bren, is it possible to love someone so very much and still hurt them?"

I reached for the bowl with the cold pasta and forked some onto my plate.

"I don't know how to explain it," he continued. "It was like I was acting separately from you. But at the same time, I felt you were always there, inside me."

I picked up my fork.

"Please," he said. "I can't even imagine your not being there for me."

There for me.

I held my fork motionless.

Had it always been like that? Probably. Me babying him, always making sure he had what he needed, while I did not ask for enough. I did not know how I was before. But when you train to be a police officer and then spend nine years being a good one, you learn how to take care of others and most definitely yourself. You learn to do it skillfully, gracefully, until it becomes a habit. And as with other habits, you go about the physical motions of the action with a routine sureness, almost a cockiness, while sublimating the inner screams. For those of us who are not perfectly balanced, when the stress is too much and the screams go unrelieved, that's when we go for our guns.

I was still holding the fork. "It's one thing to cheat on your wife—"

"Bren, I've never cheated before," Jack said gravely. "And I can't say it was a whole lot of fun, if that means anything."

"It's one thing to cheat on your wife," I repeated, "and another to purposefully act to destroy her career."

I put down the fork carefully so it wouldn't clatter and then I met his eyes.

"All the nights I came home to you and talked about . . . "

But I couldn't go on. How can you explain it to someone on the outside? The way we saw drugs as this monstrous octopus with its tentacles reaching out through the city, destroying everything it touched. How could you explain that, to us, the death and the damaged families caused by drugs produced the same sick feeling in the pit of our stomachs that the ATM Stabber did?

I took a deep breath and tried again. "All they have to do, if they want, is to find contraband in my home or my car, and I'm out of there. Every time you snort, Jack, you're cheating on me."

"I'll stop," he vowed. "I know it's hard, but I will. I just need you to believe in me."

Sure. And who was going to be there to help fix me?

"Bren, I love you so much. Tell me you still love me."

If he had smiled or reached for my hand, it would have been over. But his anguished tone and pleading eyes revealed the naked despair of a frightened man. For once in his life, I suspected, Jack understood that pretty eyes and a charming manner weren't going to be enough. Not for me. But mainly, not for himself.

I took a sip of water. "Okay. I've thought about this. I don't know if I love you. I don't know how I feel about you. I do know I'm very, very hurt and I'm scared for you."

Jack lowered his eyes.

"And I do believe in you, Jack. I know you are a shrink's dream of insecurities, but you are far stronger than you think. 'Cause no one, not Marlon Brando or Cary Grant or Robert DeNiro or Jerry Seinfeld, becomes a star without tremendous strength and determination. Talent may get you halfway to success; the other half is simply not accepting any other possibility."

"Thank you," Jack said quietly.

"So this is the deal. Betty Ford would not be my first choice, but it's probably the best twenty-eight-day program around, and I know you have time constraints with the series. You will go to Betty Ford. Until you finish the program, I don't want to see you. You may not come home. You may not call. Do you understand? Promise me, Jack. Promise me now."

His face fell. This was proving rougher than he had imagined. My husband gulped.

"Promise me, Jack. No contact until you walk out of Betty Ford clean."

"I promise," he whispered. A tear rolled down his cheek. "Then what? Tell me then *what*."

"I don't know."

Carefully, I placed my napkin on the table and rose. Jack had often joked about all the stuff they had to put in his eyes if he was ever called upon to cry. Now, as he sat there looking despairingly at me, the tears were streaming down his cheeks.

I turned for the door, but my heart was pounding so furiously I was afraid that I would faint. Slowly I walked over to him and kissed the top of his head.

And then I walked out.

As usual, I had taken care of things.

A sympathetic flight attendant brought me a steady supply of vodka and made no attempt at small talk, for which I was grateful. I was a little wobbly driving home, but I couldn't say if this was due to alcohol, exhaustion, or my emotionally wrought state. I made it to the condo without bumping into anything.

I did not check my answering machine. I did not look at my beeper. I poured a Black Russian, swallowed it whole, and promptly passed out.

I awoke with stars in my eyes, a splitting headache, and the tragic belief that I would soon die. I was tangled up on the living room couch, still dressed from yesterday. My watch read 11:15. I rolled over, stuck my face in the cushions, and tried to fall back asleep.

Only—the phone rang.

I grabbed the extension on the coffee table. "Hello?" I breathed.

"Brenden? You sound terrible."

"I am terrible." I could hear children's voices in the background.

"You have the flu?" Todd said.

Right. That's what I had said when I called the Metro desk the morning before. It was the first sick day I had ever taken.

"Yes," I said to Todd. "The flu. Will you tell them I won't be in again today? I'll never make it in."

"Sure. Can I bring you something? Medicine, soup . . . " He paused. "A coloring book?"

"Finger paints," I said. "The real gooey kind."

"Have you called a doctor?"

"Uh-huh," I lied. "He said it sounded like this twenty-four-hour thing that's going around. I'll be okay. Tell Higgins I won't be in. You won't forget?"

Todd seemed to hesitate. Maybe he wasn't sure how far he should go to come to the aid of his sick partner, or maybe he sensed something else. "I'll tell him. But are you sure I can't come by? Or Lynie can. I know Lynie wouldn't mind."

"You're so nice. But really, don't bother. I'll beep you if I feel the last rites coming on."

"Well," said Todd, unconvinced, "I'll call you later."

"Thanks, partner."

As we hung up, I couldn't help thinking, See? My partner is always *there for me*.

And I had just lied to him.

In the kitchen, I drank two glasses of water, gagged down two Tylenol, and checked my beeper—nothing there. I peered down at the answering machine: three messages. I pressed the play button and leaned my elbows on the counter. The first call was a hang-up. The second produced a familiar voice. "How was Hawaii, cutie cop? Don't worry, you didn't miss anything. But now that you're back, I'm rarin' to go. Heh, heh."

With trembling fingers, I hit the stop button. Dumbly, I stared at the machine and listened to my ragged breathing. Then I rewound the tape and played it again.

First message—the hang-up—came at 1:47 P.M.

Second message—1:53 P.M.

The third message, which I let play this time, was from Fred Lumley. The name on Amelia's prescription bottle was Dr. Charles Paine. "Can you imagine," Fred said, "going to a doctor named Paine?" That message had come in at 5:31.

I slipped the tape out of the machine and considered my dilemma. If I brought it in to Higgins or Walters, I'd have to confess I had gone to Hawaii. Otherwise, the import of the message would be lost. For, other than the Rocklins and Jack, nobody in Los Angeles *knew* I had gone to Hawaii.

Except this asshole.

Who was methodically moving in on me.

• • •

T . J . McCall was sitting in a side booth at Hamburger Hamlet on Van Nuys, reading the paper and drinking a cup of coffee. He had on a windbreaker over a pale blue shirt; his hair was damp.

He glanced up as I slid in across from him. "You look like hell, Harlow. You used to be cute."

The place was too bright; I kept my sunglasses on. "You once said beep you if I need you. I need you, T.J. Badly."

He leaned back and studied me. "What you need is Alka-Seltzer." He got up and walked away.

He returned holding a glass that made noise and ordered me to drink it. Then he signaled the waitress. "Two orders eggs over easy. Skip the bacon. Buttered toast. Another coffee for me, a Coke for her."

I grimaced. The Alka-Seltzer was disgusting. "Are you still hot for our girl Terry?"

"Between a simmer and a boil," T.J. answered. "We still can't pin her down at the time of Sally's murder, which I like. Phone company records show no calls made or received at her home, office, or cell phone. The only other car registered to her company is a station wagon. We checked the people in her office. No gray sedans. We've quietly, or I hope quietly, begun talking to her neighbors. We've got her under twenty-four-hour surveillance."

"Uh-huh," I said. "So that's it?"

T.J. grinned.

"What?"

"She met Michelle Lloyd."

"And?"

"Michelle *the nurse* Lloyd. When Dr. Lloyd operated on MacDonald Smith, Michelle would look in on him. Terry didn't like it. One day, Michelle was sitting on his bed. He was communicating by writing on a pad. Michelle was laughing when Terry walked in. She hit the roof."

"So she doesn't like women. I mean—"

"Can I finish? The night Michelle was killed, Smith was invited to a neighbor's barbecue. It was called for seven. What time was Michelle killed? According to the bank receipt, about eight-ten. At eight-forty, Smith calls from her car saying a problem's come up at one of her sites and she won't be able to make it. On a Sunday night. Who works on a Sunday night? Stop frowning at me. This is how it goes, Harlow. Piece by piece by piece. Or did you think the justice god swoops down and whispers the doer's name in our ear?"

"Yes," I said, "that's what I thought."

T.J. lifted his coffee cup. "I assume you called this meeting for a reason?"

The waitress brought our food. I stared at the greasy eggs and pushed the plate away. "Okay, what I have for you is another *piece* and a great big problem."

I told him the piece first—how Sally Sloane's gynecologist and Terry Smith's were partners, and how Terry had had a miscarriage— "but I'm not sure I buy this 'female-problem' motive. It's the kind of thing men like to think up."

"They taught you *that* at the academy?"

"No," I said soberly. "Life experience."

"Uh-huh. Well, life experience will teach you this," T.J. asserted. "The motive is in the details. Piece together the evidence, the motive shines through. Not the other way around."

I drank some of my Coke. Then I told him about the two previous crank calls and the two times a black Ford Ranger followed me home. I explained my trip to Maui as a personal matter without going into it. I offered a bit of my history with Higgins as well. Then I pulled a small tape recorder out of my shoulder bag and played the latest message for him.

"What do you think?" I said. "Is it good enough to be turned over to SID?" That was our Scientific Investigation Division.

"They might be able to fiddle with it," T.J. said, "even determine if it's a man or a woman. But we're getting ahead of ourselves. First you need a trap on your line."

"I've revised my thinking on that," I said. "He/she isn't going to call from home or an office."

"No, but if we'd had a trap, we might have found someone at the zoo who remembers a person hanging around the phone there."

"So what do you think I should do?"

"Eat your eggs."

I grimaced.

"I'll talk to Walters. He's nearing retirement and he doesn't give a shit about office politics. You go home and finish having the flu."

"But I need to come clean, T.J. I need to tell them I lied."

T.J. took the tape out of the recorder and slipped it into his jacket

pocket. "Believe me, Harlow, you will. You'll set the standard for confession from now till the end of time."

W h e n I got home, I tore off my clothes, swallowed two more
Tylenol, and crawled into bed.

The sound of a buzzer pulled me out of a light sleep. In that tran-
sitional state where you think you are functioning but are not, I stumbled to the front door and hit the intercom button. "Who is it?"

"Dr. Feel Good."

I pushed the buzzer, returned to the bedroom, threw on some
clothes, stumbled back to the living room, and flung open my front
door. A moment later the elevator opened and Todd stepped into the
hall. He was carrying a large grocery bag with a smiling face on it.

"Aren't you a little early for trick or treat?"

Todd stopped at my door. "How are you, better?"

"Come in. Thank you, yes, I am."

Except for the jackhammer that had started rattling my brain again.

"Nice outfit," Todd said, walking into the living room.

I looked down at my navy sweats. I wasn't sure what he meant by
that. He continued into the kitchen.

"What did you bring me?" I asked.

"Broth with vegetables, frozen yogurt, orange juice, diet Cokes,
and in case you're really better, a frozen pizza."

He put the bag on the counter.

"What? No enchiladas?"

Todd turned around. "Brenden, go sit down."

"Oh. Okay." I went into the living room and took my usual place
on the couch. I sat cross-legged and yawned.

"So," said Todd, settling into a chair across from me, "how drunk
did you get?"

Perhaps he had seen the bottle of vodka on the kitchen counter.
But what was the big deal? "What do you mean?" I said.

"You don't have the flu, Brenden. Tell me what's going on. And
take off those damn sunglasses."

Oops. I realized then I had left them on after I got home. I had
just collapsed on the bed and conked out. Sheepishly, I put the glasses
on the coffee table.

Todd's tone softened. "How many have you had today?"

"None." I couldn't meet his eyes. "Okay, but I was thinking about having one. I'm sorry, Todd. I'm sorry I lied to you this morning. I felt bad about it all day."

"You're forgiven. Think nothing of it. But you'd better start thinking long and hard about your drinking."

"Oh come on. I got messed up for a reason. I haven't told you what's been going on." I hesitated. "Do you want to listen?"

"Of course." He glanced at his watch. "At least we can get started."

"Hang on," I said. "Be right back."

I went to the bathroom and swallowed two more Tylenol. I had to be clear with Todd, and I could hardly think straight at the moment. I washed my face and picked up a brush. But my hair hurt.

"Does Higgins know?" I said, resuming my place on the couch.

"No."

"I went to Maui. Jack's gotten himself hooked on cocaine. Friends of ours thought it would be a good idea if we went to see him yesterday. He said he's going to Betty Ford when he finishes the film." And then I began to cry.

Todd came over and sat beside me. He began rubbing my back.

"Oh. And he found a nurse to make him feel better, too," I sniffled. "I drank all the way home."

Todd squeezed my shoulder and made me turn toward him. "Brenden, I don't care what Jack does. I care about you. I'm not going to let you mess up. You didn't just drink all the way home. You've been drinking ever since I've known you."

His deep-set black eyes bore into me. He seemed so serious and so solid. Like nothing could ever break that strength.

I gulped. "I usually have a couple after work, so what? It's not like I have a problem."

Todd began squeezing my neck muscles. "What days don't you drink?"

"What do you mean?"

"Every day you have a couple, or maybe more than a couple. It's such a habit with you. Don't you understand that you're dependent on alcohol?"

Instinctively, I slid away from him. "I think you've picked a poor time to lecture me."

Todd got up and walked to the sliding glass doors and gazed out at the ocean. In the silence, I listened to the insistent ticking of Jack's grandmother's grandfather clock.

"You know," he said, "you've always fascinated me. You're tough and you're cocky and you're totally true to yourself. That's the interesting woman in you." He turned. "But there's also a balky little girl who gets in the way and throws the woman off track. It's time to get rid of that girl."

Whatever that was supposed to mean. I folded my hands in my lap and said nothing.

"Anyway, Dr. Feel Good's gotta run."

"Okay." I stood. "I'll see you tomorrow?"

"You better."

"Thanks for coming by." I closed the door behind him.

Feeling guilty for being so flawed, I decided to soothe my conscience by doing *something*. I went back to the couch and sat down. Terry Smith, Terry Smith—what did we really know about her? That her husband died and she was a sharp businesswoman. But what was her background—what was the impetus that drove her? What did the detectives know that I did not?

I went into the den and made a phone call.

Half an hour later Mrs. Johnson from the LAPD library rang me back. "She's not in *Who's Who*, Brenden, but she is in the *Who's Who of California Business Women*. Born Terry Lee Siddins in Billings, Montana. Graduated from the School of Mining and Engineering in Reno. Married MacDonald Smith in 1984. No children. Currently is president of Smith and Company Builders."

"Well that's enlightening," I said. "What about Nexus?"

"One article in the *L.A. Business Journal*. Pretty good profile. You got a fax?"

Jack did. I gave Mrs. Johnson the number and waited—without a whole lot of anticipation—for the story to come through.

It opened with Terry being honored by the Chamber of Commerce. In her remarks to a luncheon crowd, she said, "I really want to believe this honor is reflective of the business I've brought to this city, because the buildings I make are first-rate, and because of my record of finishing jobs on time, at cost. And *not* because I'm a woman. I would hate for you to see me as a role model and set quotas requiring a percentage of your contracts go to women builders. This is not necessarily a business for women. It just happens to be what I do well."

How weird. Even in a moment of glory she sounded angry. And the story only got weirder. While working toward her engineering degree, she took an internship in a copper mine. Despite her youth and sex, she soon rose to foreman. Upon graduation, she was made vice president in charge of accounting. The owner had repeatedly told her that one day she would run the mine. But when he died of a heart attack, his widow sold the company to a Colorado firm. The new president brought in his own people and Terry was out of a job.

She moved to California and spent six years working in construction. "I wanted to learn the business top to bottom," she said. "I wanted my own company so I wouldn't get screwed again."

Only she was. After marrying MacDonald Smith, she sought loans from five banks to start her own company and was turned down—for various reasons—by all. "They demanded my husband cosign the loan and I refused," she said. "I finally did get financing, but isn't it interesting? The prejudice I faced didn't come from workmen or the people who want me to build their buildings, it came from institutions."

I massaged my temples, thinking: It isn't only women she resents.

Terry Smith is mad at the whole world.

In the kitchen, I poured a glass of Todd's orange juice—and topped it off with a shot of vodka. That was when I noticed Adam McKay's screenplay on the table. I picked it up. I could at least start it. Get the gist of it, skip to the end, report back to him, and be done with it.

My suspicion was right. Adam's story was a lethal combination of the trite and the predictable. His heroine, a female cop, spent more time in a bra and panties than in uniform. Adam must have thought we *screwed* our suspects into submission.

The villain, Eddie Rocco, had a brother on the force whom he resented (heavy psychology here, I supposed). Eddie had always been a screwup. But a superstitious one. Before he went skipping off to mail his letter bombs, he dressed in a certain way. Then he put on his good luck watch, an old timepiece his father had worn when he was a railroad conductor. He ate breakfast at the same coffee shop, ordering the same meal (heavy cholesterol), before reverently driving by all of the post offices from which he had mailed his previous bombs. When he arrived at the post office du jour, he weighed his letter on a scale in the post office lobby. Then he bought three of the latest special picture stamps (for his letter bomb scrapbook) in addition to fifty cents more postage than he needed for the bomb. He dropped the packet into the mailbox outside the post office and went off to buy himself a celebratory gift.

Then he went to a movie.

The only thing of mild interest to me was how old Eddie chose his victims. They were people who had done something to affront him. A driver who cut him off on the freeway, a girl behind the popcorn counter with an attitude, a cop who had given him a ticket for speeding (swell, Adam), and a store clerk who made the mistake of refusing to let him return what he claimed was a defective shirt.

I skipped to the end, certain that Officer Underwear would get her man.

Only, that's not what the last page said. Instead there was a note in parentheses. "Brenden, I'm almost tempted to let Eddie get away with it. But I don't think Hollywood would go for that. I'm working on the last scenes now. Any clever ideas how our girl gets him?"

You bet! I wanted to pen back, She strangles him with her *Wonderbra*.

I fell asleep thinking maybe I should get one.

awoke at eight, drank a glass of juice, and went for a run on the beach. I felt great.

Later, as I stood in the kitchen waiting for the coffee to drip, Marty Walters called.

"We're putting a trap on your phone," he announced. "It should be in place in about an hour."

This would be accomplished, as I understood it, at the phone company. They would put a device called a PEN register on my line at the switching station. When a call came in, I would notify a security person at GTE and, by telling him the exact time of the call (our clocks had to be synchronized), he could scan the computerized billing records for the point of origin. I could use my answering machine to record the call.

"So T.J. gave you my tape?" I wasn't sure how to handle this. I didn't know what T.J. had told Walters or Walters had passed on to Higgins.

"We turned it over to SID," Marty answered. "But it's iffy. I can see how you would be concerned, Brenden, but we don't have much to go on."

Stretching the cord, I managed to pour a cup of coffee. "It was the second call," I said, "in which he—or she—referred to being hand-cuffed, that made me pay attention. Also the mention of the Zodiac Killer. Whoever it is could be playing similar games with us."

"I'm not faulting your thinking," Marty assured me. "I'm just pointing out that Higgins could be right. It could be some asshole in the department who has a hard-on for you."

Like who, I wondered? I couldn't think of anyone whose name went up in lights.

"But, Brenden, don't give up. If your instincts are telling you this is our killer, there's probably a reason. Think hard and think often. Dumb as this may sound, sit down, or lie down, and relax your state of mind. Get dreamy. Then think about the calls. Or think about Terry Smith. Something you may not have quite put your finger on may be lurking in the back of your mind. Believe me, I've done this a lot, and you'd be amazed at what bubbles up."

"I'll do that," I promised.

"By the way, Higgins said to tell you roll call's at three at Van Nuys. We're going out on the hunt tonight. Maybe I'm taking the message too literally, about waiting until you get back, but I'm not going to risk it."

"Right."

"Oh, one other thing. This is classified. What the message said, the phone trap, all of it."

"What about my partner?"

"Have you told him any of this?"

"I told him about the first two calls, but not the follow-homes."

"Don't say anything else."

I scratched an eyebrow. "Um, you mentioned Sergeant Higgins." I hesitated. "So you've discussed everything with him?"

"I told him we're putting a trap on your phone, if that's what you mean."

"After he heard the tape?"

There was a silence. When Marty finally spoke, his voice betrayed no emotion. "Let me remind you of something. I'm the mainframe on this one. All information highways lead straight to me. And I am a one-way street."

I smiled. "I'll remember that, Detective."

"I've got another call. See you at three." Marty hung up.

It took me less than one cup of coffee for something to bubble up. *Now that you're back, I'm rarin' to go.*

How could the person have known? Even I didn't know I would go to Hawaii until I got home that night. And then I was iffy. I had only gone so far as to set my alarm clock.

Okay. So start again.

First mention of the trip had been at the Beachcomber. Just the Rocklins and me. At some point, Jay had phoned Jack to tell him we were coming. Presumably he'd phoned from his office in Century City or his home that night. Suzy, I was sure, would not have told anyone. Eliminate the Rocklins.

Me. I called Suzy three times from Van Nuys Station. By habit, I keep my voice low when using a work phone, and besides, I was sure I did not utter such telltale sentences as "Yes, I will be on the United flight to Maui in the morning."

I had not, obviously, told Todd. At the bar, I had spoken to Dorrie Green, Adam McKay, and Johnny. But I did not mention anything about Hawaii to any of them.

The truck stalker. Forget that one, too. Who in their right mind would camp outside my apartment all night? A serious stalker would know my habits. I sleep late.

Only one slim prospect surfaced. That something I had said on the phone to Suzy at Van Nuys had drifted into Higgins's ear.

But even for me, that line of thinking was a stretch.

M a r t y Walters looked more exhausted than the last time I'd seen him, as he put his fingers in his mouth and whistled for silence. Or maybe *defeated* was the better word. The crowded roll call room came to attention. I noticed Higgins in the front row, but apparently this was not going to be his show.

"It's possible," Marty began, "that our killer will strike tonight."

A few rows up, I spotted Dorrie Green sitting beside Cookie. I didn't see T.J. anywhere.

"I know it's Memorial Day weekend, but we're past taking chances or trying to read the mind of this wacko. It appears from the increasing frequency of the murders, the killer is in a high phase. That's why we're going to run two decoy operations, Brenden's and Dorrie's. Each will target eight banks, and four of the sixteen will be visited by both women. In addition, we're putting two OPs on the roofs of ten other banks. Our chief suspect remains Terry Smith, but I'm not in love with her yet.

"Second point. The media infestation of the Valley is worse than the medfly. Larry King had a show last night with the parents of Sally Sloane and the husband of Mary Shaunessy. Geraldo's lurking. Even the *Wall Street Journal*'s in our laps. So what I suggest is this. If you encounter a reporter slithering around a bank—"

"Shoot him on sight?" someone asked.

"I wish! But the more prudent advice is to ignore them. Don't warn them off. They're like cockroaches. They'll go into the wall for a minute then scamper right back out."

"Roach Motels! Big ones!"

"Come on, guys, I'm tired, too. Now their presence may be a help or a hindrance, depending on how you look at it, because if they're getting in our way, you can bet they're getting in the killer's way. So he—she—may be forced to lie low until the cockroaches find something else to gnaw. That's good for the city, bad for us."

Marty paused. "Okay. Brenden and Dorrie, see me. Everyone else, get ready to boogie."

Dorrie was dressed in a white tennis skirt, a T-shirt, and a navy sweater. She had on tennis shoes. Sally Sloane had been wearing baggy shorts and tennis shoes. She was the first victim who had not been wearing high-heeled shoes. But I had by now grown used to mine and decided to stay with them.

Higgins joined us. "Glad to see you're well enough to make it, Harlow." He gave me a slightly minatory smile. "But then, you like to be where the action is, don't you?"

I smiled politely.

Marty finished speaking to the sergeant who would lead Dorrie's team and turned to us. "I've been worrying ever since we started this. From now on I want you both to wear protective vests. Dorrie, you'll have to button up your sweater. Brenden . . . " He frowned.

I was wearing a cotton V-neck sweater over my skirt. A vest underneath it would look obvious.

"Ray," he said, "maybe Brenden could borrow your vest."

Higgins had on one of those khaki vests with pockets. He laughed. "I can't say it's been cleaned recently, but sure, go ahead." He slipped it off and handed it to me.

"I want you to be on the lookout for an American-made four-door dark gray sedan," Marty went on. "And Dorrie, you walk too confidently. It's okay to walk fast, but there's a difference between nervous fast and confident fast, understand?"

Dorrie nodded. "It's called a ghetto stroll. You want me to do the white man's slouch?"

"There you go," said Marty. "You just solved three hundred years of racial strife."

"But not female strife," I inserted. "We're sticking close to Terry tonight?"

234 • D i a n e K . S h a h •

"Yeah. McCall's our primary. He's out at a construction site with her now. Burbank, I believe." He handed Dorrie and me each a sheet of paper. "These are your locations and your routes. We're using two different frequencies tonight, so there's plenty of room to screw up. Brenden, you're on Tac five. Dorrie, Tac eight. I'll be monitoring both from the van. I'll be four-K-ten."

As Dorrie and I walked out together, I said, "You look a little under the weather. Are you okay?"

"I think I'm coming down with something. I don't have any energy. I hope I'm wrong, 'cause my mom's bringing my kids down for the weekend and I already requested the time off."

"You'll be fine once we get going," I said, putting on Higgins's vest. "Once, you know, the adrenaline kicks in."

M y own adrenaline didn't kick in until shortly after nine. The electricity was another matter. It had switched on as soon as I pulled out of Van Nuys Station. All of us, I suspected, were humming away on 220 current; the heart beats faster when your operation is in go mode.

"Four-K-ten. Do you read?" said Marty Walters over the police frequency.

"R-fifteen. Go," I answered.

"Pull over, park, and give me a location."

"Reading you. Riverside, two blocks east of Van Nuys."

"Sit tight."

Neither Todd nor I spoke. The electricity surged a few more volts as the minutes ticked by.

It was Higgins who broke the silence. "R-fifteen, proceed to location one."

"Copy. Ten-four." No explanation for the delay. I could only assume it was inconsequential.

The first bank, a Bank of America, was a bust. As I walked up to the machines, a car with a male and a female pulled in, followed by another car containing a male. I grabbed my twenty and hit the road.

At the second and third banks, I encountered no one. As I drove to the fourth bank I began to come down from my electric high as the futility of what we were doing sank in. Wouldn't it be better, I thought, if every bank hired a guard to work from six until midnight? Maybe we'd lose the killer, but we would save lives. Then again, I mused as I turned left onto Ventura, maybe not. The killer could simply move on—to the West Side, to Santa Monica, or south to the beach communities. Not that Operation ATM had been a total bust: according to our statistics, bank robberies and muggings at ATMs across the city were down forty-five percent over a year ago. Even robbers didn't want to risk running into the stabber—or us.

The fourth bank, a Coast Federal on Ventura, stood across the sprawling parking lot from the Great Western Bank where Amelia Lynn Grant had been murdered. Only a few cars were parked on the western side of the lot where I entered; most were grouped around the Ralph's supermarket on the Laurel Canyon side and near the Sav-on drugstore, between them, where Amelia had stopped.

I pulled into a space about thirty feet from the bank's single teller. Before I left the car I studied the backs of the buildings to the west. Two of them were banks. The closest one had its Readytellers on the side of the building along the drive-in lane from the street. Since there were no lights on the other building, I assumed the second bank's machines were on Ventura. Moving west along the boulevard for the next half mile were more banks. The killer could simply hang out right here, moving from one bank to another, waiting for the perfect victim to pick off.

Two tall standards with high-intensity lights illuminated my area of the lot. As I walked toward the ATM, I noticed a uniformed security guard languidly patrolling outside the drugstore, two buildings east of Coast Federal. He was walking away from me now . . . Terry Smith? "Check out security guard," I said softly into the mike under my sweater. "Just for fun."

I stepped up to the machine and inserted my card. As I brought my eyes up, I noticed a rectangular black glass that reflected what was behind me. A car coming in from the drive-in lane on Ventura rounded the corner as I punched in my code. It stopped and the engine died. I hit the WITHDRAWAL option. A door slammed.

I pressed $20 and checked the black glass. My own eyes stared back at me.

Footsteps sounded distinctly.

I knew the lot was crawling with cops. They could be on the roofs of the single-story buildings, in the spaces between buildings, or crouching in parked cars. Although they would have to reveal themselves to communicate with me, I could use our prearranged signal. If I needed backup immediately, I would utter "Damn" into the tiny mike I was wearing.

The money panel slid open. Now I could hear breathing behind me. Again I glanced up. But the person had to be standing to my left, out of range of the black reflective glass. I collected the twenty and my card with my left hand, and then I turned slowly to my left, presenting my left arm to the attacker, leaving my right hand free to draw my gun.

I stared into the face of Terry Smith.

In the moment it took for the brain to register and the tongue to speak, I saw that she was wearing a black zippered sweat jacket, sweatpants, and running shoes. But it was the hands that made an impression. In black leather gloves.

"Terry."

She was not wearing any makeup, and her pale face looked younger and softer. Her gloved left hand clenched, unclenched.

She said, "You know, Brenden . . . I can call you Brenden? I'm intrigued. I think *you* think I'm a suspect."

"You do?"

"Well, here I am and here you are. It makes me wonder—are the police following me?"

"Aw, go on," I said. "I just needed some cash. And I happened to be passing my bank."

"Surprise, surprise."

I glanced past her shoulder. The drugstore security guard had vanished. "You're surprised that police officers need money? Hey, in today's economy, graft doesn't go as far as it used to."

The knife would be under her jacket or in an ankle sheath.

"Just out of curiosity," Terry said, "how many female serial killers have there been?"

"How many?" I repeated.

"I don't mean crazy women who kill all their husbands. I mean Jeffrey MacDonald types or the Son of Sam or the Zodiac Killer in New York." She cocked her head and looked at me expectantly.

Cool, cool customer. The Zodiac Killer. Just like that. "Probably not many," I replied. "As a matter of fact, I can't think of one."

Who would drive around on a warm night wearing leather gloves?

"You mean," Terry said delightedly, "*I* could be the first?"

She laughed and stepped around me to the machine. From her jacket pocket she withdrew a card and inserted it. Still with the gloves on. It struck me then that she didn't need to use an ATM. There were two banks in her office building.

"Since I assume you don't carry a weapon," I said, playing her game right back, "I'll wait until you're finished. Besides, I want to ask you something. My husband's always searching for the perfect driving gloves. I've bought him two pairs and neither will do. Is that what you've got on, driving gloves?"

Terry didn't answer. She worked the machine silently. Then, as she retrieved her money, she turned and said, "Driving gloves don't have fingers, dear. They're used to protect the palms, from blisters I suppose. If you ask me, they're an affectation." She paused and looked at me carefully. "You did ask me, didn't you?"

"Right. Well—take care."

I was about to move away when, suddenly, a van came careening around the corner at a high speed, forcing me to step back. Brakes screeched and a man in a sport coat and tie jumped out, brandishing a microphone.

"Ladies! Wait up! Ted Tissler from Channel Three. Aren't you scared to death to be using an ATM?"

My heart was pounding. Jesus Christ. He thrust the mike under my chin as a camera poked out of the van window. "'Course, we're scared," I said with a loopy grin. "That's why we came together. Safety in numbers, right?"

I took Terry's arm and forced her to walk away with me. I didn't want her telling this creepo I was a cop. "You didn't want to be on TV," I said sweetly, "did you?"

"I think I may have underestimated you," Terry Smith said.

" S h e ' s like a spider, spinning her web," Marty Walters was saying. "I can't remember a serial killer who worked such a small portion of the city. Can you?"

"Maybe she wants to save on gasoline," T.J. said. "She probably uses premium." He sounded cranky.

They were sitting in the borrowed homicide office at Van Nuys Station, studying a large map of the Valley that hung on the wall. Each of the victims' homes had been circled in black; the crime scenes were circled in red. I stepped into the room.

"Can I say something?"

"Yeah," said T.J. "How about hello?"

I smiled and pulled up a chair. "Hi."

"You're looking cheerful," Marty said sourly.

"I'm actually suicidal. Now can I say something?"

No one answered me. We had shut down my decoy operation on the theory that Terry Smith had gotten her jollies for the evening, *if* she were the killer. Also, she would have figured out I was casing ATMs, and we didn't want to risk her busting our operation by following us around.

"Okay. I don't know where Terry Smith was going or coming from. But tell me why she picked *that* bank and happened to arrive when I did. Why does she even go to ATMs when she has two banks in her building? And why was she dressed like that—in killer clothes, if you ask me."

"Women care about fashion," T.J. said. "It's important to them."

"Three First Names Junior said the man in the alley wore a black sweatshirt with a hood, and Sally Sloane's eyewitness said the attacker wore something black with a hood. So please answer my questions." They were beginning to annoy me.

"Yes, ma'am," T.J. barked. "Apparently she does her business transactions with the Bank of America in her building. Her personal accounts are with the Bank of America on Ventura just east of Woodley. But she also has an account at Coast Federal. I just got off the phone with the branch manager. She's had that account for five months."

"And she just happened to be there when I was?"

"I don't know how else to explain it," T.J. said. "She went straight home from the construction site, put on the sweats, went for a run, went into the house, came out, and drove to the bank. Then she went home again. What can I tell you?"

"I think she's very clever," I said. "I think she's *enjoying* this. She even came right out and asked me if she was a suspect. She wanted to know if she'd go down as the first female serial killer in history. She thought it was pretty funny."

"She's not behaving well at all," said Marty glumly. "I'm patiently waiting for her to screw up, just once." He sighed. "I'm beginning to think she doesn't love me after all."

"You know women," said T.J. with authority. "They're fickle. But she'll come around. Trust me."

"Um, do you think you could save your female bashing for later? I'm sensitive."

T.J. grinned.

"And what about Terry's lost forty-five minutes at Parker Center?"

"She was right under our noses. Down the hall in Bunco/Forgery."

"Bunco/Forgery?" I repeated.

"Yeah," said T.J. "She struck up a conversation with a detective—Robbins, Roberts? She asked if he knew any cops who would moonlight doing security for her. He said he'd check around and gave her his card. But she never called back."

"Oh, right," I interjected. "She leaves the sixth floor, gets off on three—just down the hall here—and spends forty-five minutes talking to some guy she stops in the hall? Besides, you'd think someone in Terry's business would know people who work off-duty gigs. It's not like they're not listed in the yellow pages."

Marty drummed his fingers on the table. "What I think we need is to devise a new game plan. But damned if I know what."

"Maybe this will help you," I said. "Suppose the victims are not her primary targets, and babies, or lack of them, is not her motive. Maybe she's targeting the banks." I went on to explain about the article.

"Personally," said T.J., "I like the female rage angle better." He winked at me. "It's more genetically credible," he said.

I left them spitballing. Terry Smith was presumably tucked into her house in the care of the morning-watch baby-sitters. I stood in the parking lot, hoping to find one for me.

"Sorry, Brenden. I love you dearly, but now I have a reason to go straight home." Cookie had a cat-ate-the-bird grin all over her face.

"Sure," I said. "Well—have fun." The thought of going home to a silent apartment made me sad. I searched fleetingly for a glimpse of Dorrie Green. I didn't know what she drove.

Cookie hesitated. "Hey, are you okay?"

"I've been better."

She looked at me with concerned eyes. "Jack?"

"A little Jack, a little work, one of those days. Go. Run along."

"First you need a hug."

She was very tall and very strong and I got a bit squished. I stepped back and laughed. "Well, that did it." And I danced a little jig.

Cookie shook her head. "You're funny."

"Night."

"See you."

I stood by my car feeling somewhat lost. I looked up at the sky and was surprised to see a sprinkling of stars. Heavenly stars were sighted far less often in Los Angeles than human ones, which said something meaningful about the town. I had never figured out what.

I switched on the ignition, put on Bonnie Tyler's "It's a Heartache," and drove grimly into the night.

I t didn't take long for the night to come alive.

I was still on Van Nuys, heading for the 101, when I sped through an intersection after the light turned red. Naughty girl. A vehicle traveling several car lengths behind me had also raced through, setting off a bunch of horns. Given the speed of the vehicle, I expected it to pass me on the left. Instead, it slowed and, like an obedient puppy, fell into step behind me. I swung onto the freeway—and so did the black truck. I had my baby-sitter after all.

I considered calling the California Highway Patrol or Van Nuys to get someone out here to pull the truck over. But I knew how long it would take to get action at this time of night. The only way to be certain of a speedy response was to put out a Code 3—*officer needs help*—but that would produce a stampede of black-and-whites and a certain reprimand from the department for me.

I cloverleafed onto the 405.

The truck fell back several more car lengths. It could afford to relax. It knew exactly where I was going. So I played with the idea of taking the truck on a surprise road trip, but I tossed that idea, too. I wanted to get it on my turf.

I slowed to fifty-five and reached under the seat for my 9mm. I snapped off the safety and laid it on the passenger seat. From the glove compartment I removed a pair of cuffs. It was only then I realized that I had forgotten to return Higgins's vest. I slipped the cuffs into one of the pockets.

As I veered onto the Santa Monica freeway, I again wondered how Terry Smith had managed to turn up at Coast Federal when I did. Coincidences have never been a big selling point for me. The only logical conclusion I could reach was that she had followed me from Van Nuys Station.

I checked the rearview mirror. The truck had closed in by several car lengths. This was good. I didn't want to lose it now.

But she couldn't have followed me, because T.J. was following her, and he would have warned us. Maybe it was the simple result of our presence at twenty-six banks. If she was casing her next stalking ground, the odds were not impossible that she would have stumbled onto one of us. Was it simple chance that she had stumbled onto me?

I exited at 4th Street, but instead of turning onto Idaho, I drove on to Montana and turned right. At 7th, I made a quick U-turn. I slid up to the curb in front of an ice cream shop, shut off the engine, and slipped the semiautomatic into my shoulder bag. Inside the shop, I debated the flavors, finally choosing a mocha-and-vanilla combo. As I left, I noticed the truck was parked across the intersection on the eastbound side of Montana.

I started walking west. I was gambling that my stalker, thrown off by my behavior, would get out of the truck and follow me on foot.

At Ocean Avenue I waited for several cars to pass before I quickly crossed the street. The grassy promenade above the beach was spottily lighted, but even at this hour, joggers were out, and some of the benches were occupied. I turned right and began walking north. After a block I came to an empty bench. It faced the ocean. I put my shoulder bag down and the yogurt cup, but I remained standing, facing the street.

The Ford Ranger appeared at the corner of Ocean and Montana and, without hesitation, turned right. I put my foot up on the bench, pretending to tie a shoelace, and watched the truck drive slowly past. The tinted windows were raised, obscuring whoever was behind the wheel. I continued walking. The truck, now ahead of me, moved into the left lane. I slowed and gauged the distance to a pair of fat palm trees.

The truck made a U-turn and—trying to time it to when I was in the driver's blind spot—I slipped behind the first tree. I watched the truck pull into one of the diagonal spaces that lined the promenade. The lights went off, the engine died. A moment later, a door slammed.

I caught just a glimpse.

She was wearing black. No gloves, but now a baseball cap. And then, as she came around the back of the truck, I saw the dog. A medium-size brown dog on a leash. She seemed to deliberate before starting to walk in my direction. I pulled my head back and held very still.

The moist salty air blew gently off the water, rustling the fronds of the tall graceful palms. Soon the tinkling of the dog's tags could be heard as she passed several yards from me, but neither she nor the dog broke stride. After a moment I turned to my left and watched her continue walking north. From behind, and in her running shoes, she didn't look that big anymore. Instinctively I reached under my skirt and touched the little .380 Sigma.

I'd shoot the dog if I had to.

I gave her a good thirty feet before moving out. I kept to the grass, backtracking until I had passed her truck. Then I cut over to the street and slipped the 9mm out of my bag.

It took her ten minutes to decide she had lost me. I heard the dog tags and then the footsteps. When she came around the front of the truck and inserted her key into the door lock, I rose from my crouch position behind the car parked to her left.

"Raise your hands," I called softly. "There's a gun pointed at your head."

She was cool. She didn't jump or drop the leash or instinctively turn toward the voice. She brought her hands up slowly. And I moved in right behind her.

Shit. What the hell was going on?

"Keep 'em up and turn around. You're going to be looking at a police officer."

And when she did, I said, "Who the hell are you?"

TWENTY-FOUR

P lease, I'm not armed."

Tentatively she moved her right hand an inch or so and carefully pulled off the cap. A mound of silky blond hair cascaded to her waist. "I'm Gwen Dixon. And yes, I've been following you."

I lowered my gun and started to slip it into my bag, but then I didn't. This woman had fired a shot at Cookie and may have escaped from the Norwalk State Hospital for the insane for all I knew. I held the gun at my side. "You may lower your hands," I said formally. "And then, if you don't mind, the dog goes in the truck."

"Sure."

She opened the door and ordered the dog inside. He bounded in expectantly, ready to head for home. Gwen closed the door and leaned against it. She had one of those flawless Catherine Deneuve faces that I always found somewhat cold. Her eyes were greenish hazel, the color of mine.

"I hope we can work this out," she said. "If you report me, I'll lose my pension."

"You were fired. You don't have a pension."

"No, I do. I was dismissed with cause. I pleaded stress and I had a good lawyer."

"I hope you kept his phone number." I leaned against the neighboring car. "I want to know why."

She took a small breath. "Cookie."

"She isn't here."

"I thought maybe you were going to meet her. When you headed this way, I thought you would be meeting her somewhere else."

"Somewhere else?"

"She lives in Los Feliz."

"And what is the point of all this?"

"I don't know, Brenden. I saw you two hugging in the parking lot . . . "

"What's the name of your lawyer?"

"Why?"

"Don't try to tell me tonight was the first time you followed me. You've done it before. You know exactly where I live."

She put her hand to her mouth and nodded. Her hand was small, her fingers delicate. "Okay. I thought you two had something going. I'm crazy. I can't stop thinking about her."

She could have been crazy, I didn't know her. She certainly wasn't stable. It made me wonder how deeply the department dug into people's backgrounds anymore. Given our recent recruitment problems, maybe they took any comer with four working limbs. I turned my thoughts back to the matter at hand and how her little pieces were not adding up. I said, "How did you know about Hawaii?"

Her eyes widened with surprise. If she had been smart, she would have said she didn't know about Hawaii—what was I talking about? But I must have caught her off guard.

She laughed nervously. "It just goes to show how crazy I am. I'm working as a bodyguard for a record company exec. I drove him to the airport for his flight to New York. I saw you and I was curious. I had this sinking feeling you were going somewhere with Cookie. I followed you to your gate."

"Is that so."

"Yeah. You know you're good. I had no idea you spotted me."

"Uh-huh. And what about the phone calls?"

Again, she registered surprise. Only this time she played it smarter. "What phone calls?"

"I'll want the name of your boss, too," I said.

"No, please. Look, Brenden, I swear I'll cut this out. I've been seeing a therapist, but I need this job."

"And you need your pension. So many needs. Why the phone calls?"

She shook her head. "I don't know what calls you're talking about."

"You must still have friends in the department, or friends at the phone company. That's how you got my number. I haven't a clue how you disguised that innocent little voice."

"I swear I don't have your number. Sometimes I call Cookie, when I know she isn't home? Just to hear her voice on the machine. But I've never called you."

The dog was scratching at the window and I was suddenly aware of how exhausted I was. All of the adrenaline rushes of the night had drained me. I said, "If there's one more call or one more time I see you around, I will report you big time. Do you understand, Gwen Dixon? Are we clear?"

"Yes. I'm sorry, Brenden. Thank you."

She climbed into her Ford Ranger and started it up.

I slipped my gun into my bag and watched her drive away.

L A P D kept its staff psychologists in a holding pen on the fourth floor of a nondescript building in Chinatown. A *bank* building. Which figured. Everywhere I went, banks. I put my car in the basement parking structure and rode the elevator up.

Room 409. Despite being on the department nine years, I had managed to escape the psychologists' long reach and psyche-probing intrusions. But now, it had dawned on me, I could use some help. I twisted the doorknob and entered.

A woman seated behind a glass partition parted the panels and looked at me hopefully. "Yes?"

"Brenden Harlow," I said. "To see Ms. Lacy."

"Great. I'll tell her you're here."

A moment later the same woman opened a door and wagged a finger at me. I followed her down a short hall. She jerked her thumb. "In there."

Immediately, the office gave me the creeps. Heavy drapes drowning out the light, arrangements of dried flowers, a big comfy couch and—Ms. Lacy herself, standing over a desk. She was thin and was dressed in a proper gray skirt and white silk blouse. Her dark hair was jaw length and swung with her every move. She looked up and removed her reading glasses. "Brenden? Carolyn Lacy. Please sit down."

She came around the desk and immediately sank into a leather BarcaLounger, leaving me the couch. It had too many pillows. I shoved several aside and noticed the box of tissues on the coffee table between us.

Ms. Lacy smiled. "How are you feeling today?"

I decided to cut to the chase. "I'm fine. In case my message wasn't clear, I wanted to pick your brains about a suspect. A forty-four-year-old woman named Terry Smith."

Ms. Lacy looked at me raptly.

"At the moment we're looking at her as the ATM Stabber. She's a large woman, able to wield a knife, and she's in construction. We have a possible motive, though it's still shaky. I'm trying to get inside her head."

Carolyn Lacy laughed. "Psychologists are not mind readers, Brenden. We study behavior, form theories, and hope we're right some of the time. In this office we study *police* behavior. We're here to help you with *your* problems."

"Great. Because at the moment, Terry Smith *is* my problem. Wanna hear?"

I told her about Terry's miscarriage and wondered if, in the mind of the wrong woman, such a tragedy could lead to mayhem. I told her how I thought Terry was playing mind games with me—a sign of a bold killer's daring? In fact, I talked about Terry Smith until I was blue in the face, but Ms. Lacy just kept on looking at me. Sometimes she nodded.

"So," she said at last. "How are *you* feeling about all this?"

"Like I'm carrying around nine dead bodies in my head. Like I want all this to be over." I was exasperated. "Like maybe if you'd help me here, it *would* be."

A nod. "I understand. When you get involved in a case like this, it takes hold of your life. It obsesses your every waking moment. You want to be careful, Brenden. You need to make sure you have some balance in your life. It's easy to slip over the edge."

"And Terry Smith? What made her slip over the edge?"

Ms. Lacy shook her head. "Without talking to her, I really can't speculate. But to specifically target women who may have had abortions doesn't fit the profile. Serial killers act impulsively, and from my understanding they don't target people they know. They may target a type—people who fit a certain physical description. There may be something about the women's appearances that she reacts to or . . . " Ms. Lacy paused. "She may be angry at banks."

"Well, that narrows it down to anyone who has ever *dealt* with a bank." Then I caught myself. "Yes, that is a possibility. But why take out her anger on the customers?" I asked.

"It's a way of getting back at the banks, isn't it?"

"You mean like the postal worker who walks into the post office and randomly shoots whoever's around?"

"Not exactly. That's another type. More hair-trigger unbalanced than psychotic. The sociopath typically suffered some deep hurt early on and buried it. Something entirely unrelated to the inciting act can set him or her off, but they rarely attack the person who caused the hurt. They attack the symbol. For instance, a man who was abused or mistreated by his mother will attack women who remind him of his mother. But he won't attack his mother."

"So Terry Smith—"

"Let me ask you something." Ms. Lacy looked at me meaningfully. "Do you take sleeping pills? You might want to stop. They can cloud your thinking."

"I don't take sleeping pills."

"And watch your indulgences. If you're prone to overeating, smoking or drinking . . . "

I stood up and produced a smile. "Thanks."

Ms. Lacy followed me to the door. "Feel free to set up another appointment. I want you to know I'm always here."

Since I was in the neighborhood I decided to stop at a place I knew for dim sum. Although Chinatown is always bustling, I found a spot on the street and parked. But before I went in, I picked up my cell phone and dialed Cookie Randall.

"Hi. Got a minute?"

"Of course," Cookie said. I had never called at her home before. "Is anything wrong?"

"You tell me what you think."

I gave her a rundown on the Gwen Dixon confrontation, which had occurred two nights before. Yesterday, Memorial Day, I had "balanced" myself by vegetating at the beach. I told Cookie about the previous follow-homes but left the airport out. "The question is," I said, "how crazy is she?"

There was a considered pause. Then—"I'm crazy, you're crazy. Gwen isn't crazy."

"Meaning?"

"Shit, Brenden, you've got me in a spot. Give me a minute to think about it."

"I don't understand."

"Can I call you right back?"

I gave her my car phone number and watched the Chinese women with their string shopping bags and black parasols moving in and out of stores with names I could not read. Five minutes later, the phone rang.

"Okay," Cookie said. "You'll understand my dilemma in a minute, and yours, too. I'm going to have to reveal confidential information, so I need you to say you'll never divulge what I tell you. Ever. You have to swear on your badge and your gun."

"Jesus," I said. "All right. I swear."

"Gwen Dixon and I did have a thing. But she's not the rejected lover she claims. She's a very smart, very tough cop. Put that together with her looks and you can see her potential."

Potential? For what? "Keep going," I said.

"We weren't together that long and, frankly, she was the one who broke it off. Gwen's bi anyway. She's always had friends in high places."

"Uh-huh," I said.

"Someone somewhere in the department decided she belonged in Internal Affairs. Usually when they want to transfer a person into I.A. quietly they just remove their name from the LAPD roster. The department's so big most of us don't give it a thought when we lose track of a colleague, right? But Gwen was too well known to disappear like that. So they staged the thing with me at the airport to give them a reason to fire her. Only she wasn't fired. She was moved into I.A. for sensitive undercover work."

"Aw, go on," I said.

"I had to be told because I became part of the plot. We're still friends. We keep in touch. Not often, but she's there."

"I've never heard of such a thing," I said flatly. "You make us sound like the CIA."

"I.A.'s job is to spy on us. I guess you could say that."

"Hold it. Are you telling me she's spying on me? Officially? For what?"

Cookie sighed. "Brenden, I don't know. And Gwen would never tell me. You done anything bad lately?"

"Higgins could write a book."

"Then don't worry."

I couldn't believe this. I mean, there were times when I felt the department didn't do things as well as it should, but I never thought it was this internally devious. "They actually pretend to fire people, but don't?"

"It was news to me, too," Cookie conceded. "I suspect it doesn't happen very often."

"But it does happen, right? Now I'm going nuts. What about Adam McKay, for instance? Why's he hanging around us? Is he working I.A., too?" It would fit, the mealymouthed creep.

Cookie laughed. "You *are* getting paranoid. Before you go further, I want you to know I'm not working I.A. and never have."

"Seriously, what about McKay?"

"Forget it. He got baton happy a little too often."

"What do you mean?" I was dubious. He didn't seem heavy on the testosterone.

"I mean, that's why he was fired."

"Wait. He said he was *retired*."

"Johnny told me the story. He had all kinds of complaints against him. One was for beating a kid in South Central. Turned out he picked on the class valedictorian. Another time he got overly excited at one of those Operation Rescue rallies. I think they brought him up before a Board of Rights on that. Oh, and he shot some people, too. You know the story. Sees a guy reaching into his pants or holding something in his hand. Boom, boom! And then it turns out to be a flashlight?"

"Did you say Operation Rescue? When?"

"Mm, let's see. It was a while ago. Maybe eight years? Talk to Johnny."

"I thought you knew *everything*."

"I know to talk to Johnny. Gotta run, cutie. I'm gonna be late."

I sat there thinking. Maybe Ms. Lacy was right. Maybe I was already over the edge. But if Gwen Dixon didn't work for a record company executive, what the hell was she doing at the airport? At that hour. I could think of only two possibilities. She had driven someone to the airport and had, by chance, seen me at the Honolulu gate.

Or I was under twenty-four-hour surveillance.

T h e "War Room" was deserted when I walked in, shortly after one. Marty Walters had called that morning and asked me to drop by, saying he had a one o'clock meeting with the chief but it wouldn't last long.

The desks were piled high with eight fat murder books and mounds of additional clue sheets and reports. I cleared a space and sat down. Higgins? Had Higgins contacted I.A. about me? Was that what McKay was trying to warn me about? Oh man, I thought, this case must be really getting to me.

I studied the messy room, cluttered with all the debris that latches onto a case—like barnacles. A sheet of paper tacked to the bulletin board listed the phone numbers of the victims' families. I got up and untacked it. Then I sat down and dialed Frank Shaunessy.

A recording told me I could leave a message or try him at his office. I scribbled down the number he left and called it.

A man mumbled, "Shaunessy. Uh, sorry, I have my mouth full."

"Sorry to interrupt you," I said. "This is Officer Harlow with the Los Angeles police. Do you have a minute, Mr. Shaunessy?"

"If you don't mind sharing it with my lunch."

He sounded less angry than when I had visited him, but maybe it was merely the muffling sound of the food. I said, "I wonder if you could help me with something. You mentioned an abortion-rights rally and a cop beating a citizen. Was there an Operation Rescue demonstration going on at the same time?"

"Um, yes." I could hear smacking sounds. He seemed in no hurry to answer. Maybe his lunch took precedence over another bothersome cop. And then he said, "I can't remember who announced their demonstration first, but the other side came and the police were there. Supposedly to keep the peace."

"Would you remember the date, or at least the year?"

"Don't you people keep records?"

"It would be helpful if we could narrow the time frame, Mr. Shaunessy."

"Well, it was fall, maybe October. And it would have been on a Saturday. Say eighty-eight, eighty-nine?"

"Okay. Tell me, does the name Adam McKay ring a bell?"

The smacking sounds stopped. "It sure does. That's the son of a bitch who beat the guy, isn't it?"

"And you and your wife reported Officer McKay?"

"Wait. What is this?" Sounding suddenly leery.

"Just a few more questions, please. Tell me what happened when you tried to report McKay."

"Mary had seen his name on his uniform. I think she called headquarters and they gave her quite a runaround. Like, 'Do you know how many McKays there are, lady?' Well, she had gotten his badge number, too, so they told her to go to West Valley Station. She filled out some kind of a report, and that was the end of it."

"So you didn't get involved, it was just Mary?"

"What are you saying? Are you accusing me of something?"

"No sir, not at all. Mary sounds like she was a very concerned person. She took the time to report a police officer who hadn't even done anything to her. It isn't always easy walking into a police station to report a cop."

"Yeah. Mary was like that." His voice softened. "When she took on a project, she was relentless. She must have got four, five others who witnessed the beating to go in with her."

"Do you remember who?"

"I didn't know them, they were strangers. So what's going on? Is this guy still out there smashing people's heads?"

"That's why I wanted to call you, Mr. Shaunessy. I think he's going to be fired." In truth, I didn't know what to tell him. I wasn't even sure why I was making the call. It was another sign of my obsession, I supposed, that I needed to be doing something every minute. One day, when it was appropriate, I would call Frank Shaunessy back and explain.

Over the next fifteen minutes, I reached Andrea Wright's mother and George Croft. Except for traffic violations, neither could think of any dealings the deceased had ever had with a police officer.

I went down to the lobby snack shop to get a Diet Coke.

It was just a long shot anyway.

" T h e problem is she knows we're watching her," Marty Walters said. "So she's not going to do anything. And I'm scared to death to take her surveillance off and rely only on the stakeouts."

"Maybe we need to plant a story saying we've got a suspect in custody," T.J. weighed in. "Or we could fabricate a new sketch and say, Anyone have information?"

I sipped my Diet Coke and said nothing.

"By the way," T.J. said, "Sheila Dann had two abortions. Andrea Wright had one. None for Michelle Lloyd, Suki Kahn, Mrs. Croft, or Amelia Grant. Or Mary Shaunessy and Sally Sloane. At least that we know of."

"So much for female rage hormones," I remarked. I was still mad that they weren't taking me seriously. I thought the banks motive looked good.

Marty grimaced. "Could we conduct the war of the sexes, like, in another life? I'd like to get down to business here."

"Actually," I said, "I think T.J. may be right. If you want to give credence to sex-specific tendencies, then I may have a new candidate to play the killer."

"Gee," said T.J., "why didn't I think of that? Get *central casting* to send over the suspect."

I ignored him. "What I've got is Adam McKay. I'm only spitballing, all right? But he told me he retired from the department six years ago, did some security work, and now he's writing a screenplay. He also suddenly started showing up at the First Base Saloon. He hangs around with Cookie and Dorrie and me and Sergeant Higgins. Task force people."

Marty was looking at me with that flat, dead-eyed stare that cops are so good at. T.J. was looking at a blown-up map of the banks.

"However," I said, feeling the need to follow through, "it turns out he was fired. For too many excessive force violations, I believe. A few weeks ago, I dropped in on Mary Shaunessy's husband. He was very bitter toward the police. He said he and his wife once attended a pro-abortion rally in Rancho Park, and a cop standing near them beat a man badly. Mary reported him. Shaunessy couldn't remember the officer's name."

"And it was McKay?" Marty said.

"That's right. And I think Adam was brought up before a Board of Rights for beating someone at an Operation Rescue thing."

"Yeah, except they're *against* abortions," T.J. said.

"I called Shaunessy. He said both sides had been present that day. It was either eighty-eight or eighty-nine, in October. I asked him if the name Adam McKay meant anything and he said that was the cop. He also told me that Mary had roped four or five other witnesses into joining her in the complaint. He doesn't know their names. But if they did sign a complaint, their names would be in Adam's Personnel package."

"Anything else?" Marty had begun to doodle.

"Adam gave me his screenplay. It's a piece of dreck. About a mail bomber and a female cop. The only thing I find interesting is how the mail bomber selects his victims. People who piss him off."

The two men glanced at each other.

"I think," said Marty, "Sunday night gets more promising, huh, T.J.?"

So they had dismissed me and were back to Terry Smith. I reached for my Coke feeling like I had gone too far.

"Sunday night," said Marty, "at Dorrie's first bank, she was walking back to her car when a guy drove up. He slowed as he passed her and she saw that it was McKay. That's when I had you pull over, because he stopped to talk to her. Then he said he realized he had forgotten his bank card and drove away. In a metallic blue Caprice."

"Which could look gray?" I said.

"Which might look gray," Marty said.

"What was he wearing?"

"A short-sleeved blue shirt. No security company patch though."

"What did they chat about?"

"He asked her if she was working. She said no, she was on dinner break. He had a cell phone and a pile of laundry on the back seat, like the stranger who gave that kid Billy a ride."

For a moment, none of us spoke. Our eyes staked out different distances to stare into. I could hear voices drifting in from the other room and the ringing of a phone.

Marty's chair scraped against the floor. "Brenden, why don't you run home and get that screenplay. Maybe T.J. will latch onto something you missed. I'm going to get McKay's Personnel package. Bad cop goes badder is not exactly a novel theme."

"Yeah. Well. Neither was his screenplay," I said.

here were two messages on my machine.

One from Suzy. I hadn't talked to her since I left Hawaii on the earlier flight, and I suspected she and Jay were mad at me for walking out on Jack. But she would have to wait.

Two. The altered voice. In a way, I had been expecting it, but the sound of it nevertheless unnerved me. It said: "Poor little cop in her high-heeled shoes. Do you know what a kick I get watching you?" Followed by a pause. "We are destined to meet. Soon."

Any thoughts that this was Gwen Dixon's handiwork went right out the window. And I had never believed that one of my colleagues was doing it either. I believed I was hearing from the stabber. And he—or Terry Smith—was raising the stakes, each message using words that drew him/her closer to me. *We are destined to meet. I am destined to kill.*

I stood perfectly still listening to the words repeat in my mind, unable to stop them. I thought I could stay outside of it, especially with the phone trap, a kind of computerized third party forming a barrier between me and my fear. But this monster had invaded my home, was prowling inside of my head. There was nowhere I could go and be free of it.

I called GTE security and reported the time. Then I pocketed the tape, grabbed the screenplay, and eyeballed my way along the hall and down the stairs to the street.

There had been a space in front of my building and now I was glad I had taken it.

As I got into my car, I cast a glance at the steel mesh door in front of the garage—wondering if anyone was lurking inside.

• • •

T h e door to the War Room was closed.

I knocked and opened it. Against regulations, the room was billowing with T.J.'s cigarette smoke as he, Marty Walters, and Art Bannister sat at the tables, deep in conversation. Marty looked up. "I'll be out in a minute," he called.

I paced the Robbery/Homicide office as the minute became ten. Finally he emerged, shaking his head. "T.J. says he can't think without a cigarette. You got the screenplay?"

I handed it to him. Also the tape. Marty borrowed a tape player from a wiry detective who was working a crossword puzzle. He listened carefully, rewound the tape, and played it again. "It's funny how these calls come when you're not home."

"*I* don't think it's funny."

Marty looked at me for a long moment. "Okay, Brenden, I'm ordering protection. We'll get someone to sit on your building and maybe someone to tag along with you."

"As if hanging around with cops all day and night isn't enough." I could hear my fear spilling into my voice. Marty picked up on it.

"Relax. This is affecting all of us."

"I'm sorry."

Marty rubbed his face.

"So what's going on in there?" I asked.

"We're looking at the complaint Mary Shaunessy filed. Hang on a moment." Marty disappeared into the War Room. He returned with a sheet of paper and a manila envelope. "These are the names of the others who signed Mary's complaint. Any ring a bell?"

I looked at the list and shook my head.

"We've been going through McKay's Personnel packet, and all I'm seeing is a short-tempered bully. But to be safe, we're going to show his file photo to the victims' families tonight and to the people who said they saw a guard at the bank. I've got nothing more to lose than my mind."

"What about Terry Smith?" I said, meaning, what were they doing about her? But Marty had jumped to another track. He handed me the envelope.

"We thought," he said cheerfully, "we'd give that boondoggle to you."

• • •

S u n g l a s s e s on, toothpick protruding, Todd meandered along Coldwater Canyon into the netherworld of the San Fernando Valley. He was grouchy and filled with complaint, as in, "Shit, this Valley ever end?"

"It does if you fly over it," I replied, "but not when you're on the ground."

It was a weird place. At its southern end it bore signs of modern civilization, with Starbuck's and the Gap and Häagen-Dazs and houses and grass and trees. In its midsection, after the car dealerships and 7-Elevens ran out, it began to sprout odd places: marble and tile warehouses and sprawling single-story buildings without windows that contained God knew what. At times there were long stretches of nothing. Which is where we were now. I tried again to focus on the Thomas guide.

"I think we're getting close," I said, studying the map. "Of course, if you drove faster, it would already be tomorrow and we'd be home sound asleep."

"Oh that's nice," said Todd. "Thanks."

When I phoned Terry Smith's office the first time, I was told she was out. The second time she was in a meeting. Finally, at 6:30, she got back to me. From her car.

"I'm on my way to a site," she said. "I have to straighten out the mess my concrete pourers made. Wanna meet me there?"

"I believe she did this on purpose," I said to Todd. "She's vengeful."

Time passed, miles crawled, but eventually we found the location. It reminded me of the footage of Alamogordo when they were testing the Bomb. It was all sand—no plant, animal, or human life—and dusk had given the landscape a lurid gray pallor. A chain-link fence had been erected around the doomsday tract, and inside I could see bulldozers, trailers, Porta Pottis, trucks, and stacks of long steel rods. A large sign posted on the fence read: SMITH & COMPANY. A number of *Do Not Enter* signs had also been posted. I was tempted to obey them.

"I don't see a gate," said Todd. "Do you?"

"I think this must be what Mars looks like," I rhapsodized. "Or the dark side of the moon."

"Just tell me if I'm clear, okay?"

He had turned the car around on the sand spit bordering the

property and was now attempting to cut across two lanes of south-bound traffic to the other side so we could continue north.

"Go," I said.

At the next cross street we turned left, and some distance along it we found a gate in the chain-link. It was open slightly, but not enough to drive through. We left the car and proceeded on foot. I was wearing a bulletproof vest and my 9mm under my jacket. Todd looked better than me; he had on a sport coat and tie. A trailer was located at the northwestern corner of the property. "And there's her car," I said. It was keeping company with a station wagon and a truck. I checked the street for signs of a surveillance vehicle but didn't see one. Which meant whoever had the assignment was good.

As we drew nearer to the trailer, her voice drifted out. "But you do speak English, Manuel? Do you have a problem *understanding* it? Why weren't you here? I pay you to oversee the job. This means being here when the concrete is poured."

Manuel's voice didn't carry nearly as well, and it came out a low mumble. It was immediately drowned out by hers.

"I've got to get someone to rip out the concrete before you can come back. Whatever *that* costs, I'm billing you."

I called out sweetly, "Terry?"

The trailer door flew open. She was wearing overalls and work boots and a look that could kill. "You'll have to wait."

The door slammed shut.

I smiled. "I like the warmth, don't you?"

We stood captive for fifteen minutes. I stared at the project's centerpiece—a gaping hole that looked like a crater had crash-landed. A thick layer of concrete covered about a third of it. It struck me that there was no one else around. Maybe security was unnecessary at this point. But things in L.A. tended to disappear unless they were nailed down. Even, possibly, holes in the ground.

At last, a seething Manuel emerged. He was of medium height and had that gaunt, worn-to-the-bone look about him. His shirt was stained with sweat, and his work pants were coated with dust. He stormed past us, got into the station wagon and, raising a cloud of dust, sped angrily away.

A moment later, Terry posed in the trailer doorway, holding a can. "Beer, anyone?"

Todd and I shook our heads.

Languidly, Terry came down the two steps onto the sand. "If there have to be serial killers," she said, "why don't they ever kill people like Manuel?" She smiled impishly. "Or am I being politically incorrect?" I noticed she was wearing a cloth work glove on her left hand and two bandages on her right. I said nothing.

The silence was broken by Todd's beeper. He looked at it and frowned. "This is my second beep. Is there a phone I could use?"

It had been planned. The Robbery/Homicide secretary had agreed to beep Todd every ten minutes in the hope that it might present us with an opportunity to poke around. Terry half turned toward the trailer as if debating whether to invite Todd in. Then she shrugged. "Don't mind the mess," she said.

Now all I had to do was keep her occupied.

I was holding the manila envelope. I said, "I know you think we've been pestering you, and I'm sorry if we have. If it's any consolation, we've been pestering a lot of people. Solving cases like this can take far more time and manpower than the public is aware of. We have better technology than we used to, but finding a criminal still means . . . " I hesitated. "Finding him."

"Or her?" Terry raised an eyebrow.

"I suppose someday we'll be hunting down female serial killers, but right now we're still leaving it to the men. They're better at it."

"My goodness," said Terry, "a glass ceiling for female criminals? How unfair." She took a sip of her beer.

I looked at it covetously. I needed a shot of something, but the shot would have to wait. I opened the envelope and removed a six-pack. "Please tell me if you recognize any of these men." The photo of Adam McKay had been shot ten years before, and we had to crop it to remove his police shirt. I handed it to her.

Her face changed immediately. The relaxed smugness was replaced with a look of pure shock. "My God, yes," she breathed. "Number two. That's the security guard." She glanced up. "Have you arrested him?"

"Are you sure? No doubts at all? Because I know it was dark and he was wearing a hat."

"I'm sure. I do not forget faces, believe me. And if you let me hear his voice . . . "

"Of course. When the time comes." I no longer trusted anything Terry Smith said. If McKay was the guard, presumably another witness would recognize him.

She looked at me in disbelief. "You mean you're going to let this man run around?"

I took the picture back. "Unfortunately, we don't know yet that he killed anyone. But we've got people working on it." I paused. "Gee, those bandages. The price of working in construction?"

Terry glanced at her bandaged hand. "It's some kind of skin rash. It flares up from time to time. I have an ointment I put on my hands and I try to wear gloves." She half turned toward the trailer. "Long phone call."

"Yeah. I want to go home, too." I took a step closer to the trailer. "Todd?"

"In a minute."

I shifted from one foot to the other. "You're not afraid to be out here alone?"

"Should I be?"

I gave her a practiced smile. "Forgive me if I sound rude, but I can't imagine even a criminal wanting to be out here."

"I'm sure that's what somebody said a hundred years ago when they began putting up buildings in downtown L.A."

"So what are you building anyway?"

"A computer plant. Hardware will be designed in one part of the complex, software in another. One building will be a health club. There will be three restaurants. It'll be something."

Which is when Todd appeared.

"Sorry about that." He glanced at me. "Ready to go?"

"Thank you," I said to Terry.

"No problem." She gave me a saccharine smile.

Todd and I began walking toward the perimeter fence. It was dark now, and I had to watch my footing.

Terry's voice echoed after us. "See you at the ATM!"

Once we were in the car, I said, "She I.D.'ed McKay as the bank guard, for whatever that's worth. I mean, she must have suspected who I was showing her a picture of."

Todd started the engine. "Yeah, but she gave the description for our composite. The composite isn't far off."

"Damn. I liked her as the slasher. Now I'm beginning to feel let down."

"You can still like her," said Todd. "What do you think, Coldwater?"

"I'd take Van Nuys. What do you mean? That you found the bloody knife—or a carton of handcuffs?"

To my annoyance, Todd began to hum.

"I'm not going to beg," I said decisively.

"Beg."

"All right. Please?"

Todd laughed. "When you showed her the picture did you mention McKay's name, or did she?"

"No name was mentioned at all."

"That's interesting, because guess whose name is in her Rolodex. Under security?"

"Really?" I said.

"Maybe she met him once, took his name, and forgot. Or spoke to him on the phone. You never know."

"He did say he worked security after he left the department. But that's not all you found, is it?" I had learned to measure the size of Todd's infrequent grins. "Come on, what else?"

"Metal desk, top right-hand drawer. A yellow oval patch with blue letters that say *Mike's Security*."

"I don't believe you. You're making it up."

"You're right. The drawer contained a body."

"Where is it?"

"I didn't *take* it. We just gotta hope it doesn't go anywhere."

"Now I'm really confused. A patch? What do you think it means?"

"I think," said Todd, "that being confused is an integral part of your charm."

Obviously he was still annoyed that I had picked on his driving. I rolled down my window and pretended to ignore him all the way to Van Nuys Station.

G a r t h Brooks was lamenting his broken heart when I walked into the First Base Saloon a little after ten. The stadium was dark and the P.M. watch regulars wouldn't arrive til eleven. Two men were playing pool and only three people were at the bar. I jumped on a stool and grinned at Johnny.

"Same old?"

"Not right away. How about a Perrier with lime? I've been trudging through the Valley of Our Tears and I'm thirsty as hell."

"Sure," said Johnny. "You're early. Day off?"

"I wish." I glanced up at the TV. An overmuscled, peroxided blond was beating the crap out of a four-hundred-pound guy wearing a Hannibal Lecter mask. They had the room to themselves; nobody seemed to be watching. When Johnny came over with the Perrier, I lifted my glass. "Cheers."

He gave me an "okay" sign and smiled.

"I'm tired," I said.

"Working hard, are you?"

"It's more the nature of the work." I glanced up at the TV. Now Hannibal Lecter was straddling the blond. The blond didn't look thrilled. "I guess there are worse jobs," I said.

"Man, you really are down."

"Wouldn't you be if you came to work every night and discovered that another one of your customers had been stabbed? That's what this has been like. We've got half the department working on the ATM Stabber, the city's screaming, and we're not getting anywhere. Everyone's grumpy. Including me."

"Gee, Brenden, I didn't know you were involved in that."

"Yep."

Johnny leaned an elbow on the bar. "Are you even close?"

I shrugged. "Sometimes I think they purposely keep information from me. All I know is the part about staking out banks. And always this killer appears where we're not. It's been pretty discouraging."

Johnny nodded sympathetically while I sipped the overpriced water. "Anyway, someone . . . I'm not keeping you, am I?"

"You kidding? I'm thinking of renaming this place the Morgue."

"You'd draw an interesting crowd. Anyway, some genius sat down at the computer and fed stuff into it, and now he claims he has come up with three locations for the next kill, each with a ninety percent probability. You ask me, the only way they can come up with a ninety percent probability is if they design a deranged computer."

"Well, it sounds promising," Johnny offered.

"What's not promising is they want me to go to these banks and make withdrawals." I smiled grimly. "Say hello to the bait."

The bartender's blue eyes widened. "Jeez, Brenden, that's dangerous. Where are these banks? Are they near anything?"

"Of course not. They're in the Valley. One is a Bank of America, on Van Nuys. Another's a Great Western, across from Fashion Park. And the third is a First Interstate, at Vanowen and Van Nuys, some-

thing like that. You think they'd at least let me keep the cash I withdraw."

"They're not sending you alone?"

"Yes, I'll be operating alone." I began playing with my cocktail
napkin. "It's not as bad as it sounds. They have this suspect under surveillance. If she drives in and tries to mess with me—then I'll have
company, big time."

Johnny blinked. "Did you say *she?*"

"That's the problem, see? I mean, if they're wrong and the real
killer comes, then it's just me against him. I tried to argue with Higgins, but—"

I turned toward the door as it opened. A couple entered. I leaned
forward. "To be honest, Johnny, I'm a little nervous. And Jack is still
away. Oh well." I brightened. "So, any gossip?"

Johnny laughed. "Just Dodger stuff. You know that actress in
Harm's Way? Tammy Oakley? She was discovered in the shower with
Mr. Rookie of the Year."

"Oh, gross." I again turned toward the door. Ah, there he was.
"Hey, Johnny, I'll take that Black Russian now." I opened my purse,
snared my lipstick, and began applying it carefully.

Earlier, I had trekked back to Parker Center and reported Terry's
I.D. of McKay to Marty Walters. So far, she stood alone. None of the
victims' families recognized McKay, and the five bank customers who
said they had seen a guard were still being tracked down. Marty, who
had committed his time and resources to Terry, wasn't about to aban-
don her yet. It was T.J. who came up with the idea to plant the three
bank locations in Johnny's ear in the hope he would gossip it to
McKay. "Just for fun," T.J. said. "We need some."

I put away my lipstick as he touched my shoulder. "Why, *Adam.* I
was just talking about you. Wasn't I, Johnny? I was saying you'd given
me your screenplay and I can't wait to read it."

McKay's face fell. "You haven't read it?"

Johnny set down a Black Russian and a Corona. "She was just
talking about it," he agreed. "Good luck, buddy." And he walked away.

"You've got to read it," Adam said. "I need feedback. I need to
know what you think."

He smelled soapy clean. Beige sport coat, dark slacks, white shirt.
His fingernails were short and scrubbed. On his left ring finger he
wore a gold band engraved with an *M*. A watch peeked out from his
left cuff.

"Oh I will," I said. "I promise. But I haven't had a moment lately. And with a real killer on the loose, it's a little hard to read about one for entertainment."

"As a matter of fact," Adam said, "I finished the last scene tonight. I got so caught up in it, my heart was racing. Man, I never knew what a high it could be, writing, you know?"

"Excuse me," I said. "Did you say last scene?"

He looked sheepish. "What I gave you wasn't quite finished. I was hoping to get some ideas from you. But then it just came to me. This afternoon." He took a swig of his beer. "I decided to kill her off."

"Kill who off?" I said blankly.

Adam smiled mysteriously.

"Oh, I get it. Your killer is a woman. How clever of you, Adam. But then, once a cop, always a cop, as they say."

He frowned. "What do you mean?"

"You haven't heard? I figured word might have got back to you by now. Of course, we still don't have proof."

"You think your ATM Stabber is a woman?"

I smiled playfully. "Hey, you didn't hear that from me."

"But what makes you think that?"

I studied his face, especially his eyes, looking for signs of madness. I didn't find any.

I said, "Don't ask *me*. I'm just one of the clue dogs. But something the killer does is making the detectives think it's a female." I lifted my glass. "To women's lib and all that."

Adam glanced at his watch. "You have to read my screenplay. Then we can compare notes. Excuse me, I've got to make a call."

"Sorry. What time is it? I think my watch stopped."

He held out his wrist to me. The watch face was quite large. "Don't tell me you can't read small print anymore," I teased.

"No, it's from the thirties. My grandfather's. He was a railroad conductor and they all wore these big-face watches. It's rather valuable, I'm told." He headed for the pay phone.

His watch said 10:43. I glanced again at the door, but nobody was coming through it. I ordered another round.

"So," said Adam upon returning, "you think it's a woman. Wouldn't that be something." He picked up his fresh Corona.

"All I'm saying is you better sell your story quick. 'Cause, when our case breaks, every screenwriter in town will be scrambling to sew up the rights." I nodded. "I know how these things work."

"I'm sure you do." Adam tapped my arm annoyingly. "So when will you read it? I won't send it out til I have your input."

I glanced at the door in time to see T.J. and Art Bannister walk into the poolroom. "Tell you what," I said. "I'll read it later and I'll meet you here tomorrow night."

"Deal," said Adam. "Tomorrow."

I stood. "Hey, Johnny, put it on my tab." I hitched up my shoulder bag. "See you, *writer*."

On my way out I paused in the doorway of the poolroom. T.J. and Art were huddled in a booth, deep in conversation. Neither looked up. I slid some coins into the jukebox and pressed Carly Simon's *You're So Vain*.

It was their idea of a prearranged signal. But the choice of the song was mine.

From that point on, like a satellite that had skipped out of its orbit, I found myself drifting aimlessly through the solar system. I was still assigned to Operation ATM—as far as I knew—but the action, if there was any, was being conducted at Mission Control. Their radar failed to reach me.

The jukebox signal—T.J.'s idea—was to let him know that, yes, Adam wore the kind of watch his fictitious mail bomber did. Big deal. I knew enough about Hollywood to know that writers often put little bits of themselves into their work. So what?

"So what?" I said to Marty Walters when he called me the next morning.

"Let's save the analysis, Brenden, I'm swamped." And irritable, I thought. "We've still got Terry under surveillance. SIS will move in on our three banks tonight. There's no way to surveille McKay's house, and he'd probably pick us up anyway."

"Where is it?" I asked, wiggling my toes on the cold kitchen tile.

"He's got two acres in Canyon Country. Dirt roads. You know what it's like."

Canyon Country was several canyons removed from civilization as I knew it, even though it was home to many cops and Hollywood screenwriters. It seemed normal that Adam would live there. What did not seem normal was bringing SIS in. Special Investigations Section was the closer. It was only called in when we were sure of our suspect but needed to catch him in the act. Metro may have fancied itself LAPD's glamor division, but it was SIS that did the dirty work. Many of its members had killed.

"What can I do?" I said.

"Relax. Stay home. If Johnny didn't mention anything last night, he will tonight when McKay starts asking for you. And Higgins may drop in as well."

I was mystified. Yesterday, Walters was dismissing McKay as a short-tempered bully; what could they have dug up since? And if they did have something, why continue to track Terry Smith?

"There is one thing," Marty said. "See if you can scare up the Croft boy. Nobody was home yesterday."

"What about the eyewitness to Sally Sloane's murder?"

"He didn't see the attacker's face."

"And the bank customers who identified the guard from the sketch?"

"Two said yes, one said no, two said they didn't know. One more thing." Paper-rattling noises filtered over the line. "Call Danni Gunther. That's Lieutenant Danielle Gunther. Pacific Division. She worked with McKay in West Valley and filed a sexual misconduct complaint against him. It was dropped. Find out her story."

It was then that I began to suspect I was being given things to do while something was going on elsewhere.

"Oh, I almost forgot. Take down this number."

I picked up a pen and wrote out the number.

"That goes to the Metro car sitting on your building. You go any-where, you take company. Got it?"

"Sure."

"I mean it, Brenden. No funny business."

"I promise," I said sincerely. "I'll talk to you later."

I uncrossed my fingers, turned on my answering machine, and slipped out the building's back entrance for my morning run.

I t was a beautiful day, the air fragrant with eucalyptus and the ocean breeze cool. I took 4th to Adelaide, trotted down the 189 mur-derous concrete sloping and twisting stairs to Ocean Avenue, and headed south along the beach. I slowed my pace so I could run twelve miles instead of ten. I returned by way of Ocean to San Vicente to 3rd. When I snuck back into my apartment, I unstrapped my fanny pack, which held my gun, and dropped it on the counter. The message light was blinking.

A bunch of static and then, through it, barely audible, came the voice.

"Kind of slow this morning, huh, cutie cop? Maybe it was the weight of the gun in your fanny pack. You should try a knife." The line went dead.

The call had come in fifteen minutes before. He/she must have followed me—but how? I felt tears welling in my eyes. I never left through the back entrance. And when I went out the front, I never took the same streets to the beach. Sometimes I ran north. Sometimes I stayed on the promenade above the beach, running south. Occasionally I ran along San Vicente into Brentwood and back. Where had the monster been?

I jumped slightly as the phone rang. I let it ring five times, then I lifted the receiver.

"Hello," I said carefully.

"You're being a real asshole, you know that? I usually think of assholes as men. I don't know the equivalent for women."

I leaned against the counter and closed my eyes. "I think it's the C-word you're looking for, Suzy. But I suggest you not use it."

"What the hell's wrong with you? Jack needs your help."

"Holding his hand and saying 'Poor thing' isn't help."

"You're cold, you know that?"

"No, I'm not. I'm realistic. If Jack wants his career, and his health, and his wife, he's going to have to understand they won't be handed to him on a platter anymore." I picked up a dish towel and blotted sweat off my face. "I'm truly moved that you have so much faith in Jack," I added. "You should also have a little faith in me."

Suzy sighed. "He's here now, with us. They're shooting the last scenes on the lot. He needs to go home and get some clothes."

"Fine," I said. "As long as I'm not here."

"Jesus, Brenden. It would help him if he could see you."

"No, it wouldn't. What he wants to see is a happy, smiling wife who will tell him he's okay. Well, I'm not smiling and he isn't okay. Can I go now?"

"Asshole."

"Suzy." I took a deep breath. "I need you to be my friend. I'm hurting, too."

She was silent for a moment. Then, "Can you have lunch?"

"I wish I could. But we'll talk soon, okay? And please let me know when Jack's coming over."

I called GTE and alerted the Metro car.

Then I picked up my gun and headed for the shower.

• • •

D a n n i Gunther apologized for a busy schedule but said she'd talk to me anytime I wanted to stop by. That meant taking along Edward Chang—my bodyguard.

"Do you always drive like this?" he complained as I burned asphalt on the 405, "or are you just trying to impress me?"

"Feel free to put on your seat belt," I soothed. "The car has dual air bags. Also antilock brakes. Do you like Mary Chapin Carpenter? Bruce Springsteen? Oh, I know. Sting."

I popped in a cassette.

"I'll tell you a secret," I said as Edward buckled up. "The reason I became a cop? This. I figured I'd just keep getting speeding tickets and my insurance, well, you can imagine. But this way, I get paid to go fast." I smiled. "Cool country, huh?"

D a n n i Gunther occupied a cramped glass-enclosed cubicle. It contained a desk covered with paperwork, lunch wrappers, and a grouping of framed photographs of a husband and a child. The husband was a captain in another division. In the end, most cops married each other, then remarried another. It was that kind of place.

Danni was a streaked blonde with a trim figure that wore her uniform well. I sat in the guest chair and Edward stood by the door.

"So I hear you guys have been having a little fun," Danni began. "My problems are Venice Beach. Gang stuff. I'm a little unclear what you wanted to see me about."

"We're interested in a former cop," I said. "Your name surfaced in the form of a sexual harassment complaint. The officer is Adam McKay."

"Adam?" Danni repeated. "In connection with your case?"

I gave her a small smile. "Anything you can tell us might be helpful."

"Well he was a real son of a bitch and probably still is. I was his sergeant briefly, and that didn't go over too well. He despises women in authority and doesn't seem to get along with women in general. I don't believe he's ever been married."

"What did he do to you?"

"He mouthed off a lot. He'd make derogatory remarks in roll call. Behind my back he called me Sergeant Slut. To my face he would make a big show of saluting and saying, 'Yes, *ma'am.*' Once, I found a pretty package on my desk. There was a card that said, *For those difficult days.* It was Tampax. I was pretty sure it was from him."

"So you complained?" I prompted.

"Yes, I lodged a formal complaint. I guess Adam cried to the captain. The captain called me in and we all talked. Adam apologized and pleaded for another chance. I think he was worried because he was catching all those complaints from citizens."

Danni's phone rang and she spoke briefly into it. She hung up frowning and said, "Where was I? Oh. The thing about Adam was he could be very pleasant when he wanted to be. He was conscientious about his job, and most of the time he did it very well. He reminded me of a car. He would drive dependably mile after mile, then all of a sudden he'd hit a bump, spin out of control. Then he'd drive smoothly off."

"So you dropped your complaint?"

"I did. And I must say, he was fine after that. Not a peep out of him. At least not to me."

"You think he alienated others?"

Danni nodded. "Our paths crossed once before, at the Police Academy. He was an instructor in riot control techniques. He was pretty hard on the women and"—she glanced at Edward—"Asian officers, too."

"When was that?" I asked. "When you were a trainee?"

Danni bit her lip. "Let me think. It was a few years after I joined the department. Eighty-seven, eighty-eight?"

"Do you know if he trained recruits, too?" This would have been around the time I was at the academy, and I didn't remember McKay. People tended to remember their academy instructors.

"He might have," Danni said. "What I took was a two-day refresher course. Some of the officers complained about McKay's treatment, and they eventually transferred him out. About six months later, they transferred him to me."

We chatted a few minutes longer, until Danni had to go into a meeting. As Edward and I walked out to the car, I said, "I thought I'd drop by the Croft place. We want the son to look at McKay's picture. No one's been answering the phone, and I'd like to take a look, okay?"

"I think my stomach's settled by now," Edward said dourly.

"Oh, Edward," I said. "You're such a cutup, I swear."

• • •

N o one was home.

We sniffed around, finding a bunch of letters in the mailbox and several flyers in the driveway. I rang a few doorbells, but either no one was home or no one knew the whereabouts of the Crofts.

"Let's go back to my place," I said. "I'll call George Croft's store. School's out. Maybe they took a vacation."

Edward saw me into my apartment, then went to join his partner in the Metro car. I fixed a vodka and tonic and headed into the den.

On the desk I had left a folder with sporadic notes I had made about the case, but I saw then that I had never actually learned the name of Mr. Croft's office supply store. Something else, however, caught my eye. Fred Lumley's name and number. It was four-thirty and I dialed quickly, hoping I would find him still in his office.

"Hey, Brenden," he said. "Can you hold? I'll be right with you."

As I waited, my attention was drawn to the gallery of photographs that Jack had hung on the wall. Most were of him, taken by the *Night Watch* still photographer. But there were photos, too, from our wedding. The six years that had passed had stolen the innocence from our faces and made our eyes a little more sure and a lot less bright.

"Sorry," said Fred. "I'm preparing for a trial next week and my law clerk has hepatitis." He paused. "How are you?"

"I'm okay. I was wondering if you could help me with something though. You said Amelia didn't like some of the people at the academy. Did she ever mention an Adam McKay to you?"

"Offhand, the name doesn't mean anything. Can I ask why?"

"It's another long shot, I suspect, but we're looking at McKay, who's since been fired. Mary Shaunessy, our first victim, filed a complaint against him for use of force at an abortion rally. A female lieutenant had problems with his attitude toward women cops. She took a course he gave at the academy about the time Amelia was there. The thing is, I was in Amelia's class and I don't remember McKay."

"Wait a minute," Fred said, "you're thinking that some wacko cop who may have had a problem with Amelia nine years ago—decided to kill her now?"

"I agree. It doesn't grab me either."

Fred was silent for a moment. "You know, I just thought of a long shot myself. Amelia was a diary keeper. I've been putting her things in boxes to give to her mother. I came across a pile of notebooks. One was from her senior year in high school, so it's possible she kept a diary while she was at the academy. Tell you what, I'll look tonight. If I find anything, I'll call."

After I hung up, I made a list of the women who had been in my academy class. There had been nine of us, I remembered that, but I could recall only six, including Amelia and myself. I called Personnel to get phone numbers. They gave me three. The fourth woman had left the department two years ago, so the best I could get was her last known address. Then I called Robbery/Homicide. Neither Marty nor T.J. were in. I left messages for both.

I realized I had not eaten since breakfast. In the kitchen, I popped a frozen pizza into the microwave, poured another drink, and carried my dinner back to the den.

The first woman on my list, Katie McMurray, was working undercover narcotics. Reaching her would be tough, but I left messages on her home answering machine and with the secretary at Narcotics Division. Next I tried Ann Johnson, a patrol officer working out of 77th.

She answered on the first ring, sounding sleepy.

"It's Brenden Harlow, Annie, did I wake you?"

"You and everyone else. Try explaining to the world you work morning watch and need to sleep during the day. But, hey, Irish, how you doin'?"

"I'm fine and I apologize. I hope you can clear your head for a moment, because I need to ask you something important."

"Ask away, girlfriend. I'm as clear as I'll ever be."

"Annie, when we were at the academy, do you remember an instructor named Adam McKay? Tall, light brown hair, round face?"

"You mean Mr. Sheet?"

"Mr. who?" I wasn't sure if she had said "sheet" or "shit."

"That's what we called him, Mr. Sheet. He was like this poster boy for the Ku Klux Klan."

"How come I didn't know him if he was there then?"

"Because, girlfriend, you probably weren't required to take Remedial Reports."

I laughed. "Remedial what?"

"Some of us, mainly brothers and sisters, didn't have sufficient writing skills. So we spent some time with Mr. Sheet."

"Was Amelia Rodriguez in that class?"

"Amelia, Amelia, um . . . sure, she was the dyslexic. Sweet girl. I remember she took it so seriously. Like spelling *suspect* right would bring an end to crime as we know it."

"Annie, do you remember anything specific about McKay?"

"Just that he was a real SOB. He made it clear he didn't like blacks, and he didn't think much of women either, a real bonus for me. I remember once he called Amelia a dumb cunt, I swear he did. And she stood up and squared her little shoulders and said, 'Officer McKay, you may not speak to me like that.'"

"What happened?"

"Nothing. He just sneered and continued whatever important shit he'd been talking about."

"Were there any other women in the class?" I inquired.

"Um, no. Shirley Howard, she was the smart nigger. And the rest of you honkies didn't need Remedial Reports."

"Did you ever run into McKay after that?"

"No, thank God. They fired him, you know. I sleep a little better knowing he's gone."

I was having trouble tracking. My instincts about people are so keen I couldn't understand how I had missed the meanness in McKay. Unless, I thought, after he'd left the stress of the streets, he calmed down. I said, "Everything good with you?"

"Can't complain. I've got my man, Jimmy, and we have little Darcy, who's a three-year-old hell-raiser. Work's not bad. How about you?"

"Doing okay. I'm in Metro now."

"Metro? I'm thinking maybe Internal Affairs. So why are you asking about McKay?"

"Soon I'm going to call you back and tell you, and then we're going to make a date. Deal?"

"You got it, babe."

Next I tried Tracy Lee, an Asian officer assigned to Legal Affairs. I caught her walking in the door, and we chatted only a few minutes. The name McKay meant nothing to her, and I saw no reason to pursue the conversation. The final woman on my list, Denise Dennard, was the officer who had left the department. She was white and may not have encountered McKay. I tried Information all the same, but it had no listing for her.

I stood up, my eyes still lingering on the photographs. When the phone rang, I unreasonably hoped it would be Jack.

"Harlow, it's McCall. What's up?" The static told me he was on his cell phone.

"Where are you?"

"Camped at Terry Smith's house. She slipped our butterfly net and we've been whipping around town looking for her all day."

"All day? But how did that happen?"

"Don't know. We took her to work about eight-thirty. But it's possible she never went up to her office. We called her several times, got the answering machine. The office door was locked. I've been to a couple of construction sites, but nobody's seen her." T.J. coughed. "Tell me you have."

"Sure. We just finished cocktails. What about McKay?"

"Don't know. He's not my problem."

At least I knew now that Terry Smith could have tracked me on my run. Then again, so could have McKay.

"You heard about my phone call this morning?" I asked.

"Yeah. Your protection's got their eyes peeled. So should you. And I can't keep this line tied up."

I hung up feeling even more like a caged animal. I popped a crust into my mouth. It was just after six and I was restless.

I turned on the TV for the local news and listened as I examined our collection of videos on the bookshelves. There was the predictable recap of grisly crimes. "And when we come back," the anchorman said pleasantly, "new information on the ATM Stabber."

I half turned toward the TV. Oh really?

I took my pizza plate into the kitchen, grabbed an apple from the refrigerator, and when I returned to the den, there on our thirty-five-inch screen was a flushed Adam McKay.

I reached for the remote and punched up the volume.

"Here with me, folks, is former LAPD officer Adam McKay."

My God, I thought, he was wearing a blue short-sleeved shirt with a yellow security patch on the pocket and a policelike hat. He gazed earnestly into the camera.

"Now sir, can you tell us what you're doing here?"

"Sure, Tom. Ever since I left the department, I've been doing security work, and I thought with my background I could be helpful to some of the banks in the area where this killer has been known to strike."

"So you're working security hoping to catch this guy?"

Adam smiled self-consciously. "Actually, I'm hoping my presence will make bank customers feel safe."

"And you're working here, at Great Western across from Fashion Square?"

"It's one of the banks, yes."

"Well, thank you, Adam. Good luck. Back to you Elaine."

Jesus, I thought.

I brushed my teeth, put on lipstick, and double-locked the door on my way out.

ay Higgins was eating a sandwich and scribbling intently on a notepad. He glanced up, swallowed a mouthful, and frowned. "Harlow, what are you doing here?"

The War Room looked as if it had been through the Big One and Higgins was the lone survivor. I smiled. "I couldn't reach anyone on the phone, and I wanted to report what I learned today."

Higgins put down his sandwich and wiped his mouth with a paper napkin. "I don't recall hearing from you. To whom did you intend to report?"

I walked over to the desks. "Detective Walters asked me to keep in touch. I have some information about Adam McKay."

"What information?" Higgins looked unconvinced.

I pulled out a chair, but Higgins stopped me. "Don't get comfortable, Harlow. You won't be here that long."

Shit. Where was Marty? I said, "Do you have time to hear what I've got?"

"No, I don't. If you want, go out there and type up your report." He went back to his sandwich.

I waited a moment. "Sir, Adam McKay was interviewed on TV. He said—"

"Tell it to the typewriter." The phone rang. Higgins grabbed it. "Higgins speaking." He looked at me darkly. I turned and walked out.

For a long time, I sat in my car debating what to do. Eventually I picked up my cell phone and called my machine, hoping for salvation. I found it. "Brenden, Fred Lumley," the canned voice began. "I found three notebooks marked *Academy,* but before I could look at them, I had to run back downtown. I have them at the office now and I'll try to get to them when I can. Talk to you later."

I locked the car, tucked my Beretta into the waistband of my slacks under my jacket, and walked the two blocks to the Criminal Courts building on Temple. When I entered the lobby, I flashed my badge at the guard and walked around the metal detector. Then I rode the elevator up to the nineteenth floor.

Fred was in his office, bent over a thick leather-bound volume. I rapped on the open door. "Hi."

Fred jumped. "Oh Jesus."

I smiled. "Sorry. I was in the neighborhood. I thought maybe I could save you some time."

"Great." Fred began shuffling through the mounds of papers and books that rose tipsily from his desk. "Here you go. You'll return them?"

"I could look at them now."

Fred stood. He was wearing jeans and a sweater, and I could see the puffy circles under his eyes. "Right out there, Brenden. You can use the secretary's desk."

"Thanks." I paused. "You look beat."

He laughed. "You mean I look like hell. We were going to take a vacation in August. Drive up through Montana and Wyoming? Now I'm not sure what I'll do."

"In a sick way, the work helps," I offered.

"During the day. It doesn't get you through the nights."

"I'm sorry."

"Yeah. Yell if you have a question."

It wouldn't have taken me long to thumb through the notebooks, except that I kept getting sidetracked by Amelia's descriptions of academy life. Also by her writing, which at times was almost unintelligible. I could see the dyslexia problem in the backward letters and misspelled words.

At one point, I found an entry about me. It said, "Sqent some time today with a girl named Brinnden. Shes real qretty and seems nice but a little inTence. And unlike me, she seems to have no concurns about her uhbilties I should spend more time hanging with her!"

Poor, sweet Amelia, I thought, and wondered if I had really come across like such an ass. I sighed and kept going.

Adam McKay surfaced midway through the second notebook. I had noticed that although Amelia had made copious daily notes through the first two months of our training, the entries soon began to taper off. Some days were skipped altogether; others were recalled with a few brief sentences.

McKay was indeed introduced as the officer teaching Basic Reports, Part II. Her early notes described him as bullying, nasty, and crude. "But he seems to know how to right a good rePort and gives us good tips," she recorded. Two weeks later she noted that he had been particularly insulting to her, calling her a "dumb fucking Mexican." When she protested, he apparently told her if she couldn't take it, she had no business being in the department. "I haf to be touffer," she wrote.

I felt tears welling in my eyes, but even so, I wasn't prepared for what would come next.

For a while, Amelia thought McKay's attitude toward her was softening. He praised her progress on occasion and bantered with her after class. At the beginning of the fifth month, and what was to be the final week of this special class, McKay told her he was writing a movie about cops. One of them was a female Hispanic, and he wondered if he could talk to her that night for research purposes. Amelia, feeling uncomfortable, said she didn't know enough about police work yet. But McKay said he was more interested in her background. He asked if she would meet him at the academy lounge at seven. Amelia, thinking they would talk over a drink, reluctantly agreed.

Only, when she arrived, McKay ushered her into his car and drove her to his apartment, which at the time was in Los Feliz. At first, he was cordial, showing her his many commendations from superiors praising his work. But later she understood the inherent threat. As in, You'll do what I say because I'm important. And for two terrifying hours, Amelia did.

"He axed me to walk bAck and forth in his livingroom," Amelia wrote. "He said strut, cunt. Then hE said now walk like a hore, things like that. He tole me he was tired of police 'bullshit' and how he was going to be a big Hollywood screenriter. He tole me about the sTory he was riting about this woman cop and a mad bomber. he axed me if I would heLp him with a scene. He said the cop breaks into the bomber's aparT-ment only he's hiding in the closet and he grabs her. Then he makes her strip down to her underware. Then he ties her to a chair and makes her watch him make a bomb, witch he's going to use to blow heR up."

Amelia tried to leave, but McKay—no average citizen who could be maneuvered by someone Amelia's size—forced her onto the couch. He drew his gun and ordered her to strip. "See, I wanna get it right," he told her. With his gun trained on her, Amelia stripped down to her panties and bra. McKay then tied her to a chair. "He made fun of my underWare," she wrote. "He said it looked like a old lady's and next Time I'd better wear something sexy."

My hands were shaking as I flipped the page.

Now McKay began giving her lines to recite. Sometimes he would change them again and again. When she said them the way he wanted her to, he would write them down. At one point, she began to cry, and McKay held his gun to her head. Terrified, Amelia wet her pants. Disgusted, he untied her and pushed her out the door, throwing her clothes out the window so she would have to walk nearly naked into the street to retrieve them.

Whatever else may have transpired between them was left unrecorded. The third notebook contained only a few entries. One said, "I'm not brave. I cant take this anymore. I know I'm letting my faMily down."

The next entry was more upbeat. "I am number 2 in fiRearms."

I turned the page, but found nothing more. I stared at the empty pages and listened to the wall clock tick away the night. Eventually I became aware that I was sitting only fifteen feet from the man who had loved Amelia. I watched him writing intently on a legal pad and tried to steady my nerves. Slowly I stood and walked into Fred Lumley's office.

He brightened. "Hey, did you find anything?"

"Couple of references so far. Would it be okay if I took these home?"

Fred yawned. "No problem, Brenden. Keep me informed, okay?"

I left the building with a molten weight in my stomach and walked tiredly back to Parker Center. At the corner of Temple and Spring, a human pile of dirty laundry stepped out of the darkness and asked me for change. I gave him a dollar and silently thanked God for small favors.

Higgins's boorish behavior towards me had, at least, spared Fred Lumley another wrenching heartache.

• • •

When I got back to Robbery/Homicide, the office had cleared out and only two detectives were left, both on the phone. The War Room, still looking earthquake ravaged, was deserted. I found a type-writer and sat down.

Like Columbus, I "discovered" keys and landed on them. Except *my* keys kept sticking. I had completed only the portions pertaining to Danni Gunther and Annie Johnson when Marty Walters strode in.

He frowned. "Why aren't you home?"

His long-sleeved blue shirt was wrinkled and there was a spot on his khaki pants. He looked exhausted, his face slightly green against his thick white hair.

I said, "I couldn't reach you so I thought I'd come in."

Absently, Marty nodded and walked into the War Room. I left my two typed pages on the desk, picked up the notebooks, and followed him. "Did you find Terry Smith?"

"No." Marty flipped through a pile of phone messages before stealing a glance at the coffeepot. It was empty. Sighing, he sat down and folded his arms behind his head. "Someone from Metro with you?"

"No." I sat down, too. "I told them I was coming here and didn't need an escort. I've got some stuff on McKay. I think someone besides me should know about it."

"What did Higgins say?"

"He said he was more interested in Terry Smith."

"He's right." Marty picked up a sporting goods catalogue and stared at it bleakly. "Do you know how badly I want to go fishing? God, just give me one long weekend. Hell, a day." Regretfully, he dropped it back on the desk.

"I still think you should listen to what I have to say."

"All right. Let me make a phone call first."

I decided coffee sounded good, so while he was on the phone I made a fresh pot. I brought two cups over to the desks and waited. Finally, Marty hung up. "Thanks."

"I'll start with Lieutenant Gunther," I said, and quickly related her comments. I explained how I had come to call Annie Johnson and what she had said. "By the way," I added, "did you know McKay was on TV?"

"I heard."

"And?"

"Either he has bats in his belfry or he's a loose cannon trying to find some glory for himself. It's not an uncommon trait in a sour cop."

"I'm not sure how batty," I said, "because now if anybody says they saw him, he can say, Sure, I was on TV. Or, Yes, you saw me at a bank one day. And any potential victim walking up to an ATM may recognize him and feel safe." I hesitated. "Don't you think?"

"Brenden, we can spitball all we want. But spit doesn't fly in court. Where's the evidence?"

"Let me work him, Marty. I'll get the evidence."

The detective said nothing.

"Well, you must suspect something. You called in SIS—" Something about the way Marty was looking at me, made me stop. "You took SIS off those banks, didn't you?"

"Go home, Brenden. It's late."

"Not until you hear this." I reached for the notebooks. "These are Amelia's diaries from the academy. She was dyslexic and had to take the same remedial course that Annie Johnson did." I summarized Amelia's early comments about McKay's behavior, then I flipped open a notebook. "Listen to this."

I read verbatim the whole sordid incident at McKay's apartment. When I finished, I looked up and caught the revulsion in Marty's face. "Jesus," he said. "When was that, what year?"

"December nineteen eighty-seven."

"I can't believe he could get away with that kind of thing." He lifted his coffee cup, then decided to put it back down. "Leave the notebooks here. You can finish your report tomorrow." He began shuffling through his papers.

I stood but I didn't leave. I watched Marty look busy and wondered why he was being evasive with me and dismissive of my information. "Please," I said, "I'd like to know what's going on. Why am I being brushed off like this?"

Marty brought his eyes up to mine. "Nobody's brushing you off, all right? You're one of fifty people working their asses off on this case. Nobody's getting special attention. And when this is over, and it *will* be over, nobody's getting special credit. And you are not going to *work him*."

"Sir, I'm not asking for special credit. But look what we've got. Here's a guy who's passing around a screenplay that he coerced Amelia Grant to perform for him. And Amelia's dead. And Mary Shaunessy's dead. And now he's mugging for TV cameras. This man is telegraphing his intentions all over the place."

"My point exactly," Marty said with satisfaction. "He's all over the place. And Terry Smith is not. Good night, Brenden."

I said good night.

But I had no intention of calling it one.

I parked on Sunset and killed the engine.

The problem, although usually considered a selling point, was that the First Base Saloon had no windows. I did not want to waltz in to the disapproving glare of Higgins. I turned the radio on low and tried to get into Psychic Paul's voice-of-doom readings. Soon I was rewarded with the sight of Mr. Doom himself. With narrowed eyes I watched Higgins enter the bar.

I listened to Paul some more. Then my eye fell upon the solution. Why, what were car phones for? I dialed the number by rote.

"Johnny? It's Brenden. Don't say my name, okay?"

"Yes, ma'am. Can I help you?"

"Is McKay there?"

"Yes, that's right."

"What about Cookie or T.J.?"

"I don't think so. Sorry . . . did you say Doris?"

Man, he was good. The fine art of bartending was vastly underrated. "Could you ask her to sort of slip out? I'm parked across the street. Black muscle car."

"No problem, ma'am. Thank you for calling." He hung up.

Soon the door swung open and Dorrie, with a quick glance up and down Sunset, loped across the street. I threw open the passenger door.

"Something made me think I forgot to lock my car doors," she said as she scooted inside. "What's going on?"

"You first," I said. "Have you been talking to McKay?"

"I'm afraid so. I was hoping you or Cookie would rescue me. Instead I get Higgins, and now I'm being hit on from both sides."

"Adam, too?"

"He invited me over for a home-cooked dinner."

"Don't go. Under any circumstances."

"Shit, do I look that desperate? Anyway, he was asking about you."

"What did he say?"

"That you were coming in to talk to him about his damn screenplay. He's all puffed up over it, too. Said he's got an agent now and

he's going to get rich and live in *style*." Dorrie rolled her eyes. "No of-
fense, Brenden, but I think white guys give a whole new meaning to
the word *asshole*."

"I'll drink to that." I began chewing on a fingernail. "What's he
wearing, Adam?"

"Um, jeans, shirt, jacket. Why?"

"Light blue shirt?"

"What, you've got a thing for blue shirts?"

I grinned.

"White T-shirt. Sorry."

He'd gone all the way home and changed? Changed in his car?

I said, "So what does Higgins have to say? I mean, what do they
talk about?"

"Higgins said it had been a hard day. Their suspect had vanished,
and he needed a scotch and water bad. Then they started flexing their
little muscles at me." Dorrie made a face.

I glanced at my watch. "Okay, do me a favor." It was ten til eleven
and I was sure they would run it again. "When you go back in, ask
Johnny to turn on the Channel Two news. Pretend you're interested. I
think you'll see something fun."

Dorrie cocked her head. "Are you okay?"

"I wouldn't know. I've never had the experience. But, Dorrie? Stay
clear of Adam, please."

She gave me a long, searching look and shook her head sadly.
"Man, you must really miss your husband. But, hey, you got a thing for
McKay, no problem." Dorrie brightened. "Oh, I get it. Like how guys
need a thrill so they pick up a prostitute?"

I winked. "It'll be our little secret," I said.

T h e message light was flashing when I walked in at 11:30. I ignored it; there was no one I cared to hear from. I fixed a drink and
squired it into the bedroom. I switched on Leno and decided I needed
.a hot bath to help unwind. I turned on the water, tossed in a capful of
perfumed essence of something, then relented. Maybe the baby-sitters
had something for me.

There was one message. Please don't be Jack, I thought as I stood
over the counter and hit the play button. Alone and needing him, I
would crack if I heard his voice.

"I know you're there," the disembodied voice growled. "Hey, hey, can Brenden come out and play? You're missing all the fun, cutie cop. Maybe I'll have to come upstairs and *get* you."

I ripped the answering machine cord out of the wall and then, like a lunatic, I crept through the apartment, gun drawn, switching on lights, checking the closets. In the living room I opened the sliding glass doors onto the balcony and stepped out. Damp salt air blew across my face.

My fingers needed three tries to get the seven digits and the area code right.

"Metro. Officer Hunt speaking. How may I help you?"

"Larry, it's Brenden," I said to the old-timer who manned the desk overnight. "Can you contact the Metro car outside my apartment and have them call me right away?" I couldn't remember where I'd put the number.

"Hold tight. I'll be right back to you."

I sipped my drink. The seconds seemed like hours as I felt the monster's presence closing in on me.

"Officer?"

"Yes, I'm here."

"Well, they signed off at twenty-two hundred."

"But somebody would have relieved them," I said.

"Nope. The only Metro officers on duty are in North Hollywood on a drug bust."

"Are you sure?"

"Yes, ma'am."

"Thank you," I said.

In the living room, I chain-locked the front door, set the alarm and, thinking hard, wandered into the bedroom.

I remembered the tub just as it started to overflow.

S aturday, June 3, 1400 hours, found me imprisoned in Metro's glass-enclosed duty room answering phones. It was my third straight day of it. Higgins had not explained.

From what I gathered Operation ATM had been put on hold—at least the part Metro played. Robbery/Homicide was still heavy on the case. My platoon had been redeployed to Universal Studios to suppress a crime spree. It was vacation time: pockets were being picked, cars broken into. The day before, two East Coast tourists had been shot leaving the tram, one fatally. The mayor said it was bad for the economy.

"Metro. Officer Harlow speaking."

"You do that well," T.J. said. "But then I always had faith in you."

"I'm glad somebody does."

"How about dinner? I think I can get clear."

I hadn't spoken to T.J. since our brief conversation when he was parked outside Terry Smith's house.

"Now?" I said hopefully.

"I was thinking more along the lines of the conventional dinner hour," T.J. replied. "When do you get off?"

"Eight, officially."

"I'll meet you at the steak joint at seven-thirty."

"I said eight, hotshot."

"So when you arrive at eight-thirty, you'll be right on time, if memory serves."

"You're supposed to be feeling *sorry* for me," I said sourly, "not dissing me, okay?"

"Don't count on it." T.J. hung up.

• • •

F o r some reason, he looked especially attractive as I joined him in a booth at exactly 8:25. Maybe it was because he was wearing a shirt and tie under a tan blazer. He looked up from a notebook as I sat down.

"Early," I announced.

"I'm thrilled, Harlow. What'll you have to drink?"

"I'll buy a bottle of wine if you buy dinner. Red or white?"

"An assertive female officer. Oh stop, my pounding heart."

I grinned. "Then you buy the wine *and* the dinner *and* provide the entertainment. Especially the entertainment."

T.J. signaled the waiter. "We'd like a bottle of Cuvée 1989 now. In half an hour, we'll want two steaks, medium-rare, a platter of half fries, half onion rings, and a plate of sliced tomatoes. Thank you."

"You look great," I said. "Did you get dressed up for me?"

"No. I'm a single man. Don't get any ideas."

"Sorry." I took a deep breath. "Did any of my information on McKay leak back to you?"

"I've read the notebooks and your poorly typed report. I'm paying attention, Brenden."

"Is anybody else?"

"I think Marty is. But he's keeping me on Terry Smith and playing the rest close to the vest. We've got her back, by the way. The next day she appeared at her office around noon. We don't know where she came from or where she had been the day before. Maybe she just wanted to show a little muscle."

"Meaning she can slip your surveillance at whim?"

"It's a tough act to sustain."

The waiter brought the wine, filled our glasses, and left. T.J. had made a good choice and I went to work on the merlot with pleasure.

"So," I said, "entertain me."

T.J. smiled warmly. "Higgins doesn't like you."

"No kidding."

"I mean, he *really* doesn't like you. And he could really hurt you."

"I know that."

"He told Walters you had a personal hard-on for McKay."

"Wouldn't you? After what he did to Amelia and Danni and all those citizens he shot, beat, or insulted?"

"He told Walters that McKay said you were coming on to him at the saloon. You didn't take the rejection well."

I put down my wine glass. "Higgins said that?"

"He also pointed out there's no proof the phone calls to you were made by a possible suspect. He said your husband works with actors. It could have been staged by one of them."

"And Marty bought this shit?"

"Like I said, he plays it close to the vest. But if it's any consolation, Marty is damn good. You've produced some solid leads on McKay, and Marty can analyze them for himself."

"I guess." I put down my wineglass and played with the stem. "But I wish he would use me. I know I could play McKay. I know I could make him angry enough to act." I smiled dolefully. "After all, I succeeded with Higgins."

T.J. touched my hand. "Calm down, Brenden. This will all get worked out."

"How? Did you stick up for me?"

"I spoke to Marty, you bet. But I'm only on loan. I don't report to Higgins or to Walters. If you'll trust me, I'll guide you through this."

I smiled but I didn't mean it. I sipped my wine sulkily.

"Act two," T.J. said. "The patch your partner found in Terry Smith's desk. Interested?"

I nodded.

"We traced it to the manufacturer. Smith and Company had a hundred made up five years ago. Her husband, Mac, apparently took care of security. Back then, they were hiring their own people and they supplied them with white shirts and badges."

"That said *Mike's Security?*"

"People called Mac 'Mike,' don't ask me why."

"And McKay worked for them?"

"We went to Smith's accountant and got a look at the books. McKay was paid for two jobs."

"So he keeps the patches. That riddle is answered."

"Don't be so sure. We believe Terry used them herself."

"So McKay is just a harmless rat, if there is such a thing?"

"I think twenty, thirty cops are fired every year for stepping over the line. They don't go on murderous binges."

T.J. was right, but I was skeptical. "And people who get turned down for bank loans do?"

"Hey, you were the first to pick up on her. And connect her to banks."

"Oh, I see, you're doing this just for me."

"Four murders were committed at banks that turned her down," T.J. said.

"Was one of them the Bank of America?"

"Yes."

"Where she supposedly spotted McKay. Interesting. You think there might be a connection?"

"Brenden, we have it on tape, remember? Only one killer."

"Because she's angry at *banks*. You'd think she'd just bomb them."

The waiter arrived with two nasty-looking steak knives.

"All serial killers are basically seeking some kind of revenge," T.J. said. "And their anger is often displaced—or misplaced." He picked up his knife and gazed at it admiringly. "Man, I'd like to have a knife like this." He touched the tip to his finger. "Wouldn't you?"

"I'd like another glass of wine," I said.

E v e n on big cases, detectives keep banker's hours, or don't bother to come into the office very often. So at eight the next morning, I walked into a deserted Robbery/Homicide office hoping the War Room would not be locked. It wasn't. I closed the door, switched on the lights, and went to work. It took me twenty minutes to dig among the piles of papers and search the murder books—some of which had been dumped on the floor—before I found what I had come for. Adam McKay's Personnel package.

I sat down and skimmed it. Age thirty-nine, grew up in central California, enlisted in the army in 1975. Two years later, he joined LAPD, and for the next fourteen years he moved from division to division in a routine manner.

It was when he was in the CRASH unit in South Central that he began racking up a record for busting gangbangers—and others. Twice, when handling domestic disputes, he allegedly beat the males. Numerous complaints were lodged, but those folks rarely follow through. He had a Board of Rights hearing when he beat Antonio Gomez, the valedictorian, but his action was ruled "in policy."

When money crunch time came, CRASH was disbanded and McKay was transferred to West Valley Division. Those people do fuss. In eighteen months, he had twelve complaints for excessive use of force, including Mary Shaunessy's. The man he beat in Rancho Park suffered a broken right wrist, broken left arm, contusions about his body, and a cracked cheekbone. The witnesses said the man refused to move when McKay ordered him to. He called McKay a "Nazi pig," which I guess affronted Adam.

There was one other complaint from the demonstration. A second male and a female claimed that McKay had beat *them*. He was given a thirty-day suspension.

Next he moved to Foothill Division, but I guess he didn't like it there and the captain wasn't crazy about him either. He transferred to Newton. He and his partner were called to the scene of a liquor store robbery. While the partner was talking to the owner, McKay went out back. There was gunfire. When the partner arrived he found McKay standing over a body. McKay claimed he had identified himself and ordered the suspect to halt. He claimed the suspect reached into his pocket and pulled out a gun. There was a gun. A gun, however, without any prints on it.

Was Adam carrying a throwaway?

Adam's story did not impress the Board of Rights, which voted to fire him. The chief concurred. But the union went to court with a wrongful termination suit and won. The chief—that would have been Daryl Gates—was forced to take him back. He assigned him desk duty, but the union fought him again. In the end, McKay was given a sixty-day suspension without pay, then was dispatched to teach refresher courses at the academy.

At his next stop, West L.A., he began moonlighting, working security at upscale West Side parties. Four complaints from people who had employed him. Rude, abusive behavior. A couple of shoving matches. You don't bully those Armani folks. But since he was off duty, and since no one was actually injured, the complaints were eventually dropped.

Then, in November 1990, he was loaned out to West Valley to beef up its antigang squad. McKay supposedly caught three fifteen-year-olds coming out of a Ralph's supermarket one night. Two were carrying grocery bags. According to McKay's statement, the third kid pulled a gun. McKay shot him. The other two took off. He pursued them on foot. He claimed they ambushed him in an alley and in the struggle for his gun, it discharged. The two were DOA.

Oh man.

McKay stated one of the two runaways grabbed his gun and shot the other. Then McKay got the gun and shot the first kid. No eyewitnesses. Meanwhile, the kid who pulled a gun in front of the supermarket now lives in a wheelchair. He maintained he was in the act of dropping the gun when McKay fired. Two eyewitnesses verified the kid's story. All three were members of the Tortilla Flats gang. They had paid for the groceries.

The Board of Rights voted to suspend McKay for three months—during which time he would receive psychological counseling. Even though the chief is not permitted to increase the punishment meted out, Gates must have done something, because the board reopened the case and this time voted to fire him.

McKay sent a letter to Gates begging for a meeting and pleading for his job. He attached ratings reports from superiors praising him as conscientious, respectful, and cooperative. Gates's secretary called McKay's captain and said Gates would not overrule the board.

I went back through the package. I had been hoping to find a link between McKay and Terry Smith—a police link. Or something about McKay of a smoking-gun nature.

I closed the folder with a sigh.

Maybe Marty was right. A short-tempered bully who should never have been a cop. Except for Amelia Grant.

Her diaries scared the hell out of me.

O n the eighth day of my house arrest, I heard from Internal Affairs, as if I needed any more aggravation.

"Officer Harlow, this is Sergeant Redman, Internal Affairs. I was wondering if you could come in and speak with us."

"Um," I said, flustered. "Is this about your investigation of me?"

He laughed. "We only want to ask you a few questions. And despite the unsavory rumors you've heard, we really do have the best coffee in the department."

Oh great. An I.A. guy with a bedside manner. "Okay. When?"

"We'd like to do it tomorrow. When can you make it?"

"In the morning. I report here at noon."

"Ten o'clock?"

"Fine." I hesitated. "Do I need to bring a representative with me?"

"Probably wouldn't hurt. Thank you, Officer Harlow."

"No problem," I said.

Except that, of course, it was. I immediately called the Employee Representative Unit. Their job was to make sure I.A. didn't violate our employee rights when questioning us, whatever our rights were. A Francine Little spoke to me and told me not to worry. I worried the whole rest of the day, tossed most of the night, and arrived at Parker Center ten minutes early. What, I wondered, had Higgins done to me now?

Internal Affairs was located on the fifth floor at the end of a hall that dragged on like death row. The anteroom contained a secretary and a desk, but nowhere to sit. I waited outside like a naughty schoolgirl until, a few minutes later, a black woman in a red suit marched crisply up the hall, her heels clicking like a time bomb. "Brenden? Francine Little." She shook my hand. "How are you today?"

"Not guilty, but nervous." I had dressed for success, wearing a smart navy suit, a white blouse, and my power three-inch navy heels.

At 10:20 a tall, even more impeccably dressed man came out into the hall and smiled warmly at me. He looked like Sidney Poitier used to look, or maybe still does, and he had a white handkerchief tucked into his breast pocket. "Officer Harlow? Please come in. I'm Sergeant Redman. Francine, how are you?"

We followed him down a corridor and into a small room. It contained a block table and four chairs. Other than the fact that it was a little cleaner, it resembled the rooms we used to interrogate dangerous suspects.

I sat down.

"I did mention the coffee, didn't I? May I bring you a cup?"

"No sir. I'm fine, thank you."

There was an ominous manila folder on the table, but Sergeant Redman ignored it. I was sure it contained all of my sins, including the time I'd dropped a worm down the shirt of an annoying little girl in kindergarten.

The sergeant's teeth glowed. "Like the rest of the department," he began, "we're obliged to follow up tips, leads, any information that may suggest wrongdoing. Only, we look into *officer* wrongdoing. I'm happy to report you've been cleared, but we do have some loose ends to tie up."

Cleared? Of fucking what, I wondered.

"We wanted to find out if you were involved in drugs also," is what Sergeant Redman said.

I felt my stomach knot. Francine said, "Harris, may I have a word with Brenden?"

"Certainly."

She prodded me into the hall and closed the door. "What's this about?"

"My husband," I said resignedly. "He's been doing coke." Francine raised a troubled brow. I briefly told her the story. She nodded and we waltzed back in.

Sergeant Redman continued. "We've been getting reports for nine months about your husband. We know who the supplier is, but not the dealer who sells to Jack. Maybe you can help us with that. Our main concern, however, is you. It's not uncommon that if one spouse uses, the other does, too. That, of course, would be grounds for dismissal. And prosecution."

"I understand, sir."

"Good. Now, on May twenty-sixth you flew to Hawaii. You left in the morning and returned late that night. Quick trip, wasn't it?"

"Yes."

"And the purpose of this trip?"

"First I want to say that I lied to my superior about why I was taking the day off. I guess you know that. It was wrong, but I didn't want to have to explain."

Again the teeth glowed. "Explain to me."

"I wanted to see my husband."

"And did you bring him anything?"

Fuck you, I thought. "No, I did not. I went with friends to confront Jack. His problem was getting out of hand."

"His coke problem?"

"Yes."

"Why didn't you act before this, Officer Harlow?"

I ran my fingers through my hair, then abruptly stopped. I did not want to act flustered. "Sir, I'm afraid I didn't know. From what I'm told, he was using drugs on the set. I never saw my husband using drugs ever. I was deaf, dumb, and blind."

"Someone told you?"

I nodded. "Someone who works on *Night Watch*. Then I found a packet of cocaine in the freezer. Then Jack's agent warned me. He's the one who insisted I go to Hawaii."

"You never found contraband in your house before?"

I shook my head.

"I find that hard to believe. You are familiar with drug behavior, aren't you, Officer Harlow?"

"I thought I was, sir. But from September on, with our work schedules, we didn't see that much of each other. Toward the end, just before he went to Hawaii, he was a little moody, but that's the most I can say." Other than the runny nose, which hadn't rung a bell either.

"So what was the upshot of your visit to Hawaii?"

"Jack agreed to go to Betty Ford as soon as he wraps the picture he's on. It should be any day now, I believe."

Sergeant Redman sat there smiling at me. Like a goddam shrink.

I smiled back. Our dueling smiles clashed midway across the table.

"That's all for now," he said, rising. "We'll want to hear about your husband's progress. By the way, alcohol is *not* an illegal substance, but as you know, it can produce equally disastrous results."

Shit. Higgins. "Thank you, sir."

As I stood, he opened the door and nearly flattened me with a farewell smile.

"Next time, you must try the coffee," Sergeant Redman said.

A t last the hideous week came to an end. There had been no more stabbings, no more crank calls, and no progress that I knew of on the case. I had not gone into the First Base Saloon. I did not want to see Higgins, be spied upon by Internal Affairs, or deal with Adam McKay.

When I got home from work that Friday night, I discovered Jack had been by, which did not exactly take a whole lot of deducing. Two of his dresser drawers were open, as was his closet door, and in typical Jack fashion, he had left a pile of clothes to be laundered or dry-cleaned. There was also a note.

> Bren—
> I know you're right to shut me out, but when this is over, I won't let you anymore. I start at Betty Ford on Sunday. Thirty days and counting.
> Love, Jack.

I opened a fresh bottle of vodka and settled in to watch *The Getaway* on tape. I wondered why there weren't men like McQueen in the movies anymore.

I fell asleep still wondering.

•   •   •

D o r r i e Green phoned the next morning while I was combing the cobwebs out of my eyes. She sounded suspiciously sunny and cheerful. To be polite, I injected a human note into my voice.

"Strap on your dancing shoes, girl. We are going to *party* tonight."

"We are?"

"Lover boy invited us to a cookout. He says he sold his screenplay and wants to celebrate. Seven o'clock, his place."

"You're speaking of Adam McKay?"

"I did say lover boy, didn't I?"

"I'm afraid I'm busy." I paused. "My toenails need clipping."

"Yeah, right. Like my nappy hair needs a perm. What's wrong with you?"

I tried to consider his motive. "Is anyone else going?"

"Well, I think everyone. Last night he invited me and Cookie and Cindy—that's Cookie's new friend—and Higgins, I'm afraid. And T.J. and Gwen Dixon, which should be interesting. And he said some live Hollywood natives would be there. But he specifically said to tell you."

I wrinkled my nose and tried to figure out this new development. Maybe he wanted to lord it over us cops, show us that he had reinvented himself as a genuine big deal. Yes, that would fit. The more I thought about it, the more I liked it. An open-house invitation from Adam McKay. To poke around . . . his open house.

"I have directions," Dorrie was saying. "Unfortunately, it's—"

"I know. Two valleys removed." I paused. "So you're definitely going?"

"When you're single, you go to almost anything. Come on, Brenden. If it's terrible, we'll leave."

"All right. What are the directions?"

"Oh, great. You got a pen?"

I sighed. "And to think I don't have a thing to wear."

T h a t afternoon I checked with T.J. He assured me he would be at McKay's, "as soon as I'm done with Terry."

"On a Saturday night?" I said.

"There's a half-moon. You never know," T.J. said ominously.

The party was called for seven. Thanks to Jack, who had trained me to be fashionably late, I was just walking out at 7:30 when the

Metro desk called. "Terry Smith is trying to reach you," I was told. "She'd like you to call her right away."

I chewed this over. The number he had given me was for her office. I pressed the record button on my answering machine and dialed it.

Terry answered immediately. "Oh good," she exclaimed when I identified myself. "You can't imagine how many calls I had to make to reach you."

"So what's going on?"

"I'm at my office and I wondered if you could stop by. I have something to show you that might help with your case."

"I have to go somewhere," I said. "Why don't you tell me what it is?"

"It would be better if I *showed* you. I'm not going anywhere. I've got a bid due at ten o'clock Monday morning. I'll be here all weekend."

My mind was racing. Was she planning another stabbing and, concerned about our surveillance, did she hope to throw us off track? Or was she trying to lure me to an empty office building with the intention of killing me? "I'm not sure when I can get there," I said.

"Call me from your car and I'll alert the guard. Also, could you keep this to yourself? You'll understand when I talk to you."

Yeah, right. "Okay," I said to Terry and hung up.

I n the car I began to toy with the idea of going straight there. T.J. would be at her office building and I could alert him and he could call in the troops. But when I dialed his cell phone, I got a busy signal.

As I hurtled along the Santa Monica freeway toward downtown, I tried T.J. twice more. Another busy signal, followed by an "out of the car or out of the area" recording. Maybe, I thought, he was already en route to McKay's. I would call Marty Walters if I had to.

And then, as I was approaching the 110 interchange, it came to me. A small thing, perhaps, but it kept gnawing at me at eighty-five miles per hour. On impulse, I shot into the left lane, cutting it close, the car behind me braking hard.

I started up the 110, heading north.

C a n y o n Country, as it is so romantically labeled, was at least an hour away, even at the speed at which I travel. I rode the 110 to the

5 to the 14 to Sand Canyon Road, which got me to the Sierra Highway, and if God had intended anyone to go this far, he would have handed down a tablet saying so. By the time I found the unpaved road that Adam called home, I was ready to arrest him for excessive and criminal distance.

Cars and trucks lined the "street" fronting a sprawling ranch house, decorated with tiny white lights as if it were a Christmas ornament. I parked at some distance, and as I walked back, I searched for T.J.'s car. I had to find him right away. But his car was nowhere in sight. I could hear some country western and, as I drew closer to the house, an overlay of voices. The front door stood open.

Several people were standing beside a bar just inside the living room. After one of them handed me a plastic glass of white wine, he directed me into the dining room and out back. I was wearing black jeans and cowboy boots and a white linen jacket over a red T-shirt. I had my Beretta holstered on my hip.

The Christmas-light motif was carried out in the backyard with hundreds of tiny bulbs threaded through jacaranda trees. More lights illuminated the patio that ran around the back of the house. Beyond the lawn stood a brick barbecue pit, and Adam himself was flipping hamburgers. My eyes traveled past him. Some fifty yards away, a horse moved restlessly around a paddock. A barn loomed in the distance. Quite a few cops living in Canyon Country owned horses. If some of the public cuttingly referred to us as cowboys, they weren't far off the mark.

I turned back toward the house and immediately spotted Cookie Randall with a tall delicate blonde who could have been Gwen Dixon's twin. I waved.

"Hey," called Cookie.

I walked over to her. "Hey yourself." I smiled and held out my hand to the blonde. "I'm Brenden Harlow."

"Cindy West."

Her hand was limp. She was wearing a sheer white blouse, mostly unbuttoned, a pair of tight shorts, and white boots. She wet her pink lips and smiled blandly.

"So," I said to Cookie. "Give me a rundown."

"Well . . . those two glamor boys are producers," she said, indicating a pair of short, pear-shaped men strangling in gold neck chains. "And Mr. Smooth Dude over there—the tall one with the tan?—he's

Adam's agent. The couple by the tree are neighbors. They're nice. T.J.'s not here yet. Haven't seen Higgins. And Dorrie is somewhere. It took her exactly a minute and a half to latch on to some actor."

I noticed she had neglected to mention Gwen Dixon, who was sitting at a table eating ribs and talking to a man who had the right mustache and muscles to be a cop.

"Brenden's one of the girls I work with," Cookie explained to Cindy. "She's in Metro." Cookie looked at me. "Cindy's a little nervous tonight. She had an audition this morning and she hasn't heard back."

"Oh?" I said politely.

"Yes, for a movie. A big movie. Johnny Depp's in it." Cindy flashed a camera-ready smile.

"Brenden's married to Jack Hayes," Cookie announced. *"Night Watch."*

"Oh my God," Cindy exclaimed. "I love Jack Hayes!"

"Don't we all." I smiled wanly.

"Have something to eat," said Cookie suddenly. She pointed to her own paper plate. "The ribs are great, so's the corn."

"Okay. I'll join you in a few minutes."

I passed a table piled with food, but I walked around it and headed for the barbecue pit. Adam was talking to a man with a torn T-shirt, but he broke off as I approached.

"Hey, look who's here. I was hoping you would come."

He was wearing a long white chef's apron that was soiled with charcoal and barbecue sauce. A spot of sauce decorated the corner of his mouth. I said, "Congratulations. I hear you sold it even without me."

Adam patted me on the shoulder. "You'll get your chance. They want a new ending anyway."

The man walked away. I said, "So who's the lucky buyer?"

"An independent producer optioned it. Not much money there, but he's got meetings next week at Paramount, Sony, and MGM. They think it's going to be big."

"Isn't that something," I remarked. "And people think it's so easy to write a screenplay. But of course it's not. I mean, you've been working on yours for what? Eight, nine years?"

"Oh God, nothing like that."

"Sure you have, Adam. Collecting stuff from your police days. Anecdotes, bits of conversation. All writers do that."

"Well, sure. You can't help writing about what you know."

"It's funny though. Don't take this as an insult, okay? But I totally forgot you were teaching at the academy when I was there."

"Really?" Adam flipped a hamburger. "I don't remember. When?"

"But you do remember Amelia Rodriguez, or Ann Johnson? They used to talk about you." I stepped closer and whispered, "You left quite an impression."

Adam recoiled. "You must have me confused with someone else. Say, what do you think of my thoroughbred?" He half-turned toward the striking horse and gazed at it with pride. "Pure blood out of Buttermilk Farms in Kentucky. As a two-year-old, the talk was that he would be the next Affirmed. Then he bowed a tendon." Adam returned his attention to me. "But a thoroughbred has that purity of line. Like with people. Either you're born with it or you're not."

"Sure."

"Sneaky Pete's gonna be my trust fund for life, once we find the right mare and start breeding him."

"You must have a lucky charm, Adam. A honest-to-goodness thoroughbred. Imagine." I pointed at the barn. "And that big thing's just for this one little horse?" I didn't know the first thing about barns and had no idea if it was a big one or not. But I liked the glow the horse had brought to Adam's eyes.

He nodded. "It was here when I bought the place. I've done a little work on it. The tack room's all wood-paneled and everything. Someday I'd like to show it to you."

"Why not tonight?"

Adam tossed some fresh patties on the grill. "I don't want to ruin your appetite, Brenden, but I've got field mice."

I smiled. "Doesn't everyone?"

"Not this kind, hopefully. These little guys are carrying around some kind of bacteria. If you ingest it, it's lethal."

"Excuse me, Adam, but why would I ingest field mice?"

He laughed. "Not you. But their droppings are all over the barn. If Sneaky Pete ingests them, he would die. That's why I've got him outside. Even I won't go in there. If some of their shit dries and flakes and gets on me, I could die. The exterminators are coming tomorrow."

"Yuck," I said.

"It gets worse. I have a room in there where I work. I wanted to move all my stuff into the basement, you know, the computer and printer and stuff? But the exterminators said the basement needs to be sprayed, too."

"You have a basement? Nobody in California has a basement. There's a reason, but I forget why."

"Actually, it's a bomb shelter. It was built in the fifties when everyone was panicked over the Russians. Man, you should see it. There's like six bunk beds, only they're slabs of wood built into concrete walls. I found mattresses, blankets, candles, tons of canned food, vats of water. They even built a bathroom."

"And the mice are down there, too?"

Adam dropped a slab of ribs on the grill. "Tell you the truth, I wouldn't know. When I discovered the shelter, I got rid of everything in it. It was creepy. It reminded me of a tomb." He looked up. "Hey, how about some ribs? A hamburger?"

"Looks good."

He lifted a spatula and transferred a thick burger onto a paper plate and handed it to me. "Buns are over on that table."

"Thanks. See you later."

I helped myself to a bun, a piece of corn, and some salad. I still didn't see Dorrie, but Gwen Dixon was getting up from her table. She spoke to the man beside her, then she walked away.

I stepped in front of her. "Hi. Remember me?"

Her eyes widened. "I'm afraid I do. How are you, Brenden?"

Like me, she was wearing jeans and boots. A rawhide vest hung open over a white shirt. Even off duty, cops had their uniforms.

"Could I speak to you for a minute?"

"Sure. But let me get another glass of wine, okay?"

I pointed to a table. "I'll be right over there."

I sat down, nodded at two women and a man who were sitting at the far end of the table, and spread butter on the corn. I had been tempted to have a word with Sergeant Redman about Gwen but he hadn't seemed the type to answer my question.

Gwen sat down next to me. "I thought it would be fun to see old friends, but old friends sometimes get old."

"You wouldn't be speaking of our host?"

Gwen made a face. "Have you ever seen a more normal-looking guy? Then he writes this crap. Have you read it? I wouldn't be surprised if he were into some pretty weird shit."

"Like what?"

"Sex stuff. I don't even want to speculate."

"I think you might be right. He asked me to help him with the female cop. Frankly, she offended me."

Gwen nodded. "He tried to get into all this lurid stuff with me, too. I said, 'Adam, I've read your character, and I wouldn't have a clue what's going on with her.'"

"So he asked you to help him, too?"

"I met him for lunch one day. He said since we'd both been fired, maybe we could figure out how to get this cop in trouble. Creative retribution, I think he called it. But all he wanted to talk about was sex."

Instinctively, I glanced around for T.J. I said, "Do you remember when you had lunch? The exact day?"

She straightened as if suddenly put on alert.

"Look, Gwen, what happened at the airport, forget it. But I'd like to know if you and Adam talked about me."

"Mm." She bit her lip. "You know, you're right. He did ask about you. He said he thought maybe he had a shot at you, what did I think? I said how would I know. I said all I knew about you was that you were married to Jack Hayes and in fact—" She sat there perfectly still looking at me.

"I was on my way to Hawaii to bring him cocaine?"

Gwen blinked. She was good, good at using her face and her razor-sharp mind. She shook her head and laughed. "Now you're making me remember my undercover days. You ever worked narcotics, Brenden? Anyway, I didn't know you were going to see your husband. But I think you're right. I think that was the day I met Adam for lunch. I must have told him I was upset because I thought you and Cookie had something going. Yes, I'm sure that's what happened."

Cleverly sidestepping my reference to cocaine. I had no idea if she was telling the truth about having lunch with McKay, but the connection seemed promising.

Gwen stood up. "Now that you've got me thinking back, I remember all drug dealers I arrested who didn't even use, though of course they were engaged in unlawful activity. But it's funny, isn't it, how sometimes the biggest danger comes from people who *aren't* breaking the law." She tossed her hair and smiled. "People who ruin lives with alcohol."

I watched her walk away, long blond hair swaying at her waist. What she had told me, if I was reading the subtext correctly, was that she knew *I* knew she was working for Internal Affairs. She was telling me that maybe the books were still open on whether I had transported drugs to Jack, even though I was cleared of using. And that they were watching my drinking. I put my plate in a trash can and wandered into the house.

All of the rooms were lighted, as if Adam was intent on showing off his home. The decor was a kind of faux Western carried out with boring browns and beiges. The living room contained a large stone fireplace under a fake Remington, and a wooden horse with a good-looking saddle on it. In one corner stood a lighted barber pole, which revolved.

I continued down a beige-carpeted hall and stepped into what appeared to be Adam's den. On an old rough-hewn wooden desk sat a vintage Royal typewriter. Bookshelves were filled with detective novels, texts on screenwriting, and dozens of well-known screenplays. There was also a locked gun cabinet. In it were two rifles, a shotgun, and three .45 revolvers that could have come from the Old West.

The next room appeared to be a guest room. As I came to the last room, I found the door ajar. There was a light on. I stepped quickly inside and closed the door.

I was standing in Adam McKay's bedroom.

Unlike the other rooms, this one was filled with clutter. A queen-size bed covered with a patchwork quilt sat under heavily curtained windows in the same fabric. Two bedside tables, each with an imitation Tiffany lamp. The lamp on the left was lit, providing the only light in the room. A desk on one wall with a phone was buried under magazines and newspapers. I walked over to a tall dresser and glanced at bottles of cologne, brushes, and a jar of change. Beside it a TV rested on a metal stand. A closet with sliding wooden doors took up most of the wall to the right of the bed. Beyond that was a door, which I imagined led to a bathroom. My eyes drifted back to the closet longingly. I moved closer. I was debating taking a peek when I heard Adam's voice.

"Give me a sec, Frank. I'll be right back."

I ducked into the bathroom and shut the door.

In the dark, I found a light switch and flipped it. The bathroom was quite large and featured, at one end, a Jacuzzi tub. There was also a glass-enclosed shower with six water spigots and a lovely tiled sink set into a custom-made vanity. A mirror flanked by two period wall sconces hung over it.

I waited a moment, flushed the toilet, and turned on the tap. I washed my hands, switched off the light, and opened the door.

The bedroom was dark.

Adam must have come in, turned off the lamp, and gone out. I let my eyes adjust until I could make out the strip of light under the bedroom door. The closet could wait, and anyway, I doubted it contained what I was looking for. Cautiously, I headed for the door, but I misjudged badly and slammed into the dresser, crushing my left breast. Sharp pain radiated through me. I bit my lip, took a deep breath and, a few feet further along, fumbled for the doorknob. Slowly I opened the door, peeked out, and retreated quickly down the hall.

Beyond the foyer, the same people were still conversing at the bar. Between us, the front door stood open.

Nobody noticed me slip out.

I decided to approach the barn from the front of the house, circumventing Adam and his guests. I made a quick trip down the road to my car and retrieved my flashlight. The air had turned chilly, as it always did in this semiarid climate, even in summer. Above, the stars shone too big and too brightly. It was as if Adam, blinded by the stars in his own eyes, had created the perfect set from which to spin his lurid tale.

I retraced my steps along the road, cut across the graveled front yard, and stopped at the corner of the ranch house.

To the left, a thick tumble of bushes and trees formed a woodsy barrier between the road and the stable. I started off in a diagonal direction that would put me in the vicinity of the barn. I had no idea what Adam didn't want me to see, but the barn was where he had hidden it. Otherwise he would not have left his house open to prying eyes or gone into such detail about his scary fleet of mice.

As I broke through the woods, the barn appeared in a clearing about thirty yards ahead of me, the halo of stars above it crowned with a brilliant half slice of moon. The barn was dark, inside and out, lit only by the high-intensity lights drifting over from the paddock. Gripping my flashlight, I dashed quickly across the clearing.

The door on the road side of the barn was double-width. A concrete step, covered with a woven mat, led up to it. I doubted a horse needed a welcome mat; the horse entrance, I was guessing, was on the opposite side of the barn facing the paddock. The door was locked.

High windows flanked the door. Stepping up to the one on my left and standing on tiptoe, I tried to raise it. But it, too, was locked.

Come on, Adam, don't be a spoilsport. This is your game; you've dealt the cards. I'm in and I want to play.

I started to walk around the barn. I could try the "horse's entrance" and, if spotted, I could joke my way out of it. But suddenly I stopped and went back to the locked door. Stenciled on the welcome mat were the words *Go Away!* I smiled as I lifted it. And there, somewhat to my surprise, was a brass key.

Again, I hesitated. If the barn had an alarm system I would have to take off fast, return to the house, and lose myself among the guests. I slipped the key into the lock, turned it, and slowly nudged open the door. Neither the sound of an alarm nor the scampering of creepy little mouse feet greeted me. I stepped inside and closed the door.

It was pitch-black.

Cautiously I shone my flashlight on the floor. I was standing at the end of a long hallway with open doors on either side. To the right I discovered a small office with a desk, a phone, a chair, and some file cabinets. Taped to the walls were charts having to do with horse breeding. The door on the left led into what I gathered was his renovated tack room.

Or Ralph Lauren's.

Burnished wood-paneled walls and a few English horse prints set the tone. On one wall hung three saddles and an assortment of bridles, halters, and lead ropes. There were shelves holding shampoo, buckets, hoof picks, combs, and bottles that said *Hoof Ointment*. An old railroad clock hung on the wall above a pair of leather club chairs. Inside a cabinet, which I of course opened, I found a stack of blankets embroidered with the initials *AM*. Adam, the gentrified horseman.

I walked back into the hall and followed it until I came to three open stalls on the right. That took me to the far end of the barn, and I could see a glimmer of light through the big windows looking out toward the paddock. But to my left there was only a solid wall. He had spoken of a computer and printer. I returned to the tack room.

This time I walked through it until I came to a door. On the other side of it would be the area behind the solid wall. I listened to the ticking of the railroad clock and remembered the mice. For a moment I listened carefully. Then I twisted the knob.

Immediately two lights came on and I stood there, inside the door, staring transfixed at what lay before me. Eventually, I dragged my eyes from the far end of the long, narrow room, and methodically began to explore Adam McKay's secret trove of artifacts.

Secured on the wall to my left was a shadow box, a velvet-lined, glass-enclosed box that is presented to police officers upon their retirement. His contained the usual mementos—a service revolver that had been neutered and plated to look gold, a hat piece, buttons, rank insignias, shooting medals, and ribbons. Officers who are fired don't get a shadow box, but apparently Adam thought he deserved it and created this himself. Over the box hung a navy felt banner with our motto in yellow letters: TO PROTECT AND TO SERVE. Displayed in another glass box further along was an assortment of beautifully polished and quite scary-looking swords and knives.

I moved on to the next exhibit—a spooky life-size mannequin dressed in an LAPD uniform. Talk about a temple to his authority, oh man. Shaking my head, I turned to the other side of the room. A long worktable, set against the wall, held a computer, printer, and fax machine. Also neat stacks of papers. One consisted of drafts of his screenplay. A second contained typed notes. I glanced at my watch as I began thumbing through them. I'd been inside fourteen minutes. And then I stopped thumbing and held very still.

Five pages stapled together were entitled "Amelia 1987."

"Brought her home, tried a few things. She was so terrified I felt the most amazing thrill. At first, I felt only disgust for this sniveling crybaby . . . some police officer! But then I began to smell her fear, actually smell it, and got a hard-on. I decided I'd better kick her before I raped her!"

I winced, again feeling Amelia's pain, and went on to other pages because I didn't want to dwell on her now. Then I stopped again. This time I felt a chill right down to my toes. Underlined in red ink were the sentences *"Brenden Harlow. Thinks she's a big shit. Finished first among the women and fifth overall. Boy, would I like to knock her down a notch. Ha. Ha."*

So he *had* known of me at the academy; had he been watching me all along? But I couldn't dwell on that either. I put the pages back on the desk, lay down my flashlight, and moved a few feet further along. For a long moment, I stared at the turquoise towel with the stains on it. Carefully I lifted a corner and sucked in my breath as I stared at the bloody knife. The blade was about eight inches long—the blood was fresh.

I covered it up and fought my instinct to get the hell out of there. I still had one exhibit to go. Steeling myself, I moved toward the display at the far end of the room that had initially caught my eye.

Two vertical purple neon tubes—one on each side—lit a large square of brown paper taped to the wall. On it were drawn the concentric circles of a practice target. Taped on the circles were white cardboard squares, each neatly printed in red ink with the name of one of his victims. The squares were numbered sequentially, starting with the outer ring: *1. Mary Shaunessy, 2. Alice Croft, 3. Andrea Wright, 4. Amelia (Rodriguez) Grant,* and then on the next ring, *5. Sheila Dann, 6. Michelle Lloyd, 7. Suki Kahn.* The third ring showed *8. Sally Sloane,* and *9.,* a square, oddly, with no name. Inside the bull's-eye, was *10. Harlow.*

It captivated me, this naked display of evil, not the concept of evil but the actual hard fact of it, and I couldn't take my eyes off of my name. It was like watching a sci-fi movie in which the doomed is able to see into the future. Instinctively I found myself patting my hip for my ROVER, but I didn't have it. I would have to go out there and do it myself. "No, Adam, I don't want another hamburger. Would you please put your hands behind your back? You're under arrest."

But I seemed unable to move. And as I continued to study the gruesome target I wondered about the anonymous number nine. There had been nine murders in all, including Suki Kahn's unborn child, so maybe that was what the nine represented—the unnamed child—although, chronologically, it should have been number eight.

It was then that I heard it—the sharp intake of breath—and sensed the movement. At once, the room went black.

A hand came crushing down on my mouth, and my right arm was jacked up behind me. One of his legs shot between mine, and his heel dug into my left arch. I was immobilized.

He pressed his lips to my ear. "Hey, cutie cop. Now we're gonna write the *real* final act."

He must have had the cuffs in his pocket, because he snapped them on my wrists instantly. The cold steel of a gun barrel pressed into the side of my neck.

"You could scream and they might hear you and they'd come running and they would arrest me," he breathed into my ear. "But it would be too late for you, because you'd be dead." He clicked off the safety. "So you're going to be real quiet while I gag you." At once, the purple neon lights went on. He shoved my face into the wall and I heard a ripping sound and then a wide swatch of gaffer's tape was slapped over my mouth.

As if nobody was going to notice me missing. Asshole.

He spun me around, and in the purplish glow of neon, I looked into the empty eyes of Adam McKay.

He smiled. "How do you like the way I changed my M.O.? First the cuts to the torso, then the slicing of the neck. Subtle changes. But I know how upset cops get when the M.O. changes."

There was a door to the right of me. McKay dug into his jeans pocket for a key and unlocked it. He reached in and switched on a light. "They're gonna go bonkers with the M.O. after tonight. Come on, cutie, you're in for a treat."

He grabbed my arm and pulled me through the doorway. Even before I saw the stairs, I knew we were headed for the bomb shelter. And I thought, This is how Amelia must have felt, recognizing the madness but not knowing how far he would go.

"Don't worry about the mice," McKay said. "The ones I got are garden variety field mice. But I knew you'd fall for the bait. Besides, I needed an excuse to put Sneaky Pete in the paddock. Sneaky Pete hates the smell of blood."

He was behind me now, gripping my left elbow, and I was looking down a long concrete flight of stairs. If I brought up my boot and kicked him in the knee—with my hands cuffed behind me—I'd go flying down those stairs, and he would recover before I would. Pliantly, I allowed him to march me down the stairs.

The bulb at the top of the landing only dimly lit the entrance to the bomb shelter. I could barely make out, to my right, two slabs of wood, one above the other, which must have been the bunk beds. He put his hand on my head and pushed me onto the lower one. "Just sit," McKay said.

The air smelled rank. It was quite cold down here and damp. McKay dragged out a coil of rope from under the bed. Sitting on his haunches, gun still in hand, he stared thoughtfully at my boots. Apparently he decided to tie my ankles together with the boots on, which would make it harder for me to maneuver. He looped the rope around my ankles and, after he coiled the rope around several times, he put down the gun and finished the job. Go ahead, McKay, get your sick thrills. And don't forget my gun, asshole. You know I've got to have one.

And he did, grinning, as he stuck his hand inside my jacket and pulled out the Beretta. He studied it with satisfaction, then he straightened and shoved it into his belt.

"Get up."

I didn't know why he wanted me to stand. I figured he would leave me lying on the bed. I didn't think he intended to kill me like this, defenseless and unable to sound, through my taped mouth, the crying, dying noises he undoubtedly craved. Scowling, he grabbed my arm and hauled me to my feet, and now I could see the pure hatred in his flat brown eyes.

"I know you, Harlow. I know everything you're thinking. You're thinking, I'll get this bastard. Yeah, you are. You think you're gonna get me all by yourself with all those jerk-off cops wandering around out there dribbling barbecue sauce on their shirts and you'll show the whole fucking department what a hotshot you are."

So will you, I thought. You're going to show the department that betrayed you how you can kill a cop right under their noses.

"Only I'm going to prove that you're nothing."

He landed a right punch to my belly. I went down hard, banging my head on the upper bunk and sagging onto the floor. The air that *whoosh*ed through my diaphragm and wanted to escape through my mouth had nowhere to go, and my lungs burned. Savagely, he grabbed me and shoved me into the lower bunk. "I hope you're not claustrophobic, bitch. Because it'll be a while before you and I finish our business."

I heard his boots climb the stairs. The light went out. The door closed with authority.

Asshole. My anger had become so physical that I was shaking with it, and I lay there for what seemed a long time until my heart rate slowed and my mind began to clear. I *was* claustrophobic, and the cloying dampness of the air made me wonder about fresh oxygen. The people who built the shelter . . . how had they prepared for that?

And what was that sour odor? It reminded me of blood, but I didn't think I was bleeding. The pig probably kept his . . . bloody clothes? Was that what I was smelling?

He was right. I had swaggered into his trap a little too confidently, and he had snared me like an animal. And now, with the entire LAPD at my disposal, I was stranded on a deserted island without even a bottle to slip a message into. Stranded in this chamber of horrors with my name inscribed in the bull's-eye, my death preordained.

Fucking asshole.

I swung my feet onto the floor, still feeling the pain in my stomach and the throbbing in my head. I slid onto the floor, drew my knees up to my chin, and tried to slip my hands under my hips and up over my feet. But my arms were a couple of inches short. I grasped my heels and tried to wrench off my boots. But the rope was too tight to do that. I began to feel dizzy as the blackness and the fetid air closed in on me.

Okay. I would move, get the feel of the place, make the shelter mine. Yes. And if I were lucky, I'd find a hiding place and force the element of surprise.

Upright on my knees, I inched deeper into the cavern.

And then I stopped.

Why—he wouldn't have to come back to kill me. He could simply not return. And I would die from lack of water or air. My imagination raced as my terror intensified. And then I thought, No, Adam wouldn't do that. Where would be the thrill?

I moved on.

As best I could, I walked a straight line, and soon I came upon a second lower bunk. I sat on the floor to catch my breath and leaned against it. But something was sticking out.

I rose up on my knees and reached backward into the bunk with my fingers. Rough woolen material like a blanket. Only there was something under it, something soft, like a sweatshirt, up against something hard like . . .

Oh my God. My God.

I tried to catch my ragged breath, but as the blackness and the claustrophobia and the fear began to overwhelm me, I knew now that I had gone beyond what Amelia had. In her final seconds, her brain would not have understood what was happening to her. But I knew; he had made sure I would know.

I still have control, I told myself; don't lose control.

Forcing myself, I again splayed my fingers and felt what was behind me until there could be no mistake. The bare arm, the soft neck, the smooth skin on the face. And then, with dread, I touched the coarse, kinky hair.

She was dead. Even before I touched her neck looking for a pulse, I knew. The sour, sickening odor of Dorrie Green's spilt blood had told me that.

I crept away, fighting against my own building madness. Again I sat and brought my knees up. With numbing fingers I clawed at the rope around my ankles, mindful now of time passing. Even so, it took an eternity to untie the knot. Prying my right boot off took even more of an effort. The black calf fit my foot snugly, but my ankles were thin, and the boots, which only went up to my calves, were roomy at the top. Grunting, tugging on the heel, I progressed millimeter by millimeter, until at last, with a final jerk, my right heel broke free. The boot clumped to the floor. Hungrily I caressed the little .380 Sigma lodged in the holster on my right ankle.

I tried once more to maneuver my legs through my arms and realized it wasn't going to work. I willed myself to think. But Dorrie's lovely almond-shaped eyes and wide easy grin kept looming up in my mind. She was the anonymous number nine. But why? Why her, asshole? Did you really think you could get away with killing both of us, both last seen at your house? Rational thinking was useless. The monster had taken control of Adam's id and had twisted it beyond all human reason.

I will not panic.

Surely somebody—Cookie?—must be wondering about me. And where the hell was T.J.? Or Higgins? Oh shit. Maybe McKay had struck again, and that's where they were, poring over another ATM crime scene. Or maybe Terry Smith was up to another of her maddening tricks. Even if T.J. came, he might not notice my car parked under a leafy tree along the darkened road.

Slowly I got to my feet. Thinking, Come on, asshole, I'm ready for your final act.

Or should I say my close-up, Mr. McKay.

T i m e passed. My mouth grew parched and the stink of the place at times made me nauseous. The cuffs dug into my wrists and I had to remember to keep wiggling my fingers to keep them from growing numb. Occasionally I heard little scratching, scurrying sounds, and I shuddered and shut my eyes. Once, when my fear took control of me, I found myself dozing off.

Unless help arrived, I knew I would have only one chance—and maybe not even that.

The door creaked open. The light went on. Footsteps fell upon the concrete. I shifted onto my back, on the bunk where he had left me. Soon a pair of blue-jeaned legs, a bottle of Corona, and my own flashlight came into view.

He shone the light directly at me. "Oh, I see you got the rope off," McKay remarked. He ran his hand along my right boot and up my leg. "My, my, such a tough little cop. But I like that touch. I think I'll write that into my screenplay."

He was wearing a western shirt tucked into his jeans, and I didn't know where the gun was.

He knelt in front of me. "So what we're going to do is this. We're going to go upstairs, and you're going to take off your clothes and sit at my computer, and you, Ms. LAPD, are going to write your very own death scene." He grew thoughtful. "I don't think that's ever been done before."

I didn't want to go upstairs.

"In case you're wondering, everyone's gone. Your pal T.J. stopped by, but I told him you'd left. Cookie was mad that you didn't say good-bye, but frankly, she was more interested in her girlfriend. So, cutie cop, it's just you and me."

I stared at him with empty eyes, not moving a muscle. Maybe he had the knife, not a gun.

He sat on the floor cross-legged. "First I want to read you the part I've already written." He took a swig of beer, put the bottle down, and reached behind him. His hand reappeared, clutching a batch of folded pages. "And then we'll see what your bra and panties look like. Don't worry. I have some real nice things I bought for you in case yours aren't right." He smiled broadly. "It has to be right."

I didn't want him to tie my feet again, so I lay as still as possible. I was at the bunk's edge with less than three feet to the wall and at most three feet above me.

"Okay, here we go."

He put down the flashlight and went for the Corona. "Oh." He looked at me. "Gee, I forgot to bring you a Black Russian. I know you'd like one. A final shot of vodka." He took a long swallow from the bottle, cleared his throat, and picked up the flashlight.

"So the cop knows this guy is the mail bomber, right? And she's been surveilling him. She sees him leave his apartment and drive off. She jimmies the lock and enters the location. She's looking for plastic explosives, wire, timers, things like that. And she finds it all in a box in his closet." McKay paused and looked up. "I was trying to work in a bomb shelter scene, but it didn't feel right to me. Do you think? Well, never mind. So she's going through this box when—guess what?—the bomber, Eddie Rocco, surprises her. Kind of like tonight, you know? Only Eddie uses her handcuffs to cuff her. He tapes her mouth, ties her ankles." Adam smiled brightly. "It's called cinema verité."

I blinked, letting him know I was following.

"Okay, so here's what I've written."

He rustled the pages, found his place, and began to read aloud. Suddenly, I wanted to laugh. Here I was, being set up for the kill, and I risked going to my grave listening to this *dreck*. Fuck you, McKay. *Fuck you.*

He moved on to the next page, reading with a bit of a flair and I did it by rote, did what I had practiced a hundred times in my head. Swiftly bringing my knees up, rolling onto them, my back to him, the gun cocked and I fired blind and I fired and I fired and I fired. And the ringing in my ears and the thunderous echo in this concrete crypt was so deafening that I didn't even notice when the reading stopped.

Or did it?

No, there was a voice. Oh shit, whose voice? And pounding, some kind of pounding, followed by—silence.

I had fallen forward into a crouch, my head on my knees, and I felt the gun being pried from my fingers. He grabbed my shoulders and—I knew he would use my gun on me—he spun me around.

"Mother of God. Brenden, are you all right?"

And a second voice: "He's dead. Jesus, look at that."

I blinked dumbly into the face of Chris Leiter from SWAT.

"Sorry, this might sting," he said as he pulled the tape from my mouth. "You're not hurt?"

My eyes traveled past him. T. J. McCall, gun drawn, stood poised at the bottom of the stairs. He looked at me sadly. "I'm sorry, Brenden."

I licked my lips and got shakily to my feet and didn't look at McKay as I stepped over him.

And all I said was, "Fucking cops. They're never there when you need them."

eedless to say, Higgins was not pleased with the developments of that night, especially because he hadn't gone to the party on account of being "stressed." But since I was off duty and had clearly killed in self-defense, there was nothing even he could dream up to do about it.

The LAPD Public Relations crew put its own rather imaginative spin on the stories that appeared in the media over the next few days. Robbery/Homicide had slowly built a case against former LAPD officer Adam McKay. On the night in question, it learned that McKay would be hosting a party and sent some detectives to surveille the property. Ironically, several of the invited guests were officers McKay was acquainted with. After the guests had left, the surveillance team noticed a car belonging to a female detective. When an officer, posing as a friend of Det. Dorrie Green, phoned and asked to speak to her, McKay denied she was there. SWAT was called in.

According to the story, a negotiation was begun but McKay refused to surrender. Shots sounded and SWAT entered the house. They found McKay dead in his stable, the victim of a self-inflicted gunshot wound. Dorrie Green was found stabbed to death in a manner similar to the victims at the ATMs.

And so, with this sleight of hand, I was magically erased from the picture. Gone. "Otherwise you'll get a reputation, and people will know your face, and the public will treat you more like a celebrity than a police officer, and your effectiveness will be zero," is how Monster McGrew explained it to me three days later in his office as I sat there trying to meet his walleyed stare. "The Officer-Involved-Shooting

Team will interview you, of course. But your actions will be ruled *in policy,* and that will be the end of it." He smiled pleasantly.

"Okay," I said.

"And call Behavioral Sciences. Make an appointment to see one of the psychologists. It's mandatory. You may need several sessions."

"Sure."

"And Brenden, you might want to take some time off."

"I'll think about it, sir."

"But first talk to a psychologist. You'll be taken off active duty until you do."

Meanwhile they went through McKay's papers, and his screenplay project helped answer some of what we wanted to know. His early drafts outlined the slaying of a chief of police whom, it seemed obvious, he held accountable for his fall from glory. But as McKay's bitterness came to obsess him, a cannier revenge sprung from his twisted mind. How better to publicly humiliate the department than to go on a terrifying crime spree? Confident that he could outwit his former colleagues, he plotted his moves against theirs—with Higgins maybe leaking things he shouldn't have—and the death toll mounted. It was unclear if his earlier intentions were to vent his anger through his screenplay—and then as he became his protagonist, he decided to act out—or whether murder had been on his mind all along.

It was also unclear how he had chosen his victims, but we could only assume some, at least, were unknown to him.

Terry Smith had been no more than an example of how even skilled detectives could "fall in love" with the wrong suspect, although, to be fair, Terry did her disserviceable best to lead them on. Not to mention me, until that Saturday night when her legitimate concerns impelled her to call me.

The picture of Adam McKay we had shown her had nagged at her. In time it occurred to her that she may have known him. But she could not recall his name. Diligently she went through the records of security people her husband had hired until she came across McKay. There was no photo, but the physical description fit. She had called me to find out if this was the man we suspected and if the yellow patch she had spotted on his shirt was one of hers. Unclear if he was still with the department, she wanted to speak to an officer she could trust. Which, it turned out, was me.

Although I had been leaning toward McKay as the stabber, it was

eedless to say, Higgins was not pleased with the developments of that night, especially because he hadn't gone to the party on account of being "stressed." But since I was off duty and had clearly killed in self-defense, there was nothing even he could dream up to do about it.

The LAPD Public Relations crew put its own rather imaginative spin on the stories that appeared in the media over the next few days. Robbery/Homicide had slowly built a case against former LAPD officer Adam McKay. On the night in question, it learned that McKay would be hosting a party and sent some detectives to surveille the property. Ironically, several of the invited guests were officers McKay was acquainted with. After the guests had left, the surveillance team noticed a car belonging to a female detective. When an officer, posing as a friend of Det. Dorrie Green, phoned and asked to speak to her, McKay denied she was there. SWAT was called in.

According to the story, a negotiation was begun but McKay refused to surrender. Shots sounded and SWAT entered the house. They found McKay dead in his stable, the victim of a self-inflicted gunshot wound. Dorrie Green was found stabbed to death in a manner similar to the victims at the ATMs.

And so, with this sleight of hand, I was magically erased from the picture. Gone. "Otherwise you'll get a reputation, and people will know your face, and the public will treat you more like a celebrity than a police officer, and your effectiveness will be zero," is how Monster McGrew explained it to me three days later in his office as I sat there trying to meet his walleyed stare. "The Officer-Involved-Shooting

I rattled the ice in my glass and swallowed the remains of the Black Russian. "T.J. He's the hero. He got there late and asked for me. You were still there, I think."

Cookie nodded. "Yeah. I said you were somewhere. A few minutes later he asked me again. Brilliant me. I said, well maybe you and Dorrie had split."

"That's what McKay said, too. But T.J. said his instinct told him otherwise. He went out and found both our cars. Then he called Walters and Walters called SWAT. Even if I didn't have the gun, I think they would have gotten to me in time. But I didn't tell them that. I told them their response time stunk."

Cookie lifted her beer and clinked my glass. "To the women in blue. Wait till the world discovers how good we really are."

"Right," I said glumly. I looked up and saw T.J. coming over. "But let's not tell him."

"Tell me what? Scoot over, ladies."

"He's got a thing about assertive women," I said, bored.

"Women belong at home. Especially you," he growled, poking me. "I'll never get over how you ruined my Saturday night."

I lifted a brow. "Really? I don't remember running into you. Cookie, do you remember seeing T.J. at the party?"

"Not me."

We looked at him expectantly.

"Sheeit."

"Well, whaddya know?" Cookie declared.

I glanced at the door and was flabbergasted to see my partner. "Todd," I exclaimed. "To what do we owe this pleasure?"

He smiled congenially. "Hi, fellas. Brenden, can I have a minute?"

"Sure. Can we get you a drink?"

"Not right now." He paused. "Privately."

I slid out of the booth and stumbled on T.J.'s shoe. Todd gripped my arm and walked me out of the poolroom.

"Want to sit at the bar?" I said.

"Let's go outside, okay?"

He held the door for me. "Is something wrong?" I asked.

"My car's out front."

Todd drove a black Corvette that he had bought used and had spent more than the cost of a new one repairing.

"What's up?" I said as he closed his door.

"You're drunk."

"Of course I'm not."

"Brenden, I want you to get help. You need it. You leave here late at night, you drive the freeway like a maniac, and often the fog is rolling in by the time you get to the beach. I am not going to be the one who identifies your body. Besides, you're ruining your health, and your career will go, too."

"You're such an alarmist, Todd."

"Is that what Jack said? Just a little coke to get through the day, no big deal?"

"Cut it out."

"Look, it could be a genetic problem or heredity or—"

"You mean those crazy, drunken micks?"

"That's not what I mean. Alcohol addiction can be genetic or inherited in anybody."

"But especially in micks."

"Brenden, you know I'm right. You and Jack are locked into the same kind of behavior, and you can't see that?"

"Mr. Sigmund Freud himself. Are you finished?"

"I will be in a minute." He fell silent and stared out the windshield. "You're the best partner I ever had," he said softly, "and I don't want to lose you. As a partner or a friend. But I won't work with you if you don't pull yourself together. We're going on vacation tomorrow for three weeks. When I get back you're either sober or I'm requesting a new partner."

"Okay."

I got out of the car and went back into the bar.

I spent the next three days trying to prove Todd wrong. My increased drinking was situational, I told myself. As soon as I felt better, I would cut back.

But I wasn't getting better. I was lethargic and blue. Maybe the alcohol, a depressant, was contributing to the nightmares that stole my sleep. With a bit of bravado I tossed out all the alcohol in the apartment, bought a fresh supply of Excedrin PM, and stacked movies and trash novels on my bedside table. I unplugged the phone.

I dozed off and on but did not feel refreshed. I tried movie after movie and finished none. The novels did not hold my attention. I drank water and orange juice and ate candy bars. On the morning of the third day, I felt a spark.

I went for a long run on the beach. Later, I called Suzy. She said that Jack had eighteen days to go and a therapist at Betty Ford had told her over the phone that he was doing superbly.

Late in the afternoon I walked to the 3rd Street Promenade and caught a movie. It was a well-done comedy, and that, plus a large popcorn and a Coke, made me cheerful for the first time in weeks. It was a beautiful evening, and as I passed one of the outdoor cafés on Ocean Avenue, I impulsively decided to stop in for a glass of wine. As long as I stayed away from vodka, I theorized, I would be okay. I smiled with self-satisfaction as I sat down.

Thirty-four years old, pretty face, still a great bod—that I knew. And now—no longer coming unglued. Cheers.

F i v e days later, on a broiling Wednesday morning, I drove through Chinatown until I came to the California Pacific Bank. I turned into its underground garage and glanced nervously at my watch as I rode the elevator to the fourth floor. I was late.

But when I got to Room 409, I hesitated. I walked to the end of the hall, debated, and returned. Finally, I opened the door. The waiting room was empty. After a moment, an interior door opened and Ms. Lacy stepped out. She was holding a clipboard.

She smiled. "I've been expecting you."

"I'm not here to talk about the shooting. I'm fine with the shooting."

"I see."

"It's about something else. Not that it's a problem or anything, but . . . "

My sentence simply hung there. She did not change her expression. Then she tilted her head slightly and said gently, "But?"

I turned on my heel and walked out.

At the elevator, I pushed the button, and I could hear the car lumbering up. I had fought my way into Metro. I had, under extreme circumstances, shot to death a serial killer and perhaps saved my life. I had pressured my husband to kick his coke habit, and at least he was trying. I can do this, too, I told myself.

She was still standing with her clipboard. I stepped into the office and closed the door.

Diane K. Shah is the author of four books, including two mysteries set in 1947 Los Angeles and *Chief: My Life in the LAPD,* which she cowrote with Daryl Gates. She has been a General Editor of *Newsweek,* a West Coast editor of *GQ,* and a sports columnist for the *Los Angeles Herald Examiner.* She has also written for *Esquire* and *The New York Times Magazine.* She maintains homes in Los Angeles and New York City.